TROJAN HORSE

A Kolya Petrov Thriller

S. LEE MANNING

Encircle Publications, LLC
Farmington, Maine U.S.A.

TROJAN HORSE

A Kolya Petrov Thriller

Editor: Cynthia Brackett-Vincent
Book design: Eddie Vincent
Cover design by Deirdre Wait, High Pines Creative, Inc.

Published by: Encircle Publications, LLC
PO Box 187
Farmington, ME 04938

Visit: http://encirclepub.com

Sign up for Encircle Publications newsletter and specials
http://eepurl.com/cs8taP

Printed in U.S.A.

To Lou and Ida Katz. Always.

Acknowledgements

Thanks to James Manning, Jenny Manning Yuan, and Dean Manning for multiple readings and comments and for all your support over the years it took to get here.

1

Gina Antonia slid off the bed and wrapped a silk shawl around her nude body. She glanced at the clock. One a.m. She wasn't scheduled to call in until eight. Mihai Cuza was curled on his side, breathing evenly. A handsome man. Dark hair, aristocratic features, attractive body. He appeared younger than his real age, which was somewhere in his late 40s. Funny how a sleeping man could look gentle, almost child-like. But it was only an illusion, and she knew it. He was about as gentle as a sleeping cobra.

She picked up his phone from the bed stand and tiptoed to the circular stairs, still wearing only the shawl, and descended slowly, carefully, to the darkened office area.

She seated herself on a chair in front of a desktop computer on the far side of the open expanse. She shifted; to keep her bare bottom from sticking to the leather, she slid part of the shawl under her. Cuza had hung her clothes in an antique wardrobe with doors that squeaked. Getting her clothes out would have been the riskier option. It also would have taken time.

It had taken two weeks of covertly watching, but she finally had the password to the iPhone, which in turn held the password to the computer.

She searched, found the series of numbers and letters and, turning to the keyboard, typed them in. A click, and she was in. She attached a thumb drive, downloading a program that would allow Kolya or the tech guys back at the office to access Cuza's files. While waiting for the program to load, she remained alert and nervous. No sound

1

from the bedroom upstairs. *Do it and get out,* Kolya had told her. But what if the software didn't work? They might not get another crack at Cuza's computer. She was there; she could take another few minutes to get the information.

She went into documents and started searching.

The third document that she opened listed Cuza's plans for the next two months, to be coordinated through various European offices. *Bingo.*

She skimmed the names of the towns, in America, in Europe, one in Asia. Fifteen in all. How many people lived in those cities? How many people lived in Buchanan, New York? How many people would die immediately if the nuclear power plants in their towns melted down? How many more would die slowly of radiation poisoning or cancer?

Not in the thousands. In the hundreds of thousands.

She'd slept with a man capable of killing this many people. It had been a necessary part of the job, the only way to get close to him, but she'd done it, and she'd enjoyed it. She'd enjoyed sex with a monster.

She took a deep breath. She only knew what she now knew because she'd slept with him.

Her hands trembled with the weight of her new knowledge. Her fingers fumbled on the keyboard.

Steady. All she had to do was send an e-mail and run. She wouldn't even go upstairs for her clothes. She'd run through Soho naked if necessary.

Funny. Running naked through Soho was the sort of thing that she might have done for a laugh had circumstances been different. She liked to do things that were different. Like the time she dyed her hair pink. She'd only kept it pink for a day, but the expression on Jonathan's face…

But there was nothing funny about this assignment and nothing funny about Cuza.

Do it and get the hell out.

Had she heard something moving? *No, it was nothing.*

She accessed one of her e-mail accounts and typed Kolya's e-mail address. She typed a quick message. *Attaching Cuza's plans for fifteen towns, including Cernavoda, Romania. Oak Harbor, Ohio. Buchanan, New York. Ft. Pierce, Florida.* Then she felt the touch on her shoulder.

"Enjoying yourself?" a voice purred behind her. Cuza's voice.

Before he pinned her arms, she hit send.

* * * * *

Nikolai Ivanovich Petrov, known to his friends as Kolya, shook his blond head, scrolled down the screen, and pondered his options. If he sent Teo Lorenzo to Pennsylvania Station to watch for a mysterious woman in black, Kolya'd catch hell from his boss Margaret Bradford, head of the ECA, an agency that few knew existed—who would consider his sending a new agent a mile uptown to meet a non-existent informant to be an abuse of authority. Then, again, Kolya could simply send Teo out for a dozen bagels from the deli two blocks away. Not that Kolya wanted a bagel. He just wanted Teo, whose face peered with unrelenting enthusiasm over Kolya's shoulder, to go away.

Kolya didn't dislike Teo, but he hated this part of the job—the waiting while another agent was in danger. He preferred the active role, to be the one at risk, but right now, his role was providing backup and technical support. Gina was scheduled to check in at eight. Just in case, Kolya had monitored the phones and the computer since midnight. On the other hand, Teo had slept until seven. Easy for Teo—who hadn't lived through the other attempts to penetrate Cuza's network. Kolya vividly remembered Vasily—who had played violin—and whom Kolya had persuaded to spy on Cuza. Three days later, Vasily had been found with a stake through his body.

Normally the piano jazz emanating from his computer, Eugene Maslov, a fellow Russian emigrant from St. Petersburg, playing "The Masquerade is Over," would have a calming effect. Not now.

"You know, you worry too much."

Maybe he'd just shoot Teo.

They were holed up in a shabby two-bedroom apartment in the

West Village, designated the New York office. The computers were state of the art, but the chairs and table were plastic, and the faded green carpet smelled of mold, dust, and something undefined— maybe cat urine. But the apartment didn't bother him particularly. He'd lived in worse.

It was Alex. He hadn't seen her for two months, and he missed her: her sense of humor, her intelligence, and the warmth of her presence. He could almost hear her voice mocking him, "You mean you miss the sex, right?"

As if his thought had prompted it, his phone buzzed. *You up?*

He texted back. *For hours. Court today?*

A response came immediately. *Case postponed. Drag. Talk?*

Can't now. Later.

Call when you can. Love. Got to run.

He sent his love back, set the phone down, and returned his attention to the computer. Phone calls and texts were a poor substitution, under the best of times. It was one of the drawbacks of his line of work, the only reason he'd ever considered changing professions.

Still, he wasn't ready to give up the game.

Teo leaned over the computer and tried to tap a request onto the keyboard.

"Don't fuck with the computer, Teo." Kolya decided to send Teo on an errand to the kitchen instead of on a tour of the wilds of Manhattan. "Could you check if there's any coffee left?" He picked up a New York Mets mug and thrust it without ceremony into Teo's hand.

"Two teaspoons sugar, right?" Teo asked.

"Correct." Kolya, like many Russian Jews, had a sweet tooth. He usually didn't indulge in desserts, keeping in shape was too important, but he did like to sweeten his coffee.

Teo disappeared.

Maslov ended, and Kolya switched to Bill Evans, on the keyboard, Eddie Gomez on bass, an interpretation of "Autumn Leaves." Kolya had played a variation of the tune on Alex's piano two nights before he'd left for New York. He missed the piano, but this was the Village after all. He'd managed to find a bar where he could occasionally spend a few hours improvising on jazz standards.

A glance at the computer brought his mind back to the job. An e-mail from Gina? He clicked onto it and read her message: Cuza's plans for fifteen towns, including Cernavoda, Romania. Oak Harbor, Ohio. Buchanan, New York. St. Lucie, Florida. Flamanville, France. He clicked onto the attachment. But the attachment he opened was blank.

"Eboyanna mat." His favorite curse.

Teo reappeared, a cup of coffee in each hand. He handed over Kolya's cup and took a sip of his own. "What?"

"Attachment was booby trapped." Kolya ran a check on his computer and cursed again, this time in English. Then he shut it down. "And there was a virus on it." Cuza was smarter than they'd anticipated. Kolya switched to a second computer and checked. If Gina had done her job of inserting the software, he should be able to access Cuza's computer remotely.

"Anything come through?" Teo was at his shoulder again.

"No." Which was troubling. He searched files. Nothing.

"But if she sent the message, she got in."

"We can't access Cuza's computer unless it's online. Apparently, it's not."

"We gonna wake Jonathan?"

"You're elected."

The fact that Gina had been online long enough to send a message but had not left the computer on long enough for them to access Cuza's files was not good.

Kolya pulled out his cell and called Gina. The phone rang five times, and her voice mail picked up. He didn't leave a message.

Kolya had been against the plan. Too risky. Gina was young and relatively new in the business. Asking her to screw Cuza was a little over the line of what he found acceptable, even in their line of work.

But Jonathan was the team leader, and Jonathan had made the decision. Cuza liked a certain kind of woman. Gina had been the closest match of the available ECA female agents. Well, nothing else had worked, and they needed to get into Cuza's computer. But if Gina were discovered, Cuza would take it as a personal affront.

So, he worried. He didn't know her well; this was the first time they'd worked together, but he'd liked her sense of humor—and aura of rebellion. When they'd discussed the operation in her office decorated with prints of Renaissance paintings and pictures of her mother, sister, and cat, her hair had been dyed pink—to make a statement, she'd said. She'd dyed it back before attempting the infiltration of Cuza's organization.

She was good. She'd be fine. She was just so young.

He sent a text: *lunch?*

No response.

She'd done her job and she should have left immediately.

"*Eboyanna mat.*" He repeated the Russian curse, involving mothers and sex.

He thought about the message with the booby-trapped attachment. Cernavoda, Romania; Oak Harbor, Ohio; Buchanan, New York; St. Lucie, Florida; Flamanville, France.

What would interest Cuza in Ohio? In Illinois?

"What's up?" Jonathan Egan strode over to the computer, coffee cup in hand, bleary eyed, and positioned himself with a view of the monitor. Despite the fact that he had just woken up, Jonathan could have passed for a model: dressed in designer slacks and sweater, brown hair immaculate. He looked like what he was: the trust fund descendant of an industrialist, the privileged son of a former Senator who regarded Jonathan's employment by an intelligence agency as an insult. Kolya also knew the reality beyond the appearance: Jonathan was a dedicated operative, a loving father, even if his marriage hadn't lasted, and a good friend. The only real friction: music. "Turn off the damn jazz. Can't you listen to something from the 21st century?"

Kolya ignored the insult.

"Gina sent a message with an attachment that self-destructed. She should have gotten out immediately. Nothing else from her. No texts. No calls. No response when I tried to reach her."

"You think she's in trouble?"

6

"Good chance."

"OK, then." Jonathan nodded. "We go in."

Kolya turned off the computer, stood, slid his HK .40 caliber compact from its holster, ejected the magazine, and checked it. Twelve rounds. He slid the magazine back into the butt of the gun, reholstered, tugged his shirt down to cover the bulge, reached for his sweater on an adjacent chair, and pulled it over his head.

Jonathan didn't bother to check his gun; he simply shrugged into a jacket.

Kolya fished a set of keys out of his pocket and tossed them to Jonathan. "The van's in the garage across the street."

2

The pain was fading, and that was good. A tiny corner of her mind told her that she was dying, that her senses were going, and with them, the pain.

Gina Antonia was only twenty-three. There were so many places she hadn't gone, things she hadn't done or seen. She'd wanted to take her mother to Florence, a promise to a mother who'd scraped out a living as an art teacher to support Gina and her brother. Gina'd bought the tickets. January. They were going in January.

That thought had flashed through her mind in the seconds before the pain took over and became everything.

She had heard Mihai Cuza's voice murmuring through her own screams as they pushed the stake through her.

Then there had been nothing but the agony consuming her. No regrets, no sadness, just agony.

Now, pain was receding. She was grateful for that, but that tiny corner of her mind argued with her to hold on. Her mother. This will kill her mother. *Momma.* She was going to Florence with her mother. Her mother was a painter. They were going to see the Uffizi Gallery and paintings by Raphael and Fra Angelico. They were going to sit at a café together and drink cappuccinos and talk the way they used to when Gina was in high school.

* * * * *

Greene Street in Soho was not particularly busy, not even during rush

8

hour, but since it was Manhattan, legal parking spots were in short supply. They parked the van in a bus stop directly across from the warehouse that had been transformed into Cuza's loft.

They exited the back of the van and headed for the door to the building that now housed an art gallery on the bottom floor. According to the records, Cuza owned the entire building, but he occupied only the third floor. They jogged lightly up the stairs to the door that marked Cuza's premises.

Jonathan rang an unmarked buzzer and moved to the right side of the door. Kolya, to the left of the door, slipped out his gun, snapped the slide, and held the gun against his chest.

Jonathan tried the handle, which turned in his hand. He pushed the door open with his foot.

Their footsteps sounded hollow on the wooden floors and the sound bounced off bare white walls. The living room was spacious, sparsely furnished with a Boca do Lobo leather couch and matching loveseat in the center, lit by a gold and crystal floor lamp. They first checked a large maple desk against the far wall, with a matching filing cabinet. Nothing. Drawers empty. Wires for Internet, but no modem or computer.

Kolya pointed to a kitchen area at the back of the loft, and Teo headed for it. Kolya climbed a circular wrought iron staircase to a loft area and found an empty bed and an empty antique wardrobe. No clothes. No personal effects. If Gina had ever been there, she was gone.

He leaned over the rail of the loft and looked down. In an open space between the desk and the sofa, Jonathan knelt and examined the floor. Kolya hurried down the stairs and knelt next to Jonathan.

"Clorox," Jonathan said.

Kolya felt the floor. "Not completely dry."

He stood. There was nothing more they could do here.

Was there a chance that she was still alive? He doubted it, but some people lived for days after being impaled.

Jonathan remained on one knee. "Goddamn it!"

Kolya's own anger rose, but he tamped it down. This was neither

the time nor the place. "We have to leave. We need to try to find her."
He knew the odds against finding her alive, but they had to try.

"Find her?" Teo was amazed. "She could have been dumped
anywhere. In Manhattan. In New Jersey. Staten Island."

"Cuza doesn't dump people. He displays them. I doubt that he
would have attempted to leave the island with her in the back of a
van. My guess would be that she's somewhere in Manhattan."

"One of the parks, maybe." Jonathan rose and holstered his own
gun. "Central Park or Riverside Park. Let's go."

They moved quickly toward the door. Kolya pulled his phone from
an inside pocket, but Jonathan's hand on his wrist stopped him.

"You can't call the police. Margaret's orders. You know that."

"To hell with Margaret." Kolya had never felt so frustrated by
the constraints placed on them. He had never been so frustrated by
Jonathan. Jonathan had always been more inclined to follow the rules
than Kolya, but Kolya generally put up with it. He was not putting
up with it now.

"Just exactly what you do plan to tell them? They'll think you're
crazy. You think they're going to believe you if you don't tell them
who you are. What you are."

Kolya knew as well as Jonathan that an anonymous call into the
police to report a woman being impaled would be considered a prank.
Still, he didn't have anything better to suggest. There were only the
four of them on the team. There were only the four of them in New
York.

Three of them, he corrected himself. They couldn't search the whole
island.

But there was a chance the police would search, just as there was a
chance that she was still alive. The New York City police would have
the resources to find Gina more quickly than the three of them could.

Not much of a chance in either case. But, damn it, they had to try.

Teo joined in. "Jonathan, it's Gina's life we're talking about."

"She's already dead. Even if we find her, she'll be dead."

"You don't know that."

"Goddamn it, I do know it." Jonathan's voice broke. "We've been after Cuza for a year. He doesn't leave people alive. Compromising the operation isn't going to save her. If we don't find out what Cuza's up to, there could be a lot of other people dead."

Jonathan, guilty at allowing Gina to go ahead with the plan and convinced she was already dead, was rationalizing. Gina's sacrifice would be justified if they could succeed in uncovering Cuza's plans. Conversely, her death would be worse than meaningless if the operation failed.

But the two were connected. If they found her alive, they would know what Cuza was doing. Cernavoda. Oak Harbor. Buchanan. St. Lucie. What connected them?

"Impalement doesn't kill immediately." Kolya's voice was quiet. It wouldn't help if he also became emotional. "It's only been a matter of hours. We can't abandon her. And Gina could tell us what she found. If she's alive."

Back on the street, they slowed their pace. Remain inconspicuous, even when a young woman's life was at stake. Secrecy was essential to what they did. Kolya knew it and accepted it. Up to a point.

"The hell with it," Jonathan said. "Call. For whatever the hell good it'll do."

Kolya checked both directions on the street before he opened the door to the van, his left hand tapping numbers on the phone. Kolya spoke quickly and disconnected before his location could be pinpointed.

* * * * *

David Fuller, known on the street as Frick, looked the part of a drug dealer—bald, muscular, a tattoo of a dragon on one exposed arm, a tiger on the other. He sat at a table next to the window of the restaurant four doors down from Cuza's building and poked a fork into his eggs. He'd ordered dry scrambled eggs and bacon. He'd been served runny eggs and sausage. And, the breakfast special cost ten dollars. New York. God, sometimes he hated the place.

Three of 'em. A young guy, a tall slender blond guy, and a slightly shorter guy with brown hair. He watched them enter the building while he poured ketchup on the eggs and sausage. They wouldn't find anything. He'd already been over the damn place to make sure it was clean. Still, the three of them inside, poking around, made him nervous.

He could call the police and report three prowlers, but he couldn't really see the point, other than fucking with them—and they might figure out that someone had been watching. The coffee shop would be a logical place to ask questions. No, he'd let it go.

He finished the eggs, held out his cup for a refill of coffee, and was halfway through it when the three men emerged from the building and returned to the van. He'd know them next time.

3

They drove north on Eighth Avenue, heading for Central Park. At 8:30 on a Sunday morning, traffic was light, even close to the Lincoln Tunnel. Teo, at the wheel, knuckles white, kept his eyes fixed on the road. Next to him, Jonathan argued with Ross, head of the agency's technical section, on an encrypted phone.

Kolya, in the back of the van, logged into the New York City Police Department's network and scanned for any news.

"They didn't take my call seriously," Kolya said.

Jonathan, phone still pressed against his ear, glanced over his shoulder, his expression I-told-you-so.

Kolya turned back to the laptop keyboard. He began to type. The New York City Police might eventually be able to trace the all-points bulletin back to his computer—assuming that they located his computer—but he doubted that the department had the necessary technical expertise to immediately detect that the bulletin was unauthorized.

"What're you doing?" Jonathan asked.

"Making them take it seriously."

"Can it be traced back to us?"

"Hopefully not." Kolya could hear screaming from the other end of the phone. Ross hated it when Kolya hacked other governmental agencies. Ross had almost as much of a secrecy fetish as Margaret Bradford. Kolya also suspected some professional jealousy. Hacking was Ross's department. "Tell Ross to fuck himself."

They continued up Central Park West.

They were near 96th Street when the report came through. Kolya read it twice to be sure. "Cross the park," he told Teo. "The entrance near 103rd Street."

* * * * *

They parked the van on Fifth Avenue and walked to where five blue and whites, lights flashing red, lined the road. They halted, back far enough not to be spotted by the police who were securing the scene. Detectives would arrive any minute, along with the medical examiner, and representatives of the prosecutor's office.

Gina remained where Cuza had left her, six feet off the ground. The stake that held her had been shoved into her body between her legs, and the tip of the stake protruded from her chest.

From where they stood, Kolya could see her naked body, but he couldn't see her face. He was grateful for that at least, although with the wind in their faces, even at a distance, he could smell the blood and the excrement.

Teo stumbled behind a tree and vomited.

"There's nothing we can do here." Jonathan's voice was strangled. "The two of you need to fly back to Washington. Immediately."

Jonathan would be the one to call Margaret Bradford. She in turn would discretely arrange for the release of Gina's body, and Jonathan would bring her home. Then they would turn their attention to Cuza.

"We're going to kill that son-of-a-bitch," Jonathan said.

* * * * *

That night, Kolya dreamed he was in St. Petersburg, in front of a fountain near the Neva River, eating a dish of chocolate ice cream while a blonde woman smiled at him. He heard a scream, and turned. A few feet away a slender dark-haired man pushed a stake through Gina.

He woke and remembered where he was. Washington. Alex's townhouse in Georgetown. Next to him, Alex curled on her side, dark curly hair half obscuring her face. He gently brushed a curl back from her forehead and resisted the urge to wake her. She had a tough job and needed her sleep—he shouldn't disturb her just because he had nightmares.

It was what always happened. In the *dyetskii dom*, he'd learned to keep his emotions under control. To do otherwise invited attack. He remembered that first year after his mother's death, the tauntings, the beatings, and worse, until he learned to fight and to conceal anything that could be interpreted as weakness.

But control had its price, and he paid at night.

He slid into his jeans and padded downstairs to the kitchen. He found the vodka in the freezer next to the chocolate chip ice cream.

The liquor burned coldly down his throat. He cradled the glass in his hands, unable to dispel the remnants of the nightmare.

He could have stopped Gina from going ahead. He should have spoken up. It was a stupid plan, and he knew it was dangerous. He knew she could get killed.

He tried not to think of the way she'd died, of her pain and terror, but the dream pushed itself back into his mind.

He finished his drink and poured another. He deliberately turned his mind to the other image from his dream. His mother always put in an appearance in his sleep after any traumatic event. Funny, when he was awake, he could barely remember her face. After all, it had been years. More than twenty years since she'd died from the flu.

Wasn't it absurd to die of something so ordinary?

But now, he tried to remember something besides her death. Something concrete. He could remember her laugh better than her face. Mozart. She loved to play Mozart. He could picture her hands on the keys. He remembered her outrage when she caught him playing Ellington. Other images flashed in his mind. She held his hand in a noisy crowd near the *Nevskii Prospekt* on a never-ending summer night. The White Nights. They sat under a tree in the park next to the *Muzey Zheleznodorozhnovo Transporta*, and the air smelled of lilacs.

The hospital smelled of rubbing alcohol and bleach.

"Enough." He banished the memory.

He returned the vodka to the freezer and washed out his glass, his mind returning to the events of the past day. To Gina's last message. Fifteen towns. Cernavoda, Romania; Oak Harbor, Ohio; Buchanan, New York; St. Lucie, Florida; Flamanville, France. What did it mean?

He found his computer in the living room and opened it up. Signing onto the Internet service, he Googled Buchannan, New York.

The name of Buchanan had not been familiar, but the name Indian Point was.

A chill went through him.

Was it possible?

He checked Cernavoda, followed by Oak Harbor, followed by St. Lucie. He checked every one of the fifteen towns, and in every case, there was one thing in common. Every town had a nuclear power plant.

What exactly was the bastard planning?

He sent an e-mail with his findings to Ross. Someone in the technical section needed to check it out as quickly as possible.

Suddenly exhausted, he closed the computer and headed back to bed. Alex had rolled onto her back, and the sheet slipped down to her waist. He carefully pulled the sheet up and tucked it around her. She murmured but didn't wake. He slid out of his jeans, crawled into bed, and stretched out on his back. His mind went back to Gina and to Cuza, but now he concentrated on something quite different from the nightmare or the meaning of her last message.

How had Cuza discovered that Gina was a spy?

Did Cuza simply catch her trying to get into his computer? Maybe. On the other hand, they had gotten close to Cuza on several other occasions, and every time, something went wrong. Vasily in Romania. Cuza had impaled him as well. Then there was the recruit in Paris who'd been found with his throat cut three days after he'd called Jonathan. There was the Ukrainian who didn't even get in the front door.

Cuza was either very lucky or he was receiving information. If so, from whom?

Kolya watched wisps of moonlight dance on the wall.

Start with the people who knew about this mission and the others. Jonathan? Absurd. He'd known Jonathan too long, since the days in the FBI. They'd gone through training together, worked together on busting the Russian mafiya in Brooklyn, and been recruited into the ECA together, what was it, nine years ago? He'd been best man at Jonathan's wedding, and Jonathan had accompanied him when he buried his cousin. Teo. Kolya hesitated on that one. Could Teo's enthusiastic routine be an act? If so, it was a good one. But Teo had had no opportunity to alert Cuza to Gina's true identity. More importantly, Teo hadn't been in the agency when Cuza murdered Vasily. Or when Paris fell apart. Ross? Mark Leslie? Neither of them knew about Vasily.

He made a mental list of the people who knew about every operation that had been blown. The list inside the agency was short. Bradford. Her secretary. What about the technical section? Ross and his people. Did they know?

There was the Intelligence Committee. He thought about that one. It was worth checking out.

* * * * *

There was no sign over the door. The building could have been an apartment complex or a business office in one of the more expensive areas of D.C. except that there were no signs and no names. Just a black façade and a larger than usual satellite dish on top of the building. Nothing indicated that it was the office of the ECA, the elite of the intelligence agencies, established by executive order, the director answering only to the President of the United States.

Kolya entered through the nondescript door to the lobby. Inside, he tapped a four-digit security code into a box and spoke his name. Inside, a receptionist with chin length blonde hair and perfect eyebrows sat behind a desk decorated with flowers and a picture of a Labrador puppy. He glanced at her, recognized her as the regular receptionist, and paused before a second door. He placed his palm in the appropriate spot, and the door opened.

In the cafeteria on the first floor, he purchased a large cup of coffee and dumped in two teaspoons of sugar. It wouldn't be strong enough to compensate for the lack of sleep, but it would do for now.

He jogged up one flight of stairs.

The second floor was the technical section, ruled over by Greg Ross. Kolya pushed open the door to a small office. Mark Leslie occupied Ross's desk, hands on the computer keyboard. Mark, in his early thirties, overweight, with a wispy brown beard and hair down to his shoulders, munched on a chocolate chip muffin and washed it down with a can of Diet Coke that had left a ring on the wood desk. Napkins were wadded up on the desk next to the computer and decorated part of the floor.

If neither Mark nor Ross had been there, Kolya might have taken the opportunity to go onto Ross's computer and poke into Ross's personal log. But since Mark was there, Kolya would play by the rules.

Kolya leaned against the door and cleared his throat. Mark looked up.

"I was looking for Ross," Kolya said.

"Cafeteria. You know he always eats breakfast there. Can't imagine why. The food stinks, except for the sweets. So what the hell happened in New York?"

"We don't really know." But he was also thinking about it. "Do you have anything for me? Did the software work? Could you open the attachment?"

"No to both." Mark broke off a bite of his muffin and munched it down. He gestured invitingly at the plate. "You want any?" Kolya shook his head. "Okay then, like you thought the attachment was booby trapped not only to self-destruct but to destroy the hard drive of any fool who opens it. And no go on the software. My thought—he shut it down and destroyed the computer before we could download any of his information."

"A reasonable assumption. And the towns that Gina listed?"

"Yeah, you were right, they all have nuclear power plants. Maybe they're potential targets. Maybe Cuza's planning to crash some planes or something."

"Cuza works through computers. It's how he got his money. It's why we're trying to break into his network."

"You can't just hack into a nuclear power plant. Anyway, we've alerted all of the plants. They're running checks as we speak. You know they've all got great firewalls. I tried getting in and couldn't."

"If there's an inactive virus on any or all of the systems, they won't find it. Or if there is a glitch in the software. Cuza could have planned this years in advance. We don't have any idea who his people are or where they are."

"Even if you're right, we're warned. Security has been upped. Meantime, you locate Cuza and get into his system and find out just what the hell he's up to."

Mark made it sound simple. Technical had failed to get in with phishing e-mails or other hacking techniques. Kolya's team had been working on infiltrating Cuza's organization for almost a year, and every time they got close, someone died. "I'm willing to hear suggestions."

"Ross says he might have a lead." Mark nodded at the computer. "An investment company that he thinks might be a front. In New York."

"E-mail me the address, would you?" He'd check it out himself. It could mean another trip. He returned to the other open question. How had Cuza found out about Gina? "I was also wondering," Kolya said in as casual a tone as he could manage, "Who else in the agency knew about the operation."

"I knew and Ross. Bradford. Why?"

"Just curious."

Mark was not stupid. "Do you think someone leaked details about the operation?"

"Not really," Kolya lied.

"Well, it wasn't anyone in this office. Believe me. Nobody else knew what was going on. Bradford played it close to the vest."

Of course, if Mark were the leak, he would say that, wouldn't he? Kolya liked Mark, despite his messiness, liked his competence and general friendliness, but that didn't mean he wouldn't double check. For now, he let it ride. "I was also wondering about the latest intelligence from the NSA."

The NSA, the information gathering mega-agency located in the suburbs of Maryland, conducted the most massive electronic eavesdropping operation in the world. The NSA also controlled ECHELON, a multinational surveillance network that intercepted worldwide communications and searched for pre-programmed keywords or addresses. It was a little known secret that Ross had also linked into ECHELON itself, which was the reason that Kolya liked to use Ross's computer. It was also one of the sources of the friction between Ross and Kolya.

"The report's not in yet." Mark scarfed down the rest of his muffin and returned to his computer, whistling an off-key version of George Gershwin's "Summertime." Kolya winced at the rendition.

Kolya looked over Mark's shoulder at the monitor and was curious. "What are you doing?"

"Creating a virus. Not to use. Just to see if we could do it."

"We?"

"Ross and me."

Kolya continued to watch. Mark, uncomfortable under his gaze, saved his work and squarely faced Kolya. "Don't you have anything better to do?"

Kolya did, but he was interested. "If I get a virus on my computer, I will not think it funny."

"I told you. It's not going anywhere. Just an internal exercise. I've got work to do, so let me alone. If you want to get Ross, try back a little later. I'll tell him you stopped by."

Kolya shrugged and gave up. He also had work to do. If Mark and Ross wanted to create viruses, it was their business. "Tell Ross to call."

* * * * *

Kolya tapped his fingers on the desk, mentally improvising with Dave Brubeck, "Take Five" playing on the computer, as he began his search. There had been rumors that Cuza had some sort of financial office in

New York. He ran another search on its history. The Balkan Financial Group had been in existence five years, and a well-known backer of Cuza, a doctor Emil Stanescu, had invested heavily in the group.

Excellent. Kolya began probing the defenses. He sidetracked for a few minutes to run names and dates from the list he had mentally compiled the night before.

Then he turned to nod a welcome as Jonathan, with a grunt, dropped into the second chair in Kolya's small office. Jonathan hadn't shaved, and his eyes were bloodshot.

"You were right. It was a fucking stupid plan."

Kolya hesitated. Jonathan was obviously feeling guilt. As he should be. It had been a stupid fucking plan, and they should have been more concerned about a possible leak. He turned back to the computer. "Do you want me to disagree?"

"Do you?"

Kolya shrugged. "Not really."

"She did agree to do it, knowing the risks. I mean, we are in a dangerous business."

"We are, and it's important to get Cuza. Still...."

"Still." Jonathan put his head in his hands. "Margaret thought it was a good plan."

Jonathan Egan was one of the few people who dared to call the head of the agency, Margaret Bradford, by her first name. But, then, she had been a frequent visitor to his childhood home in Washington, as well as to his parents' summer place in Mystic, when Jonathan's father chaired the Senate Intelligence Committee, back before the ECA, when Margaret still headed Operations for the CIA.

"Bradford doesn't always have the concern for our lives that she should." Kolya glanced over at Jonathan. "But you're right. Gina knew and accepted the risk. I went along with the plan, too. And blaming Bradford or you won't bring Gina back. Maybe we should concentrate on getting Cuza."

Kolya turned back to the computer. After five minutes of watching Kolya type, Jonathan spoke. "What've you got?"

"A possibility in New York." Kolya nodded at the screen. "But I'm not having any luck getting onto the site. Have you considered the possibility that it wasn't an accident? That we have a leak?"

"Yeah, I've thought about it. God, I'm tired. Vasily. Paris. Gina. It would fit."

Kolya pulled up a document he had typed half an hour earlier. He printed it and handed it to Jonathan. Jonathan skimmed it.

"I've cross checked," Kolya said. "That's everyone who knew about all the operations."

"Shit. Us. Bradford. Half the Intelligence Committee. How'd you get the attendance list of the Intelligence Committee meetings?"

"Don't ask."

Jonathan studied the paper. "You don't think Margaret?"

"Why bother sending us out only to have us fail? It makes no sense. No, I would look into three members of the Committee. Ben Smithson, Carl Ford. And the Chair of the Senate Intelligence Committee."

"Corey Manion? I can't stand him, but I don't see him as a traitor." Corey Manion was Jonathan's ex-wife's current lover.

"He's one of the few at all of the meetings. Oh, and the President."

"Oh, come on, Kolya. The President?"

"I'm Russian. I always suspect government officials."

"So we tell Margaret at the debriefing this afternoon. What're you doing tonight? Do you want to go out drinking?"

"Not particularly. It won't help."

"Like hell it won't."

"Did it help last night?"

"Didn't drink enough."

"Don't you have Dylan tonight?"

"Nope. He's going to a friend's birthday party. I'll call Teo. We can do the bars in Georgetown. Maybe we can pick up a couple of women. Or Teo and I can. You've got a woman."

"You should decide whether you want to get stinking drunk or get laid. The two tend to be mutually exclusive." Kolya's only desire was to spend the night with Alex, preferably in bed. But he was concerned about Jonathan. Jonathan was taking it hard. "I'm up for a night of drinking, but not at a bar, Jonathan. Spies do not get drunk in bars."

* * * * *

Ross walked into his office two minutes after Kolya Petrov exited, glared at the napkins on the floor and at the crumbs on the desk, but Mark was oblivious. Weren't gay guys supposed to be neat? "How's it coming?"

"Good." Mark brushed his fingers to get the crumbs off. The chocolate had left a smudge on his fingers. He picked up a napkin and wiped his hand. "I think we've got it nailed. By the way, Kolya was in here looking for you."

"Kolya Petrov?"

"Only one Kolya in the agency."

"Did he see the program?"

Mark shrugged.

Ross felt a surge of anger. If there was anyone he didn't want to see the program, it was Kolya Petrov. Ross put a hand in his pocket and pulled out a stick of gum. He unwrapped and popped the gum into his mouth. "Did…Petrov…see…the…program?"

"He saw me working on it. So what?"

"Did you tell him anything?"

"I told him we were designing a virus for the hell of it. He said something about not wanting his computer infected. What's the big deal, anyway? He's got clearance."

"Not for this, he doesn't. Until Bradford okays it, there's only two of us on this job. You and me. Have you got that?" Ross chewed furiously, his words punctuated by the popping of gum. "Get back to work. And clean up this mess. Where the hell do you think you are?" He noted Mark's look of chagrin with satisfaction, but disciplining Mark was a secondary consideration. He needed to talk to Bradford.

4

Frick rested his elbows on the table and watched the waitress, dark hair and clothes, weave toward him, a look that Frick found appealing until she smiled to reveal rotting teeth. "Mr. Enescu will be here in a moment." She placed a mug of beer, a nearly raw hamburger, and spiced fries in front of him and returned to the kitchen, still swaying, but Frick had lost interest.

He ignored the hamburger and drank the beer until Radu made his appearance. Radu, in his late thirties, owned the restaurant-bar—in name at least—although Frick knew Cuza to be the real owner. It was through Radu that they had made contact with Cuza—or rather Cuza had contacted them and offered what turned out to be a steady stream of reliable information on drug and weapon smugglers from Eastern Europe.

Radu slid into the seat across from Frick. He handed over a picture and a piece of paper. Frick glanced down at the picture of a young man. "Vitalija Salev," he read.

"Arms smuggler from Belarus," Radu said. "The Count has informed me that he's arriving in the U.S. with a load of MANPADS. Surface-to-air missiles."

"How? Where?" This was big information.

"By ship. Port of Newark. Two days from now, on a tanker under the Albanian flag. The details are there." Radu nodded at the sheet of paper.

"You're sure of this?"

"Our source is highly reliable. The weapons are concealed under

24

crates of raw steel." Radu's smile revealed bleached teeth. "Isn't this worth coming out for an early lunch? You don't like your hamburger?"

"I like my meat well done. This is a little bloody for me." Frick pushed the bun down. Red liquid oozed out.

"So send it back. You're a friend of the owner." Radu snapped his fingers. The dark haired woman slunk back and removed the plate. "Well done," he told her. "And bring me a Westvleteren as well."

The small bar was known for its fine Belgian ales, a fact that Frick found peculiar, given the owner and the manager. "Who's the buyer?"

"You'll have to ask Mr. Salev. I don't have that information."

"Where are the weapons from?"

"You'll enjoy this." Radu smiled again. "The missiles originated in the United States and were sold to a third world government which, in turn, sold them to various parties. They eventually wound up in Mr. Salev's hands. So, the weapons are coming home to roost, so to speak."

Frick suspected that he was being tossed someone whom Cuza wanted to get out of the way. Still, and yet, intercepting MANPADS was big. Very big. If the tip panned out, it might even be worth the bargain he had struck with the devil.

"Okay. Thanks. We'll check it out."

* * * * *

"What is so important?" Margaret Bradford stared at Greg Ross. She was dressed in a tailored blue suit and a white silk blouse for her two o'clock meeting with the President of the United States. She had little time on a meeting day, and the loss of Gina had put her in a foul mood. To top it all off, her daughter Amy had begged her to come to her granddaughter Maddie's school play that evening.

Well, damn it, she'd wanted to go. But she couldn't just walk out of the office at four in the afternoon. She was the head of an intelligence agency with a murdered agent—an agent who had passed on the locations of fifteen towns with nuclear power plants, three of which were in the United States.

A large-scale nuclear accident at any one of the plants would be a disaster. The possibility of an incident at all of them was a scenario she didn't even want to contemplate.

Now Ross had insisted on a meeting. Annoying.

"I've, um, designed a Trojan horse."

Ross reached in his pocket and pulled out a piece of cinnamon gum. She frowned at him, hurrying him, but he didn't notice.

"If we can trick Mihai Cuza into running my Trojan horse on a computer in his network, it will give us access to his complete files."

"Chewing gum is a bad habit, Mr. Ross. It will rot your teeth, and it annoys people. Just how do you propose doing that?"

Ross spat his gum into his hand, wrapped the chewed gum in the silver wrapper, and stuck it into a pocket. "Get him interested in accessing our computer network—through a fake website and portal. After what happened with Gina, I think he'll want to know what we know about his operations."

Of course he would want to know, but she wasn't about to give information to a madman. "You'd let Cuza onto our system?"

"Nope. That's the beauty of the whole thing. He'll think he's getting stuff that he's not. He'll be getting chicken shit, fake info, while our virus loads—and we get the crown jewels from him."

"Interesting, Mr. Ross. But let's get down to brass tacks, so to speak. How do you propose getting Cuza to download your Trojan? Your plan to insert a software program onto his computer failed once."

"That's because he was watching for that type of attack. If he thinks he's getting into our network instead of us trying to break into his, he won't have his defenses up. And...."

"And?"

"And we have a complicated security system for him to get through—that would make it impossible to hack into our fake portal. Then we give him an agent, an agent up on the "security system." Have the agent get Cuza onto the site."

"And you think Mihai Cuza would accept an agent who showed up on his doorstep, offering him this free information?" She shook her head. Gina's failure had alerted Cuza to the ECA's interest in him.

"I wasn't suggesting that an agent simply show up on his doorstep offering free goodies. Cuza has to think this is his idea."

"So we understand each other… what are you suggesting exactly?"

"That we allow Cuza to kidnap an agent and then force him to get into our system—thereby leaving Cuza's network wide open for us to download his data. I was thinking of Kolya Petrov— he's good with computers."

She eyed Ross with new appreciation. It was a ruthlessly brilliant plan, but she was surprised that Ross had the guts to propose it.

"Petrov's one of my best agents."

"Yeah, I know, but it should be someone who's good with computers – and he doesn't have any family."

Ross didn't add what she knew: that he didn't particularly like Petrov.

"I see. Do not discuss this with anyone else. Inform Mr. Leslie that it is under the highest classification. To be known only by yourself, Mr. Leslie, and me. Thank you for all your hard work, Mr. Ross. That will be it for now."

He leaned on her desk. "We could get Cuza with this."

She controlled her distaste. "Thank you, Mr. Ross." She didn't watch him leave.

Ross hadn't thought of the obvious problem with his little scheme: how to get Cuza the information that would induce him to kidnap an agent. But she had a few ideas of her own—thanks to Jonathan and Petrov. Jonathan had informed her of Petrov's theory that a mole inside the Intelligence Committee was giving information to Cuza. When she put all the data together, it was the only thing that made sense in light of the failed attempts to penetrate Cuza's organization.

Somewhere, someone was leaking information.

It was something she could use. Between the mole and the Trojan horse, they'd get Cuza.

5

Mihai Cuza listened to Mozart as he ate, the 23rd piano concerto, an excellent interpretation, in the dining room of the penthouse on the upper East Side of Manhattan. He didn't particularly like Jews, but he admired Horowitz's technique.

It was a pleasant room. An antique walnut table was set for three with white china rimed in gold. Paintings of the Eastern Carpathian Mountains hung on the walls. The apartment was not in his name: that would have been unwise. Thankfully, he'd only taken Gina to the loft in Soho—she hadn't known that he had another place in the city. Or known of his other business operations in the city. Even so, given the ECA's current interest in him, New York wasn't secure. He would be heading back to Romania in a few hours on his private jet—and he'd stay there until things cooled down.

"Nice wine, Mihai." Dr. Emil Stanescu, middle-aged Romanian-American, seated at the far end of the table, finished off the last of the 2000 Bordeaux.

Max sat silently between them. He was not drinking.

Max's father had been a member of the Departmentul Securitatii Statului, the hated and feared secret police in Romania under the Communist rule, and Max followed in his father's footsteps. Having sworn his allegiance to Cuza, Max employed his talents to create a strong Christian Romania, under Cuza's leadership.

Cuza wasn't about to state it out loud—nor allow anyone else to do so—but he'd made a mistake. His romantic impulses had nearly allowed a spy to penetrate his organization. Gina had been beautiful,

28

intelligent, and artistic. He had even thought that she might be the one who would share his life and his life's work.

He hadn't felt so strongly about a woman since Marie, who'd been murdered during a mugging by a street thug that the government should have executed. Her death had inspired him to his present work, and he turned his love for her into love for the country of his ancestors.

But his thoughts kept returning to the woman who had betrayed him, and the people who had sent her to seduce him.

She had made a fool of him. No one would laugh, no one would mention it, but he felt the humiliation. He had checked into her background, but obviously, not closely enough.

Never again. He would not allow himself the luxury of a romantic entanglement again, not until the operation was concluded and the election over. It was too close to the completion of his plans.

On his return to Romania, he would check up on Ion Georgescu, who needed constant attention, like a two-year-old. Cuza regretted the necessity of using a front man. He should be the one running for president of Romania. After all, he was descended on his father's side from Voivode Janis Zapolyai, the leader who gained independence for Transylvania in the sixteenth century. On his mother's side, he was related to the great leader Vlad Tepes, known to the uninformed as Vlad the Impaler, who drove the Turks out of Walachia in the fifteenth century. In honor of that ancestry, he executed his enemies by impalement—useful in instilling both fear and respect. His life's work would be to restore Romania's greatness. But he would have to be too public if he ran for office. For now, he needed to be behind the scenes, running the show, with a fool like Ion to put on a good public face.

His thoughts were interrupted by the sound of his phone ringing. He picked it up and checked—yes, a call to take.

"I'm glad you've recovered the MANPADS. Now, in turn, I want to know what this agency has on me. I don't want any more surprises."

Frick's voice on the other end sounded strained. "I should

be getting an update this afternoon. After the meeting of the Intelligence Committee."

"We'll speak then."

* * * * *

President Thomas Lewis, PhD in political science from University of Chicago, and a former Senator, a trim man in his late fifties with an air of intelligence and dignity, sat behind the desk in the Oval Office. The room never ceased to impress Margaret Bradford, who had seen the arrival and departure of at least three presidents. Margaret had despised the previous occupant of the office, although she was too much of an old hand to have displayed anything that might have allowed him to discern her attitude. Lewis, however, was acceptable, even if he at times demonstrated an annoying tendency to micromanage.

Lewis gestured her to a chair opposite his desk and nodded at his Chief of Staff, who left the room. "You said it was urgent, and only for my ears. You got me for twenty minutes."

"Thank you, Mr. President. There are several matters to discuss." She had considered various ways to approach the subject—and decided on a blunt attack. "First, I believe that someone on the Intelligence Committee leaked information on my operative to Mihai Cuza. I discussed the details of the operation in our last meeting, and she was dead less than twenty-four hours later."

He shook his head. "Could be coincidence. Cuza is smart —and operatives make mistakes."

"Once. Maybe. I thought someone had made a careless mistake the first time it happened in Paris, two days after the Intelligence Committee was informed. The second time, in Romania, seemed suspicious, but it could have been a combination of operative error and bad luck. There was a young Ukrainian, too. That's three. Gina— makes four. And Gina Antonia was very good. There are only three members of the Committee who were present at all meetings, and two of them are heads of intelligence organizations. I need your permission to investigate—discretely. This is especially critical in the wake of Ms. Antonio's last message." She then detailed the e-mail that Kolya had received and the concern that nuclear power plants could be targeted. "Whatever Cuza's planning would not be obvious—which is why we need to get inside his network."

He leaned back in the chair. "So, you have two issues, now. The first, a possible mole on the highest level. And second, finding out what Cuza is up to."

"Actually, I wanted to talk to you about the interplay of the two. Using the mole to get inside Cuza's network."

He drummed fingers on the desk. "Interesting. So you're thinking of feeding Cuza fake information through the Intelligence Committee?"

"Close." She hesitated. How willing would Lewis be to go along with her plan? Did he have the requisite ruthlessness? He was a college professor. A college professor who'd devastated his opponent in the campaign. She forged ahead. "My technical people have designed a Trojan horse that would allow us access to Cuza's files. However, as always, we need to get it onto a computer connected to his network. Our attempts to get someone inside failed. Our attempts to hack his computers failed. So maybe instead of our trying to break into *his* computer, our play should be to entice him to break inside *our* computer."

Lewis' brow was furrowed. "I'm not following you. You'd let Cuza have access to classified information?"

"Of course not." She waved a hand. "He'd only have access to an elaborate parallel system through a fake portal—but he has to think it's real. He has to think we have information that he wants. And he has to think that getting our data is his idea."

"And you would do that how?"

She'd hoped he'd made the necessary leap, but he hadn't. She had to lead. "Allow Cuza to believe that he is forcing one of my operatives to give him access to our data. We know we have a mole. We use the mole to give Cuza the information that would not only incentivize him to get hold of ECA data—but would allow him to kidnap one of my operatives."

31

"You'd set up one of your own operatives?" Lewis pronounced the words slowly, as if not fully believing what he'd heard.

"That would be the plan."

"Do you have a particular agent in mind?"

"Nikolai Ivanovich Petrov. He's reasonably good with computers. And he has no family." Therefore, no grieving relatives with the incentive to pry out the truth should Petrov not return. A girlfriend, yes, of whom he was very fond, but the girlfriend was a factor that could also be used, if necessary.

"Petrov." Lewis sounded the name out. "Russian?"

"He was born in Russia, but he's very much an American. He came over when he was a teen." She wanted Petrov's allegiance on the record. She owed him that much.

Lewis drummed a pen on the oak desk. "Have you said anything to him?"

"No. I needed to clear it with you. I'll be asking Petrov to volunteer not only to be kidnapped but to allow himself to be tortured. He'd have to hold off long enough under torture to make it appear real when he does give in."

"What if Cuza uses chemicals?"

"Truth serum is a myth. All chemicals can do is lower inhibitions. It's hard to get anything but nonsense out of a trained agent under chemical influence."

"But if Cuza used chemicals on Petrov, Petrov might reveal the Trojan horse inadvertently." Lewis clicked the pen, looked down at a piece of paper in front of him, and scribbled a note in the margin.

"Yes. Tricky isn't it? Petrov would have to conceal the Trojan horse both under chemicals and under torture. And it'll be difficult to judge just when he should give in. How badly does he allow himself to be hurt? A mistake in judgment, and we've thrown away an agent for nothing." Margaret was slowly but surely leading Lewis to the conclusion she had reached.

"Would Petrov agree to do it?"

"Possibly. Of course, you might remember what happened with Thompson five years ago."

"I wasn't in office then."

She told the story.

Jake Thompson had been an agent for the ECA, who had volunteered for an almost certain suicidal mission in Yemen, allowing himself to be captured by a newly formed Islamic cell with a chip implanted in his arm, so that American special forces could locate and destroy the group with an on-the-ground raid. He'd either lost his nerve or given in under torture, but the end was the same. He told his captors not only of the plan but of the identity of the informer who'd alerted the ECA to the existence of the group. Thompson and the informer were killed; the special forces unit walked into an ambush, and six of them died.

"I had trusted in Thompson's strength of character," Margaret said. "I was wrong. It's impossible to know how anyone will react, no matter how well trained, no matter how dedicated, under torture and the possibility of almost certain death."

Lewis pursed his lips. "Would it be technically possible for Petrov to know how to access the system but not know about the Trojan horse or that it's a fake portal?"

"I'm informed that it would be."

"So, don't tell him."

"It's a hell of a thing."

But it was what she wanted him to suggest. It was what she had already worked out as the best possible option. Thompson had demonstrated that there was no other way. Only now, it was the president's decision, as well as hers.

"Do you have a back-up plan if he doesn't break?" Lewis would ask the question that she didn't want to answer.

"I do, but hopefully it won't be necessary. Most people break eventually, given enough pressure. Still... it's not a guarantee." She'd hold off on the back-up plan, but she knew it would probably come down to another betrayal. She hated the idea, as she hated to deceive Petrov, but she had to make the hard decisions.

The possibility of Cuza's engineering multiple nuclear accidents, the number of people who would die as a result, was real enough to be worth the sacrifice of one person, or even two, and enough to justify what she might have to do.

"But why search for the mole if you're going to use the mole?"

"Because if we know the identity of the mole, it'll be easier to feed him fake information. And as soon as the operation ends, we can remove him so he'll do no further damage."

"Okay." Lewis nodded. "Go."

He had given her what she wanted: absolution. "And two more conditions: First, that once we have downloaded all of Cuza's files, you allow my agency, with whatever help may be necessary, to attempt to retrieve Petrov alive." Not that there would be much chance of success. She expected Cuza to kill Petrov once he no longer had any useful information to offer. Still, planning to rescue Petrov made the betrayal more palatable, even if the end result were the same. "Second, that you never reveal that we deliberately allowed Petrov to be captured."

Whatever happened to Petrov must not cost her the loyalty of her other agents.

"Of course." Lewis waved a hand. "To both. I don't want a shadow on this office either. And, certainly, I would prefer to retrieve the man, once his mission is accomplished. Preferably alive, but if he dies, we will give him the hero's funeral that he'll deserve. And you can have whatever you need to get him back." He checked his watch. "Can't keep the Joint Chiefs waiting."

She stood and smoothed her skirt. "I will arrange matters on my side."

"Good. I'll expect a full report on the agency's new advanced computer files and Mr. Petrov's whereabouts at the next meeting of the Intelligence Committee."

6

Alexandria Feinstein carried the pizza into the living room of her Georgetown townhouse, which she'd purchased from the proceeds of a class action several years earlier. Jonathan Egan slept on the couch, a glass of scotch resting on his chest, which she removed and placed on a coaster on an end table. Teo lay under the piano, his drink next to him on the hardwood floor. Kolya sat on the bench in front of the grand piano, improvising on "Waltz for Debbie," by Bill Evans, an empty shot glass on a coaster.

She set the pizza on the coffee table, slid next to Kolya, and rested her cheek against his shoulder. He smiled and continued to play.

"I play the violin," Teo volunteered from under the piano.

"Mazel tov." Kolya played an E minor seven chord and swung into an elaborate arpeggio.

"I thought he was out cold." Alex peered under the piano. "Jonathan is."

"I played in the college orchestra." Teo's voice echoed hollowly. Alex knew from Kolya that Teo was fluent in fifteen languages and had been recruited straight out of the University of Michigan, where he'd graduated at the tender age of eighteen.

"Again, mazel tov." Kolya hit a series of chords, going down the scale chromatically from E minor to A minor, and then switched to a Duke Ellington tune, "Satin Doll."

"Wanna pass the vodka?" Teo's voice floated up.

"Not particularly. I don't want you throwing up on Alex's floor."

"Won't throw up," Teo said. "You know what's weird about this job?

35

Can't tell anybody. My parents have no idea what I do for a living. My mother asks me how the job's going, what I'm doing, where I am, and I'm making stuff up about the IRS. It feels weird. Feel weird to you, Kolya?"

"Not really."

"What do you tell your parents about your job?"

"Not an issue."

"They don't ask?"

Alex felt a slight tightening of Kolya's arm muscles, but his voice was calm.

"No."

He switched melodies again to "Moonlight in Vermont." Alex lifted her head from his shoulder and looked at Kolya.

She had known Kolya since law school, and although their romantic involvement was of more recent vintage, she had considered him a friend since that time. She had a flash of memory: of Kolya sitting next to her, asking her interpretation of a legal phrase. She had been attracted on that first meeting: the good looks, the shy manner, the quiet wit. But she had been engaged, so she limited herself to "friendship." And after the engagement ended, she had kept in touch, but only as a friend, afraid, she supposed, of losing him completely if they made the move from friends to lovers.

Not that she hadn't thought about a possible closer relationship. But they had been in different cities, and in different lines of work. It was after she had made the move to D.C. for a brief stint as counsel for the ECA that they met up again. Initially, she kept her distance, not wanting to be involved with an agent of the organization that she represented. Once she had moved on from the ECA to start her own law firm and found the Center for Defense, a non-profit dedicated to freeing the wrongfully convicted, matters had progressed.

In the course of an eleven-year friendship and a one-year intense involvement, she had pried from him only the most basic facts about his childhood, and most of what she did know, she had learned back in law school when he was younger and more open about his past, before his job choice solidified his personal reserve into a professional secretiveness. She didn't even realize that he was Jewish until she'd known him a month, not that it mattered to her, although it made her mother happy that she was for once dating a nice Jewish boy – who worked for the IRS.

She knew his childhood had been difficult, just as she knew that he'd been up most of the previous night after telling her that Gina, whom she'd met and liked, had been killed. Playing jazz, as much as the drinking, was his version of therapy.

Teo continued to ask questions.

"Really? They never ask what you're doing when you're out of town for months?"

"They're dead."

There was an awkward pause, or it would have been awkward had either Kolya or Teo been sober.

"Sorry."

The moment passed. Kolya returned to "Moonlight in Vermont."

Teo hiccupped. Alex peered under the piano. "Teo, go to bed. You go to sleep there, and you'll be stiff tomorrow. Guest bedroom is up the stairs, first door on the left."

"Whaddabout Jonathan?"

Alex glanced in his direction. "If he wakes up, he knows where the other guest bedroom is located."

Teo crawled out from under the piano and staggered up the stairs.

"Cut him a break, Kolya. He's not so bad."

"Maybe not. But he's annoying."

She shook her head. "Okay, be a son of a bitch, beat up on the kid. I'm going to put the pizza away, take a shower, and go to bed."

"I want to play for a few more minutes."

He concentrated on the music, and she slid off the bench. She took a long and luxurious shower, and when she emerged from the bathroom, he was stretched out on top of the quilt, fully dressed, eyes closed. He looked so young when he was asleep, deceptively innocent. She sat on the side of the bed and leaned over to brush the light blond hair from his forehead. As she did, his arms circled her waist and pulled her down into a kiss, his mouth tasting of vodka.

She broke off the kiss. "Are you okay?"

"I'm a little drunk."

"Not what I asked."

"I know. It's my answer, though."

"I know you can't share operational details, but I'm here if you want to talk. About Gina. About anything."

"I know that too. But talking doesn't help."

She'd expected that answer. "What would help?"

In answer, he reached for the tie on her bathrobe—and then looked at her with raised eyebrows.

"The answer is yes, but I thought you were drunk."

"A little drunk. Not too drunk."

"Then I suggest you get undressed."

He conceded her point and stood. He yanked off his shirt, slung his belt with the holster over the chair, removed the gun and slid it into a holster that he had attached to the back of her bed. He finished undressing and tossed his clothes on an armchair next to the bed.

He lay down and pulled her next to his hard body. Winding fingers through her hair, he kissed her deeply and roamed slowly down her body, her throat, her breasts, then he moved lower, teasingly, slowly nuzzling and kissing, until she was ready, more than ready.

She tightened her fingers in his hair and pulled his head up. "Now, love," she said in a hoarse voice. He positioned himself, and she wrapped her arms around him, pulling him down into her, feeling his mouth on her neck, his chest against her breasts, moving with his rhythm, forgetting everything but the moment.

7

Three men were seated on the far side of the long conference table in West Wing of the White House—their usual Thursday meeting. Margaret Bradford looked around the table, noted absences—the House representative, Homeland Security, the DNI—and found her own seat. She was fine with the absences since all those present were the ones under suspicion for being a mole. Nor did the absences change the purpose of the meeting—disinformation.

Ben Smithson, Director of Central Intelligence, once her boss, bald, with a pretentious goatee, and an insufferable air of superiority, swiveled his steel gray eyes in her direction. "Heard you lost one, Marge."

"That is correct." She refrained from comment on his use of a nickname she despised. She hoped that Ben Smithson was the traitor.

Carl Ford, Director of the FBI, turned to her. Sandy brown hair and glasses, he had a mild manner that belied his determination. He'd come up through the ranks of the FBI—as she had come up through the ranks of the CIA. She'd known him for twenty years—and liked him. It would be sad if it were him. "Do you need any help? The FBI has more manpower than the ECA."

"Thank you for the offer, Carl. But no."

"Sorry to hear about your agency's loss." Corey Manion, the new Senator from the State of New York, good looking, considered a Presidential prospect a few years down the road, sat next to Carl. "No one I knew, I hope. Not Egan, was it? Or that fellow with the accent."

The Washington world was a small one. The Senator knew both

39

Jonathan Egan and Kolya Petrov personally because he was sleeping with Egan's former wife, who also happened to be his speech writer. Margaret and everyone else at the table were aware of the affair, which was not a big deal, except perhaps to Jonathan.

"Thank you, Corey. Mr. Egan and Mr. Petrov are both fine. But further explanations should wait until the President joins us, don't you think? Where is he, by the way?"

"Budget dispute," Carl Ford said.

The words had barely left his mouth when the door swung open, and President Thomas Lewis strode in, waving at the others to remain seated. Lewis seated himself at the head of the table. "Sorry for the delay. I had the Speaker of the House on the horn, and I couldn't get him to stop talking. Shall we get down to it?"

Reading glasses perched on the bridge of her nose, Margaret sorted through the papers in front of her. "Let me start with our attempt to locate and neutralize Mihai Cuza."

"Let me just register my opinion once again that the United States has no national interest at stake related to Mihai Cuza's activities." Smithson, pompous as ever. "Cuza is trying to replace the current Romanian president with his own candidate. It shouldn't concern this administration."

"What evidence do you have that Cuza is planning some sort of terrorist activity in the United States?" Ford asked.

"How about the fact that he murdered my agent?"

"Which is a terrible fact—but you don't know if the murder was related to any security concern in the United States. Maybe the murder was personal. Wasn't she sleeping with him?" Ford persisted.

"We know that Cuza's dangerous. We know that among other thing, he intends to discredit the current Romanian government for its alliance with the U.S."

"If you're that worried, have him taken out. We can do that, Margaret, if your team has a weak stomach for it," Smithson said.

"My team is quite capable of taking out anyone the CIA is capable of taking out." She was aware that at least some of her agents might balk at assassinations, but Smithson didn't have to know. "But taking him out won't necessarily stop an attack. We need to get into his files. That's what my operative was trying to do—get into Cuza's files."

"And which she failed to do. If this is a matter so critical to the security of the country, then professionals should handle it, professionals in an organization big enough to have back-up teams and intelligence analysts in place." Smithson's real problem was not with the reasoning behind the Cuza assignment, but with the staffing—by her agency, not the CIA.

"An agency so big it's been penetrated by moles repeatedly."

Smithson looked like he'd been slapped.

"Enough." President Lewis held up a hand. "Obviously, Ben, you are never going to agree. But this is my decision. As always, Margaret acts under my direct orders, and she has my confidence. Can we cut to the quick, Margaret? What is your next step?"

"We have reason to believe that a financial office in New York is really a front for Cuza's operation. We've also compiled a database on every known link to Mihai Cuza, going back twenty years, and we have a team combing through it right now. We have a program assessing every move and every contact Cuza ever made. And also, my tech team is setting up a new security protocol that will allow any agent to access our system from any computer."

"And?" Lewis asked, his fingers tapping the table.

"We're going to be sending someone to our office in New York to follow up on Cuza's contacts—and to field test the new security system." She looked around the table, gauging the reaction. She could tell nothing. Whoever the mole was—he was very good.

"Have you worked out the details?" Smithson asked.

She really hoped it was him.

"Not yet. I'm assigning personnel later today."

She caught the President's glance and smiled at him. She made the first steps towards the trap. Now to ready the bait.

* * * * *

Mihai Cuza stroked the nose of the Arabian mare and offered her a carrot. She tossed her head and then accepted the treat. It was nice to be back. Riding his mare was one of the benefits of being home in Romania. The scenery was another.

From the meadow where he stood, he had a spectacular view of the Carpathian Mountains, until recently almost deserted, except for the small villages where Romanian peasants had lived for thousands of years. Now, with the arrival of entrepreneurs in the country new estates dotted the hills, although the general population remained desperately poor. Not that he felt crowded: His own property of a thousand acres of forest and mountains, along with his stables, his house, and his back-up generator for the inevitable power blackouts, provided both privacy and luxury.

"Sir?" It was Max, followed by Ion Georgescu, a stocky man with military bearing, a trim grey beard, and pale blue eyes.

"No difficulty on the roads, I hope. It is still too early for snow."

"No, no difficulties. No car trouble, no wolves."

Cuza knew that this corner of Romania still had occasional difficulty from wolves, and he also knew that Georgescu was nervous in the mountains. "You don't need to be concerned about the wolves. They haven't eaten anyone this year."

"I wasn't really worried about the wolves," Georgescu said.

"Just about being seen with me."

"My being connected to you publicly may not be the wisest course politically. Although you are known to many as a patriot, others are uncomfortable. The Americans could cause difficulties, especially if you insist on killing them. That young woman in New York."

"She was a spy working for the same American agency as the man I impaled here."

"I don't care who you impale here." Georgescu dismissed the murder with a wave of his hand. "No one cares what you do here in the mountains. But an American agent? In New York? That would make it awkward politically if it were widely known that you're backing me."

"I'm not backing you, Ion." Cuza's tone remained pleasant. "You're fronting for me. Remember. It is an important distinction."

"Still, I'm the one who has to face the public. The questions. And what if the Americans come after me?"

Cuza ran the metal stirrups up under the saddle. The mare needed to be walked, and the groom was nowhere to be seen. He didn't want her to suffer because Georgescu was having a nervous fit. Cuza grasped the bridle and started to lead the horse toward the barn. Georgescu followed. "The Americans will do nothing except nicely try to get information from you. Just keep up the fiction that you know nothing of me—or the people who work for me."

It wasn't actually fiction. Georgescu knew only a handful of Cuza's people, none of his contacts in other countries, none of his other addresses, none of the false names under which he traveled.

"You're not planning anything that would embarrass me?"

"No, just keeping track of our adversaries." That was partly true. He needed to know what his enemies were doing. This ECA was proving itself to be difficult. But this also was not to be discussed with Georgescu.

The groom ran out from the barn, alarm on his face. He bobbed his head in apology as he took the horse's bridle. Cuza would let the man's lapse pass without retribution.

Cuza took Georgescu by the elbow. "Let us go in the house. You will stay for lunch, won't you? My housekeeper is a fine cook—she's prepared *pui Cimpulungean*. And I'll introduce you to Doctor Stanescu, who flew in from New York with me. He'll be dining with us."

* * * * *

Georgescu had scurried off as soon as he had finished eating his chicken stuffed with smoked bacon, sausage, garlic, and vegetables. Cuza didn't mind: He needed Georgescu —a popular white nationalist who was campaigning against the foreigners and globalists who were ruining Romania—but the man had no culture—no appreciation of music or good food. Worse, he had complained about his wife for a good part of the dinner and ruined what otherwise would have been an exceptional meal.

Cuza had just lifted a forkful of his dessert and paused to listen to a melody that he loved when he became aware that Max stood behind him. He finished the bite and washed it down with a sip of coffee. "Any word on the American agents?"

"Nothing. But I just got off the phone. It appears the ECA has developed some sort of database on you." Max settled himself in a chair opposite Stanescu and helped himself to a cup of coffee. "And they're setting up a new security system."

"I have some of the best hackers in the world working for me. Get them on it."

Max drank coffee. "If it doesn't work—apparently there may be another way. The ECA is sending an agent to New York to test out the system—and to track down people who've had contact with you. Maybe we could intercept the agent."

Cuza nodded. "Tell Frick of our interest in the ECA's plans. It's annoying that the ECA is in possession of the names of the towns where we're targeting the plants."

Stanescu poured himself more brandy. His speech was already slurring. "I take it you haven't mentioned the plan to Ion."

"It never came up."

Ion Georgescu neither knew nor needed to know about the fifteen nuclear power plants that would experience meltdowns or near meltdowns. It was a perfect plan. Georgescu, at Cuza's direction, opposed expanding nuclear power plants in Romania—the opposition supported it as a way to combat global warming and to earn revenue. Once the accidents occurred, the Romanian public would turn on anyone supporting nuclear power. Ion could properly express his indignation at the folly of the present government. And Cuza, who had invested heavily in companies that cleaned up radiation from spills or accidents and in green technologies, would not only watch his candidate sweep into office but would substantially increase his net worth.

8

Margaret Bradford sat at her oak desk decorated with a crystal vase filled with the flowers of the day and a silver framed picture of her granddaughter, although no one ever thought of her as a grandmother. The walls were decorated with framed Vanity Fair prints of writers from the 19th century. She must have owned a dozen of them, and she rotated through them periodically. The writers of the day: Ruskin, Arnold, and Browning. All English—all boring, even to Kolya, who'd majored in English literature in college.

That she'd called the surviving members of the New York expedition into her office again was a little unexpected. After all, they'd been debriefed. They were working on developing other leads to locate Cuza. But had something turned up at one of the nuclear power plants?

They were arrayed in leather chairs in front of Margaret's desk: Jonathan, the favorite, dead center—Kolya to Jonathan's right, with Teo on the far left.

Kolya had questions, but he waited while she tapped something on a phone, opened a file and shuffled papers. Then she finally spoke.

"Gentlemen, given that we have two distinct problems, the possibility of a mole as well as determining Mihai Cuza's plans, I've decided to split you up. Jonathan, I am assigning you and Mr. Lorenzo to investigate three members of the Intelligence Committee—The Director of the CIA, the Director of the FBI, and Senator Manion. Those were the only three, along with the President, who were present for the discussion of the details of your mission. Discretely, please. I am also putting three other agents at your disposal—Elizabeth Owen, Marty Davis, and Pete Menendez."

Kolya stirred in his chair. "And me?" He was a little surprised to be split off from Jonathan, with whom he normally partnered.

Margaret turned her gaze on him. "Ah yes, Mr. Petrov. Please report to Mr. Ross. I want you trained on a new computer security system. Next Friday, you're to go to New York to follow up on leads to other members of Cuza's New York organization, and while you're there, you can field test the system. Eric White will rendezvous with you on the following Monday. The two of you can then decide if additional field agents are needed."

"I thought Eric was tracking nuclear material sold by North Korea."

"Is there a problem, Mr. Petrov?"

Kolya preferred to work with people he knew well, not merely for social reasons. In life and death situations, he liked knowing the capabilities of his team. He didn't have anything against White; he just didn't know him very well. "No."

"No sending him on a tour of Little Odessa in Brooklyn."

"I only send new agents on tours." Kolya and Jonathan had already sent White out on a non-existent mission five years earlier.

"Yes, I recall Mr. White's visit to the Supreme Court," Margaret returned. "You do it again, Mr. Petrov, and I'll accept your resignation."

Kolya found the level of hostility unsettling. He knew she disapproved of initiation pranks, but she'd ignored them in the past. Why was she suddenly aiming at him?

"The tours are an agency tradition," Jonathan objected. "And I'm in on them, too, Margaret."

Bradford turned to him. "I wasn't addressing you. I am aware that you and Mr. Petrov have been co-conspirators. However, it is to cease."

With an effort, Kolya maintained his composure. "I will consider myself warned."

Audrey bustled in, placed a tray with a teapot and a flowered mug, inscribed with the words *World's Best Grandmom* on Margaret's desk. She surveyed the three men and sniffed.

"Thank you, Audrey," Margaret forestalled any comment.

Audrey sniffed again and stalked out.

Margaret poured her mug of tea and measured in a teaspoon of sugar. "That will be all." She picked up the receiver of her phone. "Mr. Egan, I want a daily update on your progress. Mr. Petrov, report to Mr. Ross. Good evening."

* * * * *

"So, what is this new system I am supposed to learn?" Kolya asked Mark Leslie.

Mark's tone was subdued. "Instead of signing onto the system with a simple password, I designed a system that will randomly choose ten security questions out of a possible two or three dozen or so questions that you have to answer for access. Each question has to be answered within thirty seconds, and a wrong answer will shut down the system for twenty-four hours. It will allow you to establish a link with our network with a computer not previously identified, and since the questions are never the same, it will be impossible to hack."

"Will I have to go through the program every time?"

"As long as you use the same device, even if you turn it off, the system will recognize your device and let you on with a simple password. But the password will change with each session, and you'll be informed of the new password at sign-off. You up to starting tonight?"

Mark continued to avoid meeting Kolya's eye. Kolya felt uneasy. Was there something he was not being told?

Don't be paranoid. He remembered Jonathan's frequent admonition to the same effect, and with an effort, pushed down his doubts.

Kolya suppressed a yawn and glanced down at his watch. "Fine. Just give me half an hour to get some dinner and make a phone call."

* * * * *

It was a rainy Friday morning. Rain splattered against the windows, and on K Street, black and red umbrellas bobbed along the sidewalks five floors below the conference room where Jonathan had assembled the team. Elizabeth Owen, Marty Davis, Pete Menendez, and Teo Lorenzo had also brought their breakfasts and their beverages to the meeting.

Elizabeth, slim and athletic with short black hair and a warm brown complexion, looked at Jonathan. "Petrov not joining us?"

"Nope," Jonathan said.

"Too bad. No one livens up a party like Petrov."

"You got a problem with Kolya?"

Elizabeth had had a brief affair with Kolya that he'd taken seriously but she had not, although she'd been noticeably pissed off when he'd moved on.

"He's a little too caustic for my taste."

"Kolya's all right. Get over it, Liz." Marty Davis, thinning light brown hair and just the hint of a middle age paunch, whose southern accent crept in when he wasn't trying to hide it, also knew the history. "Can we move this along?"

Jonathan turned a pen in his hands. "You all have been briefed by Bradford. We have the delicate duty of finding a mole. It's especially urgent because of Gina's last message."

Three heads nodded soberly. Everyone knew of her murder and of the possible threat to a nuclear facility.

"I worked for Ford when he was Assistant Director, before I was recruited by the ECA." In his late twenties, Pete Menendez, black hair and black eyes, had been with the agency for three years.

"So did I," Jonathan said. "And Kolya. In New York."

"Don't see him as a mole."

"Me neither," Jonathan said. "But he's one of the three we have to check."

Elizabeth ticked off the main points. "We've got a U.S. Senator, the Director of the Central Intelligence Agency, and the Director of the FBI to investigate, and the five of us. Can we pull in other agents to do footwork?"

"We can use our people to do groundwork, but we can't tell them the nature of the investigation. It's on a need-to-know basis."

Marty laughed. It wasn't a good laugh, just enough to indicate skepticism. "You expect us to investigate members of the Intelligence Committee without any of them finding out? You're crazy."

"I know a couple of guys on the inside to check out Ford and Smithson," Jonathan said.

"One of them Steve Kowolsky? Our tours in Moscow overlapped by a year or so." Marty shook his head. "He's a mean ol' son-of-a-bitch."

"Think he won't help?"

"He'll help. He loves to catch spies. But he's got his own agenda and his own ideas. You ask him for help, and you don't know what the hell you're going to get."

9

At every nuclear power plant, the details differed, but the idea was the same. Control rods were raised, and the three percent of uranium-235 in the fuel rods began to undergo induced fission, capturing neutrons and splitting into new atoms. The resulting energy drove the steam turbine, which spun a generator and produced power.

Nuclear power was safe, or so the experts said, because of all the safeguards programmed into the system. If the core temperature remained stable, and the cooling systems worked, everything was fine.

The core temperature, the coolant system, and the external radiation were all monitored by computers, with a back-up analog system. But as long as the computer system operated normally, few operators bothered to check it.

The recent alert from an American intelligence agency had caused concern at fifteen plants. Security had been increased, and checks performed on all systems. Nothing abnormal or wrong.

Anyway, when did American intelligence agencies get it right?

* * * * *

Jonathan found Kolya tapping on the keys of a computer. Kolya glanced up, nodded an acknowledgement of his friend, and returned his attention to the screen.

"Having fun?"

"Nothing I like better than computer games." Kolya typed for another minute and hit enter. "The damn thing is timed. If I don't

50

get an answer in quickly enough, everything I've done to access the system cancels. What are you doing here in Siberia?"

"Looking for you." Jonathan perched on a desk. "The kid may be a whiz at languages, but he's not much of a hacker. I need to get into Capital Tennis Club. I'm going to try to meet up with Kowolsky at his club."

"Accidental meeting?"

"More or less."

Kolya held up a hand, leaned forward, and read the screen. He typed again.

"What're you doing?"

"Ross and Mark cooked up this new security system," Kolya said. "Random questions and answers." He typed again. The screen went blank. "*Eboyanna mat.*"

"Why are you doing this?"

Kolya pushed his chair back and picked up a cup of coffee from Mark's desk, where it had left a brown drop on the fake wood. Kolya flicked the liquid with a forefinger and then brought the coffee up to his lips.

"It's an elaborate security system to allow access to our central computer from a new device. This is only a test. If I were really trying to sign on in the field, I'd be shut out for twenty-four hours after a mistake."

"Sounds kind of fun."

"I would be pleased to trade assignments with you. So, you want me to hack into the Capital Tennis Club and find out when he's playing?"

"If you don't mind a break."

"Ross will be unhappy. So I'll do it. My office?"

"Sure. Why not?"

Kolya stood, stretched, and followed Jonathan into the hall.

"And I wanted to talk to you," Jonathan continued as they walked down the corridor. "I don't know what the hell was wrong with Margaret."

"The most likely explanation is that she suspects me of being the leak."

"You're still after Cuza, aren't you? If she really thought you might be leaking information, she would have quarantined you from anything to do with him. And she would have told me to keep you away from what I was doing. She did neither."

"Then it was simply personal? Maybe because I'm the only Russian in the agency."

"You're not Russian, you're an American."

"Yes, but ethnically I'm still Russian. And Jewish."

"She doesn't have anything against either. Shit, Kolya, she was just in her boss from hell mood. Has nothing to do with your ethnicity. She just gets like this sometimes."

10

From her seat, Margaret could see out the window to the lawn of White House where a Secret Service agent walked Lewis' Irish setter. Around the conference table, the full Intelligence Committee—but it was the presence of the three suspected moles that mattered. They were there. The President was there. It was time. With the President's approval and help, she was about to set up her own agent. He gave her a nod. It was her turn to update the committee. She took a breath and started.

"We have new information on Cuza's activities in the United States, and we are cultivating an informer inside Cuza's organization." It was something of an exaggeration. Still the possibility of an informer would certainly intrigue Cuza. "We are checking out some names and addresses of possible Cuza associates in New York. Meanwhile, our new security system is about to go online. We're combining the two efforts, the search for Cuza and a field test of our new program. I'm sending one of my most senior operatives, Petrov, to work out of our safe house in New York. He'll be responsible for surveillance of a financial institution connected to Cuza and following-up on other information provided by the informer. Hopefully, we'll soon understand the significance of the fifteen towns."

The Committee, of course, didn't know the real reason that she was sending Petrov to New York. Margaret wanted Petrov isolated from her other agents, so that any attempt to kidnap him would neither be foiled by the unexpected presence of Petrov's friends nor result in the loss of additional agents.

"Petrov knows how to work this new security system?" Lewis asked.

"He's being trained on it right now, along with several other agents going to the Middle East and Asia." That was also a lie, but she needed Cuza to think that even if Petrov disappeared, the system would continue to be operational.

"When's Petrov going to New York, Margaret?" Lewis prompted. "Given the danger posed by Cuza, maybe the FBI should also be aware of when he's arriving and what he's doing. For additional security." He glanced over at Carl Ford, who nodded.

Margaret turned to Carl, trying to act casually, as if she hadn't expected the question. "He'll be taking a train to Penn Station on Friday. He should get there at around ten in the evening, and he'll be staying at the safe house in the West Village."

Carl nodded. "Have him check in with us when he gets there."

Which would of course defeat the whole purpose unless Carl was the mole, but the details were out there. She took another look at the faces of the three men she suspected of betraying the United States, one of whom would probably be on the phone to Cuza in the next few hours. It was the first time she had ever hoped for a leak.

* * * * *

Bob Smith, a large man in his fifties who appeared elegant in a well-cut suit despite his size, played poker with five other men in the back room of a bar popular with FBI agents, one of the few in D.C. that accommodated both cigar smoking and drinking. A dish of peanuts and a mug of beer sat at Bob's left elbow, a smoldering cigar balanced on the edge of an ashtray in front of him.

Bob fanned his cards. "Shit. You dealt me shit. You dealing from the bottom of the deck, Mike?"

Mike denied cheating.

"Shit." Bob tossed one white poker chip onto the pile and spotted Jonathan. "I'll be damned. Egan. What the hell you doing here?" He gestured with his beer. "Sit. You bring money?"

"I don't play penny ante poker. You play for real money and I'll think about it." He took a chair from a neighboring table.

"Yeah, I know. This shit ain't for rich guys like you. Crummy little ten-dollar pots."

The man next to him raised with two blue chips. "Call or fold."

Bob tossed two blue chips onto the pile and blew cigar smoke over the table. "Call." He had a full house.

"You got a few minutes?"

Bob gathered in the chips and stacked them carefully. "Five minutes."

Jonathan followed him into the men's room. Bob checked that the stalls were empty and took his position by the urinal.

"What'd you want?" He unzipped his pants.

Jonathan stationed himself at the neighboring urinal and followed suit. "We may have a problem of the Robert Hansen variety."

"We, buddy boy? You back in the Bureau?"

"We, the people of the United States of America."

"Oh, that we." Bob zipped and moved to the sink to wash his hands. "So you think there's a spy. Based on what?"

"Couple of things. Gina Antonia's murder, for one." Jonathan turned the tap on, squeezed a dollop of soap onto his palms, and washed.

"Heard about that one." Bob hit the hand dryer with his elbow. He slowly rubbed his hands under the blast of warm air. "One of the possibilities in the FBI? High placed? Someone you'd have trouble tailing or bugging."

"Carl Ford."

Bob laughed, a low soft sound. "Shit, you want me to spy on the Director. Are you out of your mind? Hell no. Pure and simple. Not that it hasn't been fun seeing you, Jonny, but no. No. No. No."

"You owe me. You owe Kolya." Years earlier, Jonathan and Kolya had saved Bob's life in a shoot-out, shortly before leaving the FBI for the ECA.

"I'll get my ass busted for this. You don't just investigate the Director of the FBI."

"I can't. But you can. You can check his calls, his visitors, and he doesn't even have to know. If he's clean, no one has to know, and I hope to God he is clean. I like Carl. You've checked on high level people before."

"Not this high." Bob reached into his jacket and brought out a cigar and lighter. He bit off the end of the cigar, spat it on the floor, stuck the cigar in his mouth, and flicked the lighter. He blew a stream of smoke at Jonathan. "What the hell makes you think it's someone on the Intelligence Committee?"

"We've been after a guy—Mihai Cuza—trying to get information about possible cyber terrorism attacks—and every time we get close, it blows up on us."

"You checking your own house? It would be pretty damn embarrassing if I'm snooping around our Director and the mole turns out to be an ECA operative."

"We're checking. Still, I don't think the leak's from the agency. I think it's the Intelligence Committee."

"What the hell," Bob said. "I never investigated a Director before."

Jonathan chuckled. "Look at it this way. Now Kolya and I'll owe you. Won't that be a relief after ten years?"

"How's Kolya doing, anyway?"

"Same as always."

"Haven't seen the bastard for a while. You tell him to drop by for poker some time."

"He hates poker."

"I know. A goddamn intellectual, lousy at poker. That's why I like playing with him. He always loses. Funny guy. Risks his goddamn neck all the time, one of the best for undercover work, but can't play poker for shit." Bob shook his head.

"Maybe he doesn't take poker seriously."

"Maybe. And maybe he takes money seriously and doesn't care about getting killed. You notice that no one's used the bathroom for the past ten minutes?"

"Funny about that."

"Yeah, funny," Bob said. "Especially in a bar full of men drinking beer. Let's go."

Jonathan led the way out of the bathroom. Leaning against the wall just next to the bathroom door, arms crossed, was Kolya.

"How many guys you turn away?" Jonathan asked.

"About a dozen," Kolya said. "All very annoyed."

"Hello you goddamn son-of-a-bitch," Bob said. "Want to play a hand?"

"Are you fucking kidding?" Kolya said. "No."

11

Mihai Cuza frowned at the rug on the floor of the living room. Someone had spilled red wine on the white portion of the gold, white, and green hand-woven rug. Beauty was important to Mihai Cuza, and to see something beautiful carelessly ruined bothered him.

He pointed the stain out to Max.

"Do you know how much that rug cost me, Max? Thirty thousand American dollars. Get someone to clean it up, would you?"

Max's expression, if any, was unreadable. "I will get someone on it. Is that all?"

"No." Cuza shifted his gaze from the rug to the view outside the large picture window. The leaves on the bushes just were starting to turn gold and red. Fall came early in the Carpathian Mountains. "It seems the ECA may have some interesting information on their computer about me. Their director claims to have an informant, which I question, but I need to be sure. They also don't seem to understand the reason for the list that Ms. Antonio sent before we killed her. We've had no luck hacking into their network." Cuza watched a small golden bird settle on a bird feeder. The mountains were home to numerous species of birds, and Romania hosted thousands of other species migrating from Europe to warmer climates. "We need the cooperation of someone who knows how to get into the network. An ECA operative who can access the network will be in New York Friday night. I think we should invite him for a visit. Take a number of our people and contact our New York organization."

"Do you have a description of him?"

"We have a picture. Over on top of the table. The man in the middle."

Max picked up the photograph and studied it. "The blond?"

"Yes. Nikolai Ivanovich Petrov. Russian immigrant to the United States, and a former FBI agent. Petrov is also a Jew, or so I understand."

"A Jew and a Russian. Perfect. He should be easy to take."

"Don't underestimate your opponent."

"I don't plan to underestimate him. But I will enjoy taking down a Jew. There's too many of them still, controlling the money, controlling the media. They'll rule the world if we don't fight back. Romania isn't going to be great again until we're rid of them."

"I agree, and enjoy yourself. Still, make sure he remains alive, and in sufficiently good shape to provide information." Cuza handed Max a sheet of paper. "That's the Amtrak train he's arriving on and the address where he'll be staying. We need to do this quickly to confirm the security of our plans. The date is getting close."

* * * * *

"I hear we're going to be working together." Eric White, a heavy-set redhead, carrying a tray with a tuna sandwich, potato chips, a cup of coffee, and a piece of apple pie, greeted Kolya in the cafeteria. Eric spoke six languages fluently and had a master's from Georgetown University in International Relations. "You mind?" He indicated the empty seat at Kolya's table.

Kolya was eating a bowl of tomato soup and reading the *The Washington Post* on his phone. He clicked it off. "Not at all." Although Kolya tended to be more solitary than not, he saw no reason to reject a friendly gesture.

Eric inspected the top piece of toast on his sandwich. "I told Rita rye bread."

Kolya looked at the sandwich. The bread was wheat. He sympathized. "Take it back."

"It's not worth getting up." Eric ate a corner of the sandwich. Kolya knew what he meant: it wasn't worth arguing with Rita, the cafeteria manager. Rita was six feet tall, two hundred pounds, and didn't take kindly to complaints. "I hear I'm working with you on this Cuza thing."

"Correct." Kolya sipped a spoonful of soup. "We are to set up in the agency apartment on Washington Street."

"Nice," Eric said. "I like New York. The city that never sleeps. Restaurants. Plays. Music."

"Good jazz."

"So what's the plan?"

"The Balkan Financial Group in New York has some connection to Cuza. Couldn't hack in, so I'm going up on Friday and figure out a more conventional approach. Also, I'm supposed to try out the new security system for the network."

"Sounds good. Want to catch that bastard Cuza. You go to Gina's funeral?"

Kolya nodded.

"Didn't you love how Bradford stated that she was a great asset to the IRS? We even have to be buried under false pretenses."

Did it really matter what was said at the funeral? He thought of Gina's mother sobbing in the front row.

"You do anything to the kid that was on your team, what's his name, Lorenzo?"

"Me?"

"Yeah, you. Don't give me that innocent look, Nikolai. I remember five years ago when I first came to the agency, you and Egan called me up and told me to go sit in the Supreme Court gallery with a red carnation in my buttonhole. I sat there until the damn place closed, listening to the most boring shit I ever heard in my life. I still owe you on that one, bud."

"It was good for you. It taught you to be skeptical of orders." Kolya allowed himself a small smile. "And the Supreme Court is important to maintaining our democracy."

"I'm just glad I'm not a lawyer. So, I'm heading to New York on Friday." Eric crunched his last potato chip. "My sister lives in Queens. She just had a baby. Her fourth."

"That's a lot of children." Kolya mentally contrasted his home with Rifka, as a doted upon only surrogate child, to his time in the boy's home, when he shared a room with nine other boys. At the boy's home, there had been continual noise, never enough food, and the only adult attention was negative. Rifka had not been rich, but she had indulged his interests in books and music.

"I came from a big Catholic family. Two brothers, three sisters. We had to wait for the bathroom, but we were never bored. You don't have any kids, do you?"

Kolya finished his soup. "I don't."

It was true, for how long, he wasn't sure. Alex would like children. He hadn't decided. "Your wife is pregnant, isn't she?"

"Due in the spring." Eric looked at the mayo that had dripped onto his fingers from the end of his sandwich. He reached for the napkin. "God this stuff is messy. You driving to New York?"

"I have a ticket for the train. Seven o'clock." Kolya didn't want to offend Eric, whom he liked and with whom he would be working, although he would have preferred to read on the train. "There should be empty seats."

12

When the alarm rang, Kolya flipped the switch and glanced at Alex, who was still asleep. Resisting the urge to kiss her outstretched arm, he pushed himself out of bed and headed for the bathroom.

He let the warm water on his face finish the job of waking him. They should have gone to sleep earlier. Five hours was not enough.

Toweling himself dry, he smelled toast and fresh brewed coffee. He pulled on his robe and padded barefoot into the kitchen. Alex, uncharacteristically, was cooking.

"What are you doing up? It's only six." He stroked back a strand of hair that had fallen in her face and traced a finger down her cheek.

"You're up."

"I don't have a choice. I have to get to the office." He poured himself a cup of coffee and stirred in sugar.

"I need to go home and change my clothes. And I wanted to say goodbye."

"I said goodbye last night so you could sleep." He leaned against the counter, cradling his cup between his hands.

"It was so much fun, I thought I'd say it again."

"It won't be quite the same." He gave her a half smile over the rim of his coffee cup. It had been good. Dinner had been wonderful, and after dinner they had walked through the chill of an October night to a small jazz café. Afterwards, they had returned to his apartment for a leisurely session of lovemaking.

She whisked the eggs vigorously. "I'll drop you at the office on my way home, so you won't need to walk. And you could use a decent breakfast. Don't give me that look. I am perfectly capable of cooking scrambled eggs."

"If you say so. But just so you know, there's a fire extinguisher in the cabinet on top of the refrigerator

In the bedroom, he pulled on a blue polo shirt, a white sweater, and a pair of jeans. He settled his holster around his waist before retrieving his HK. After checking the manual safety on his semi-automatic, he placed it in his holster and pulled his sweater down to hide the gun.

Returning to the kitchen, he accepted a plate of eggs and toast, which he carried to the table. Alex joined him a minute later.

"Thank you for cooking." He lifted a forkful of the eggs. Overcooked. He tried extra salt. It didn't help. He added pepper.

"You're welcome. I overcooked the eggs a little."

He bit into the toast.

"And the toast," she added.

"I noticed. I'm perfectly happy to cook, and I'm better at it."

"It's six in the morning. I made you coffee, and I made you breakfast. So, you going to eat or you going to *kvetch*?"

"I wasn't *kvetching*, just observing." At least the coffee was good—strong, the way he liked it. He hesitated, only for a moment. "I thought perhaps you might want to join me in New York next weekend."

"While you're on assignment?"

"It's a low-risk operation. Not much different from working here. I can take a personal day on occasion. I thought perhaps we could do some jazz clubs and visit the diamond district. If you're interested."

"Jazz clubs and the diamond district. I'm intrigued by the combination." But she was smiling. "Care to elaborate?"

He stirred sugar into his coffee. "I should think it obvious. New York continues to be one of the best venues for jazz—and I want to buy you a diamond ring."

She reached across the table. He took her hand and kissed it. "You do have to actually say the words, Kolya."

She knew. They'd been building to this moment for the past year, longer as far as Kolya was concerned. Still, she wanted him to be explicit. He could do this much; after all, he was committing to a lifetime with her. "I am asking you to marry me, Alex."

"So this is the talk we were going to have about the future?" But she was still smiling.

"Is there anything else that needs to be said?" He thought of something else, and then added it. "Other than I love you."

"Probably not. At least not now. Sooner or later, we will have to talk about my concerns about your job over the long term. In any case, since I love you, too, I'm willing to take the risk. As long as it's a big diamond."

"Do remember that I am a public employee." He was smiling back at her. "But I promise to reconsider my profession should it affect our marriage." Not that he could foresee any. He was in a dangerous profession, but while he might risk his life on occasion, it shouldn't impact their relationship.

He finished his breakfast and carried his plate and cup to the kitchen. She followed, dumping the coffee while he did the dishes. He picked up the garbage bag, tied it off, and washed his hands. He'd drop it in the dumpster in back on his way out. "I've got to get to the office. Ross asked me to be there by 7:00."

"Can you call me at any point?" They walked to the door, his arm around her waist.

"I should be able to manage it. I'll text when I get in and then call tomorrow morning around nine. You'll be home?"

"Or at the office." She glanced at his living room, and her eyes moved from the small upright piano wedged against the wall, to the books piled on top of the piano and on the floor. "Do you suppose we could live at my place? Much more comfortable. And I have a better piano."

"I can't afford your townhouse, and I intend to pay for half our home." He slipped on his jacket and picked up his suitcase and his books. "Even if I concede the points about comfort and the comparative quality of our instruments."

"You want me to give up a three-bedroom townhouse in Georgetown for a one-bedroom apartment on 17th Street so that your male pride won't be offended?"

"It does sound unreasonable when you put it that way. We can argue it out when I get back." She would, too. She argued everything.

13

Max descended the stairway at Penn Station, New York, to a darker hall, where passengers disembarking from New Jersey or points south could head for the subway.

He saw two of his men on the far side, also watching.

Max unfolded his newspaper and positioned himself in a corner. He counted up the men he had looking out for the Russian: a total of sixteen men, counting himself. Petrov might be a professional, but he wasn't getting by all of them.

* * * * *

Kolya glanced out the train window as the Amtrak train rattled along the tracks from Newark to New York City. Ten o'clock at night, and only headlights from passing cars and streetlights on city roads clearly visible. Then the train eased into the tunnel that ran under the Hudson, and the view turned to black.

Kolya picked up a volume of Yeats, which he had wanted to read and which had rested on the seat for the entire trip while he had chatted with Eric and read e-mails on his phone. *I will arise and go now, and go to Innisfree.*

"What're you reading?" Eric asked.

Kolya read the line out loud.

"You're a strange guy, Kolya."

"Because I like Yeats?"

"That among other things. But I guess we're all a little strange in this business. What're you doing in the city tonight?"

Kolya consulted his watch. "A late dinner. I didn't have time to eat before I left. Then I'm heading to the Village and the apartment."

With a screech of the brakes, the train shuddered to a halt. Kolya tapped a quick message to Alex, promising to call later, retrieved his black sports bag from the overhead luggage rack and zipped his book inside, and then swung his laptop bag over his shoulder.

Eric pulled down a white and tan suitcase and a box wrapped in bright yellow paper, decorated with butterflies and balloons. "I'll catch dinner with you, if you can stand my company another hour or so."

Kolya nodded agreement and preceded Eric off the train. The crowd was ahead of them: packed against the stairs. The two men were among the last up the two flights to the central waiting room.

At the top, Kolya surveyed the scene. A board announced train arrivals and departures; shops lined the far walls, offering a variety of donuts, coffee, newspapers and pizza. Passengers, bags dumped carelessly at their feet, waited impatiently.

With his customary caution, his eyes swept over the crowd one last time. He noticed a man in a dark gray suit, on the far side of the enormous waiting room, similarly scanning the crowd. Their eyes met, and the man glanced away. Kolya felt a cold chill on the back of his neck.

He studied the man's appearance, the way the suit jacket hung on his shoulders, and recognized the shape of a gun in a shoulder holster. One of Cuza's people? He shook off the thought. No, an undercover officer, most likely. Penn Station was filled with police and soldiers with guns, standing guard, and they were backed up by plain clothes officers.

Even if the man were illegally carrying a gun, he was probably nothing more than an ordinary criminal. No reason to think that the man worked for Mihai Cuza or anyone else who'd have an interest in going after him.

Kolya surveyed the crowd, uneasy. His well-developed sixth sense continued to signal an alert. He could notify one of the nearby officers in uniform, but he didn't want to draw attention to himself. And, if someone was in fact interested in him, the danger wouldn't be just from one man. There'd be others, and he might not make them all. Better to just get out of there.

"There may be trouble. Keep your eyes open."

"What did you see?"

Kolya inclined his head backward. "There was a man with a concealed gun. I may be mistaken, but he appeared to be very interested in me."

Eric shifted the bag and the present, freeing his right arm. They moved quickly through the station to the stairs leading to Seventh Avenue. At the top, Kolya turned around. The man had disappeared.

"Hey, stop worrying so much. You think Cuza has any reason to know about you and this new security system?"

"Probably not."

"So relax. It's a nice day. Early October in New York, sixty-five degrees, beautiful evening. What could be better?"

A short man stood to the right of the staircase, solely occupied in watching the crowd. Kolya tried to quell his suspicions. It could be completely innocent.

The man looked directly at Kolya and turned his head quickly, retrieving a phone from his coat pocket.

"*Fuck*. Eric, move."

Kolya turned on his heel and quickened his pace. Eric trailed behind.

Heading south on Seventh Avenue, Kolya considered the options. If the two men he had spotted were watching for him, then they could be following or setting up an intercept ahead. *Hail a cab.* New York cab drivers were wild enough to lose any potential tail. If there was a tail. If the men were after him. Was he being paranoid?

On the corner of 31st Street, he turned and waved for a cab. Flowing towards him was a sea of traffic: yellow cabs intermingled with vans and private cars, but none of the cabs with the light that signaled availability.

A block behind them, three men halted. One of them was the

man Kolya had spotted at the top of the stairs from Penn Station.

Kolya no longer questioned what they were doing.

The light changed. The men remained motionless as Kolya continued to face in their direction, hand raised.

Three of them. He turned and glanced across 31st street to Eighth Avenue. Two more figures headed in their direction. Innocent pedestrians? Reinforcements?

Eric was a decent shot. The two of them could probably take the three closest men, but there would be a risk to bystanders. Also, the two men approaching from a different direction might not be the only back-up.

He peered up Seventh Avenue at the row of cars halted for a light. If no cabs were available, they would have to shake off the men on foot. He shifted his bag and regretted that he had packed a favorite sweater and laptop.

Eric, beside him, muttered. "I see them. Shit."

The light changed, and the cars started to move again. "Now." Kolya dropped his bag and tossed the laptop into the path of an oncoming truck. Tires crunched the laptop, and horns blared discordantly. He darted across Seventh in front of the traffic, barely avoiding being hit by irritated drivers.

He reached the far side of the Avenue and ran down 31st Street, Eric keeping pace behind. On Sixth Avenue, he turned right and ran to 30th Street, where he turned left. He checked over his shoulder. Several strides behind, Eric signaled Kolya to wait.

Kolya halted, gun in hand. Eric bent over, winded. The three men had not turned the corner.

"We need to move." Kolya still saw no sign of the pursuers.

"I'm good." Eric straightened. "You think we lost them?"

"No."

Kolya turned and started off at a slow jog. Eric followed.

The doors to the shops were closed and shuttered. Bars crisscrossed glass windows where manikins displayed the wares. The shop closest to them displayed silk dresses on faceless plastic bodies.

Kolya increased his pace to a run, followed by Eric, down 30th

Street to Broadway. On Broadway, they turned right again, with a fast left onto 29th Street.

Kolya slid into the shadow of a doorway, holding his gun across his chest, Eric next to him. Two minutes, and several men reached the corner of Broadway and 29th, close enough for him to hear the voices.

"*Unde?*" One of the voices asked the direction in Romanian.

"*Drept inainte.*" Straight ahead was the answer.

The language eliminated Kolya's doubts as to the identity of the pursuers. The hunters continued south on Broadway, however, instead of turning left. Kolya remained frozen in place, his heartbeat thudding in his ears, waiting to see if they doubled back, or if more pursuers were following.

"Who the hell are they?" Eric asked in an undertone. "Romanians?"

"Yes."

He gave it another five minutes and then stepped out of the doorway, jogging down 29th Street, away from Broadway, his gun clenched in his right hand.

Eric followed at a slow trot. At the corner of Fifth Avenue and 29th, Kolya halted. He listened first and then peered cautiously around the corner. No one was in sight in either direction.

A car passed, and he sprinted across the street, half expecting a bullet out of the darkness. Kolya turned left and continued to jog to the intersection of Fifth Avenue and 30th. Eric trailed him.

On 30th Street, he checked both ways, saw nothing out of the ordinary, and slid the gun out of sight, under his sweater. "We could split up. You head up to Grand Central Station. I'll double back and go on to the apartment."

"I don't think so. They're after you, aren't they?" Eric holstered his own gun.

"Apparently. Unless they're after you."

"You're the one who knows this new security system for our network. And they don't look like anybody I know."

"Exactly. Which is why they will probably follow me and not you."

"And which is why I'm making sure you get to safety before I head out to Queens. How'd it look if you get killed while I'm at my sister's?"

"Embarrassing."

"Damn right." As they jogged across the street, Kolya did a 360 turn, checking for movement. "So we assume those were Cuza's people, and they were after you. How'd they know what train you were on?"

"Lucky guess?"

"Or a leak."

"Or that."

They were walking briskly now.

"If there's a leak," Eric said, "maybe the location of the apartment's blown as well."

"I've thought of that myself."

"So don't go there. Come with me to my sister's in Queens."

"If they're after me, do you really want me at your sister's house, with her four children?"

Eric considered this and shook his head. "Probably not. What are you going to do?"

"Dinner." Kolya checked his watch. It was almost ten-thirty, and he hadn't eaten since noon. "Running makes me hungry."

"Sounds like a plan."

"I know a place on First and 34th Street. Decent enough food. And not close to where we saw any of them."

"And after we eat, you can find a hotel."

"If Bradford authorizes it." Kolya doubted she would. Even if she did authorize it, he'd have to at least make an attempt to access the agency apartment, where there was sensitive and expensive equipment, which should be destroyed if there were any risk of it falling into the wrong hands.

* * * * *

With a powerful stroke, Elizabeth slammed the ball over the net toward Jonathan. He returned it, and she lobbed it over his head. He ran backward and smashed it down the line. She hit it to the other side of the court, and he sprinted at top speed and just missed the ball.

71

Jonathan watched McIntyre and Kowolsky play on the neighboring court. Dan McIntyre, tall, potbellied, and slow, had a decent forearm but no backswing, and Steve Kowolsky, short and sturdy, chased each ball down with a grim determination.

Jonathan motioned Elizabeth to the net.

"You feel like having dinner? Before we head back."

"That's why you asked me to the net?" Her voice was cool. "Not to discuss tactics?"

"Yeah, sure. Tactics. I want to discuss tactics. But I also want to ask you to dinner."

"Maybe. I'll think about it. Right now—business."

"Right. Hit in the direction of other court. I'll miss and bump into Kowolsky on my way to get the ball."

They returned to their respective baselines. He balanced on the balls of his feet, racket held at the ready. She smashed the ball. It careened at an angle to the far side and bounced onto the adjacent court, hitting Kowolsky in the thigh.

Jonathan gave a nod of appreciation and trotted over to the next court. Kowolsky was cursing and rubbing his leg where the ball had hit.

"Sorry." Jonathan held out his hand. "Steve Kowolsky, what a surprise."

Kowolsky narrowed eyes at Jonathan. "Egan, isn't it? Who the hell are you playing with, Wonder Woman? Jesus, that hurt."

"Isn't it funny what a small town Washington is?" Jonathan ignored Kowolsky's comment. "I've been thinking of calling you, and here you are, coincidentally, on the court next to mine. You got a minute?"

Kowolsky shrugged. "Why the hell not?" He turned and shouted at McIntyre. "Taking five, Dan. Hit a few with Serena Williams here?"

Kowolsky fed quarters and punched the machine. A bottle of Poland Springs clanked down. He twisted off the cap, sat at a table directly in front of the shaded window, and balanced the chair back on two legs. His sparse red hair, mingled with gray, was plastered to his head. "You've got exactly sixty seconds to explain what you want, and why the hell you couldn't call me if you wanted to talk."

"If I'd called you, there'd have been a record. I need you to check out the possibility of a mole in the Company. High level mole."

"I kind of figured you wouldn't be playing spy vs. spy with me otherwise. So who do you suspect and why?"

"We've had operations blown, operations that only a few people knew about."

"Which people?"

"There's three we're watching," Jonathan said. "Smithson, Ford, and Manion."

Kowolsky choked on his water. "Smithson? Ford? Christ."

"Yeah. Three operations were blown and those three members of the Intelligence Committee were the only ones outside the team who knew about them. The President agreed to the search for a mole."

"Well, fuck." Kowolsky looked through the darkened window at McIntyre and Elizabeth. Elizabeth lobbed the ball over McIntyre's head. "Look at that woman play. She any good in bed?"

"I wouldn't know. And that's a fucked-up thing to ask."

"Hell, fuck political correctness," Kowolsky grunted. "So, you want me to check up on Smithson? Question—on the ECA—you had the same team on all the operations that were blown?" Kowolsky said. "I'm guessing you were on it. Who else in your fun little gang was working with you?"

"Gina Antonia."

Kowolsky's only reaction was to take another swig of water. He had heard about Gina. "And?"

"Teo Lorenzo, Nick Petrov." Using the despised nickname for Kolya didn't fool Kowolsky for a second.

"Nick Petrov. You mean Nikolai Ivanovich Petrov, your Russian pal, don't you? You check whether he's your leak? Kolya. Yeah, that's it. That's his name. I remember from the time I met the two of you, where was it, Afghanistan. Five years ago. That son-of-a bitch never goes by Nick. He uses his Russian name." Kowolsky stared at Jonathan with his small eyes.

"Of course he does. He's not trying to hide anything. But I know

73

you. I used the English version of his name so you wouldn't go off on a tangent, but there you go anyway."

"Maybe, rich boy, because I know them. You pal around with Petrov for a while and you think you know Russians. You don't know Russians, boy; I know Russians. I know them through and through. When there's trouble in the world, just count on it, the Russians are involved."

"As I said before, Kolya is a naturalized American, even if he was born in Russia. He's been in this country since he was fourteen."

"They get them early, you know, the Russians. Indoctrinating them. Training them. Petrov was in some kind of state school, too, wasn't he?"

"This has nothing to do with Russia or Petrov."

"Yeah?"

"Even if it did, Petrov is an ECA agent and his loyalty or non-loyalty is ECA business. All I'm asking you to do is to check your own house."

"I know what you're asking me to do. Understand this. The security of this country is my business. And if some Goddamn Russian is leaking information, I don't care what agency he works for or who he's friends with." He stood, indicating the end of the conversation, and picked up his racket. "Now I'm going to go play the last ten minutes of my match."

14

"Good pastrami." Eric was eating pastrami on rye bread with mustard and a side of fries. Kolya was eating a grilled ham and cheese. "You eat food like that and someone's going to mistake you for a *goy*. No offense."

"Were you under the impression that I was religious?"

"Not really. Just giving you a hard time."

"I get enough of that from Alex's asshole brother." Alex's brother disapproved of Kolya for not being a practicing Jew, for being an introvert, and for not earning enough money as an "accountant" at the IRS.

"Yeah, my in-laws are assholes, too."

Kolya took another bite of his sandwich. He knew rather than felt that he had to eat. More important was the coffee. The deli had good coffee, and, anticipating a long evening, he was already on his second cup. After ordering their sandwiches, he left a message on Bradford's cell.

The restaurant consisted of a deli counter and five tables. The two of them chose a table next to a refrigerator filled with bottles of Snapple and designer water. A small thin man with a mustache served the sandwiches and two cups of coffee. He now leaned against the cash register, chewing on a toothpick, at enough of a distance that he couldn't overhear the conversation.

"You going to just sit here until she calls back?" Eric dipped a fry into a mound of ketchup.

"That's the plan."

"Do me a favor. When Bradford calls you back, don't mention that I'm here."

"Are you worried that you'll lose your weekend if she knows you're with me?" The phone in the inside pocket of his jacket rang. He pulled it out. "Petrov."

"Mr. Petrov," Margaret Bradford said. "Where are you?"

"In a deli in Manhattan. I just spent the evening playing an elaborate game of hide and seek with Mihai Cuza's men."

"Explain."

He did so, leaving out any mention of Eric.

"Is that why you haven't accessed the agency apartment?"

"If Cuza knew I was arriving in New York by train, if he knew that I had something he might want, then he might also know the location of the agency apartment."

"Are you certain that it was Cuza's men and that they were after you? You do have enemies in New York, who would be all too happy to kill you."

"Yes, I know. Certain members of the Russian mafiya don't remember me fondly. But the language the men spoke was Romanian, not Russian."

"It could have been coincidence. Perhaps they simply happened to be in Penn Station—and someone recognized you from your visit to Cuza's loft."

"There were at least five men waiting at Penn Station. After spotting me, they followed for several blocks. If they were waiting for someone else, why follow me? Why bother, even if I was recognized, unless I had something they wanted."

"I'm not convinced that this was anything other than a coincidence. We knew Cuza had people in New York. Are you certain that you weren't followed to the train in Washington?"

"No, I can't be completely certain. But in any event, I see no need to take unreasonable chances. Standard operating procedure would be to find another location."

"I don't agree that going to the apartment would be taking an unreasonable chance. In any event, we have equipment there. Didn't you compile our intelligence on Mihai Cuza on the computers in that apartment? We don't want that information in Cuza's hands. Just on the off-chance that Cuza's people are actually looking for us."

"No, we wouldn't want Cuza to have it." All files had been deleted, but he had not had the time to go into the hard drive and write over the material. Data might be vulnerable to someone who knew how to retrieve files, and Cuza would either know how or employ people with that knowledge. And if Cuza got hold of an ECA computer, he might be able to hack into the ECA network. The new security protocols only applied to new connections.

"So you need to double check the security of that computer as well as of the apartment, don't you?"

With a sigh, he agreed.

"I will arrange for several available operatives to meet you at the apartment in a few hours, but I need you to make a preliminary assessment on security. Just approach carefully. If you spot anything out of the ordinary, back off."

Kolya returned the phone to his pocket. She was probably right— he'd been spotted at the train station in Washington or New York. Unlikely anyone would be planning to ambush him at the apartment.

"You can catch the Number Seven to Queens." Kolya finished the last of his coffee, leaving half the sandwich. "Back-up will be meeting me in a few hours."

"Like I told you I'm hanging in until you're in a secured location. We'll get to the apartment, check it out, and then I'm on my way."

"Fine." He was pleased. He'd not been looking forward to heading out alone.

* * * * *

Kolya and Eric descended into the subway, purchased passes, and waited for the local line. A half-empty train rumbled into the station five minutes later. They rode to the East Village where they exited the subway and headed east, toward Second Avenue. Kolya continually checked the surroundings. There were people out enjoying their Friday evening, but he saw nothing to raise concern. After a few blocks, they cut north and then turned west, walking slowly along Morton Street, checking windows, pausing frequently. No one else stopped, no one seemed interested in them.

While the center of the Village still hummed with life close to midnight, a few blocks west, pedestrian traffic dwindled down to one or two people.

On Washington, a block from the apartment, they turned right, halted, and surveyed the street. Completely deserted. No moving cars. No pedestrians. The apartment was in a commercial area, wedged between an office building and warehouses for Federal Express, perfect for the purposes of the ECA, given the hours and activities of agents. Still, that very isolation gave Kolya pause. It would be a perfect place for an ambush.

They proceeded slowly, alert to every shadow, every sound. A block to go. A dumpster blocked half the street, wedged up to the pavement, and they'd have to pass it to reach the apartment.

Kolya noticed the increased darkness: all of the streetlights from the dumpster to the end of the block were out.

Kolya stopped and turned. None of the streetlights were out in the previous block. Given the earlier events of the evening, he found that suspicious. Then, despite the darkness, he caught a glimpse of a moving shadow on the far side of the street, as if someone had ducked out of sight behind a car.

He stopped, put out his left hand, and touched Eric's elbow. At the same moment he reached under his sweater, pulled his gun from the holster, and clinked off the safety. He held the gun straight down by his side, his forefinger parallel to the gun barrel.

It might be nothing. A pedestrian. A drunk. He might be paranoid. But he was taking no chances.

He cast a glance over his shoulder. Seeing no threat from behind, he began to back down the sidewalk, away from the dumpster, alert for an attack. Eric followed suit, also with gun drawn.

Tires squealed, and he spun, seeing the headlights of a van heading the wrong way on Washington, straight toward them. Simultaneously, a voice called from the far side of the dumpster, "Petrov, both of you put your weapons on the ground and raise your hands. If you do, neither you nor your friend will be hurt."

A shadow emerged onto the sidewalk, and a shot skimmed off the cement between them.

Kolya returned fire and dove for shelter between the dumpster and a Lexus parked with its bumper three feet from the metal end as more shots were fired.

Eric fired twice and followed. He landed next to Kolya and put a hand up to check his chest. The hand came away bloody.

"Shit."

"Fucking shit." Kolya saw the blood spread across Eric's jacket. He peered around the edge of the Lexus. The van stopped thirty feet down the street, and men sprinted to the cover of parked cars on either side of the street.

One of the attackers stood in the open, his shape dimly visible. Stupid. Very stupid. Kolya leveled his gun, aimed for the head, and fired twice. The man staggered and fell. Kolya swung his gun to aim at a head poking up from behind a car hood on the far side of the street and pulled the trigger twice more just as the man ducked.

Kolya glanced around the corner of the dumpster. Two shapes, flattened against the side of the dumpster, were creeping forward. He fired. They ran back.

Kolya checked Eric. Sitting on the ground, back to the dumpster, Eric clutched his gun with his right hand, the other pressed against the right side of his shirt. The shirt and the hand were covered with blood. A shoulder wound. He'd live—if he could get to a hospital in time.

"Think we're in trouble?"

"Maybe." Kolya reached into his jacket pocket for his phone. He tried the ECA's emergency line but was met with silence. He tried again.

After the second try, he knew. The signal was jammed. Kolya cursed in Russian and dropped the phone back into his pocket.

"Now I know we're in trouble." Eric's voice was weaker.

"If we can hold out, someone will call the police." Even in this deserted section of Manhattan, there were apartments nearby. How long since the first shot? Felt like hours but was probably just a minute or two.

Eric coughed. "We could give up."

"Do you know how Gina died?" Kolya still had five rounds in his gun and a second magazine in his pocket. "I'd prefer to be shot."

"So we sit here and shoot until we're killed—or until we run out of ammo, in which case, we get captured. Then, Cuza impales us."

"We could each save one round to shoot ourselves."

"I'm Catholic. Can't shoot myself."

"Then we can shoot each other. It won't be suicide."

"Don't…care for that…either." Eric's voice was halting, breathy.

Kolya turned his head. Eric gave Kolya a grim smile. Kolya leaned to take a better look and didn't like what he saw. "Or I could surrender. They appear to want me, not you. You keep my gun and your gun, and they'll take me and leave."

"You're just full of great ideas tonight. Negative on that one, too." Eric eased against the dumpster.

"Or I make a run for it. Maybe I can get out of range of the jamming device."

He might not make it, but it would be a chance. He was a fast runner, and if he could get reception, he could call for help. And maybe they'd follow him and leave Eric alone. Back wedged against the dumpster, he cautiously stood, and judged the distance to the closest doorway.

"Get back down, Kolya. It's suicide." Then his voice sharpened. "On the right."

Startled at Eric's words, he swirled as a man on the other side of the street fired. He didn't feel pain from the bullet that hit the side of his right leg several inches above his knee, but he felt the impact. He fell heavily, and his legs slid under the Lexus. Hands shaking, he returned fire. Eric fired over him. The gunman fired again and ducked out of sight.

"Eric, all right?" There was no response. Kolya could feel the silence.

80

Eric, either unconscious or dead, was slumped against the side of the dumpster.

His leg refused to move.

He pulled himself into a sitting position and leaned against cold metal. They could come at him from two sides, but his back was covered by the dumpster, his front by the now bullet-ridden Lexus.

His upper right leg throbbed, and blood spread across the dark fabric of his jeans. His short grace period was ending, and the pain starting to build. He took deep breaths to stop his hands from shaking. This block was commercial, but there had to be apartments close by. It was Manhattan. There were apartments everywhere. It had only been a few minutes at most since the encounter had started, but someone must have heard the shots. Help would come. He had ammunition and could hold them off.

Unless, dizzy and nauseated from the pain and loss of blood, he passed out before help arrived. He put his head down to his knees.

Footsteps approached from the far side of the dumpster. He straightened and steadied himself to shoot. The footsteps retreated. He touched the side of his jeans, and his hand came away red. He ripped off a strip of his jacket lining and bound it tightly around his wounded upper leg. It wouldn't do much, although the pressure might slow the bleeding enough to keep him conscious until help arrived.

Eboyanna mat, it hurt.

Just how many men were out there? Two men had shot from the left. Five men had exited the van. He had shot one. That left at least six.

He felt a breeze against his face. What had Eric said? Something about a lovely October evening in New York.

Time was running out. He had to try something. Eric would die if help didn't arrive soon.

He felt in his jacket pocket for his phone. It was an exercise in futility, but he tried anyway, with the same result as before. The signal was still jammed.

How long had it been?

"You're surrounded Petrov. Your friend is injured. We only want you. Surrender, and we'll leave him alive."

He had considered surrendering, but only when Eric had been conscious and able to protect himself. Cuza's men would not want to finish off Eric badly enough to risk walking into a bullet. But Eric unconscious was another matter. He had no illusions about what would happen to his defenseless friend. This wasn't the fucking Boy Scouts.

He also knew what would happen to him if he surrendered. Cuza didn't obey international laws prohibiting torture.

He heard movement on his right. A shadow moved on the far side of the dumpster. He fumbled in his jeans pocket. The last round was chambered, ready. He released the empty magazine and with the palm of his hand, pushed the fresh magazine into place. Thirteen rounds left.

Footsteps on the far side of the dumpster. Not yet. Every round had to count. He held his breath and listened. He lowered the gun and aimed.

One man poked his head around the corner. Kolya held his fire. A second man emerged. Both had guns aimed in his general direction, but neither had located him in the shadows.

Kolya shot the first man between the eyes. The other ducked back around the corner. Kolya squeezed off two more shots and missed.

Down three rounds.

He heard the words, "The son-of-a-bitch killed Joseph," in Romanian. He didn't catch the rest.

The voice was back.

"You're making this difficult, Petrov, and you're injured."

The voice grated on Kolya. He leaned left, ignored the pain that shot up his leg, and peered around the corner. From his angle, he could see the legs of two men hiding three cars back. Kolya checked his pockets again, although he knew the gun held the last of his ammunition.

Stupid. What had he been thinking when he left Washington with only one extra magazine? He knew what he had been thinking.

Alex. The irony struck him, but he couldn't afford to let his mind drift in that direction. He couldn't think of love or marriage or regrets, not in the middle of a gunfight. Survival—his and Eric's—required that he concentrate.

Kolya placed his fingers against Eric's neck and felt the pulse. At least Eric was alive. There was still a chance.

Where were the police?

He had ten rounds left, not much, not with at least—what—five—six men on the other side. The Beretta on his ankle was a .22, appropriate for close defensive use or an assassination. In this kind of a gunfight, he'd be better off throwing it.

Eric's gun had fallen from his hand to the sidewalk, out of reach on the far side. If he reached for it, Kolya would expose his head and torso to the gunmen.

He looked again at the legs that were visible where gunmen sheltered behind a car. It was a clear shot, but a leg wound wouldn't kill and might not even take a man out of the fight. He didn't want to run out of ammunition, but everything he could do to discourage them and to stretch out the time increased his and Eric's chances. He aimed, squeezed off a shot, and heard a yelp and a curse.

"Petrov?" It was the annoying voice again.

Kolya heard whispers. He strained to catch the few words in Romanian. Annoying Voice ordered men to rush him. Someone else was against the idea.

Kolya rested his gun against his chest and waited. He shivered, cold despite his sweater, leather jacket, and the warm night.

A noise on his right. He turned and fired at a face poked over the hood of a car. He missed.

Another curse.

He was down to eight rounds. He checked his watch. How could it only be five minutes since the fight had started?

He hoped Annoying Voice would poke his head up next, but he was losing his concentration. Black spots swam before his eyes.

A few more minutes and they wouldn't need to rush him. The makeshift bandage on his leg hadn't contained the bleeding. Another wave of nausea and dizziness hit him, and he briefly closed his eyes.

He shook his head violently. If he passed out, both he and Eric would die. All he had to do was stay awake long enough for help to reach them.

But he was losing the battle, and he knew it. The street swirled around him. More black spots. *No, don't. Can't.* It was his last thought before the street faded to black.

* * * * *

He woke and found himself lying on his side, sprawled into the street. He had been out long enough for his attackers to realize that he was incapacitated.

Five men stood in front of him, guns pointed at his chest, his own gun held in the hand of a stocky man with thinning blond hair.

"Heckler and Koch compact. Nice." He was the owner of the annoying voice.

"I like it." Kolya tried to keep the fear and pain out of his voice. He blinked and pushed himself up on an elbow. "I believe this is where I surrender."

"Don't have too many other options, do you?" The man removed the magazine from Kolya's gun.

Five men stood on the sidewalk, directly over Eric's prone figure. One, a large man, bald, with a silver earring in one ear, and a semi-automatic in his hand, knelt and put a hand on the side of Eric's neck.

"Still alive," he reported.

A cold chill ran through Kolya. "He didn't see any of your faces. He's been unconscious." Kolya pushed into a sitting position, mindful of the guns pointed at him. "You wanted me. You have me."

"And three of my people were shot. Two of them are dead," the blond man said. "I will have to tell the Count, and he will not be happy."

"I shot your men."

"Petrov did do the shooting, Max." The bald man stood. "Our faces weren't seen. This isn't necessary."

Max clicked the magazine back into the butt of Kolya's gun. "I dislike loose ends."

"I didn't agree to this," the bald man said.

"Too bad." Max aimed across Kolya at Eric's head. "My decision."

Kolya tried for the Beretta on his ankle; but four men grabbed his arms and wrestled him out into the street and onto the paved road. His arms were yanked behind his back; his face shoved into the street.

"That was stupid. Did you really think we'd let you get another gun? Or that we'd shoot you? We have other plans, you Jew bastard. I'm being kinder to your friend than to you." Max walked the few paces back to Eric, aimed, and pulled the trigger. Eric jerked sideways. Kolya closed his eyes.

The man returned to Kolya and kicked him in the ribs. "Check him for any other weapons," he said to the men holding Kolya's arms. "Then get him into the van."

After a search, Kolya's wrists were pulled behind his back and cuffed tightly. He didn't bother to struggle. The odds were too uneven— there were too many of them. Conserve strength and wait.

The bald man looked at the body of one of the men Kolya had shot and back at Kolya. "Body works." He walked over, bent down, patted Kolya's pockets, and found the wallet. He took a handkerchief from his own pocket, covered his hand, retrieved the wallet, and Kolya's phone. He unbuckled the band of the watch on Kolya's wrist. He pointed back at the body he had examined a moment earlier. "Put Joseph's body in the trunk of the car and let's get out of here. And put this in Joseph's pocket." He handed off the phone.

Kolya realized what he was doing. "You're wasting your time. My agency will never believe it."

"Sure they will."

Kolya looked at the bald man, and recognition clicked. Kolya now knew the identity of the mole, for all the good it would do him. He kept his face blank of emotion and took deep breaths to calm the trembling of his body.

Two men yanked him roughly to his feet. His right leg buckled. His arms were caught. Unable to walk, he was dragged toward the van where he was shoved and pushed inside, his jacket and sweater sleeves pushed up, and a needle inserted into his arm.

"A precaution." Max pressed the plunger and shot a clear liquid into Kolya's vein. "Once he's out, take off the cuffs. Just in case we're stopped on the New Jersey Turnpike."

The other men piled into the van; a driver jerked it into motion. Kolya counted. Thirty seconds since the injection. Sixty seconds. He heard the distant sound of sirens as the van turned down Hudson toward the Holland Tunnel—the police—too late—saw swirling lights, fought against the encroaching darkness, and lost.

15

Elizabeth pried snails from their shells with a tiny fork and dipped them into the garlic butter. Jonathan had never liked the damn things: too rubbery. He preferred the truffle pate, thickly spread over buttered French bread. But whatever she wanted. Jonathan was just pleased that she'd accepted his invitation to dinner after the successful approach to Kowolsky.

The waiter approached, smiling. Jonathan was a regular. In perfect French, Jonathan ordered the duck in orange sauce. Elizabeth ordered the salmon, also in perfect French. The waiter filled their wine glasses and left. Average price for dinner for two was over three hundred dollars—before drinks.

"So you're paying for this, right?" Elizabeth asked.

He poured another glass of wine. "I don't want to offend your sensibilities."

"Buying me dinner doesn't offend my sensibilities. You come from a long line of wealthy white people, and you have a trust fund. My parents were teachers at an inner city school in Detroit—and I had to go into debt to get through college. I couldn't afford this place."

"When you put it that way, of course I'm paying." He sipped the wine. "I was planning to, anyway. My small contribution towards resolving the problem of economic inequality."

"You think economic inequality is funny?" But she looked amused, not annoyed. He hoped he was reading her right.

"Okay, clear the air. I'm rich. I'm white. I'm a centrist politically. I'm straight and cis gendered. All in all, a boring person."

"Yeah, I know all that. I also know that you joined the FBI to spite your father, the Senator, and that you screwed around on your wife—and regretted it. And you have a son, Dylan, who you don't see as often as you should."

"Shit, is there anyone who doesn't know why my marriage broke up?"

She swirled the wine in her glass. "You work with spies."

"And, by the way, I see my son as often as possible. Now: what I know about you. You're extremely smart, ambitious and not interested in a serious relationship."

With a flourish, the waiter set the entrees in front of them. Elizabeth picked up her fork and tried the salmon, artistically displayed on a bed of wild rice and mushrooms. "Close. Did Petrov tell you that I'm good in bed?"

"Not the type of thing he discusses."

"Big of him."

Jonathan noted the bitter tone.

"I thought you weren't interested in a serious relationship. He was—so he moved on. Why still mad?"

She shrugged. "I liked him—and he dumped me."

"You wanted it both ways? Holding on to him while not committing?"

She looked at him through narrowed eyes. "Like what you did? Holding on to your wife but not committing."

"That's fair."

"So, are you curious?" She finished her glass and smiled at his raised eyebrows. "Whether I'm good in bed."

"A little."

"I'm a little curious about you as well."

* * * * *

Frick was seated in the third row of the minivan, squeezed next to the unconscious man slumped against the side window. Petrov was breathing, and that was all that mattered. Frick had spent the first half hour of the drive applying pressure to the bandage wrapped around Petrov's leg, and the bleeding had almost stopped. If Petrov died now, it would be from the drugs or from shock.

Too bad about Petrov's friend. Too bad about Petrov, for that matter. It was a tough business, and people got hurt.

"When's the drug due to wear off?" Frick asked.

"He could wake up any time within the next half hour to hour," Max said. "The Jew son-of-a-bitch so much as twitches, and you shoot him up again."

The van held six men. Frick and Petrov were in the back. Frick had his hand on a hypodermic needle in his jacket, although he was uncomfortable with injecting more drugs, not knowing the proper dose or the possibility of negative reactions. He'd removed the handcuffs after the drugs went into effect just in case they were stopped. A man sleeping in would not rouse suspicion. A man in handcuffs could raise questions and might lead to a confrontation. Thankfully, Petrov showed no signs of stirring.

Radu flipped on the windshield wipers against a mist of rain and turned onto a road that ran alongside a river. One of the two other cars used in the operation followed with three men who were also flying to Romania. After the drop, Radu would return to Manhattan with the van. Frick would take the second car north to meet up with the car carrying the remains of the luckless Joseph.

Frick wiped his sleeve across the fog on the window. Radu pulled into a parking lot in front of a two-story building with a sign, "Walker Aviation."

Glaring white light illuminated the parking lot and the Gulfstream on the other side of a steel fence topped with barbed wire. Beyond the fence, blue lights lit the runways and a small control tower blinked.

Petrov had shifted his position, but his eyes were still closed, his body slack, his breathing even. One arm lay against the seat; the other, across his chest.

"Even if he's awake, he's injured and he should be groggy," Max said. "Anyone asks—he drank too much. Just stay close with the hypodermic."

Two men outside the car each took an arm and pulled Petrov forward. Frick pushed from the third seat, and they managed to get Petrov's inert form out of the sliding door. The two balanced him between them, an arm over each of their shoulders.

Cursing the tight quarters of the back of the van, Frick slid his way out in time to see Petrov slam an elbow in the side of the head of one of the men holding him. Frick didn't see what happened to the second, who crumbled to the ground an instant after the first.

Petrov took one step on his bad leg and fell. He rolled toward the two men on the ground.

"Shit." Frick launched himself from the van.

Max exited from the passenger side of the van, too far away. Radu was just opening his door.

Petrov was going for the gun that had fallen from the waistband of the man closest to him. Frick got there and kicked the gun away. He kicked again, aiming for Petrov's midsection. Petrov caught the foot in midair and twisted. Frick went down hard on his ass.

"Fucking bastard." Frick scrambled to get space between them, but Petrov held onto Frick's leg, and they rolled together. Petrov knocked Frick's head against the pavement, and Frick slammed a fist into the side of Petrov's face.

Petrov's arm sliced at his face. Frick barely managed to block the motion, the blow numbing his left arm. Frick punched, and Petrov deflected it. A second punch connected with the side of Petrov's face. Petrov aimed the side of his hand at Frick's throat. Frick blocked it and grabbed Petrov's arm. Petrov jammed a knee into Frick's genitals. Frick saw swirling white specks and curled his legs up toward his chest. Petrov rolled off Frick and towards the gun.

Max got there first and kicked Petrov in his bad leg. Four men grabbed Petrov, dragged him up from the ground, and held him. Max's arm went around Petrov's throat, holding him immobile and cutting off his air. Petrov gasped and struggled.

Frick sat up slowly, rubbing the back of his head. He saw with satisfaction that Petrov's face was bruised and his leg bleeding freely again.

"Give him the shot," Max hissed. "Now. Before one of the immigration agents in the trailer notices anything."

Frick yanked Petrov's shirt up, sank the needle into his hip, and injected the contents. He stood back to watch the drug take effect.

Max released Petrov's throat. Petrov's head went forward, and he gasped in a breath. Frick watched Petrov's eyes glaze, but he saw something else in Petrov's expression: recognition. He leaned forward and spoke to Petrov in a low voice.

"Do you know who I am?"

"Fuck you." The words were slurred.

"Do you know me?" Frick persisted.

"Your mother sideways on a horse." Almost unintelligible words were spoken in a language that Frick assumed was Russian before Petrov's eyes closed, and he went limp.

Frick trailed the four men half carrying and half-dragging Petrov through the building. The pilot sat in a lounge area with a large window overlooking the airfield, drinking coffee. He looked at the group without a change in expression and then followed them out to the plane.

Inside the jet, Petrov's hands were cuffed behind him. He was dumped in a window seat and secured with a seat belt. His head lolled to the side. Frick looked at Petrov with a grudging respect for his adversary. The anger over Petrov's escape attempt dissipated, and he felt a flash of regret. A capable agent. What a waste.

But he'd done this before. He'd betrayed that young woman to her death. He'd let Max murder an unconscious man. But he'd had no choice.

He exited the plane with Radu and watched as it taxied and took off into the night sky.

He ached. He smelled of gunpowder and blood. All he wanted was to get back to his apartment and take a shower. But he had to tie up loose ends first.

16

"**Jazz? You are supposed** to be practicing Bach." Her short blonde hair framing her face, she frowned down at him. He tried to play the piece in front of him. But his hands refused to cooperate, no longer painful, simply numb. He flexed his fingers, but the numbness spread into his wrists and his arms.

When he looked up again, his mother was gone.

Kolya woke. His head ached, he was nauseous, and his right leg felt as if it were on fire. His shoulders hurt. When he tried to shift his position, he realized that his hands were secured behind him. Where was he? He blinked. His head was turned toward a small circular window. Outside the window was a dark sky. An engine vibrated.

He closed his eyes to orient himself. It took another minute for him to focus, and then he remembered. Eric White was dead; he had been shot, kidnapped, and drugged. He remembered waking in a van and feigning unconsciousness. He had recognized one of the men who had captured him—the one who prevented his escape—but now he struggled to remember the man's identity as he became more awake and more uncomfortable.

The nausea was getting worse. The drugs… had to be the drugs. He put the question of the man's name out of his mind for the moment. *Bozhe moi*, he felt sick. He opened his eyes and turned his head. Next to him sat the stocky blond man—Eric's murderer—Max, smoking and reading a newspaper.

Kolya's seat reclined: his legs were up on an extended section, his body covered with a blanket. The leg hurt, but the nausea overwhelmed any other sensation. He struggled to sit up but made it only as far as his elbows, restrained by the seat belt around his waist.

"We've got another five hours flight, Petrov," Max said in a bored voice. "Lay back and relax."

"I need to sit up. I'm going to be sick."

"Another goddamned trick. Jews are just full of them." Max blew smoke in his direction.

He didn't answer. He turned his body towards Max, leaned as far as possible, and began to retch. He was dimly aware of Max jumping away, swearing, but he continued after his stomach was emptied, after there was nothing left to bring up. Finally, the heaving stopped.

A short young man with bleary eyes stumbled down the aisle with a roll of paper towels, soaked up the mess, dumped the towels into a garbage bag, sprayed, and wiped down the seats.

The man yanked Kolya's head back and wiped off his face with a water dampened paper towel.

Max stared at Kolya. "While everyone's up, can we do anything for you?"

"A bathroom."

As the nausea subsided, he became more aware of his other discomforts and pains. The injured leg remained top of the list, probably either a hairline fracture or the bullet lodged against a nerve, but he also had an uncomfortably full bladder. Max eyed him without speaking. Kolya could see the calculations. The second man spoke a simple declaration of distrust in Romanian.

"I don't trust the bastard." Max spoke in English. "But I don't want him pissing on the seat. Cuff his arms in front and give him a bucket."

The second man put Kolya's seat into an upright position, pulled him forward with a jerk, and uncuffed his hands. The sudden elevation made him dizzy but moving his arms was an immense relief. Kolya closed his eyes and rotated aching shoulders. Pinpricks ran up his hands to his arms as the circulation returned. He rubbed both wrists and forearms.

"Put your wrists together now," Max ordered.

He held out his wrists in a show of compliance. Max clicked the metal restraints closed and handed over a small bucket. Aware of the guns trained on him, Kolya pushed the blanket down and fumbled with his zipper.

Finished, he returned the bucket.

Max stubbed out the cigarette and lit a fresh one. "Give him some water while you're up." The second man took the bucket and headed toward the back lavatory. When he returned, he had a cup filled with water. He handed it to Kolya, who drained it in three gulps, returned the cup, leaned back, and pulled the blanket up to his shoulders.

Max settled himself on the cleaned chair. "Put your hands outside the blanket so I can see them."

He complied, since he was under too close observation to test the possibility of freeing himself. Still, it was a relief to not be lying on his arms, to have even limited use of his hands. He might be able to do something if the opportunity arose.

Max checked the handcuffs and picked up his newspaper again. "We've got a long plane ride ahead of us, which means you'll get water and you'll need to pee. Which means we'll let you use your hands. Just remember: keeping you alive doesn't mean I can't make you hurt even more than you already do. You try any stupid stunts like the one you pulled at the airport, and you'll be sorry."

"I already am sorry." He wasn't sorry for his effort, just sorry the attempt had failed. Kolya closed his eyes. He was exhausted and in desperate need of sleep but to relax enough to sleep, he had to get all thoughts of his present situation out of his head. Simply closing his eyes was not restful. He immediately visualized the evening, the chase through Manhattan that ended with Eric's death. He fought down the flood of rage and thought instead of the obvious use for his wallet, phone, and watch. Would the agency believe him dead? If they believed him dead, the belief would become reality: there would be no search—no rescue—and he would be killed. *Think of something else—something pleasant—Alex*—that thought was also painful. Something impersonal. A book.

His mind retrieved a Yeats poem: *I will arise and go now, and go to Innisfree.* He started at the beginning of the poem and forced himself to try to remember each word of each line. Before he reached the end of the first stanza, he was asleep.

* * * * *

Frick arranged the body in the front seat as Cuza's two men stood and watched.

"You could help."

One shook his head. "I don't like this. Joseph should have a funeral."

"He'll have a funeral. He'll just have it under another name." Frick didn't add the obvious: that there wouldn't be much left to bury.

He strapped Petrov's stainless-steel watch on the wrist of the corpse, shoved keys into the pocket of the pants, picked up the five-gallon gasoline can, poured gas onto the seat of the car, onto the corpse, and held his breath against the fumes.

The car was in a parking lot for hikers on the side of a mountain road circling through the Delaware Water Gap. To Frick's left, the trail ran straight up the mountain.

The Ford Explorer stood twenty feet away, far enough that the flames wouldn't reach it. Frick retrieved Petrov's wallet, still wrapped in the handkerchief, from the pocket of his jacket and tossed it five feet away from the car. He regarded the tableau. One last detail. "Do you have Joseph's gun?" he asked the man closest to him.

He handed it to Frick.

Frick checked it. It was a .45 caliber Glock. He walked over to the dead man, cocked the gun, placed the muzzle against Joseph's mouth, and fired, shattering the teeth and the skull. He'd drop the gun in the Delaware River on the way back to New York.

Frick opened the window and slammed the car door. The two men piled into the Ford and waited.

Frick walked five feet back, and with a pen, lifted the handkerchief from the ground. The wallet remained where it had fallen. Frick wrapped the handkerchief tightly around the pen and fished in his pocket for matches. He waited until the cloth ignited before tossing both through window onto the corpse. He ran. As he reached the car, he heard the whoosh of the gasoline flaring behind him.

He turned and surveyed his handiwork. The flames roared, engulfing the entire car. As they drove off, he heard the sound of an explosion.

17

"The wallet is Kolya Petrov's," Carl Ford said. "His driver's license and credit cards inside. Fingerprints outside."

Saturday morning and Margaret was in the office and at her desk, waiting for the call that had finally come, but with news that she didn't expect. She fought to keep her emotions under control. It wasn't her fault that Eric White had been killed: she'd told him not to meet up with Petrov until Monday. How could she possibly have known they'd be together? She had a flash of anger at Petrov—unfair, she knew. But Petrov should have told her White was with him. If Petrov was dead as well, so was the elaborate plan she'd worked out with Ross and the President.

"Phone?"

"Bits of metal that might have been a phone were found in the wreckage of the car. We checked cell towers. There's no reception at the burn site, but Petrov's phone was traced north from New York to where it went dead—about ten minutes from where the remains were found."

"And the body?"

"Too badly burned for a positive identification. His watch survived. Initials NIP. Also two bullets and some metal keys. Right now, we're working on a theory that someone in the Russia mafiya recognized him. It's the type of thing they would have done."

Her mind continued to reject the conclusion. If Cuza had indeed conducted the kidnapping, why would he kill Petrov like this? Without even questioning him. "Can you extract DNA?"

"We'll see if we can extract anything from the bones, but it's unlikely. The general body type would match. From what's left of the body—the victim was a male, around six feet tall, slender frame."

Damn. Damn. Petrov wasn't the type to submit tamely to a kidnapping. He would have tried to escape—and he might have forced his captors to shoot, preferring a bullet to what else he might face.

"Fingerprints?"

"None besides Petrov's on anything."

The whole thing was too neat. The wallet preserved, but with no fingerprints except for those of the victim. The body totally destroyed. Why set the car on fire?

Because it wasn't Petrov's body. Of course. Cuza would need time to question Petrov. With Petrov missing and presumed in unfriendly hands, the ECA might change its computer system or try to rescue him. If the ECA believed Petrov was dead, then the computer codes would remain in place. And no rescue attempt.

It was something to cling to, even though she wouldn't know for sure until the DNA results on the remains came back. If there were any results to get. Or until Cuza downloaded the Trojan horse.

"All right, Carl. It is probably Mr. Petrov's body, but try for DNA confirmation."

"Fine. We'll need something for comparison. Hair. Blood sample. Toothbrush."

"I'll see what we can get from his last physical. If necessary, I'll send Jonathan Egan to his apartment. Sad. Petrov was a good man."

"Ever hear him play the piano? I went out to a bar once with Egan, Petrov, and the rest of the team. After about four vodkas, Petrov started playing piano. Professional level."

"I tried to get him to play for the office holiday party, but he never would. Never came to it, either."

"Well, he was something of an introvert. Weird, considering that he chose this profession."

"I know."

* * * * *

"He's dead? You can't be serious. He wasn't supposed to die, not until he got the Trojan horse up." Ross, the first one she'd called into her office, searched his left jacket pocket but came up empty. No gum. "I've been monitoring the system since last night just in case—and it's for nothing?"

"I'm touched by your grief, Mr. Ross." With a sigh, she leaned back in her chair. "I think it possible that he is dead. It's also possible that Cuza wants us to think he's dead. So, unless informed otherwise, you will continue to monitor the system. You will also inform Mr. Leslie of the situation. I intend to tell the rest of the agency that I am certain of what I am not certain: that Mr. Petrov is dead. Any hint that anyone in the agency thinks otherwise could be disastrous. Also, I need you to keep an eye on in-coming and out-going e-mail, texts, and phone calls—especially anything going to Mr. Egan."

* * * * *

Jonathan knew that there'd been a death. He'd been called in to Margaret's office on a Saturday morning, and he'd seen the faces of other agents on his way to her office. She looked unusually subdued. He took a seat and waited.

"Mr. White and Mr. Petrov were ambushed last night. Mr. White was shot dead on a street in Manhattan." She paused and finally looked him in the eyes, but he waited to hear her say the words. "I'm sorry, Jonathan. Mr. Petrov's body was found early this morning."

"Christ." Jonathan slammed a fist into the arm of his chair. He felt tears rise in his eyes, and he fought them back. He waited until he could trust his voice. "What happened?"

"All I have is that Mr. Petrov and Mr. White were ambushed near the apartment in the Village. Mr. White died at the scene. Mr. Petrov was taken away and murdered."

"Who identified his body?" Jonathan felt the aura of unreality and tried to keep his voice under control.

"The New York office of the FBI. The body was burned."

"Burned? But he was recognizable?"

"Not from the remains. There wasn't much left, but I'm confident of the identification."

Maybe it was a mistake. Couldn't it be a mistake? "If the body was that badly burned, how can you be sure that it was Kolya? Was there a DNA match?"

"Jonathan, we'll try to run the DNA, but it might not be possible. Even if we can't, it doesn't change anything. He was kidnapped by the people who shot Mr. White, and his phone was traced close to where the body was found. His wallet was on the scene. A watch with his initials was on the body, along with keys. You can check if they're his. It was a male, similar body type. You have to accept it. Kolya is dead. I know you were close. I'm sorry."

Jonathan stood and walked to the window. It was a pleasant day. Sunny, warm. He put a hand against the window and studied the pattern of traffic on the sidewalk below. The glass felt cool under his palm and fingers. They had been friends and partners for almost ten years. Kolya'd always had his back—and vice versa—until last night—when someone murdered him. *And what was I doing while Kolya was dying? I was having sex.*

"Cuza?" he asked.

"Not necessarily. As Carl Ford reminded me this morning, it could have been the Russian mafiya."

He swung from the window. "Carl Ford? For God's sake, Margaret, he's one of our suspects. You're going to accept his word that the body is Kolya?"

"Even if he's the mole, what would be the motive for lying?"

"Maybe Cuza knows about the system that Kolya was working on and was planning to field test in New York. Maybe Cuza kidnapped Kolya, not just to kill him, but to obtain information. In that case, the body… the wallet… could be intended to mislead us."

"And how would Cuza know to kidnap Mr. Petrov? Knowledge of the system is confined to only those in our agency with top-level clearance. No one on the Intelligence Committee knew of the security protocol. And even if Cuza knew about it, knew that Mr. Petrov was working on it, how could he possibly have known when Mr. Petrov was going to New York? No, Jonathan, it doesn't compute."

"But it could have been Cuza. We went to Cuza's loft in Soho. Maybe there was a camera —and they identified Kolya." There was only one thing for him to do. "I'm going to New York. To make sure it's Kolya. I know you're convinced, but I'm not. And if it's him, I mean to find out who's responsible. We take care of our own."

"No, Jonathan. We are not a law enforcement agency."

He paced back to his chair. He had to move, had to do something, anything.

"Jonathan, I'm authorizing a trip to New York for you and a small team, but only to identify and bring back our people. You're not to try to find the killers. You have duties and responsibilities here."

"Put someone else on the hunt for the mole."

"No. It's your assignment. Beyond that—I cannot allow you to go chasing bad guys in New York."

He crossed his arms. "How are you going to stop me? Fire me?"

"I'm quite aware that you could and would pursue the issue as a private citizen. But if Mr. Petrov was killed by old enemies, the FBI would be the most logical organization to track them down. If it was Mihai Cuza's people who killed him, you have a better chance through finding the mole."

"Fine." There was logic to what she was saying.

"One other thing…" Her voice stopped him in the doorway. "Mr. Petrov's girlfriend. It might be better coming from you, but I know how much you hate this particular job. Would you prefer me to notify her?"

Oh God. He didn't know if he could stand it, but he couldn't let anyone else tell Alex. "I'll do it. When I come back." If Kolya were dead, he would be just as dead when Jonathan returned, but Alex would have one more peaceful night.

18

Kolya felt the change of pressure, heard the grumbling of the engines and the grinding of the landing gear. If it was Romania, given a ten to twelve-hour flight, it would be late afternoon.

He had dozed for most of the flight. His captors had eaten scrambled eggs, toast, and coffee a few hours earlier but had not offered him anything. It was just as well. The nausea had diminished, but it was still there. The pain in his leg continued to build, and the handcuffs cut into his wrists. But as uncomfortable as he was, he didn't look forward to the end of the journey. He didn't expect any improvement in his situation.

The plane bumped onto the ground, and he turned his head towards the window. Not an airport, just a clearing with a runway in the middle of a forest. A Land Rover and a Mercedes were parked at the far end of a cement landing strip, next to a metal hanger. A dirt road paralleled the strip and wound into the trees. A desolate place, not a chance of escape.

"Get up, Petrov." It was Max.

Kolya turned his head on the seat and looked into Max's light gray eyes. The barrel of his own gun was aimed at his chest. He considered a try for the gun and knew he wouldn't make it. He needed the gun within grasping distance.

"Go fuck yourself."

He hoped that an angry Max might strike out with a fist or gun, which would put him closer and off-balance. But he was disappointed. Max stepped aside, and four men dragged Kolya out of his seat and off the plane.

Outside, the temperature was sharply colder. Kolya was blindfolded and shoved into the back of the Land Rover, a man on either side of him, a gun against his ribs.

The ride was bumpy. Not a paved road. Romania had some of the most deserted forests and mountains in Europe. He had spent several weeks traveling the country with Jonathan, and he remembered both the beauty and the isolation. He also remembered the young Romanian they had recruited.

The car lurched to a stop. The side doors swung open. Fresh air and the smell of a pine forest poured into the car. His stomach tightened in dread. His arms were grabbed, and he was dragged out of the car, up three steps, and into the front hall of a large house.

The blindfold was yanked off. The driver of the car dumped keys on a table near the door. Kolya was in a large open hallway, with Italian stone floors, a huge chandelier on the domed ceiling two flights above, and a stairway circling upward. He could smell smoke from a fireplace, and the odor of chicken, sautéed garlic and onions from the unseen kitchen.

Kolya focused on the man in front of him: thin lipped with dark hair, wearing jodhpurs and a plaid jacket. Mihai Cuza.

Strains of music wafted from the room that Cuza had just exited, and Kolya identified the piece: Stravinsky: "The Firebird."

He must have spoken the name of the piece unconsciously. Max smashed him across the face. "You speak when you're addressed."

Cuza approached, smiling. "Now, Max, he was showing an appreciation of music. You know, I don't care for very many Russian composers. But I like Stravinsky. He is… interesting. Welcome to my home, Mr. Petrov."

"A little modern for Romania, isn't it?"

"Were you expecting Dracula's castle? Dramatic but too drafty. The house was built thirty years ago for the former head of the Securitate." Cuza pointed out the chandelier. "Hand blown crystal. What do you think of it?"

Kolya tilted his head to look at the delicate glass. "The Met. It's a replica."

"I go to the opera whenever I'm in town. The Jazz Festival would be more to your taste than opera, though, wouldn't it?"

How did Cuza know about his taste in music? Kolya's mind flashed back to his capture, to the man who had helped kidnap him—whose boss knew Kolya personally.

Max was impatient with the charade. "He killed two of our people."

"You made a nuisance of yourself, Mr. Petrov," Cuza said.

Kolya licked dry lips. "Sorry?"

Max smacked him again. Cuza surveyed Kolya. "You will be staying downstairs as my guest for the present. Dr. Stanescu?"

A second man, shorter, stouter, carrying a glass half-filled with ice and a golden liquid, had followed Cuza from the living room. "Emil, if you don't mind. Mr. Petrov needs attention."

Stanescu gave Kolya a once over. Kolya tried to return the look, but his focus had become blurry. "How fixed up do you want him?"

"Enough that he's not in imminent danger of dying. But no need to make him too comfortable."

* * * * *

Waiting at the airport, Jonathan hit the call button on his phone. *Answer, damn it.* The second time, Bob did. And he wasn't happy.

"Jonathan, I'm on the 17th hole. It's Saturday. SATURDAY! Tomorrow I spend with the wife and kids. I got one lousy day a week to play golf."

"Kolya was killed in New York last night." The words were hard to form. Somehow telling the news gave it a reality. "Bradford just told me."

"Jesus. You're kidding."

"Wish I were."

"Damn, I liked the son-of-a-bitch. Must be a tough one to take. You guys were pretty close."

"Yeah." What else was there to say?

"Hold on a minute, I'm picking up my goddamn ball. A hundred bucks. Hey, Tom, go ahead and putt out. I'll meet you at the clubhouse. I'm walking, what the hell do you think I'm doing?" Jonathan could tell from the sound that Bob had moved away from his companions. "Egan, this phone's about as unsecure as they come."

"I know that."

Bob voice changed to business. "Okay, I did what you asked. Bugged the target's office and phones. Tracking down every call he's made in the past month on his cell. You think that there might be a connection between what we talked about and Kolya's death."

"Possible."

"I'll going in now. I come up with anything, where can I get you?"

"I'll be in New York."

"You bringing him back?"

"Yeah." Jonathan suddenly felt tired and old. "And I have to make sure, you know, that it's Kolya."

Interference scrambled the connection for several seconds, and Jonathan waited.

"How'd Bradford get the news?"

"Your guy called and told her."

"So, the plot thickens. I'll check it out."

"Thanks."

"You're welcome. Drop by on poker night sometime. And Jonathan, I'm really sorry about Kolya."

* * * * *

Situated at the bottom of the stairs was an upscale recreation room: a walnut bar with leather bar stools, a stone fireplace, a marble floor, an upholstered couch with a woven throw across it; a coffee table with an old fashioned landline in front of the couch; a wide screen television; a set of golf clubs in the corner. Max opened a panel in the wall and inserted a key. Wood paneling swung open to reveal a second, much smaller room.

They had transitioned from rec room to prison, walls and floor of gray cement, streaked with dark brown dirt, and lit by a bare bulb screwed into a fixture in the ceiling. A sink stood in the far corner and a heavy wooden chair against one wall. On the floor, against the other wall, several blankets were spread. A chain hung from the wall above the blankets. In the center of the room, another chain and a pair of manacles dangled from the ceiling.

Kolya was dropped onto the blankets, which stank of mold, dust, and dried blood. Even with the blankets underneath, he felt the cold.

Stanescu shone a light into his eyes and took his pulse from the side of his neck. "I need to give him a shot of antibiotics, check his blood pressure, and put in an I.V. It would help if his jacket were removed. And he can relieve himself."

"In the meantime, he could kill you."

There would be a level of satisfaction in killing any of them, including the doctor who was only patching him up in preparation for torture, but what was the point besides a faster death? He wasn't there yet. "I am aware what would happen if I tried."

Stanescu nodded. "See, he's reasonable. There's one of him and five of us. Six, if you count me, which I would prefer you didn't, since I'm not a violent man."

Max knelt to unlock the cuffs. A bucket was fetched, and Kolya relieved himself. By now, he was less self-conscious about the men watching him. A new level of reality had set in and small indignities were accepted. Of all the things he would be facing, loss of privacy was not the worst.

"Your jacket."

Kolya zipped his pants, slid the jacket off one shoulder and raised himself off the floor enough to slide the jacket out from under him.

Max picked the jacket up and tried it on. It was too tight for his stocky build. Max muttered and tossed it onto the chair.

"Sweater, too. Easier than rolling up your sleeves. And belt."

Kolya pulled off the sweater. He unbuckled the belt with the empty holster and pulled it out from under him.

Stanescu fumbled in his bag for an alcohol swab, a hypodermic, and a plastic fluid pack, attached to a tube with a covered needle at the end. He swabbed Kolya's upper arm, jabbed the hypodermic into a muscle, and injected the contents.

After several false tries, Stanescu inserted a needle into a vein inside Kolya's elbow. He taped the needle in place, and a guard held up the bag of fluids.

Kolya braced himself as the doctor touched his upper leg and peeled away the stained bandage. The doctor produced a pair of scissors from his medical bag, cut away part of the jean fabric, squeezed, and poked. A flash of new pain.

"Hurt?" The doctor probed again.

"Not too bad." Kolya gritted his teeth.

The doctor chuckled. "You're a lousy liar. Bullet didn't go all the way through. Looks like it's in there against the femoral nerve. He isn't going anywhere, not walking anyway."

Kolya had already guessed that a nerve was involved. He stared at the ceiling at the manacles dangling from the wooden beam as Stanescu began bandaging the wound. He turned his head to look at the streaks of brown dirt on the wall. Dried blood, not dirt.

Stanescu wrapped the leg tightly enough to prevent bleeding but not so tight as to cut off the circulation. He finished and went to wash his hands in the corner sink.

"That should do it for now. Can't take the bullet out unless I knock him out, and it'd make a mess. Also, there's more of a chance of infection if I start digging around in his leg. How's it feeling, Petrov?"

"Wonderful." Kolya's leg did feel a bit better, but he was colder. The bag of fluid was almost empty.

"Another few minutes, I think, then we can leave Petrov and go to dinner." Stanescu picked up his drink from the floor and took a swig. "By the way, are there any more blankets?"

Max signaled another guard, who grumbling left the room and returned with two wool blankets.

Better, but he was still cold. Stanescu knelt next to him, pulled the intravenous needle from his arm, and taped cotton against the vein to stop the bleeding. Kolya pulled his sweater back over his head.

"Take your shoes off," Max ordered. "Shoes, socks, and the ankle holster. Off."

He stripped off the items. One of the men picked them up and stood back.

Max approached, holding the handcuffs. "We can do this easy or hard."

Kolya looked at the handcuffs, and then at four guns, two pointed at his middle, two pointed at his head. He offered his wrists without a word. The handcuffs snapped shut and the chain from the wall locked on the handcuffs. He settled on the floor, pulled the fresh blankets up over him, and watched as his captors filed toward the door, speculating in Romanian about the dinner menu—*rasol moldovresca*—boiled chicken with horseradish and sour cream. Kolya was starting to feel hungry, but he also knew that he wouldn't be having dinner. Water was essential to maintaining life, but a man could live quite a long unpleasant time without food.

They left him a cup of water and the bucket within reach. Kolya heard the key in the lock on the other side of the door and the faint sound of footsteps moving away.

At least they had left him alone. Maybe they had reason to be confident, but he'd see. He tested the handcuffs, first, and then the chain. The handcuffs were locked tight and the chain, around four feet in length, was securely locked to the cuffs and planted in the wall. The chain was long enough that he could reach the bucket or the water, or turn on his left side, if he wanted to, but not so long that he could move around his prison.

What he needed was a thin, flexible wire. If he could pick the lock on the handcuffs, he could hop, crawl or roll to the door. If he could get that open, maybe he could make it to the phone in the other room. Maybe someone had even left a gun in an accessible location. Even the golf club could be a weapon.

He did a mental inventory of his clothes: cotton sweater, polo shirt, and blue jeans. Nothing that would be of use. He cursed his lack of foresight.

But he wasn't supposed to be on the kind of assignment that

might land him in hostile hands. Just going to the New York safe house should have been low risk, a milk run, which was why he had had no official back-up.

How could this have happened? How could Cuza know about the computer network—how could he know of Kolya's New York trip?

It didn't matter. Focus.

What about the rest of his things? How thoroughly had they searched him? Did he have anything left in his pockets? His wallet, in which he had kept a folded thin piece of wire, just in case he ever needed to pick the odd lock, had been confiscated in New York, but did he have anything else he could use?

Keys. His car had been in the shop a week ago for an oil change. He hadn't bothered to remove the identifying tag that the shop had put on his key, a tag attached with a small piece of... twisted wire.

He patted his pants pockets frantically. He remembered sliding the keys into his front right pocket after locking the door to his apartment—and then he remembered kissing Alex goodbye, her lips, warm, sweet. Engaged. He was engaged to Alex, and he'd never see her again. He'd been so goddamn stupidly happy, just a few hours ago. But he couldn't think about Alex. Focus on the keys.

He felt nothing on the outside of his pants. Turning his right hand sideways, he managed to slide it into his pocket despite the handcuffs and chain. With the tips of his fingers and his thumb, he pulled the fabric into his hand until he had explored every inch. Back pocket, no, he was too much of a New Yorker: valuables— keys, wallet—went in front. He tried the left front pocket just in case. No, nothing.

Had they taken his keys while he was unconscious? Of course. His keys would be with his wallet and his watch: his personal items would all combine to convince the ECA that he was dead.

Eboyanna mat. He yanked in fury and frustration at the chain that held him. But the chain didn't give, and the struggle hurt his wrists. He wasn't going anywhere, he finally acknowledged, and let his hands fall on his chest. There was nothing he could do except direct his thoughts. As long as he could keep his mind elsewhere, he had some level of control. They could hurt him or kill him, but only he could let them inside.

The anticipation of torture was part of the torture. He ran his repertoire of jazz standards through his mind and selected Dave Brubeck, "Take Five." He chose a key, pictured his hands on the keyboard. His imagination played the first chord and swung into the theme, hearing the sax and the drum. He improvised against unheard melodies.

19

Jonathan took a deep breath as the morgue attendant slid the first drawer open. Yes, it was Eric. Teo took one glance and walked to the far side of the room.

"Can we see the other body, please?"

She walked to a second drawer and slid it open to reveal a zipped body bag. She unzipped it and waited. Jonathan took a deep breath, moved to the drawer, and looked down. Marty followed.

The charred remains were barely recognizable as those of a human being, let alone those of Kolya Petrov. There was a fragmented charred skull and blackened bones. The acrid smell of smoke still clung to the remains.

He hadn't expected much, but somehow he had hoped he would know if the burned bones were that of his closest friend. All he felt was revulsion and pity.

Teo stayed on the far side of the room. "Is it Kolya?" His voice quavered. Jonathan couldn't blame him. He could barely keep his own nausea down.

Marty answered for him. "Can't tell by looking, Teo."

With an apologetic look, the morgue attendant handed him a small plastic bag. Inside were blackened keys and the stainless steel husk of a Movado watch. Initials N.I.P. on the back. Nikolai Ivanovich Petrov.

Jonathan looked over at Marty and Teo. "Let's go for a walk. I need some air."

He was desperate to get away from the morgue. The image of the remains would stay with him, but at least he could escape the smell of formaldehyde, the closed in windowless room, and the silent, accusing presence of the dead.

* * * * *

Several hours later, they were at the Delaware Water Gap, where the remains had been found. The car was a blackened hulk of metal.

"The gas tank exploded as well." Les Thompson, an FBI agent with whom Jonathan and Kolya had worked years earlier, walked by Jonathan's side.

Jonathan examined the road that wound around the mountain, just to the side of the parking lot. It was a lovely spot. Across the road, he could see a stream winding through the woods. The trees were just beginning to turn red, gold, and orange. A few golden leaves drifted down over them.

"Where was the wallet found?"

"Over here." Les paced off five feet from the wreck of the car. Jonathan followed and squatted down to examine the pavement. He couldn't tell if there had been another car, two other cars, one person, five people.

"Blood on the wallet?"

"Some."

Kolya had kept his wallet in a front pants pocket. So how'd the blood get from Kolya's head to his wallet and how did the wallet wind up five feet away? Maybe one of the killers had taken out Kolya's wallet before shooting him and then dropped the wallet on the way to the car. Hell, it didn't make any sense.

Jonathan took out his iPhone.

"No reception here unless you've got a satellite phone," Les said. "No towers and lots of mountains. Wait until you get out of the park."

"It can wait." Jonathan replaced it in his pocket. The agency gave out satellite phones when necessary, but he hadn't taken one for this trip. He could check messages and e-mail when they were out of the mountains.

Bob Smith clicked off the phone. Egan was either out of range of a tower, or he'd turned his phone off. How the hell can you be out of range in New York City? No way was he going to send a text.

He tried again. The computerized voice informed him again that Jonathan Egan was unavailable. He picked up a cigar from his desk, bit off the end, and spat it into a garbage can.

Bob didn't know anyone else at the ECA, not unless he counted Kolya Petrov, and Petrov wasn't exactly available either. He knew Margaret Bradford's name, but he'd have to go through layers of shit to get to her, and he'd still probably wind up with some deputy or other, and then God knows who he'd be talking to. And it could get back to Ford. No, this was too damn hot to entrust to anyone but Egan.

He toyed with the idea of contacting the Deputy Director but decided against it. The first priority was to save Kolya Petrov's life, and the ECA would have a better chance of mounting an operation in Romania.

He still couldn't believe it.

The Director knew that Petrov had been taken to Romania where he'd be interrogated and ultimately killed. But Bob had no idea where to even start looking, and from the conversation, it didn't sound as if the Director knew, either. The only one who might be able to locate Petrov quickly enough to save his life would be this Frick guy that the Director had been speaking to.

Frick. Who the hell was he? There weren't a lot of clues in the conversation. Bob chewed on his cigar.

It was clearly someone currently under cover in New York. Deep cover. *Okay, time to go hunting.* He put the thumb drive with the incriminating conversations into his shirt pocket, chomped down on his cigar, typed the password into the computer, and began to search.

It took another hour to find three likely candidates: agents who operated undercover in New York and who had been with the Bureau for at least ten years. He pulled up the first file and skimmed downward.

It had details on every assignment since the man had graduated from Quantico, but not a damn thing to indicate that he was Frick or knew anything about Romanians. He exited the file, took the cigar out of his mouth, considered lighting up, decided against it, and placed the cigar on the side of the desk.

The second file was equally unenlightening.

He opened the last file and started to read. David Fuller. Fifteen years with the Bureau. He had received uniformly good evaluations. He had worked directly with Carl Ford, when Ford had been in charge of the New York office, in a bust of a Columbian drug ring. There was a glowing evaluation by Ford.

Bob chomped down on the cigar and gave in. He pulled a matchbook from his pocket and lit up.

He went into a separate file, highly classified, input Fuller's name, hit the enter key, and waited. It only took a minute.

Fuller had spent time getting himself accepted on the street. He started gathering evidence on a gang importing heroin from Turkey. The operation had continued beyond the original scheduled termination because of additional information that Fuller had obtained on possible terrorism attacks, the source unidentified. Fuller had been responsible for obtaining the tip that had led to the discovery of the MANPADS arriving at Port Newark.

Fuller was known on the street as Frick.

Bob scanned the file, signed onto the Internet, typed Egan's e-mail address, and wrote: "Petrov is alive, being held in Romania. Turn your damn phone on. Bob." He attached the file and sent it.

He'd call Egan again after he left the office.

20

Kolya woke from an uneasy sleep at the sound of footsteps in the other room. The sky outside the high barred window was black. His leg ached, and he was chilled and stiff from sleeping on the floor.

He gave one futile tug at the chain before the door swung inward. Cuza had come this time, along with the guards and Max. Stanescu knelt down to take his pulse, the tips of his fingers on Kolya's wrist, and then pushed up Kolya's sweater sleeve to wrap the blood pressure cuff around his arm. Kolya read the upside-down watch as Stanescu listened with the stethoscope. Midnight. It would be five o'clock in Washington. Saturday night, wasn't it? October—October 9? Alex would be heading to her brother's home in Silver Spring for a dinner party in honor of a great aunt. He imagined being there, watching Alex weave among her difficult family members.

Stanescu removed the blood pressure cuff and folded the stethoscope back into his black bag. He checked the water cup and handed it off to one of the four nameless men standing against the wall. "Get him more water."

The man moved away at the same moment that Cuza spied the leather jacket that had been tossed on the wooden chair. He picked it up and slid it over his tailored shirt. Kolya had a flash of memory, of Alex presenting him with the wrapped box on his last birthday.

"The government must be paying you well. This is an expensive jacket." Cuza buttoned it. "A good fit. I hope you don't mind, Mr. Petrov, but it seems a shame to leave it down here. You see, we can proceed in a civilized manner. You have had medical treatment, and

I've allowed you water and blankets." Cuza waited for a response until it was clear there would be none. "I expect you to answer when I speak to you."

There was no point in refusing to speak, as long as he said nothing of consequence. "I wasn't aware that you said anything requiring a response."

"An acknowledgement is polite if nothing else. I expect politeness from guests."

"Guests? You chain your guests to a wall in the basement?"

"When necessary."

Kolya looked at the chain dangling from the ceiling and the blood on the walls. "How often is that?"

"Now and then. Three or four special guests, like you, although you are a little unique. I understand you have certain knowledge—about a new security system developed by the agency that employs you. If you help me to access the ECA network, I will not only release you alive, without further harm, but put fifty thousand dollars in your name in a Swiss bank account."

"Betraying my country should command a better price."

"You're not an American. You emigrated to live a more comfortable life than you could in Mother Russia. Accepting my offer will simply further that end." Cuza paused. "I am willing to negotiate the amount. I know Jews like to negotiate. Name a price."

Even if he wanted to make a trade, money for information, Kolya'd never see a penny. Cuza would agree to any amount and then kill him after his usefulness ended. In any event, any information Kolya gave to Cuza would allow him to kill more people. He would die either way, but he could refuse to take others with him.

Still, he considered agreeing as a stalling tactic —but he was just too tired to play the game.

"I told you, Voivode Cuza," Max said from against the wall. "He won't deal."

"So I see," Cuza responded. "Mr. Petrov, let me just clarify that you have no interest in selling your knowledge."

"None." A wave of nausea hit him, and he shut his eyes, fighting it.

"Emil?" Cuza's cultured tones directed his inquiry toward the doctor.

"Some additional discomfort probably—and notice I said probably—won't kill him. Unless he loses too much blood, which could be dangerous."

"We will be careful."

"Since you asked me, I would recommend waiting. Let him rest for now. The man is injured."

"We can let him rest for the night, but I think he should have something additional to contemplate. Is the leg broken?"

"Can't be sure without an x-ray, but I don't think so. The weakness and pain seem to be from the bullet lodging near or against a nerve."

"The golf bag in the other room, Max. One of the irons should do. Lower leg or knee. I apologize, Emil. I know you hate to duplicate effort. But a broken leg shouldn't cause additional blood loss, and you don't have to set it. At least not immediately. Just keep him alive."

Kolya's eyes snapped open and focused on Max, who approached, golf club in hand. He shifted his gaze back to Cuza and tried to conceal his fear.

"You're still with us, Mr. Petrov?" Cuza said pleasantly. "I thought you were asleep. You understand what is going to happen? You have five seconds to agree to cooperate or Max will break your lower leg and shatter your kneecap."

Kolya pushed himself up on an elbow and then into a sitting position, his gaze fixed on Max. The chain attached to the handcuffs on his wrists was just long enough that he would have a chance to grab the club before it struck his leg.

Max stepped back and looked at Cuza. "He's going to try to grab the club."

"Can't have that." Cuza signaled the other men.

The four guards grabbed Kolya, pulled him prone onto the floor, yanked his arms over his head, and pinned him down. Max bent over and pulled the blankets off Kolya, tossing them to the side.

"Mr. Petrov? Have you changed your mind?" Cuza's voice remained pleasant, cultivated.

Kolya swallowed hard in an unsuccessful effort to control his voice. "There is nothing wrong... with the mind I have. I... see no reason to change it."

"Very witty, Mr. Petrov. Proceed, Max."

Max swung the club, smashing the middle of Kolya's lower leg. Kolya cried out in agony, and his body jerked as the bone snapped. Sweat broke out on his face, and the lights in the ceiling swam. He remained grimly conscious.

"The knee?" Max inquired.

Cuza held up a hand. "Well, Mr. Petrov?"

Kolya took a deep breath and then another. God it hurt.

"Mr. Petrov?"

He tried to still his trembling limbs, not wanting Cuza or Max to see how much he hurt. It took a monumental effort, but he managed to speak clearly and distinctly. "*Yob tvoyu mat'*!"

"What did he say?" Stanescu asked.

"He told me to perform a sexual act on my mother," Cuza said. "That was rather rude. Max."

Max swung again, and Kolya felt the flash of white pain and heard his own scream as the club impacted his knee. The men holding him released his arms, but he didn't move. His breath came in short gasps, and his heart pounded.

"Well?" Cuza demanded.

To Kolya, the voices seemed to come from a great distance.

"Enough for now." Stanescu's voice sounded faint. "Leave fresh water where he can reach it."

Blankets were pulled up to his waist. He pulled his arms down and hugged them into his chest to warm himself. The immediate shock was passing. Although the pain was building, he was aware of his surroundings again.

"Emil?" Cuza's voice.

"Checking his pulse," Stanescu reported.

Kolya felt the unwelcome touch of Stanescu's hand on his wrist. He summoned all of his reserves, jerked his elbow sideways into Stanescu's chest, and knocked the air out of him. It wouldn't accomplish anything, but the effort gave him momentary satisfaction. Stanescu gasped and sat down hard. Kolya collapsed.

Max started for Kolya, but Cuza held up a hand. "Tomorrow, Max. I suggest you leave him alone, Emil. He's alive and not appreciative of your efforts."

"I was treating him, damn it. Doesn't he know that?"

"He knows exactly what you're doing. He'll survive the night without your attention. Just to be sure, I'll have a man look in on him periodically. If he seems to be in serious distress, you'll be called. Don't drink too much. In the morning, then, Mr. Petrov. We can continue our negotiations then."

They filed out one by one, leaving the light on.

Kolya felt the broken leg swelling, and he wished futilely that he would pass out. Unconsciousness would at least be a temporary relief. But the pain that he wanted to escape wasn't enough to cause him to black out. It kept him awake, conscious, thinking about the next morning. No, he would not think about it. He had known the situation since his capture, but he had managed to divert his mind until now.

But his leg hadn't been shattered until now. The bullet wound had hurt, but not like this. Even if he freed his hands, he couldn't move enough now to get to the next room. Merely shifting his position sent a wave of fresh agony radiating from his leg up through the rest of his body.

Through the haze of pain, he tried to focus on a piece of music. He thought of tunes he had played, what was it, two nights ago in his apartment, Alex's head on his shoulder. For a second, his memory was so vivid, it was almost tactile. While he hurt too much to feel desire, he still remembered everything about that last night, the touch of her lips, the feel of her breasts, the way she moved. *No. Don't think about Alex.* But, he did, for a moment longer, and then he let go and returned his thoughts to music. "Moonlight in Vermont."

The pain broke through. He lost his focus and fought to control his thoughts. He'd had broken bones before; the limb would swell, it was painful, but it could be survived. But his mind wouldn't listen and whispered that tomorrow would be worse, not better and that this time he would not survive. But all that was beside the point. The objective was not to survive, but to hold out. He could and would.

He pushed the thought of the morning out of his mind. Bill Evans.

21

Bob Smith drove onto the Beltway, heading north to Bethesda and home. The more distance he put between himself and FBI headquarters, the better he liked it. Bob increased his speed, switched into the middle lane, and passed a red Mustang on his left that had been hogging the fast lane. When he cut back into the far-left lane, the mustang driver flashed his headlights.

Goddamn idiots on this road.

So, what should he do? He wouldn't be safe as long as he was the only one who knew the truth. It wasn't just his own safety, either, that concerned him. He was the only one, besides Carl Ford and this Frick guy, who knew that Petrov was alive. He'd sent Jonathan Egan an e-mail, but that wasn't enough.

He had to get in touch with Egan, and he had to do it soon.

A car cut in front of him within inches of his bumper, and he leaned on the horn. The promised rain began, drops scattering across his windshield.

He turned on his lights and his windshield wipers. It was raining lightly. The wipers smeared dirt across the glass. While watching the road, he punched dial, for Egan's number.

The rain was falling more steadily now, the wipers thumping in a regular rhythm. The red Mustang, now next to him, tried to pass, but the car hydroplaned in the water on the road, spinning out of control.

* * * * *

As soon as the plane landed, Jonathan checked his phone. No messages. No e-mails. Four calls from Bob Smith. He quickly hit all the numbers he had for Bob Smith but hung up without leaving a message on voice mail.

The plane came to a thumping halt, and the lights flashed back on in the cabin. He called Elizabeth.

"Anything up?"

"Not really. Bradford made the usual arrangements, with the consent of White's wife. White's funeral is set for Tuesday. Petrov's still to be arranged."

Willis Funeral Home handled ECA arrangements unless the family had another preference. "Have you heard anything from Bob Smith?"

"Nothing."

"See if you can locate him."

"Will do. You coming back to the office?"

It was after eleven, and he felt as tired as he'd ever felt in his life. "Not unless there's something urgent. I'm heading home, belting down a couple of bourbons, and going to bed. If you find something out tonight, give me a call. Otherwise I'll be in early."

A pause.

"Have you spoken to Alex Feinstein?"

"Tomorrow. Can't face it tonight."

"Can't blame you. Tough day."

It wasn't so much her words, as her tone. No emotion. "God, Elizabeth, don't break down on me now."

"Screw you, Egan, you bastard."

"Any time. Except tonight. I'm not in the mood."

22

"Petrov. *Trezeste-te!*" **This voice** was unfamiliar. The words repeated in English. "Wake up!" Accompanied by a kick to his side.

He blinked his eyes at the wooden beam in the ceiling, not knowing where he was, aware only of waves of pain from his swollen leg. Usually he woke up quickly, but between his injuries and the lack of sleep, he was groggy. Streams of sunlight beamed down from the high window in the far corner. What day was it? He worked it out. Sunday, October 10.

One of the men who had captured him, who had been on the flight from the United States, stood nearby. Kolya didn't know this man's name but remembered him as the man at the top of the stairs from Penn Station. Kolya lifted his head to check the small room.

Only the two of them. The door into the other room was open.

The man wore a gun, tucked in his prominently displayed shoulder holster. Kolya had never liked shoulder holsters. The guard, though, was the type who would sport a shoulder holster: young, macho. It would be so easy to take that gun away if Kolya could move. Or if the man came close enough.

It was an idea.

His hands, even if cuffed and chained, were in front, and the chain had enough give.

The reality was that he wouldn't be able to escape. He would still die. They'd shoot him, or worse, wait until he ran out of ammunition and take him. He dismissed the last possibility. If he got his hands on a weapon, he would not be taken alive again. Still, it was a preferable alternative, and before they killed him, he would take some of them with him. With any luck, he'd get a shot at Max or Cuza.

He didn't have any other options. Either lie there, helpless, waiting to be tortured, or go for the gun.

As if sensing Kolya's thoughts, the man moved back a step.

"You are awake, Petrov?"

"More or less." Kolya pressed hands against his eyes, rubbed, and ran his tongue over his teeth, absurdly regretting the lack of a toothbrush.

"You get to eat now. Voivode Cuza will be down soon."

Kolya turned his head. On the floor next to him was a metal plate with a few scraps of fatty meat and a slice of bread. The plastic mug that he had drained during the night was filled with water again. Kolya pushed the blankets down, closed his eyes, and shifted slowly and painfully to his left side, lying on his good leg. He rested and then leaned up on an elbow, careful to keep his lower body still.

He reached for the bread. It was stale but even so he had to remind himself not to eat quickly, that food on an empty stomach could cause cramping. Even chewed slowly, the bread was gone too soon, not making a dent in his hunger. He eyed the meat, strips of fat and bone with only a hint of what had been a steak still clinging to the grizzle. He wouldn't give scraps like that to a dog. He drank the water in the mug and availed himself of the bucket. Pushing the bucket away, he lay back down and watched the guard with his peripheral vision.

"Eat the meat." The guard leaned against the wall. "You are lucky to get that."

"I—am not—feeling—very well." Kolya inserted pauses to sound feeble and ill. He wasn't completely feigning: he was weak, hurting badly, and feeling unwell. Not so unwell that he couldn't get the man's gun. But for that, he needed the guard to believe him even more debilitated than he was.

The guard seemed to believe him and found it funny. "You will feel worse soon. Eat now while you can."

"It will make me sick."

Kolya concentrated his entire mind on the gun and the guard. He shifted his weight so that he could more easily move his upper body and watched the guard through half closed eyes.

"Okay." The guard shrugged. "You do not want to eat. I am taking the food away." He pushed off from the wall and approached.

Kolya readied himself, tensing his muscles. *Four feet away, three feet. Just another foot.*

"Gheorghe, if you bend over to pick up that plate, you idiot, he'll have your gun. You'll be dead, and you'll deserve it for being a fool." Max's voice in the doorway.

The guard sprang back. All the tension went out of Kolya's muscles, and he sagged against the floor. Almost. Another second. Another foot. *Poshol k chortu,* Max. Go to the devil.

"He's hurt. Sick. He wouldn't be able to take my gun."

"Sure he would. With no trouble whatsoever. He's not incapacitated, and his hands are in front. He hasn't given up, yet." Max entered, followed by four more men. "He was watching your every move." Max came within Kolya's view but not his reach. "You were going to try it, weren't you, you fucking Jew?"

Kolya opened his eyes all the way to stare back at Max. "No. As the man said: I am unable to walk. It would have been suicidal."

Max kicked Kolya's swollen right leg. "Now you can pick up the plate," he said to Gheorghe as Kolya twisted, gasping in pain. "Go ahead, fool. Take the bucket and empty it, too."

Gheorghe scurried forward, picked up the plate and the bucket, and disappeared.

The flash of white pain eased back to the persistent throb that he had been enduring since waking, and Kolya was able to calm his breathing. Cuza drifted into his peripheral view. He wore jodhpurs—again—and mid-calf black boots. He carried a white china coffee cup in his left hand, in his right, a matching plate with a croissant, butter, and a small knife. Cuza seated himself in the wooden chair against the far wall, setting the plate on one arm. The coffee in the cup was steaming.

"Good morning. There's nothing like a cappuccino after a brisk gallop to start the day off right. Any new developments?"

"Gheorghe nearly got himself shot. Nothing else."

"Ah." Cuza raised a cultivated eyebrow. "Mr. Petrov was abusing our hospitality?"

"He was thinking about it."

"Were you?" Cuza focused on Kolya.

Kolya shrugged. "Think of me as helping to weed out the less intelligent of your thugs."

"You should recall that you are a guest, Mr. Petrov. I am already put out with you for killing two of my people. Have you given any additional thought to cooperating?"

"*Du te dracului!*" Kolya spoke in Romanian, switched to English, and repeated the phrase. "Go to hell."

"You really need to learn to watch your language, Mr. Petrov." Cuza set down the coffee, and buttered his croissant. "Baked fresh every morning. I have a French pastry chef as well as my regular cook. She whips up the most fabulous desserts." Kolya turned his gaze from Cuza to the wall, resolved not to watch the show that was being put on for his benefit. "Hungry, Mr. Petrov?"

"Not at all." Yes, I'm hungry, you *govnyuk*, and you know it. He could eat the entire croissant in two bites and still be hungry. And the coffee, god, a cup of coffee would taste so good. *Choke on it, Cuza.*

"He didn't eat the meat," Gheorghe said.

"It was pretty disgusting," Cuza put more butter on the croissant. "I didn't think he would, but I was curious. He ate the bread?"

"Yes."

"Good. He's had some calories, but not enough to fill him." Cuza slowly chewed the last two bites. He picked up the coffee cup and studied Kolya, who, in turn, studied the wall. "He still thinks he might get away or be rescued. Don't you, Mr. Petrov?"

Kolya watched a spider climb the wall to the ceiling. It was a small yellow-white spider, and it spun out a thin white thread between the wall and the ceiling. *How do spiders learn to spin webs?* He didn't know. He had never been interested in insects, but now he was curious.

Cuza turned in his chair, following the direction of Kolya's eyes, but failed to notice the spider. "Your agency is preparing your funeral as we speak. Your badly burned body has been transported back to Washington. There will be no rescue."

Kolya had realized the reason for the appropriation of his wallet, his watch, and his keys.

"And you're still not tempted to cooperate? A hot meal, a warm bed, medical care doesn't tempt you?"

Kolya returned to watching the spider, which had attached two more threads to its web.

"Oh, all right." Cuza took a sip from his cup. "Obviously, we have a way to go toward breaking him. Dr. Stanescu has suggested that we refrain from additional blows to his leg, as a blood clot could prove fatal. I don't want either his hands or his head injured. When he finally cooperates, he will need both. Max, as we discussed."

Two men gripped his left arm, two men on his right. Max knelt down, fished into a pocket, and came up with a key. Inserting the key into the lock on the chain, he clicked it open. He looked Kolya in the eyes.

"I'm going to enjoy this."

The four men dragged Kolya across the floor by his arms, unlocked the handcuffs, stripped off his sweater and shirt, and pulled him to his feet. Every nerve in his leg screamed in protest. His wrists, stretched straight over his head, were locked in the manacles attached to a chain that was just long enough for him to stand. He rested all of his weight on his left leg, but even the change of position and slight pressure on the right leg was excruciating. Despite the chill in the room and the removal of his shirt, he was sweating. Max left the room.

"We did the adjustment to the chain prior to your arrival, Mr. Petrov, based on your height. It looks about right. I thought an old-fashioned flogging to begin. It's simple. Traditional. Have you ever seen a Jamaican cart whip? Quite a collector's item. Do you know that the British government made it illegal for slave drivers to use it to administer any more than ten lashes at one time. We'll start with twenty and move on from there to more creative possibilities. Of course, Mr. Petrov, we will stop at any point that you agree to cooperate. Do you understand?"

"*Yob tvoyu mat.*" Kolya's voice shook.

"Again, Mr. Petrov? Can't you come up with a more original insult?"

What the hell did it matter? "Not an insult. Just a commonly known fact about your sexual proclivities."

Max returned. Kolya's stomach tightened, and he braced himself.

Cuza lifted the white china cup. "For that you get fifty lashes. Max, whenever you're ready."

The whip slashed across Kolya's back, and he choked back a cry. He gripped the chain above his wrists, keeping his weight on his arms, trying to keep from losing his balance and putting pressure on his broken leg.

"One," Max counted loudly.

The second blow felt harder than the first, sending fresh pain reeling throughout Kolya's body.

"Two," Max said.

* * * * *

Kolya told himself that his back was almost completely numb. It wasn't, but he hoped that his mind would pick up on the suggestion. After all, pain was in the mind, wasn't it?

He counted the blows along with Max. Twenty-five or six wasn't it? He hung limply by the wrists, now, no longer able to grip the chain, unable to decide whether his leg or his back hurt more. Twenty-five more. He focused on the end of the beating. Then— what? But whatever Cuza had in mind, he could hold out. He had to.

Cuza, after the first few blows, moved the heavy chair back two feet, careful to remain at a sufficient distance from any splattering of blood.

"Slowly, Max. He'll feel it more if you go slowly. Awake, Mr. Petrov?"

Kolya licked his lips, tasting salt and blood. Must have bit his mouth. He couldn't even feel it, too overwhelmed with the pain in his back and his leg. He tried to focus his mind on something neutral to distract himself: music—the chord progression in an Ellington song, "Satin Doll"—but all his mind could register was pain.

Let it stop.

But it wouldn't, not unless he surrendered.

"Satin Doll." Start with D minor seven. He pictured his fingers on the piano keyboard, playing the chord solid, then inverted. Improvise in the D minor scale. What were the notes, and then he lost his train of thought as the whip struck him.

He took a deep breath and focused. The D minor scale. "Satin Doll." He couldn't remember the next chord. What was it? He should remember: It was one of Alex's favorite songs; he had played it for her often enough.

Stop it. Don't think of Alex.

The whip struck him again, and he shuddered from the force of the blow. Dizzy. Losing too much blood. He twisted his hands in the manacles. But his hands were too large and the attempt merely hurt his wrists.

"Claire de Lune." Alex had the music in her piano bench. How could he have forgotten? He found it flipping through her music, and he had asked her to play it. She refused. She never liked to play in front of him. His fault. Alex, so confident in a courtroom. Had he made her nervous? *Alex, I'm sorry.*

He groaned loudly, nothing in his mind but the pain, but then he fought back, refocusing on "Satin Doll." D minor seven to F major seven. That was it. From F major seven, the melody went down a step to—to—

"E minor seven," he mumbled, not even aware that he was speaking out loud. He flinched as he was struck again.

Cuza heard the words and stopped Max momentarily. "E minor seven, Mr. Petrov? Are you trying to distract yourself with music?"

"A major seven."

"He's not answering you," Max observed.

"I noticed. Well, although it is less than polite, it is not unexpected. Mr. Petrov, agree to cooperate, and, even though he's enjoying himself, Max will stop."

Kolya forced the words, but his voice was only a whisper. Cuza stood to hear.

"*Ya...tebya...mat.*"

"Very nice, Mr. Petrov. Now you've screwed my mother."

"And—she—was—good." He would have invented details, but he didn't have the energy.

Cuza didn't hear him and looked inquiringly at Max. Max obligingly restated Kolya's last comment.

"Really, Mr. Petrov, I am shocked. Continue, Max. Harder. If you're getting tired, someone else can take a turn."

"I can manage." Max lashed the whip.

Thirty or thirty-one. Kolya couldn't hold music in his head anymore, couldn't hold any thought. There was nothing between him and the pain. Black spots whirled in front of him, and nauseated, he closed his eyes, hoping he would pass out.

"Thirty-five." He heard Max's voice behind him, but it sounded fainter. "Thirty-six."

The black spots grew larger and turned white.

The white flakes swirled in a delicate dance as they cascaded to the ground. He had always loved walking in the snow. He tried to remember the name of the town in Vermont. Alex walked a few feet ahead, and he quickened his pace to catch her. He called her name, but she didn't turn. The snow fell harder and faster, and he could only see a few feet in front of him. It was deep, knee deep, and he could barely move his legs through the drifts.

"Did he say someone's name?"

"I didn't hear anything. He didn't move the last two times I hit him," Max's voice barely penetrated Kolya's consciousness. "You awake, Jew?"

Kolya remained silent, only part of his mind hearing the question.

"He may have passed out. Try water."

Water splashed in Kolya's face and brought him back from the edge of consciousness. Coughing, he started and blinked. His head rose momentarily, and then shivering from the cold, he let his head droop, eyes closed once more. The water had had the desired effect.

He was awake enough to be aware of how much he hurt.

Max slashed. "Forty," he counted.

"He's passed out again." Gheorghe said.

Kolya hadn't, but he had no reason to contradict Gheorghe. If they believed him unconscious, they might stop. It would be a temporary reprieve, possibly only long enough for them to toss more water on him, but he was desperate for any relief.

As he had hoped, the flogging halted. Cuza, with a sigh of exasperation, pushed himself out of the chair, and examined Kolya, who didn't move.

"He may not be completely out, but he's close."

"Could be faking," Max said. "He's fooled us before. Fucking Jews are full of tricks."

"Now, Max, Dr. Stanescu did warn us about too much blood loss. He was already injured." Cuza's footsteps sounded behind Kolya. "He is a bloody mess, isn't he? Rinse him off."

The water that hit Kolya's back startled him into full awareness again.

Behind him, he heard Max. "Ten more to go. Keep going?"

"Of course, Max. It is important to follow through. Otherwise, one loses credibility."

They revived Kolya twice more before Max finished. After the last blow, he hung limp in the chains, wet, bloody, and barely conscious. After Kolya's wrists were released, he collapsed. The men dragged him across the room, back to his original location on the floor, snapped the handcuffs closed and tossed the blankets on him. Shivering under the blankets, he blinked weary eyes open, staring at the wall six feet away, and gingerly flexed sore wrists against the cuffs.

He heard Max laugh above him. "There's a bucket, so you don't piss on yourself. Take a nap. We'll be back. The Count doesn't want the chicken roulade to get cold."

The words didn't have the desired effect; he was so miserable that he no longer felt hungry. The dark spots swirled in front of his eyes again. Grateful for the respite, he slid into the darkness.

23

Jonathan woke at six, swallowed two aspirin for his splitting headache, and lurched into the shower. Fifteen minutes later, he was in his car. Half an hour after that, he was at the ECA. He found Elizabeth, dressed in jeans, at the computer in her office.

"Who's in?" He seated himself in the extra chair.

"Our team. Bradford. Ross. The usual Sunday support staff."

"Margaret? Ross? Why?"

"You asked who's here. I happen to know. I don't know what they're doing."

He understood why Margaret might be in at quarter to seven on a Sunday morning. But Ross? What was he up to?

Whatever. Ross's hours weren't his concern.

"What do you have for me?"

"You requested that I do some checking. I have information on Bob Smith. He was in a car accident last night. Driving at high speeds in the rain."

"Shit. Shit. Shit. He's dead, too?"

"No, I didn't say that. He's in George Washington University hospital, critical, but alive."

"Damn. Of all the goddamn bad luck. If it's luck."

"There's only a one in three shot that Ford's the mole, Jonathan. You know that."

"You don't think it odd? Kolya dies; his body unidentifiable. Margaret's given the news by Carl Ford, and the next day, a guy checking out Carl Ford is in an accident."

"Coincidences do happen."

Her manner was angry. He could ignore her anger or deal with it. But they were on the same team. Tension between them made working together difficult. One of them had to make the overture, and he suspected that it wouldn't be her.

"Sorry about last night, Elizabeth. I was out of line."

"Do you think that's going to do it? A simple 'sorry?'"

"But you could have been a little nicer. I was bringing back Kolya's body. I know you had a history with him, and it ended badly, but for God's sake, he's dead. He could be difficult or rude, but he was my best friend and my partner for ten years. And Eric—I wasn't close to Eric, not the way I was with Kolya, but he was a good man."

She looked away. "I suppose I could have been a little more sympathetic."

"You think you can still work with me?"

"Why not? I'm a professional. Just keep it on that level."

* * * * *

Margaret Bradford read the two sentences on the printout and then glanced up at Ross.

"And Jonathan will be unable to detect either that you deleted a message or you were poking in his e-mail and phone?"

"Yep."

"Good. Who sent the e-mail?"

"Some guy at the FBI Bob Smith. Smith was in a car accident last night after sending the e-mail—he's in a coma. We couldn't have arranged it better."

"We don't have to worry about him for the moment. And we know the identity of our mole." She considered. Petrov, confirmed to be alive, had been a prisoner for at thirty-six hours. The question was—how long before he gave in? "No sign that the Trojan horse has been activated?"

He shook his head.

The date was October 10. The Romanian elections were scheduled for November 1, a date that was creeping up. Whatever Cuza had planned would occur before that date.

The time for intelligence gathering was short. However distasteful she might find it, knowing the identity of the mole made it easier to implement phase two.

* * * * * *

Jonathan had just pushed his chair back from the desk, when he saw Teo Lorenzo standing in the doorway of his office.

"You're going to talk to Alex, aren't you? I'm coming, too."

"You don't even know her."

"Sure I do. I got drunk under her piano. Remember? I just thought—" Teo hesitated and took two steps into Jonathan's office, "I just thought you'd like some moral support. And I want to be there for Alex. Maybe I can be of some help."

"What the hell, come on." Teo was right. Jonathan hated this job. He put on his sports jacket and picked up the blackened keys from his desk. The first stop would be Kolya's apartment.

* * * * *

The brandy was a little known French brand. Cuza could afford more expensive brandies, but he liked a bargain as well as any other man. He sipped it and savored the pleasant afterglow of a fine meal.

"I just received the latest poll numbers," he said to Stanescu, who was eating a crème brûlée. "They're saying the election is so close that it can't be called."

"So are you still going ahead with the plans?"

"Of course. The prospect of a nuclear disaster will be so terrifying that no one will vote for a government planning to build more plants." Besides, there were his cleanup companies to consider. "Have you been downstairs?"

"Not today. I assumed that if there were an emergency, you'd let me know."

"Not an emergency, but I would like you to check Mr. Petrov after you finish your dessert."

"No change from last night?"

"He wasn't quite as witty." Cuza helped himself to a cigar. "But his attitude remained unhelpful."

"He'll break," Max said. "I guarantee it."

"Perhaps. Eventually. But I am concerned that it may take too long. We need to confirm the security of our operation, and for that, we need access to his agency's computer. He's already resisted longer than I would have thought. I've had guests downstairs on other occasions. None of them were quite so stubborn."

"He's a trained agent," Stanescu said. "More likely to resist than one of the local peasants. You have to know what motivates him."

Max looked at the cigar and smiled thinly.

"Torture doesn't always work. What do you know about his personal life?"

"It's a thought." Cuza'd give Radu a call in New York, ask him to find out what Frick knew or could find out about Petrov. In the meanwhile, they would continue with Max's methods.

* * * * *

Alex Feinstein put down her phone. He'd texted that he'd arrived in New York—and then nothing. No response to her texts either. He hadn't called as promised. Okay, she knew the drill, knew there were times he couldn't communicate, but he'd said it was a low risk operation. *God, let him be all right. Let him be safe.* Once she heard from him, she'd kill the son-of-a-bitch for worrying her, but now she just desperately wanted that reassurance.

Her line of thought was interrupted by the doorbell. Who the hell could it be at ten o'clock on a Sunday morning? Kolya had a key. Stopping at a mirror in the hall, she glanced at her reflection. With her fingers, she hurriedly smoothed down the thick dark mass of hair. Otherwise, she was decent enough, even without shoes, in jeans and a dark blue tee shirt.

Jonathan Egan and Teo Lorenzo stood on the top of her stairs. "Jonathan," she said, pleased to see him. "Teo."

Jonathan's expression didn't change. "May we come in Alex?"

She looked at Jonathan and then at Teo, and she realized why they had to be there, two of them, wearing the type of expression that can only be described as funereal. "Hell no, you can't." She tried to shut the door as if the act would keep the news out.

But his foot was in the way. "Alex, please, we need to talk to you."

With a deep breath, she swung the door open again. She stared at him mutely, and he stared back at her. Teo turned away.

"Don't say it, Goddamn it."

"Alex. I'm so sorry."

"No." She shook her head. This wasn't happening. She was dreaming, a very bad dream. "No, he can't be dead." Teo was crying. "He can't be. He can't be."

* * * * *

Margaret Bradford turned the cup of tea in her hands, staring at the words, *World's Best Grandmom.*

The point of allowing Cuza to capture Petrov was for Petrov to access the fake system. Cuza had not yet accessed the system, which could only mean that Petrov was continuing to resist. She should have factored in his stubbornness. So, like it or not, the next step was logical, even if it meant another death on her conscience. But how many deaths could be prevented if Ross got into Cuza's computer system? That was always the equation.

Nasty job. Maybe consider retirement herself after all this was over. A nice little cabin in Maine—or maybe on Martha's Vineyard. Yes, with a view of the ocean. The grandchildren could come play on the beach—and she could spend some time with them—the time she had never spent with her own children.

She pictured the beach and her favorite grandchild, Meg, three years old, with strawberry blonde hair, as she picked up the phone and dialed. "Carl." Her voice was warm. "I'm calling to give you the details on Mr. Petrov's funeral."

"Yes, of course. I'll send out a memo as well. There's a number of people who worked with him in New York who would want to attend."

"The funeral's scheduled for Wednesday morning. 9 a.m. at Willis. Sad. Such a capable young man."

"Always sad. At least there's no family."

"No, no relatives, although Mr. Egan had to give the news to Mr. Petrov's girlfriend."

"Girlfriend?" Carl Ford asked. "Serious girlfriend?"

"As I understand, very serious. Lovely young woman, an attorney. You might have heard her name—she was in the media for that innocence thing over in Virginia. The poor girl's just devastated."

24

Kolya reclined on the white couch in Alex's living room, reading. He glanced over at Alex, working on a pile of papers at her desk, her face obscured by her dark hair, and considered just how to coax her away from her work and into the bedroom.

"She's lovely, Kolya." Twelve years old, Dmitri Lemonsky, his once best friend, sat next to him on the couch. Dmitri lowered his voice conspiratorially. "Yelseyev is looking for you."

Before he could answer, Dmitri disappeared. Kolya treaded water in the ocean. Mystic Connecticut. What the hell was he doing here? This had to be Jonathan's idea of fun. Bring Alex, we'll stay at my parents' house. It'll be a nice weekend.

A wave caught him, and he broke up from the ocean, coughing.

He floated up to consciousness, dimly aware that he was not swimming, that he was lying on a floor, ill and aching. Someone had thrown water on him to rouse him. But the effect was momentary, and he slipped back into a half-dream.

I'm not swimming. He struggled to remember. Not—

"Why's he so wet? Has he been swimming?" Idiot. Anyone could see he'd been swimming.

"We had to wake him, and we cleaned him while we were at it." There was a laugh. Kolya didn't open his eyes, but he became conscious enough to know the speakers. Not Jonathan, it was that *kozyol yobannity* Max. And the drunken doctor.

"Obviously effective in rousing an injured man. I would have suggested internal application of water. He's probably lost another

138

pint or two of blood, and he's soaking wet. Get a towel."

Kolya swam into fuller consciousness as his head was lifted and a cup of water pressed to his mouth. He swallowed greedily and drained the cup, still not fully awake, only aware enough to know that he hurt and he was still thirsty.

A hand on his wrist took his pulse. The doctor—what was his name—Stanescu—what? "Talk to me, Petrov. I want to know if you are capable of being coherent."

"No." He tried to return to the dream. It had not been a pleasant dream, but it was preferable to this reality. A hand on his shoulder shook him slightly, reminding him of the pain in his back.

"Fuck you." It was an inelegant insult, but it was as much as he could manage.

There was a sharp prick in his upper arm.

More awake, Kolya blinked his eyes open to see a blurred outline of Stanescu, removing the hypodermic from his arm. It took another minute for his vision to clear. Kolya shifted his position in a futile attempt to ease his injured leg.

He was freezing, soaking wet, and his entire body ached, although the pain was most acute in his leg and back. The blankets had been removed, probably before the water was dumped as part of the effort to rouse him. He wondered how long he had been unconscious.

"You look awake," Stanescu said. "Took long enough. Need to piss?"

Kolya found enough energy to answer in the affirmative, although the simple act of unzipping his pants with hands that he couldn't feel took an enormous effort. Nor could he find the strength to raise himself. After finishing, his eyelids slid closed again.

"Time to take your temperature. You going to cooperate, or do I need the guards?" Stanescu removed a thermometer from his bag as he spoke.

It wasn't important enough to resist. He took the thermometer and placed it under his tongue.

"Well?" Max reappeared from wherever he had been lurking.

Stanescu indicated the thermometer. "He might have a fever—which would also explain why he was so difficult to rouse. Some of his injuries seem be getting infected. Turn over on your back, Petrov, I need to look at your leg."

Kolya failed to respond, and Stanescu repeated the request, louder.

"I'll get him to turn over."

Kolya recognized Max's voice. Deciding that assistance from Max would hurt more than moving by himself, Kolya slowly rolled from his side onto his back, his eyes still closed, the thermometer balanced under his tongue. As his raw back met the floor, he recoiled, muscles tensed, and he teetered on the edge of consciousness again. But after the first shock and the wave of dizziness passed, the cold of the sodden blanket underneath him was soothing.

Stanescu's light touch on his leg jolted him again, and his teeth clenched down on the thermometer.

"The wound looks infected. Lower leg's a mess. Bone's broken and the kneecap's shattered."

"Should be. I hit him hard enough," Max said. "He shouldn't have an infection. I thought you were giving him penicillin."

"Antibiotics don't completely replace the human immune system." He reached up, removed the thermometer, brought it down in front of his face, and peered over his glasses. "101.

I'd say it's up to the Count whether or not he wants to risk killing him. Although he does have a good steady heartbeat, and he looks like he's not in shock. Blood pressure's low, though. He shouldn't lose any more blood."

"I'll inform the Count. He'll make the decision on how to proceed." Max disappeared from Kolya's line of vision.

The moronic Gheorghe appeared and dumped a towel on Kolya's chest.

"You should dry off," the doctor observed as Kolya simply closed his eyes again, exhausted. "You'll be warmer. If it's too much effort, someone can help."

"No… thanks." He didn't understand the point: he was lying on wet blankets, and his jeans were sodden. He made half an effort to dry himself, rubbing the towel against his damp hair, and drying his chest. It didn't do much good: he was still wet, and the blankets that had been covering him were on the other side of the room. After returning to his side, his broken leg positioned on top of his good leg, he flexed his wrists and tried moving his fingers. His hands were numb, either from the cold or the restraints.

Stanescu checked Kolya's wrists. "The cuffs are tight because your wrists are swollen. It's probably a little uncomfortable."

A talent for the obvious. Kolya closed his eyes again and drifted toward darkness. The doctor continued to talk, but his words snapped Kolya fully conscious again.

"Can cause nerve damage. There's even a name for the nerve damage from tight handcuffs. Now what's the word?"

"Permanent damage?" The question slipped out before he could stop himself, his mind registering what the damage would mean for his music at the same time registering the absurdity, under the circumstances, of caring whether or not he would be able to continue to play piano.

"Could be. The longer the cuffs are on, the greater the chance any damage would be permanent. They seem unnecessarily tight. Gheorghe, do you have the key?"

Stanescu loosened the cuffs, and Kolya felt tingling in his hands as circulation returned. He also became aware that Stanescu was piling the blankets back on top of him. It was a mixed blessing. The touch of the cloth on his back was painful, but he was warmer.

"You know," Stanescu said in a half whisper, "you're sick enough that I might be able to get them to postpone questioning you."

Stanescu was playing a variation on the good cop, bad cop technique. It was a game, but Kolya could play along. Maybe there was a chance that the next torture session would be postponed.

"But you have to give me something. Tell me the name of your informer."

There was no informer, at least no current live informer. Kolya was willing enough to give him something useless.

"Gina Antonia."

Cuza, followed by Max and two more men, entered the room. "The name of someone we haven't already killed," Cuza said.

Cuza's riding attire had been replaced by an outfit that could only be described as business casual—a cashmere sweater over a shirt and gray slacks. He also wore Kolya's jacket, which Kolya determined to be a demonstration of their comparative situations rather than a fashion statement. His face remained as politely pleasant as before, as if he were circulating at a cocktail party.

"He's not going to tell you anything, Emil." Cuza addressed the doctor in Romanian. "You know the critical question: is he likely to die on me if I continue his interrogation?"

"It is a possibility. I would avoid anything would cause an additional loss of blood."

"You can stay to monitor his condition."

"If I get a drink."

"Help yourself." Cuza indicated the other room and smiled down at Kolya. "Unlike you, I don't appreciate games."

Max and the other guards dragged him off the floor and chained him again in the center of the room.

"Mr. Petrov, you haven't answered me." Cuza reached in the pocket of the jacket and fished out a cigar and a silver lighter. Cuza rolled the cigar between his thumb and first two fingers, holding the lighter in his left hand, as if weighing a decision. He flicked the lighter and lit the cigar.

Kolya's eyes closed, and he took a deep breath, trying to steel himself, his heart hammering.

"Last chance before Max takes over."

"*Mat—tvoyu cherez—sem' vorot s—prisvistom.*" Kolya voice was barely audible.

"Let me see if I can work that one out. Fuck my mother, through seven gates, while whistling. Very inventive. Max."

The cigar burned against his chest, and the flash of fresh pain racked through his body. Crying out, he jerked at the chains holding him.

"Had enough?" Max burned a new spot.

Bile rose in Kolya's throat, and he saw black spots. He welcomed his increasing dizziness, hoping he had only a few minutes more of consciousness.

"His hands?" Max asked.

"No, not the hands," Cuza said. "He may need to operate a computer. Besides, he's a musician. An artist, or so I understand. I'd like to hear him play, if we can ever persuade him to be sociable. Other body parts are less important, to me, if not to Mr. Petrov."

"Fine." Max unsnapped the top of Kolya's jeans.

The imminent personal invasion brought Kolya back to life. He grabbed the overhead chain, held on, his entire weight on his arms, and, despite searing pain through his right leg, managed a front snap kick with his left. Even in his condition, he felt a momentary satisfaction at knocking Max halfway across the room. It was a short-lived victory. Max stood up, eyes glinting with fury. Kolya was beaten on the legs and held while his pants were unzipped and pulled down below his hips. Max applied the cigar to Kolya's genitals. Kolya screamed, gagged, and retched. Max continued, and Kolya continued to scream until his voice gave out. The black spots grew larger until there was nothing but darkness.

He lay on the floor, once again chained to the wall. His jeans, drier, but still damp, had been pulled up and fastened, and he was wrapped in dry blankets. The sodden blanket on the floor was gone. The room stank of urine, vomit, and burned flesh.

He felt terrible beyond any words to express it. Every inch of his body hurt. He swallowed hard, trying to moisten his dry throat.

Stanescu touched his neck, taking his pulse.

"Take—your hands—off—me—or—I'll—kill you." It wasn't a realistic threat. Kolya didn't think he could lift his head by himself.

Stanescu removed his hands. "I don't think he wants me to touch him." There was fear in his voice.

It was almost funny.

Cuza's footsteps sounded nearer. Kolya felt him standing overhead, staring downward. "So? He probably doesn't want us torturing him either. You have to treat him. If he dies, I'll be very annoyed."

So dying was a possibility. Encouraging.

"He's breathing, what do you want?" Stanescu's voice was decidedly more slurred than earlier. "I don't think he's likely to die immediately."

"We're stopping for now. I need to check some e-mail and make a few calls. We'll be back in a bit, Mr. Petrov. Meanwhile, Emil, do what is reasonable medically —short of pain relief."

"You want me to set his leg?"

Cuza considered. "I think that would come under pain relief."

"He could lose the leg if it goes untreated too long."

"If he cooperates, he'll be treated. If he doesn't, losing his leg will be the least of his worries." Cuza patted Stanescu on the shoulder. "Give him some antibiotics, Emil, and don't worry so much. He can't really kill you. Gheorghe, the room stinks. Spray some air freshener, would you?"

Kolya barely felt the two shots. He heard the sound of an aerosol spray and smelled canned pine. It added to but did not mask the other odors.

"I'm leaving water where you can reach it, Petrov." It was Stanescu's voice. "I'll be back a little later."

"Enjoy your nap," Max said. "I'll be keeping you up the rest of the night."

He lay without moving until his tormentors filed out of the room and locked the door behind them, and then he slid his hands down the inside of his pants to check the damage. There were several large burns on his penis and his testicles, but everything seemed to be intact. Not that it would ultimately matter. He withdrew his hands and pulled the cup of water over. Lifting his head half an inch off the floor, he sipped the water slowly and spilled some from shaking hands. After setting the cup down, his eyes closed again against the glare of the overhead lights. He was beyond the ability to focus his thoughts, but as he drifted mentally, he heard the notes of a Mozart piano concerto, the Twenty-Third, his mother's favorite, faintly filtering through the ceiling.

25

Frick cracked the door of his apartment and saw Radu. "Not now. I'm busy." Frick was watching the New York Giants get the shit beat out of them, as he was preparing to cook chili. The last thing he wanted was another chat with Radu.

"You said you'd call back, but you didn't. You want to talk with me in the hall?"

Frick unhooked the chain and swung it open. "Not really." He led the way to the living room, where a pot, a cutting board, a knife, and onions lay on the coffee table. The television blared; the Giants had just lost ten yards. Frick sat on the couch, picked up the knife, and returned to chopping onions. "I helped you capture the guy; I faked his death for you; what the hell else do you want? Hey, stupid," he shouted at the Giants' quarterback, "throw the goddamn ball!"

Radu peered at the contents of the pot. "Interesting. What is it?"

"Cincinnati chili." He scraped the bits of onion from the cutting board into the pot. "So what do you want?" Frick picked up the pot and headed for the kitchen, where he put the pot on a burner and turned on the heat. Radu trailed behind.

"Like we talked about earlier: we need personal information on Petrov—to break him."

"I thought Cuza and Max were experts at persuasion."

"Petrov is stubborn. The Count thinks that he may need motivation beyond physical pain. I understand he has no family. But perhaps there's someone he cares for."

"Like a girlfriend, you mean?"

145

"Exactly."

"And you'd kidnap the girlfriend, parade her in front of Petrov, and kill her if he doesn't give in?"

"We are planning a better future for millions of people. Sometimes people are hurt in the process. It's not that the Count enjoys killing women."

"That so?" Frick took the pepper down from the shelf and dumped another teaspoon into the chili. "The name Gina Antonia ring any bells?"

"That was different. She was a spy and a whore."

"If you say so."

"I do say so, and you said you would look into whether Petrov had any personal involvements that might make him vulnerable."

"Did I?" Frick gave the chili another swipe with the spoon. The meat was still raw or he would have tasted the mixture. "You know, it's one thing to kidnap an intelligence agent to get information. It's quite another to go after his girlfriend. It's outside the rules of the game."

"Rules of the game? The ones who win make the rules. We have already violated these so-called rules with what we've done to Petrov."

"Maybe so." Frick put a lid on the pot and turned down the heat. He stalked back to the living room and slouched down in the couch. Radu dogged his steps but remained standing.

"Petrov has a girlfriend. And you know her name, don't you?"

The crowd roared as the Giants' wide receiver caught a fifty-yard pass. "Now, run, you bum!" Frick shouted.

"Answer the question."

"Okay, then yeah. The Director called me earlier today."

"The Director has been a good friend. We don't forget our friends."

"I'm not feeling very friendly."

Radu picked up the remote and turned off the television. "Let me make myself clear. We need to get into the ECA computer network, and we need to do it soon. Petrov isn't giving in. Max may be able to break him, or he may not. Either way, it's taking too much time. However distasteful you find the idea of kidnapping Petrov's girlfriend, something else must be done and done quickly. You're involved. So is your boss. What do you think would happen to you—and to him—if this became known?"

Married to them. I'm fucking married to all of them. But he saw no way out. Frick picked up the remote and snapped the game back on. "Petrov is involved with a woman named Alexandria Feinstein. She's a prominent attorney—involved in some sort of innocence project. She lives in Georgetown."

"Good." Radu settled on the couch. "There's another five minutes in the fourth quarter. After that, we will eat your chili, and then we will drive together to Washington D.C."

"Have a wonderful time. You don't need me."

"Sure I do. You're FBI. You might be able to get her into the car without a struggle. It would be more difficult for our people. Someone might notice if she's forcibly abducted."

"I'm not using FBI credentials for this."

"I'm sure you can come up with something on the drive. And you can accompany me to Romania afterwards."

"Now why would I want to do that?"

"I don't have anyone else available. No one who's able to take a couple days off and fly to Romania. The woman may cause trouble on the plane, and it's a long flight."

"Doesn't have to be me."

"The Count specifically requested your assistance."

"Whatever." Frick slid lower on the couch.

* * * * *

"What's that?" Alex Feinstein, huddled on the sofa hugging her knees, looked at the cup held in Teo's outstretched hand. Jonathan and Teo had spent the afternoon with her, for which she was grateful, and with the help of half a bottle of the vodka that she kept in her freezer for Kolya, she kept herself together.

"Oolong tea. And we could order some food. It's almost dinner time."

"Don't want any goddamn tea." She pushed the sleeves of the overlarge sweater back up on her arms—Kolya's sweater. It was a plain blue cotton pullover that he had left at her house, and she imagined it as still holding some of his essence. "Don't want any goddamn food either." She turned to Jonathan, who was nursing a scotch. "I want to see him." It was the fifth request.

"No, you don't." Jonathan shook his head. "I always thought the Jewish tradition of not viewing the dead was sensible. Remember him as he was in life."

"But you saw him, right?" She reached for her glass on the coffee table and almost fell over.

"Yes."

She turned to Teo. He stood there, a hangdog look on his face, holding the damn teacup. "You see him, Teo?"

"No."

Teo looked at Jonathan.

"Alex, I know this is hard," Jonathan said. "But you don't want to see him." Jonathan drained his glass.

She shut her eyes, and there he was, lying next to her in bed. She could visualize his face, every inch of his body, but she'd never see him again, and in time the memory, so vivid now, would soften and blur. In that fading, he would die again for her, and the thought was unbearable.

She opened her eyes to Jonathan's concerned face and Teo, hovering, uncomfortable and awkward, at a distance.

For a moment, she hated them both as she hated the ECA and the whole espionage business. Kolya could have been a lawyer. They would have married, had children, and lived out their lives together. Instead, he had to be a Goddamn spy, and now he was dead.

She stood unsteadily and made her way over to the piano. "You can go, Jonathan, very kind of you to stay all afternoon." She sat on the bench and started to finger the keys. "Moonlight in Vermont," how did it go? She played a few notes, but even sober, she didn't have anything approaching Kolya's skill. Now, she couldn't even pick out the tune. She slammed her fist on the keys.

Jonathan put his hand on her shoulder. "Alex, is there anyone I can call to stay with you? Your brother, maybe?" He seated himself next to her on the piano bench.

"No, not my brother. I don't want my stinking brother. Kolya wasn't rich enough or Jewish enough for my brother. I want to stay in my own home."

"How about we get you to bed?" Jonathan put an arm around her.

"No." She couldn't face the bedroom where she had slept with Kolya. But sleep sounded appealing. "Couch."

Jonathan guided her back to the couch, found pillows, and tucked a quilt around her. There was a ringing sound, and she tried to focus on it. The phone that she kept for business continued to ring, and she started to get up. But Jonathan was ahead of her.

"Stay there, Alex." He lifted the portable phone off a side table. "No, I'm sorry. Ms. Feinstein is resting. I'll give her a message."

"I can take it." She held out her hand. He looked at her dubiously but handed the phone over.

"I'm calling you about the Robinson case." The voice was male and unfamiliar.

Homer Robinson was on death row in Virginia and had consistently maintained his innocence.

"Who are you?"

"The name's Jones."

"And your connection is what?"

"I'm a believer in justice."

"Good for you. And?"

"I've got a witness. Says Roman Yoblonsky confessed to him. You interested?"

Roman Yoblonsky, she ran the name rhythmically through her mind. Roman. Roman. Roman was the main witness against her client, and the person she suspected of being the actual killer. Her mind clicked into work mode.

"Very."

"He'd like to meet with you. Tonight."

"Tonight? No, not tonight. I've had a death in the family."

"Tonight," the caller insisted. "Or not at all. This guy's only in town one night. He worked on construction with Yoblonsky, and he's leaving tomorrow. Can we meet somewhere private. Maybe around ten-thirty. He's afraid of being seen."

She wanted to curl up in a ball and never emerge. But it was her responsibility. Kolya. Kolya would want her to carry on. She'd be sober enough in three and a half hours to talk to a witness. She hesitated, but she could defend herself. "Come to my house." She gave the address and then she hung up.

"Are you nuts?" Jonathan asked. "Working tonight?"

She pulled the comforter back over her. "It's a man's life at stake. An innocent man's life. Kolya'd want me to do it. I'll just nap here on the sofa and I'll be fine. It'll be fine." Except that nothing would ever be fine again.

She found the television remote and clicked from station to station, landing on an old Katherine Hepburn, Spencer Tracy movie.

Jonathan looked down at her. "We'll stay the night if you want, Alex."

"No." She closed her eyes and listened to the dialogue. Katherine Hepburn was a librarian; Spencer Tracy, a computer expert. It was witty, but it couldn't keep her attention. Still, it was noise.

"How about we stay until your meeting?"

"Nope. You'll scare my witness."

"No, we won't," Teo put in.

Teo, sweet Teo. "Witnesses are funny."

"Witnesses can also be dangerous," Jonathan said. "You don't know who the hell this guy is."

"Jonathan please, I'm not a fool. I've been threatened, and I know how to protect myself. I have a gun. Kolya taught me how to shoot." Mentioning his name started the tears again. "Thank you, Jonathan, you've been kind. You, too, Teo. I really want to be alone."

"You can call me any time." Jonathan patted her shoulder. "In the middle of the night. Anytime."

"You're a good friend. Thanks."

He hesitated. "There're some arrangements that you should go over. I'll call you tomorrow."

She knew what arrangements he meant. She quailed at the thought and buried her head under a pillow.

* * * * *

The good thing was that he couldn't stay conscious for more than a few moments. At least it was good for him, if not for Cuza. It was particularly frustrating to Max, who grew angrier every time Kolya was brought around again.

Max had switched to a cattle prod. With each contact, Kolya's heart jolted and his muscles contracted. He didn't have enough voice left to scream.

"I need a stronger current," Max insisted, but Cuza negated it.

"I don't want you to stop his heart."

Whatever else Max said in response merged into the white flash of another shock.

"Stay awake, you Jew bastard."

Just before Kolya blacked out again, he reflected on the absurdity that passing out had become an act of defiance.

* * * * *

Steve Kowolsky didn't mind working at six o'clock on a Sunday evening since he didn't have anything else he wanted to do. The only things that he really liked were work and tennis, and he needed a partner to play tennis. So, he might as well come in on a Sunday as not.

He had promised Egan to check on the possibility of a mole leaking information about the ECA, and followed up with an investigation into Ben Smithson's activities. As far as Kowolsky could tell, Smithson was clean.

He'd warned Egan that if he started an investigation, he'd finish it, wherever it took him. Now, as he looked at the inter-office summary of intelligence, he knew which direction to head.

The report from the FBI had given details on the death of Kolya Petrov, who had allegedly been shot to death, his body burned beyond recognition. The ECA was concerned about a mole, and, viola, an ECA agent who had access to all the information that had been disclosed was dead under mysterious circumstances where his identity might never be verified. Petrov wouldn't be the first suspect to fake his own death and disappear before charges could be filed.

He'd never liked the smart-mouthed Russian. The few times they'd run into each other, Petrov had been a major pain in the butt. Like that time in Afghanistan. Of course, Egan had been in on that little game, getting an informer out from under the nose of the CIA and into the clutches of the ECA.

If he proved Petrov to be the leak, he'd be doing Egan a favor.

* * * * *

They waited until he dozed off before waking him again. Someone was shouting, but he was too tired and ill for mere noise to rouse him. A light shown in his face didn't do it either.

They threw water on his face, kicked and prodded him until he finally blinked eyes open.

Dmitri returned, twelve years old, lit a cigarette and blew the smoke in his direction, along with Arkady, Kolya's other friend at the *dyetskii dom*. The two of them were talking, heads together, and Kolya could see them looking over at him.

Part of him knew it was a hallucination.

He closed his eyes and was kicked awake again. The third time it happened, he didn't bother to close his eyes, fixing his gaze on the far wall where the spider sat in the middle of its now complete web. The spider was black with purple spots, eyes glowing red.

Jonathan leaned against the wall. "Do you know where you are?"

"Yes." It was a lie. His voice was hoarse, almost a croak. He swallowed hard, trying to moisten his throat enough to speak. "I'm— seeing things, Jonathan."

"What are you seeing?"

"Dmitri. You—should remember Dmitri." Only when Jonathan had met Dmitri, Dmitri had been in his twenties. He coughed, his throat too dry to continue, and he was out again.

When he came around, Jonathan held his head and gave him water. Kolya drank and focused on the figure in front of him. Not Jonathan. Stanescu. He recoiled.

"*Eboyanna mat,*" he croaked.

For a moment he knew himself, knew where he was, and then he lost it again.

With Jonathan in Afghanistan, he hid in a cave in the mountains, trying to smuggle an informer over the border without either the terrorist cell or Kowolsky knowing. It was cold in Afghanistan. That's why he was wet, he'd fallen in the snow. *No, not Afghanistan. Romania.* Jonathan was watching him. "How did you get here?"

"Plane. Same as you." Jonathan buttoned his jacket. "Aren't you cold?"

"Yes."

"All you have to do is cooperate. You could be warm and dry in a bed, and I could be sleeping, but, no, you have to be stubborn." Then Bradford stood next to Jonathan, holding a cup of tea in her *World's Best Grandmom* mug.

This was wrong.

"You're here, too?"

She drank from the cup. "Who do you think I am, Mr. Petrov? How long has he been like this?" she asked Jonathan.

Kolya still had enough presence left to realize that his mind was blending dream and reality. He wasn't talking to either Jonathan or Bradford, but to his torturers. Had he said anything he shouldn't?

"Off and on for about an hour. He's been talking to imaginary friends."

"Is he faking?"

"I don't think so," Jonathan told Bradford. No, not Jonathan. Kolya blinked and refocused. Stanescu, the bastard, talking to who? Cuza, of course. "Even if he agrees to cooperate, he'll be useless like this. At least let him sleep."

"I suppose you're right," Cuza-Bradford stooped down to look in Kolya's face. "We want him disoriented, but not unable to function. Sleep, Mr. Petrov. We'll have something very special for you soon."

* * * * *

Frick turned right on 28th street to avoid the inevitable crowds on M and drove up the hill to Olive. Only a block from the main tourist strip, the street was quiet, deserted, a few stray leaves blown across the sidewalk. The three-story brick townhouse in the middle of the block between 29th and 30th streets was dark. Frick pulled over to the curb and parked two doors down from the house. "Maybe she's out."

"Or sleeping," Radu said.

Frick took a breath and pulled up the door handle. Radu got into the back seat.

Frick climbed the three steps to the door of the townhouse and rang the doorbell.

A woman opened the door. Her features were delicate, pale skin flawless, and her large dark eyes would have been beautiful except that they were rimmed with red and had the haunted look of a person who had recently received bad news. She wore jeans, a man's blue sweater that was too large for her, and a jacket, her hands thrust into the pockets.

"Miss Feinstein?" Frick had seen her on television after the exoneration of a man two days from execution. She was prettier in person. Petrov had good taste.

"Yes. And you are?"

It wasn't until she spoke that he realized she was only a little drunk, that the hours since he had called had allowed the alcohol to work through her system. "Jones."

"Where's your friend?"

"He's a little uncomfortable coming in. He'd prefer to talk to you in the car."

"I'm a little uncomfortable getting in the car of someone I don't know and who hasn't given me a real name. You and your friend can come in to talk. There's fresh coffee, and I can take notes better in my living room than in a car."

He looked again at her stance and her jacket and realized that she held a gun in the right pocket.

She watched him walk to the car. He yanked the back door open and spoke quietly. "She's not buying it. We got to go inside."

"Just grab her."

"Apart from the possibility that a neighbor could call the cops, she's got a gun. I suspect that she knows how to use it. We have to go in."

They followed her into an elegant room: a red and gold oriental rug, a beige silk couch, two wood and silk green chairs flanking the couch, a dark wood coffee table in front of the couch, a television discretely displayed inside a solid wood cabinet, and a Yamaha grand piano taking up the far corner.

Frick moved to the piano and pressed down one note. "Nice piano." He didn't know anything about music. "You play?"

"A little, but not that well. My fiancé...."

He turned his head toward her and saw tears. She dashed the back of her left hand across her face. Her right hand remained in her pocket.

Petrov had a reputation as a jazz pianist.

"I'm sorry. Is it your fiancé who died?"

She nodded. "Please sit. Can I get you some coffee, Mr. Jones and Mr....?"

"Enescu. Radu And, no thanks."

"Romanian name, isn't it?"

Hell. Radu was one hell of an operative. Couldn't even make up a Goddamn name. "I'd love some coffee," Frick said. "Can I help you?"

"Not necessary. How do you take it?"

"Black."

She nodded and disappeared.

When she returned, she carried two mugs. She set one down on a coaster on the coffee table in front of Frick. Radu seated himself on one of the green chairs, and she on the other.

"Mr. Enescu, suppose you tell me what you know." She put her own coffee on a coaster, set her phone up to record, and picked up a pen and legal pad.

Frick had coached Radu—and he hoped Radu could act the role.

"Well. It's like this, you see, I was on this job with Yoblonsky." Radu shot a nervous glance at Frick.

"What job?" she interrupted.

Frick slowly put his hand into his pocket and carefully removed a small vial. He leaned forward and picked up his coffee cup. Alex Feinstein was watching Radu, not him. If he got too close to her, she might react, but he was a safe distance from her. Her coffee, however, was not.

"It was this construction job…" Radu rolled his eyes towards Frick, and Frick could see his discomfort.

Frick's thumb flicked the lid off the small vial.

She watched Radu critically, with an occasional glance at Frick. "And?"

"And we'd have a few beers after work and talk, you know, this and that, and then you know, one night, he told me."

If he made the move now, she would see him, so he waited and sweated. Miraculously, she scratched her pen on the paper, frowned, and rose. "I need a new pen. Excuse me." She walked over to a briefcase against the wall and took out a pen. In that brief moment, Frick passed his hand over her coffee and emptied the vial. She returned, took her seat again. He picked up his own cup and drank. *Your turn, honey.*

Instead she watched Radu shift in his seat. "You have the date?"

"Last summer. July."

If she didn't drink the coffee, they'd have to wrestle the gun away from her and inject her. They were due at a private charter jet in an hour.

"What did he say?"

"That he was the real killer."

"You're not giving me many details, Mr. Enescu." She finally lifted the coffee to her lips and drank.

Frick tried not to watch.

"That's all. Just that there was some guy in prison—for what he had done."

"That's it?" Alex set down the cup and narrowed her eyes at Frick. "Your role in this is what?"

"I'm just a friend. Radu told me about it, and I'd read about the case."

She picked up the cup again. Frick picked up his own coffee to encourage her. He took a large gulp, but she took only a small sip.

He looked at his watch.

"Are you in a hurry?" she asked. "You keep looking at your watch."

"No." He shook his head. "I know it's getting late."

"What did you have to drink at the bar?" she asked.

"When?" Radu asked.

"When you went out with Yoblonsky."

"Beer?" he asked.

Alex Feinstein picked the cup up and drank more coffee. "You seem to be asking me."

Radu was having trouble keeping even the limited details straight. *Just a few more minutes.* Frick watched her drink the rest of the coffee.

She frowned down at her pad of paper. "It's not much. You're willing to testify, correct?"

"That's why he's here." Frick watched her put a hand to the side of her head. "Are you all right?"

"A little dizzy. I was drinking earlier."

"I know. You had just received bad news about your fiancé. What was his name?" Frick asked.

She blinked eyes that were becoming unfocused. "Kolya."

"That's short for Nikolai, isn't it?" It didn't hurt to double check that they had the right woman. It would be a little awkward if they discovered halfway to Romania that the fiancé for whom she was mourning was not Petrov.

"No one calls him that." The words slurred together.

"Petrov's an unusual last name. Where's he from?"

She staggered up from her seat. Her hand dove into her jacket pocket, and she took out the gun, a .22 caliber semi-automatic. She

157

held it as if she knew how to shoot. "You show up on my doorstep with a song and dance about a public case, and you know Kolya's name. Who the hell are you?"

Frick cursed his own ineptitude. She'd be out soon, but before that, she could shoot them both. He held up both hands. "Hey, you told me his name. What are you, crazy?"

She shook her head. "I told you his first name." But he could see the tiniest doubt. With the drug impairing her judgment, she was wavering.

Radu chimed in. "You said Kolya Petrov."

She put a hand on the back of the chair, her body now visibly wobbling. "No, I didn't."

"You did," Frick insisted. "What are you worried about anyway? Was he running drugs or something?"

"He—he worked for the IRS."

Was it possible that she didn't know what Petrov did for a living? No. She would not have been so alarmed at Frick's knowing Petrov's name unless she knew what he was.

"What's wrong with me?" she asked, the gun in her hand drooping toward the floor. She shook her head, and her gaze fell on the coffee. "You son-of-a-bitch." She went down onto her knees; the gun dropped from her hand, and then she gracefully curled onto her side, as if she were a cat.

26

At six a.m. Monday morning, Elizabeth sat alone at a table for four and slowly crunched a bacon and egg sandwich. She spotted Mark Leslie entering the cafeteria and waved. He waved back, and five minutes later, appeared at her table. She eyed his Diet Coke and apricot Danish and picked up her newspaper to make room.

"You're here early."

"Not really." He clattered the tray down. "I'm just grabbing a bite before I leave. I've been on since six last night."

"Doing what?"

"Don't ask." He waved a hand. "You don't want to know."

Or aren't cleared to know. "This happen often?"

"Since Friday. I've got a question to ask you. How long does it take to break a guy?" He took a bite of his Danish.

"I don't do interrogations as a rule," Elizabeth said. "But, it depends on the guy. And what's done to him."

He looked like something was bothering him, but there'd been a lot of deaths in the agency in recent weeks. Two funerals in the next two days.

"You going to the funerals?" he asked, as if reading her mind.

She shrugged. "Haven't decided. You?"

"Probably not. Too busy. Did you know Bradford's creating a Deputy Director position?"

"Everyone does."

"I've heard Egan might be up for it." He looked slyly at her. "Or you."

159

"You know this how?"

"I read everyone's e-mail and texts. Periodically. Sometimes we keep a closer eye, if Bradford orders it."

Everyone was informed about the lack of privacy, but she hadn't really thought about the fact that Mark and Ross would know everything that went on in the agency. "You must be cleared for everything if you do that."

"I'm cleared for stuff I don't want to be cleared for." His mood darkened again. "You ever question whether you're doing the right thing when you follow orders?"

"No."

"Never?"

"No."

"I do sometimes. I wish I didn't." He checked his watch. "Shit, Will's already left for work. Haven't seen him except in passing for three days. Hope he's fed the cats."

Will was Mark's husband.

"Anyone at the ECA ever give you trouble about being gay?" There were a lot a macho types hanging around, and she could well imagine harassment or worse.

"Once about eight years ago." He popped the tab on his Diet Coke. "We had a recruit who'd been a special op guy. Didn't think that intelligence services should employ gays. He gave me a hard time on a couple of occasions."

"What happened?"

"He got a very special new recruit tour of the gay bars in the D.C. area, and he quit."

"Egan and Petrov?"

"Of course."

"I never heard about this."

"It was kept under wraps. We're a secret agency, you know. Shit. Goddamn it to hell." He slammed the palm of his hand on the table.

She was surprised by the sudden outburst. "What?"

"Kolya's a good guy. He and Jonathan helped me out, and I'd forgotten all about it."

His use of the present tense didn't escape her. "I liked him once. But he showed himself to be a jerk."

"Oh, come on, Liz, be fair. You wanted him, didn't want him, whereas he wanted a relationship. You didn't. Besides, he's been in love with Feinstein since before he came to the agency—when he was in law school."

Present tense again. Elizabeth's mind clicked. And why was he so agitated at remembering that he owed Petrov? "Petrov told you all that?"

"No, of course not." Mark finished his Coke. "Kolya never talks about his personal life. Most of it I put together from reading e-mails and office gossip." He gave her his first smile of the morning. "As for Kolya and Alex—Jonathan told me. What do you think of Egan?"

"What do you mean?" She tensed.

"I always thought he had a nice ass. I was curious about your opinion."

She had to laugh at that one. "I hadn't really focused on it."

"If I were a woman, and wanted a fun, not too serious relationship, I'd check out that brand." He pushed his chair back, as if he were aware that he was talking too much. "I should get going."

"See you around." Elizabeth watched his retreating figure as she mulled over the conversation. Something was going on. What was it, and what was she going to do about it?

* * * * *

Margaret looked out the window behind the President. Beyond the green lawn, she could see a glimpse of the fence that separated the White House from the blocked off section of Pennsylvania Avenue. "I called Carl Ford yesterday to give him the details on Mr. Petrov's 'funeral.' I mentioned that his girlfriend was distraught over his death."

"You told Ford her name?"

"And she didn't answer her phone this morning. I called three times."

"So you think she's also been kidnapped."

"It's the logical deduction."

"It's a hell of a business."

"I think you should have Delta standing by for a hostage extraction. As soon as we're in Cuza's system, you can give the go-ahead."

"Can't your own people do it?"

"We do covert and undercover operations, but we don't usually mount assaults on enemy positions. My people are capable but not up to the standard of Delta or the Seals for this type of operation. There's not much of a chance that we'll get Mr. Petrov and Miss Feinstein out alive, but we should optimize the chances."

* * * * *

It was a trendy restaurant in Chevy Chase, glass and plants and water fountains. The politicos hung out there, so it would be the restaurant of choice for Jonathan's father to have a meeting with Corey Manion. Corey remained a suspect, and as such, the meeting was of interest.

Jonathan sat alone at a table for two, unfolded his newspaper, and ordered scrambled eggs and coffee. Across the room, Teo conversed animatedly with Elizabeth. Several tables away, Corey studied his watch. Jonathan felt the stir in the restaurant and watched the familiar, white haired figure stride through the restaurant. Jonathan waited while the former Senator Egan handed his menu over to the waiter before sauntering over to the table where his father sat in animated conversation with Corey. Jonathan loomed over the pair.

"Well, well." Jonathan seated himself without being asked. "Hello, Dad. I didn't know you were in town. I was just having a late breakfast and saw you come in. You should have called. Hello Corey." Jonathan secured a miniature microphone to the underside of the table.

His father scowled at him. "The last time I called you, you were out of the country, god knows where."

"I'm in town now. As you see."

"Yes, I do see. And what are you doing here?"

"Breakfast."

"At nine o'clock on a workday? You just happen to show up in the same restaurant as me? That's bullshit. You never do anything by accident, Jonathan."

"Me? What about you? What're you doing in town? What're you doing with him?" He nodded at Corey.

"We're old friends." Senator Egan mustered some dignity.

"You don't have friends." Jonathan stirred milk into his coffee. "You have connections. Only this one's a member of the wrong party."

"I've always been able to reach across the aisle in friendship."

"Yeah, sure. To get someone in your pocket."

"The very least I expect from you is respect. If not for me as a father, then for my service to the country as a Senator."

"You weren't serving anyone but yourself, Dad, so don't give me that."

"I suppose you think you're serving your country. You and that so-called friend you brought up to Mystic."

"You couldn't possibly be referring to Kolya Petrov, could you?" Jonathan said in tones of pure ice.

"Yeah, your Russian friend." The former Senator turned to Corey. "He only got into the FBI because he knew half the people in the Russian mafiya. Then the ECA recruited him. Don't understand it. He's a socialist, as well. He told me that I had more money than was good for me."

It sounded like Kolya. "Well, you do."

"Now you're defending a communist."

"Democratic socialist."

"A commie."

"Shut up, John. The man died in the line of duty." Corey turned to Jonathan. "I'm very sorry, Jonathan. Petrov was a good man. Was he killed in New York?"

Jonathan froze. "How'd you know where he was?"

"Usual way. Margaret mentioned it during a briefing."

Jonathan pulled his chair close to the table. "What exactly did she say? Take a stroll, Dad." His father didn't move.

"Why don't you just ask Margaret?"

163

"I'm asking you. My friend was murdered. I want to know what you know and when you knew it."

"John, maybe a stroll wouldn't be a bad idea." Corey Manion turned to his former mentor.

"I don't feel like a stroll."

Teo appeared, a notebook in hand, and announced himself to be a student at Georgetown University. "Could I ask a few questions for my term paper, Senator Egan?"

Egan Senior, surprised and flattered, turned to Teo as Jonathan grabbed Corey's arm and pulled him out of the chair and out the door. The sidewalk was empty, and Jonathan was comfortable that no one could overhear.

"From the top, Corey."

"I don't understand, Jonathan. Bradford gave the Intelligence Committee a detailed briefing on a new computer system at the ECA. She mentioned that your friend was trained on it and was going to New York to try to track down Mihai Cuza?"

"Did she mention Kolya's specific travel plans?"

"Yeah, she told us he was going to New York last Friday on a seven o'clock train and that he'd be at the agency safe house in Greenwich. Why?"

Jonathan's head spun. "Just a security double check. Keep this to yourself, would you?"

Corey looked puzzled but he nodded.

Jonathan rejoined Marty and Elizabeth in an agency van parked a block from the restaurant.

"What the hell is going on?" Marty asked.

"My question exactly," Jonathan said. Teo joined them two minutes later.

"Did Bradford get Kolya killed?" Teo asked after Jonathan filled them in on the conversation.

"We're just full of good questions this morning," Jonathan said. "And I don't have any answers. Maybe Margaret does." He glanced behind him at Elizabeth. She said nothing.

* * * * *

Steve Kowolsky smiled in what he hoped was a charming manner at the woman behind the front desk of the funeral home. She didn't look charmed. He shrugged and removed his credentials from a coat pocket. She was unimpressed.

"I can't let you have access to the body."

"Sure you can." He indicated the lab technician standing next to him. "We're just going to get a small sample of bone."

"You're CIA. We're under contract with a different governmental agency to arrange the funeral. You need their authorization."

"The ECA doesn't need to know. No one will know. It's not like you can have an open casket, is it?"

The woman shook her head again. "You got a warrant?"

Steve Kowolsky had had enough. "Listen, sweetheart," he leaned on the desk with both arms. "This is a matter of national security. You're going to give me access to Petrov's body now, or you're going to find yourself answering questions at CIA headquarters."

* * * * *

Margaret was on the phone with the ECA team in Pakistan when Jonathan stormed into her office. She pointed to a chair, but Jonathan folded his arms and continued to stand. "Call back in twenty minutes, Ethan," she said into the phone and hung up. "So, Jonathan, what is so urgent?"

"You told the Intelligence Committee where Kolya was going and what he was doing in New York. You even told them what train he'd be on. Jesus Christ, Margaret. You knew there was a mole. You violated security on Kolya's travel plans, and now he's dead."

Margaret almost let her relief show. So, that was it. Bad, but not as bad as she had feared.

"Jonathan, I informed the President privately of Mr. Petrov's mission and plans. He chose to reveal it to the Intelligence Committee."

"The President violated security?"

165

"Yes, the President. He's not a professional, Jonathan. He's a politician, not a very bright one at that."

It was not an unbelievable lie, especially not to a man like Jonathan Egan, who had spent his life despising politicians.

Jonathan wasn't appeased. "And you let Kolya go out without warning him."

"He was informed of what the President did, and he took appropriate precautions."

"Appropriate precautions? He didn't change his travel plans. That would have been an appropriate precaution."

"I suggested it, but Mr. Petrov had a meeting set and decided against postponing his trip, despite my urging. As you know, Mr. Petrov had a stubborn streak."

"Stubborn, yeah, he was stubborn. But he was also careful."

"Which was why he had back-up."

"All right. Maybe he would have gone anyway. But it changes the odds on who took him out. It changes the odds on whether the body in Wills Funeral Home is Kolya's."

She shook her head. "You're reaching. I'm sorry Jonathan, but it doesn't change anything. It doesn't change the fact that Mr. Petrov's keys, watch, and wallet were on or near the body. How did you happen to be discussing Mr. Petrov's schedule with Corey Manion?" She switched topics, hoping to throw him off balance.

"We were planting a microphone at the table where he was meeting my father."

She raised her eyebrows. "You discussed Mr. Petrov's operation with Senator Manion in a public restaurant, and you come in here accusing me of breaching security?"

"Manion is part of the Intelligence Committee."

"And under suspicion. You had no business discussing anything with Senator Manion. Jonathan, you're off this assignment. Mr. Petrov's death struck too close to home, and you're acting unprofessionally. I'm sending you to Pakistan. I know you'll want to attend Mr. Petrov's funeral. Take a couple days off, then you head out." She picked up the phone and dialed Audrey. "Audrey, get

Elizabeth Owen up here." She hung up the phone and turned to Jonathan. "Ms. Owen will take over as team coordinator." Elizabeth Owen was ambitious, probably had her eye on the soon to-be-created Deputy Director position. She would be easier to steer in the wrong direction.

* * * * *

Elizabeth found Jonathan in his office, shrugging into a jacket. He glanced briefly at her as he picked up the cell phone from his desk.

"Congratulations." His voice was dry. "You're on your way up the career ladder."

She rocked back on her heels, her hands in her pants pockets. "I didn't ask for this, Jonathan. Look, the Pakistan operation is also important."

"Yeah, of course. Everything we do is important. What did she tell you to do?"

Elizabeth thought back five minutes earlier to the terse meeting with the head of the ECA. Bradford hadn't promised her the job of Deputy Director, but she had made it clear that Elizabeth was in the running. The important thing was not to be distracted from the objective, which was the long-term security of the United States. At present, those security interests required a step down in the search for a mole on the Intelligence Committee.

"Mr. Egan will have trouble accepting the order, in the wake of the murder of Mr. Petrov," Bradford had said. "Which is why I am asking you to take over as team leader and to stall until Mr. Egan leaves for Pakistan, after which time your team will be reassigned."

Elizabeth understood: don't ask questions. But she had them. She hadn't said anything when Jonathan uncovered the fact that the Intelligence Committee knew of Kolya's travel plans, but she had thought back to her conversation with Mark Leslie. Something was on Mark's conscience. He felt guilty about something to do with Petrov. And, he had referred to Petrov in the present tense—as if Petrov were still alive.

It was all very interesting, although she was not yet certain what she intended to do.

Jonathan had followed up on what appeared to be a breach of security. As a reward, he was being posted off to Pakistan. She had no interest in winding up in Pakistan—and yet, what had happened to Petrov was troubling her as well. Whatever her feelings about Petrov, he had been—was a fellow ECA operative. If he was alive, she owed him the effort that he would have made for her. But was it worth her career?

Jonathan was on his cell. He switched it off and pocketed it.

"That's the third time I've tried Alex Feinstein."

"She's grieving. Maybe she's not up to talking."

"Yeah, maybe. And maybe I'll drop by her townhouse, go inside, and check things out."

"You've got a key to her place? Don't tell me she was unfaithful to poor Petrov."

Jonathan crossed his arms and glared. "I've got Kolya's keys, and he had a key to her place. That was an incredibly bitchy thing to say. What is it with you?"

Despite herself, Elizabeth was embarrassed. Why did she say something so nasty? Jealous? After all Alex Feinstein had taken away Petrov. Or was it the possibility that Egan was feeling something other than friendly concern for Petrov's girlfriend? Either choice made her feel petty and stupid. "Sorry. This is getting to me, too. What are you planning to do?"

"Just see how she's doing."

"You're not going to repeat what Manion said?"

"To Alex? What good would that do?" Jonathan asked as Teo burst into his office.

"Tell me it's not true," Teo said.

"For a secret organization, news gets around quickly."

"I told Marty," Elizabeth said.

"Who told me," Teo said. "Why are you leaving the team?"

Jonathan put his hands in his pockets. "That's for Margaret to answer."

"Does it have anything to do with Kolya's death? Something funny's going on, isn't it?"

"If there is, you'll find it out. With Elizabeth as team leader," Jonathan said. "Meantime, I'm going to go. I've got a few things to check out."

"I'm coming with you," Teo said.

Jonathan nodded and then looked at Elizabeth. She read an invitation in his look, but it was an invitation she wouldn't accept, not yet.

27

Kolya slid in and out of blackness, in too much pain to fall into a deep sleep. It had been hours since they had left him—maybe a day—his sense of time was as damaged as the rest of him. He thought that Stanescu had come in once or twice, taken his pulse, checked bandages, given him a shot, but even of that, he wasn't completely sure. The basement cell where he still lay on the floor, covered with the stained blankets, was silent and had been that way for hours. The sky outside the high barred window was just starting to turn dark. Another night was starting.

He knew he had woken several times and noted the dark of the windows, but he couldn't pin down whether he had slept through the day or woken several times in the same night.

How long since he'd eaten? He couldn't remember that either. What did it matter? Any feelings of hunger had long since faded into the dull background. Water was a more pressing need, and his captors hadn't refilled the small cup he had been given after the last torture session. Thirst was constant, nagging, making it hard to swallow.

At least he was alone. Cuza wasn't even bothering with a guard. They had reason to be confident. He had no hope of escaping nor of putting up much of a fight, even if his hands had been free.

He heard voices on the other side of the door and distinguished Cuza's cultivated tones among them. He was dismayed to realize that he was shaking. The fear that he thought he had conquered flooded back. He tried to control the trembling, but he was sweating, too. With the desperation of fear, he found enough energy to try his restraints.

He twisted his hands and tried to feel the lock of the handcuffs with nearly numb fingers. He touched part of the cold metal and located the lock in the center, but there was no give in the handcuffs, and his fingers were useless. The chain remained fixed to the handcuffs and to the wall. There was nothing he could do, except feign unconsciousness as the door opened and footsteps approached. What it would be this time? Electric shock? More burns? Another broken limb?

Or… he could give in. Give them what they wanted, and then they would kill him quickly. It would be better than dying slowly—either under torture, or left to die of his injuries, or impaled, if Cuza got tired of the game. *Just give up, stop fighting. Let Cuza have access to the damn computer.* The temptation was almost overwhelming. He was so tired, and he hurt so much. What the hell did he really care? Give in and he could fall into the comfort of empty darkness.

He fought down the impulse with difficulty. It wasn't the certainty that he'd be killed as soon as Cuza had what he wanted that kept him resisting. He was going to die either way; he was already half there. But he couldn't let himself give in. Innocents could be killed—and it would be his fault. An easier death wasn't reason enough for him to help Cuza. Dying with his self-respect mattered more than dying painlessly.

His internal struggle over, he waited for the games to begin again. The group halted, but one person with light footsteps continued to approach. A woman, he identified by the sound of the footsteps, but no woman had been present during any of the other torture sessions. Why would Cuza bring a woman to watch? It took all of his concentration to will himself to remain still, eyes shut, breathing slowly, even as he felt the woman bending over him and then kneeling down next to him.

"Oh God. Kolya." It was a voice that he almost didn't recognize, not expecting it and not wanting it, a voice that didn't belong there.

He blinked his eyes open and saw Alex kneeling in front of him, her face angry and shocked. He closed his eyes again. It was his mind, tricking him. It was another hallucination.

"Kolya?" she repeated.

He opened his eyes again. The woman still looked like Alex, but he refused to believe it. "No." He weakly shook his head. "You're not here."

"He's been hallucinating off and on." Stanescu explained to a bald man with one earring, whose face was familiar.

Then he felt her hand touch his face and smooth his sweat-dampened hair back from his forehead, a familiar and intimate touch. He started to believe in her reality and that was even worse. "No." This time the word was in horror and protest.

"It's me. Really. You look terrible."

She was so beautiful.

"I'm—fine."

"You're full of shit." Her voice was gentler than her words, and she placed the palm of a cool hand on his forehead, her gaze traveling down the blanket covering most of the damage. He closed his eyes briefly, the touch of her hand on his face both soothing and painful.

"You're burning up. Sons of bitches—" Her voice trailed off and she started again. "What's wrong?"

"Shot. In the leg. Not life threatening."

Her gaze traveled to his legs, concealed under the blanket. She bent her head. "I thought you were dead. I thought I'd never see you again."

"I'm—sorry." He was both sorry for her pain and sorry that he hadn't already died. If he were dead, she wouldn't be here—she'd be safe. "Did they hurt you?"

"No."

Behind her: Max, Gheorghe, four men whose names he had not learned but who had helped in his capture and torture, Stanescu, the bald man, and of course Cuza. Cuza seated himself in his usual spot and made a gesture of impatience.

"Are you satisfied that your fiancée is really here, Mr. Petrov?"

Kolya intertwined the fingers of his right hand with Alex's.

"It's quite simple. I'll be brief. You will either cooperate, or I will have Miss Feinstein shot in front of you. It would be a shame; she's quite lovely. But it's your choice."

Kolya hesitated. If he cooperated, Cuza would have valuable information—information that could lead to the loss of other lives. It was the same choice he had faced ever since his capture, with one difference. Alex would die with him.

Yet he couldn't simply refuse—couldn't just let her be killed in front of him. He thought that he had prepared himself for the worst that could happen. He had been wrong. He could stand anything else they could do to him, but he couldn't watch them kill her.

"Let her go. Once I know she's safe—I will—cooperate." Play for time: it was the only tactic that came to him. Even if the time were only minutes.

"You're not in a position to bargain, Mr. Petrov. Besides I've come to know you since you've been my guest. Your cooperation would disappear the second you thought Miss Feinstein was safe. We could play the game, you know. I could pretend to release her, but really won't, you could pretend to cooperate, but really won't. Then we'd be right back here, with me threatening your lover, and you stalling. So let's pretend we've done all that and get to the point. Yes? Or no?"

Kolya was out of ideas, so he told the truth, directed at Alex, not at Cuza. "He'll kill us anyway—even if I cooperate—"

If nothing else, he wanted her to understand why he couldn't save her.

Cuza also directed his next words to Alex. "No, Miss Feinstein. Mr. Petrov is incorrect. I assure you that neither of you will be killed if he cooperates. You have my word."

Kolya still hesitated, not convinced that his cooperation would do anything but buy them a brief period of life, yet unwilling to say the words that could cost Alex her life.

Alex picked up on his hesitation. "Kolya, maybe he won't kill us. It is possible, isn't it?"

"They shot—Eric White—in cold blood." Kolya raised himself on an elbow, to be more emphatic. "He—was unconscious and—they blew his brains out. His wife is—pregnant." He was dizzy. The room swirled and went dark. When he opened his eyes, Alex was pressing a damp cloth against his forehead.

"You scared the shit out of me. I thought you were dying."

"I black out sometimes."

"Stay lying down then."

He gave a half-shrug in acquiescence. "As you wish."

"Mr. Petrov, your associate was killed in the field. It is regrettable that he died, even more that he had a pregnant wife, but Max has an understandable aversion to leaving someone behind who could provide information," Cuza said.

"As—we could."

"I didn't say you'd be free to go. Not immediately anyway. But you'd be together with this lovely young woman in a secured room upstairs, with good meals, medical care, even music. A few months of comfortable captivity. That doesn't sound so terrible, does it?" Cuza's voice flowed over Kolya like honey, and he wanted to believe it.

He was losing his Goddamn mind. But maybe, just maybe there was a chance. Maybe they would want other intelligence information from him. Or to trade the two of them. Maybe. It was possible, wasn't it?

No, it wasn't possible.

"He—impaled—Gina," Kolya told Alex.

This reference only angered Cuza. "That particular incident involved a personal violation of trust. I do not appreciate being made to look like a fool. Was it your idea that she go to bed with me?"

Alex's gaze shifted from Kolya to Cuza and back to him again. "More Jonathan's style than yours."

"Doesn't—matter—" Kolya was beginning to lose concentration.

"Jonathan?" Cuza inquired politely.

"He frequently works with Kolya. His sexual morality is a little looser than Kolya's."

"Alex, don't. Don't tell—him anything."

Alex ignored the instruction. "I don't want him to kill you or me because Jonathan came up with one of his usual hair-brained ideas. Typical Jonathan. What a jerk. And why the hell wasn't Jonathan backing you up, Goddamn it?"

He tightened his fingers on hers, as if his grip could stem the flow of words. Had she gone crazy? No, she was trying to protect him, to turn Cuza's anger at Gina's infiltration. Maybe even trying to change his mind by questioning Jonathan's loyalty. Still, the question wasn't a bad one. What was Jonathan doing? But Bradford had assigned Kolya to the new computer system; Bradford had broken up his usual partnership.

Cuza turned back to Kolya. "Mr. Petrov, this has been an amusing digression, but it's getting late. I want an answer, and I'd like it now, please."

Alex intervened. "You can't expect him to make a rational decision. For God's sake, look at him. I don't think he's even fully conscious, let alone capable of making a life and death decision."

Cuza was unmoved. "Except for the initial shock of seeing you, he's been perfectly rational. He's weak and in pain, but he's conscious."

"He may be conscious enough to know I'm here, but he can't make a decision this quickly. Give me a little time with him. He hasn't actually refused. He's a stubborn son of a bitch, but I can sometimes persuade him." She gave Kolya a half-smile, as if they shared in a private joke, as they so often had, a joke about her always arguing, always the lawyer. Even now, she had to be the lawyer, now when their lives hung in the balance. "He's more amenable to persuasion than to force. Which you've obviously discovered by now. They're not even looking for you, Kolya." Alex turned back to him. "Jonathan came to my home and told me that you're dead. He's not looking for you."

"They—rigged a body with—my wallet and keys. Probably—burned. Unrecognizable. Jonathan—probably—does believe I'm dead." This was all beside the point. She wanted him to give in, and he wanted her to understand why he couldn't. He looked directly into her eyes and summoned all his energy to explain. "This isn't about Jonathan. Or about whether I love you. Or even about whether—they'll let us live. The only reason I've resisted—the only reason I'm still resisting—even with the risk to you—is the possibility that my cooperation will cost other people their lives."

"Possibility? Not a certainty?"

"Not absolutely certain."

"So, this isn't the moral equivalent of giving the names of resistance fighters to the Nazis?"

"We—suspect he's planning—to sabotage a nuclear plant. Maybe a number of plants."

Alex kept her focus on Kolya. "If you withhold the information he wants, would that stop a nuclear accident, even if that's his plan?"

"Perhaps not. Perhaps. Not certain."

"But our own deaths are certain if you don't cooperate."

"So it appears."

"Then it's a certainty versus a possibility. I'm not arguing that you should trade our lives for those of other innocent people. I'd just like to think that if you allow them to kill us, that you're not doing it for one of those governmental secrets that will be discovered anyway, and won't really make much of a difference to anyone."

She was so smart, and he loved her dearly. "I don't have the strength to argue."

"She makes a lot of sense," the bald man standing behind Alex interjected. "Petrov, you're going to let her die for nothing. If you're doing this out of loyalty to your agency, you should know it's misplaced. The head of the ECA was so stupid and so casual with your life that she gave us the information we used to capture both you and your fiancee."

The name came to him. David Fuller. Turncoat FBI agent who had tackled him, preventing his escape that first night.

"Fuck your mother," he said.

"Margaret Bradford told us about the computer system. She gave us your schedule. How do you think we found you? We knew where you were going and when. She gave us Miss Feinstein's name. Bradford's careless about security and not worth your loyalty."

"*Eboyanna mat.*" But the statement resonated. How had Cuza known about the new system? How had he known Kolya's schedule? How had Cuza known about Alex?

It was a lie, a lie designed to break down his defenses. Carl Ford was the mole. Fuller was Ford's man, and Fuller's very presence here and now attested to that—but was it possible that Bradford had given information to Ford? But why would Bradford do that? She knew— had to know—that Ford was one of three suspects for the mole. Even if not a deliberate betrayal, someone had breached security. It had to be Bradford. Who else knew?

It could be someone else in the ECA. A handful of people knew his schedule, knew Alex's name and relationship with him.

None of this made sense. It was just another interrogation technique. Deceive the subject into thinking his friends betrayed him.

"I'm waiting, Mr. Petrov," Cuza said.

"He's thinking about it," the bald man said. "Give him a minute."

The period preceding his capture flooded back into his mind. Why had he been trained on the new system and sent out virtually alone to New York? Eric—poor son-of-a-bitch—wasn't scheduled to check in with Kolya until three days later. And Bradford had insisted that he continue on to the New York office, even after he had described his pursuit by Cuza's followers.

Had she wanted him to be captured?

Bradford knew, as Kolya did, that there was a mole in the Intelligence Committee. But Ford—and Fuller—didn't know that they knew. Fuller would assume that any disclosure by Bradford was inadvertent and stupid. Fuller was using that to try to undermine Kolya's loyalty.

But if Bradford had disclosed to Ford or the Intelligence Committee any information about Kolya, his mission, it had to have been a deliberate act on her part—to pass on information that would give Cuza the opportunity to—what—to capture him?

But why?

If his head were clearer, he could figure it out. All he could do now was play out the hand and not reveal that he had previously known of a leak from the Intelligence Committee.

"He's had a minute. Max," Cuza said.

Max removed a gun from a holster under his arm and placed the barrel against Alex's temple. Her gaze locked on him. "Kolya, please. Be sure it's worth our lives."

He wasn't sure, not anymore, not if Bradford had wanted him to be captured. There was only one thing of which he was sure.

"No." He saw Max's finger tighten on the trigger. "*No*, I'll cooperate," burst from him as the gun clicked - empty.

Kolya reached his chained arms to pull a shaking Alex to him. He pressed his lips against her hair. Whatever was going on, he had made his decision. He would betray the ECA and his country.

"I knew that Mr. Petrov just needed the right motivation to be reasonable," Cuza stood and headed toward the door. "Max, take the handcuffs off, get a shirt on him, and get him upstairs on the computer. I've got a phone call to make."

The adrenaline rush over, Kolya collapsed back onto the floor, unable to move even when his wrists were finally released. He heard Alex say his name as he faded out.

"Get up, Petrov." It was Max's voice. A foot prodded his leg.

"Not that way," Stanescu said. "Not if you want him to work."

He felt a burning in his arm and opened his eyes. Alex was still at his side, her hand still twined in his, but she had moved to allow Stanescu to inject him.

"That's the second time he's blacked out since we came down here." Her voice was low and worried. "What's wrong with him?"

"He's injured, and I believe he has an infection. Once he's finished upstairs, I'll immobilize his leg, get some food into him. He'll be okay."

"You haven't given him any food?" Kolya recognized the dangerous tone.

"He's been given food," Max said. "He refused to eat it."

Well, strictly speaking, it was the truth. Kolya remembered the strips of fatty meat that he had been offered, what was it, one or two days earlier?

Stanescu said. "The stimulant will help temporarily."

The injection helped wake him, but it did nothing for either his dizziness or the pain. He raised himself on an elbow, pushing back the blanket that covered his upper torso, heard a muffled exclamation from Alex, and realized that much of what had happened to him had been hidden by the blankets.

"It looks worse than it is," he told her.

"Like hell it does." She pressed her lips together and shifted to take a better look. "Where's your shirt?"

He nodded in the direction, and she turned to look at the filthy polo shirt and sweater, which had been kicked into a corner. She shook her head and pulled off the blue sweater she was wearing.

He shook his head in turn. "You'll be cold. Just get me my Goddamn shirt. Please."

"It's filthy. You can't wear anything that dirty. Your back is stripped raw. And this is your Goddamn sweater anyway. You're the one with a Goddamn fever, and you can Goddamn wear something clean and warm."

"Fine." He accepted the sweater, sat up slowly, ignored the rush of dizziness, and gingerly pulled it over his head. It was a soft cotton knit, but it still chaffed. He looked at Stanescu. "I can't walk. If you want me to go anywhere, I'll need help."

"Your bitch can help you," Max said.

Alex was half a foot shorter and fifty pounds lighter than he was. He was afraid of hurting her, but she didn't hesitate. She slipped an arm around his waist, careful not to touch his back. He put his right arm around her neck and pushed up with his left arm and leg, keeping his right leg as still as possible. The change of position brought a white flash of pain. He didn't make it to a standing position.

He came to long enough to realize that Fuller and another man were carrying him upstairs.

The next time he woke up, he lay on his side on a leather couch in what appeared to be a large office. The sleeve of his sweater was pushed up, and an intravenous needle attached to the vein in his elbow, a bag of fluids hooked over a floor lamp.

Alex sat on a straight-backed wooden chair next to him. On the other side of the room was a gleaming walnut desk with a desktop computer, and in the executive chair in front of the computer Mihai Cuza sat typing. Stanescu, in an armchair in front of a bookshelf, looked up from a leather-bound volume.

"How are you feeling?" Alex asked in a low voice.

"Terrible."

Max, seated in front of the door, watched him. Frick and another man leaned against the door and talked in low voices. On the far side of the room stood two other men who had served as his guards. Their pistols were holstered, but over their shoulders were slung Galil Mar assault weapons.

Stanescu closed his book and came over to remove the needle and place a Band-Aid over the puncture. "That should keep you going. I'll need to drug you to set that leg. You'll have to put up with the discomfort until after you're done on the computer."

The question was whether the discomfort would be ended by medical treatment or by a bullet through the brain. But he didn't voice the question, not with Alex two feet away from him. She was worried, but she had more confidence than he did in their possible survival. *Let her keep hoping.*

She cradled a white china cup in her hands, apparently having made the decision to accept hospitality. Her gaze met Kolya's.

"Coffee?" Kolya asked.

She nodded.

He extended a hand. She turned the cup and placed the handle in his grasp.

"It's got milk, no sugar. You don't like it this way."

"Right now, I don't care." He propped himself up. It had a dark rich aroma and evoked pleasant memories of Sunday mornings. The first sip, even with milk, no sugar, tasted wonderful.

Cuza turned from the computer. "Ah, you're awake again, Mr. Petrov." He stood and motioned to the chair. "Frick and Radu will move you over here."

Kolya took another sip of the coffee and handed it back to Alex. "Are you going to be able to do this?" she asked him.

"Yes." He doubted he'd be able to make it through the computer games—doubted he could remember the correct responses—or that he could remain conscious. But on the general theory of lessening Alex's anxiety, if not his own, he put on a show of confidence that he didn't feel.

180

Frick and the second man moved over to the side of the couch.

The transition was awkward and painful but not as bad as he had anticipated. Surprisingly gentle, Frick helped Kolya settle in the chair in front of the computer and propped his leg on a footstool.

Sitting up was more problematic. He was dizzier, more nauseous than he had been stretched out on the couch. He leaned on his elbows, focused with difficulty on the computer screen in front of him, typed in the access number, hit enter, and waited.

"How long will this take?" Cuza's voice was directly behind him as he input his access code.

With an effort, he kept all emotion out of his voice. "A few minutes."

"And it works—how?"

He closed his eyes, rested his head on his hand, and waited for the beep of the computer that would signal the first question. "There's ten timed security questions, randomly selected."

The computer beeped, and he blinked at the screen. Composer of *The Brandenburg Concertos*. He remembered this answer. He typed Howard Shore.

"That's the wrong answer, Mr. Petrov."

"No." He hit enter. "Factually wrong. Correct for access. All of the answers are factually incorrect." He felt more and more tired.

Poem on the fall of Man by John Milton.

He typed, *Stopping by the Woods on a Snowy Evening*. Enter. The dizziness was worse. "Could I have some water?"

"I don't want you to have water so near the computer," Cuza responded. "Finish first."

If I can finish, you bastard. He glanced toward Alex as he waited for the next question. She read his expression, stood, and moved toward him.

"Don't bother him, Miss Feinstein," Cuza said.

"He's not looking well. Kolya?" Her hand gently touched the top of his shoulder.

He watched the screen. The next question, Author of *Pride and Prejudice*.

Jane Austen, but, no, that was the right answer, so it was wrong.

What was it? He thought desperately. He looked at the clock, thirty seconds left. It was a joke, he remembered, a joke involving 20th century history.

The room was swirling around him. His head went down onto the desk, *just for a second*, and he was out.

When he lifted his head, the screen was blank. "*Dermo*," he cursed and hit the enter key to pull the program back up. The program had shut itself down.

"You'll have to start over." Cuza's voice was cool.

"No field access will be accepted for twenty-four hours." Kolya turned to face him, aware that there would be consequences for his failure.

"Twenty-four hours?" Cuza repeated.

Max moved towards him, red-faced. "The bastard did it on purpose to stall. Just another of his tricks."

"No. I passed out. I apologize." Kolya almost choked on the words, hating the part he was playing almost as much as he hated Max and the rest of them. But he had already surrendered. His job now was to prevent Alex from suffering from his failure. He felt a tightening of her hand on his shoulder in support.

Max glared. "He's faked us out whenever he got the chance. He's a Jew. You can't trust them. Ever."

He started for Kolya as Cuza held up a hand. "Wait." He scrutinized Kolya's face. Kolya returned the look impassively. "It's possible that Mr. Petrov was not faking. He does appear quite ill. However, on the possibility that he was not ill, but obstructing, some discipline should be imposed. I'll leave the choice of punishments to you, Max. Just don't damage him in any way that would impede accessing the system tomorrow." Cuza turned to Stanescu. "Emil, after Max has finished, return and do what you can medically for Mr. Petrov. He has twenty-four hours to recuperate. I do not want him passing out tomorrow. In the meantime, would you care to accompany me to dinner?"

After Cuza and Stanescu left, Kolya focused on Max, who picked up a fire iron. "Alex," he said in a low voice, "step away from me."

The two Romanian guards had their assault weapons pointed at him.

"No." Her voice was quiet but firm.

Frick pushed himself off the door. "This is stupid. Max, the man's half dead. You beat him up, and you're likely to kill him."

"And your concern is what?" Max stopped three feet away from Kolya, the iron balanced in both hands.

Frick held his hands up. "Hey, I don't like the guy, He beat the shit out of me, remember? But hurting him anymore would be counterproductive. Both of us want to know what's in the ECA's computers."

"And if there's no punishment, he'll pull something else. But you're right, I don't want to kill him." His glance shifted from Kolya to Alex, and Kolya's stomach turned over.

"If you touch her, I will fucking kill you."

"You know you curse too much, Petrov. Anyone ever tell you that?" Max smiled. "Just to show how fair I am, I'm going to let you choose your punishment. Either I break your other leg, or I fuck your woman in front of you. Which do you prefer?"

A chill went down Kolya's back. "Break my leg," he said without a moment's hesitation.

Max's smile grew larger. "Not so fast. She gets to vote, too."

Kolya grabbed Alex's hand, protectively. "It's my decision, Alex."

"What am I, a potted plant? You think I'd let him break your leg to protect my virtue? Do you think I'm some sort of vestal virgin? He won't be the first asshole I ever fucked."

"No." Kolya couldn't let her sacrifice herself for him.

"So, we have a tie," Max continued to grin. "Both of you willing to sacrifice to protect the other. Very sweet. I guess I'll just have to be the tie-breaker. Petrov, you've made your willingness to endure pain quite clear. The only thing that really gets to you is a threat to your woman."

"If you touch her," Kolya said. "You can forget about me cooperating."

"I could just kill her," Max said. "Which is what I was about to do before you agreed to cooperate."

"Enough," Frick said. "Let her alone, Max."

Max turned on him, his face an ugly mask. "You're part of this."

"No, actually, I'm not. We have interests in common, but I'm not a member of your fun little gang. I've done a lot of stuff I'm not particularly proud of for you people. I draw the line at rape. And there's no need. You've made the threat. Petrov believes you'll do it. The threat'll be a guarantee of future good behavior. And if you break his other leg, we're going to have to keep carrying him, which is a nuisance—if you don't outright kill him."

Max took a step toward Frick.

"We need Frick," Radu interposed quickly. "He's our link to the Director."

"Fine." Max's face was an ugly mask. "I don't want to fuck a filthy Jew, anyway. She gets off this time, Petrov. But the other men here aren't as fastidious. Next time, they all get a turn. Then we'll kill her. And while Frick's got a point about having to carry you, you need a reminder of who's in charge." He kicked Kolya's broken leg hard. Kolya screamed as the bone separated. Pain enveloped him, but before he blacked out, he felt a surge of relief—that Alex wouldn't be touched—for now.

28

"There's a toothbrush." Teo emerged from the bathroom connected to Alex Feinstein's bedroom. "Where do you think she is?"

"I don't know," Jonathan said. "She didn't call into work either."

He went back downstairs and checked in the kitchen. Two coffee cups were washed and stacked in the drainer. The kitchen was clean and unremarkable.

"You think something might have happened to her?" Teo persisted. "She had that meeting with a witness last night."

Jonathan honestly didn't know what to think. There was no sign of struggle, but it was unlike the responsible woman he knew to disappear without a word to her office. Then, again, maybe this was how she dealt with grief. But there were too many things that just didn't add up: Kolya's questionable death, the disclosure by Manion that the Intelligence Committee had known of Kolya's trip, Bob Smith's accident, Jonathan's transfer off the team, and now, Alex's disappearance.

It was too much to all be coincidence.

* * * * *

Elizabeth Owen pushed open the door to Mark's office at five minutes after six. He slouched in front of the computer and played chess in a chat room.

"You supposed to be doing that?"

"Nah. But what Ross doesn't know won't kill him. I minimize

185

every couple minutes."

She looked over his shoulder at the game. "Black or white."

"White."

"You're losing."

"I noticed. What's up? You want the NSA printout? Ross should have done that."

"He did. You hear about Egan?"

"Congratulations. Assuming you wanted it."

"I want it. Even though it doesn't mean much."

"It means Bradford trusts you to keep a lid on things."

"That's my impression, too. Did you know that the search for the mole on the Intelligence Committee is being quietly discontinued?"

"Now there's a surprise. I might just have a heart attack and fall over from surprise." Mark moved his mouse and clicked. "I've got the bastard's queen." He was about to be checkmated anyway. Two more moves, and he exited the chat room in disgust. "Don't you have anything better to do? No offense Elizabeth, but you don't usually hang out with me."

"No one else is here. Egan's mad at me. Marty and Pete went home. Teo's following Egan around. I'm all alone by the telephone."

"So leave. Nothing's breaking. See a movie. Eat dinner. Pick up a man. Pretend you have a life."

"No use pretending. No movies I want to see, and I'm sick of men."

"Sleep."

"Why sleep when there's caffeine?"

"You know the shit's going to hit the fan in a couple of days. We're going to need everyone available to be rested and ready to roll."

"Really? Just what shit are you referring to?"

"Theoretical shit. Hey, as long as you're hanging around, feel like getting me a diet soda from the cafeteria. Throw in a piece of cheesecake."

"Right. Cheesecake and diet soda." She headed for the cafeteria.

Cheesecake was one of the better offerings—Rita brought it in from a local bakery. Elizabeth selected a slice of strawberry cheesecake for herself as well as one for Mark.

Bearing a tray with the desserts and a diet cola, she made her way back to Mark's office. She removed her cheesecake and handed the tray over to Mark.

"Super." He dug in.

Elizabeth ate a strawberry. "Pretty good. You know where Rita buys this stuff?"

"Nope, that's one of the biggest secrets in the agency."

"Almost as big a secret as the fact that Kolya Petrov is alive and a prisoner undergoing interrogation?"

He had just forked a chunk of cheesecake into his mouth. He choked, coughed, grabbed the soda and swilled a mouthful. "How the hell do you know that?" he demanded when he was finally able to speak.

"I didn't actually know until now. You just confirmed a guess."

"God, I did, didn't I?" He grabbed his head. "Ross's going to kill me. He's going to cut me into little pieces, and then he'll send me to jail for a million years."

"He can't both kill you and send you to jail. Anyway, he doesn't have to know." Elizabeth picked another strawberry off her plate with her fingers and ate it delicately. "I want to know what's going on— and then I'll decide what I'm going to do."

"I tell you anything else, and I'm going to be in even deeper shit."

"You don't fill me in, and the first person I'll call is Jonathan Egan. The second person will be Margaret Bradford."

"Christ. How'd you guess?"

"There's been a lot of suspicious things going on. You used the present tense to refer to Kolya; you asked me how long it takes to break a man, and you acted very guilty when you remembered that Kolya had defended you. Your turn. What the hell's going on?"

He sighed. "It's like this. Ross and I designed a Trojan horse. If we can get it on Cuza's computer, we can download all his data. Ross figured if Cuza thinks he's hacking into us... because he's forcing someone... Kolya's good on computers."

She put the cheesecake on the desk as the implication sunk in. "You son-of-a-bitch. You fed Petrov to Cuza."

He squirmed. "Ross thought up the plan, but Bradford and Lewis made the decision. I just went along with it. You have no idea how bad it was, sitting with him for days, knowing what was about to happen to him."

"You poor baby."

He flushed. "Okay, I could have warned him. But Ross threatened me if I said anything—violating National Security and all. And Ross said that we'll get Kolya out after the Trojan is activated."

"And that's why you're watching the computer around the clock, so that you'll be able to download Cuza's files."

"The download'll be automatic. As soon as Cuza accesses the system. I'm here to get the information as soon as it comes in, and also to alert Bradford to okay a rescue."

"Where is Petrov?"

"Romania, somewhere. Wait, I'll show you." Mark pulled up a file and hit print. He removed several sheets and handed them over to her.

"Bob Smith sent this. I'll be damned." She read through the pages and looked over at Mark. "Doesn't say where in Romania. Do you know?"

Mark shook his head. "No, I figured you field types would get it out of this David Fuller guy or maybe it'll be on the download of Cuza's files."

Her mind went through the logistics of finding Fuller, persuading him to give up Petrov's location—if he even knew the location—planning and mounting an assault. "We'd never get there in time. Petrov'll be dead before we even know where he is."

He looked at her anxiously. "So what are you going to do? You can't tell Jonathan. If he makes a move to get Petrov out, it'll blow the whole plan."

If Jonathan knew, he'd take the next flight to New York and be sitting on Fuller's doorstep. If Fuller could be persuaded to cooperate and give Petrov's location, a rescue might succeed. If Elizabeth told Jonathan what was going on....

But doing so involved personal risk. Bradford would be furious at the breach of security. She'd expect Elizabeth to come to her, and she'd expect Elizabeth to toe the line.

So, what to do?

Elizabeth didn't particularly like Petrov, but she didn't want him to die, either. She did like her job, and she would very much like the title of Deputy Director.

Help a colleague or help her career: that was the choice.

She picked up the cheesecake and, almost without noticing, finished it.

"Well?" Mark asked.

"I'm thinking."

29

Frick flipped the channels, searching for a sports event he could stand. He found a cricket game on British television, soccer on a Spanish station, and bicycling on a French station. He switched to CNN, propped his feet on the coffee table, and, balancing his Scotch and water on his stomach, leaned back to watch a report on a small child rescued from a well.

He was in the recreation room in the basement. On the other side of the wall was the room where Petrov had been held and tortured. Petrov was currently in a drugged sleep in a bedroom upstairs, his girlfriend with him. He'd helped carry Petrov up the long flight of stairs and then taken a walk up the mountain to try to clear his head—and his conscience.

It hadn't worked.

The Scotch was Glenfiddich, good stuff. Frick thought about going upstairs to sleep, but it was only six-thirty, Eastern Standard Time. If he went to bed, he'd just lay there, thinking about Petrov and Feinstein.

Petrov had looked like shit. It was one thing to send a man off to be tortured. It was another thing to see the results. Even worse, he felt responsible for putting Alex Feinstein at risk. Kidnapping Petrov was bad enough, but by signing up with the ECA, Petrov'd agreed to put himself in harm's way. Alex Feinstein hadn't. Girlfriends, family should be off limits. And yet, he'd helped kidnap both of them.

He had managed to stave off the rape and hadn't helped them torture Petrov, but he hadn't escaped the blow-by-blow description

190

of Petrov's ordeal that had been provided by Gheorghe during dinner. He rattled the ice cubes in his glass.

"You really shouldn't add ice to single malt." Cuza's cool tones sounded from the top of the stairs.

Frick squinted his eyes and concealed his surprise at the company. "I know, but what the hell?"

Cuza descended, strolled to the bar, and poured himself a shot of scotch, straight up. "I had planned to speak to you in the morning. I'm surprised you're still up. Is your room comfortable?"

"Very, thanks. I haven't adjusted to the time change."

"Takes a day or two." Cuza seated himself across from Frick in an armchair.

Frick picked up the remote and clicked off the television. "Nice place."

"Yes, I enjoy it. Beautiful views. You can climb to the top of the peak in half an hour. Did you enjoy your walk?"

"I did, but I didn't get too far."

"I wanted to let you know that I understand your intervention to prevent Max raping Miss Feinstein—this time."

"Max told you."

"Max didn't have to tell me. Every room in the house is wired." Cuza sipped his scotch. "I thought Miss Feinstein might suffer the consequences for Mr. Petrov's failure, but I agree that the threat is probably enough—for now. Miss Feinstein is innocent of anything except loving the wrong man. But sometimes these kinds of things are necessary, if distasteful."

"Necessary?"

"Necessary. Mr. Petrov is a very dangerous man. He needs to be kept under tight control. He might have been attempting to stall. I wouldn't put it past him."

Frick drank more scotch. "Hell, he couldn't even sit up. It was hard to believe that he was the same guy who nearly took me apart last Friday."

"He's the same man. Injured and ill, but still defiant. Even when we brought in his fiancée, he tried to play for time."

191

"But he gave in. He was cooperating."

"Until the moment that he passed out—or pretended to pass out. Whether he did or didn't, he was taught an important lesson. If he knows that Miss Feinstein will pay for any failure on his part, he'll be anxious to please. The power of love is remarkable, isn't it? But if he fails to cooperate fully—you will not intervene again."

"Will that matter after tomorrow night?" Frick drank the last sip. "Aren't you planning to kill both of them as soon as he gets you into the ECA computer?"

Cuza examined his glass. "Does that bother you?"

"Nope, doesn't bother me." Frick pulled himself off the couch and wandered over to the bar to help himself to another scotch. He dropped in two ice cubes and filled the glass. "Seems like kind of a waste, though. Petrov's a smart guy. He has all sorts of information about the ECA—stuff neither I nor the Director would know anything about. He knows their people, their tactics. He could help understand any information you download from their computer."

"I thought that you wanted him killed immediately. Max said that Petrov recognized you."

Frick shrugged. "I'm not sure if he recognized me. He just looked at me funny. But it doesn't really matter. As long as he's here, safe and secure, he's not a threat to me or to Director Ford. And as you've pointed out, he's going to behave himself to protect his girlfriend."

"What you say is correct; he may possess valuable information beyond the ability to access this computer system. I'd like to have some assurance, though, of just how cooperative he's likely to be."

Frick returned to the couch and picked up the remote. "I'd say you've got him pretty well broken. As long as you've got his lover for leverage, he'll do anything you want."

"Maybe. Accessing a computer system is something he can't fake. But he could and probably would give me false information that I'd have no way to check."

"And maybe not. I saw Petrov's face last night when he thought Max was going to rape Feinstein. I don't think he'd risk it."

"Test him. Ask him a question you know the answer to but he'd normally lie about it. A truthful answer would demonstrate that he is under sufficient control to be of continued use. Can you think of an appropriate question?"

"The name of his partner is something he'd conceal. You already know that Petrov works with Jonathan Egan, but Petrov doesn't realize that you know. Petrov tried to shut up the woman when she said something about Jonathan arranging for the honey trap. If there's anything a guy like Petrov would try to protect, it's the identity of a fellow agent, especially since they're also friends." And Petrov, if he had in fact recognized Frick, would know that Frick already knew the identity of his partner. Frick could only hope that Petrov would be intelligent enough to play along.

"Fine." Cuza nodded his head. "Petrov's under sedation at the moment. In the morning, he should be able to talk. You go have a little chat with him. If he's truthful, perhaps I'll keep him alive for a while."

*   *   *   *   *

At Jonathan's stone Tudor home in Chevy Chase, Maryland, purchased with money from a trust fund, Jonathan searched his phone contacts while Teo searched for snacks in the expansive pantry next to the kitchen. Teo emerged with a box of Lucky Charms, a month expired, that Jonathan kept on hand for the occasional visits with his son. Teo picked out colored marshmallows, and Jonathan dialed two of Alex's close friends. Neither had heard from Alex. He flipped through his contacts and dialed three more acquaintances and Alex's brother.

None knew her whereabouts. Jonathan gave up. He had run out of people to call and out of ideas. He watched Teo rummage through the cereal box.

"Can we go eat dinner then?" Teo asked.

"What do you mean we? Go home, Teo."

Teo shook his head. "I'm going to hang with you for the evening."

Lucky me, Jonathan thought, as the doorbell rang. Teo started for the door, but Jonathan beat him to it.

Elizabeth Owen stood on the doorstep, her hair damp from the soft drizzle. "Glad I caught you." She stepped inside. "You've got the boy wonder here, too."

"This is a surprise," Jonathan said. "What're you doing here?"

"Visiting the Egan estate. Wanted to know how the rich and infamous live."

Jonathan did not comment on the fact that she had not only previously visited his house but his bedroom.

She strolled into the living room and seated herself on the couch, legs crossed, top leg swinging. Jonathan followed and sat on the other end of the couch. Teo perched on the arm of an overstuffed armchair. "What's new?" she asked.

"Not a lot," he said. "Except that Alex Feinstein's disappeared."

That got her attention. "Disappeared? Not as in visiting a friend or family?"

"Disappeared. Didn't call in to her job. Didn't call her brother or any friend."

Elizabeth sat up straight, fury on every feature. "The bitch. I thought she was low, but this is the absolute bottom."

Jonathan stood. "A hell of a thing to say about Alex, considering what she's going through. Get out, Elizabeth."

She looked up at him. "Chill, Jonathan. I was not referring to Alex Feinstein. I was referring to Bradford." She fished in her coat pocket. "I've been debating what to do. I thought I'd see what you had found out, what you were thinking, and then I'd decide. I've decided. Here." She handed him several pieces of folded paper.

He unfolded the paper, read the e-mail address from Bob Smith that was on top, and looked at her. "Care to explain?"

"I ran into Mark Leslie in the cafeteria, and he said things that started me wondering. This evening, I tricked and bullied him into telling me what was going on. He went through your e-mail when you were in New York and then deleted this message."

Jonathan read the brief note. "Jesus Christ. Kolya is alive. I knew it." He felt a quick rush of relief, a lightening of spirit, followed immediately by heightened tension.

194

Teo peered over his shoulder as Jonathan flipped through the rest of the pages. "This is some FBI guy's file."

"It is. Which means that the mole is Carl Ford." Not his top concern at the moment. "Bob doesn't give any details on where Kolya's being held. Or how he was captured." Jonathan's attention returned to Elizabeth. "If Mark Leslie knew that Kolya was alive, Margaret knew. What the hell is going on?"

"Margaret set him up to be captured in order to get into Cuza's computer."

"Holy shit," Teo said.

"Okay, give me the whole damn story," Jonathan said.

Elizabeth explained. Jonathan listened, stood, walked to the fireplace, and paced back to the couch. He glanced over at Teo, whose face had gone ashen.

"Lovely business, we're in, eh, Teo?" His attention returned to Elizabeth. "So Kolya wasn't informed."

"No," Elizabeth said. "They thought he might not volunteer or that he might not hold out long enough after his kidnapping to make his capitulation realistic. They figured he'd give in eventually with enough pressure, even if he didn't know."

"Goddamn it to hell," Jonathan exploded. "He won't give in. He's the most stubborn son-of-a-bitch I know. He'll let them strip off every inch of his skin before he gives."

"But he'll cooperate to save Alex Feinstein if not himself. I was wondering how Bradford could guarantee that Petrov would cooperate? Not until you mentioned that Alex Feinstein was missing did I figure it out."

"What a bitch," Teo exploded. "Let's get them out."

"Hold on, boy wonder," Elizabeth said. "Just how do you propose we do that?"

"We find this Fuller guy, and we find out where Cuza's holding Kolya."

"Then what?" Elizabeth asked. "Even assuming we find Fuller and he knows Petrov's location. No offense, but if I'm ruining a promising career to save Petrov and Feinstein, I'd prefer to not

195

screw it up. I don't trust that the three of us could pull it off."

"Once we know where Kolya is," Jonathan said, "I call Margaret and persuade her to send us to Romania with a special op team. First things first."

30

Kolya woke, panicked from a nightmare, but he realized that Alex was sleeping next to him. He could smell her shampoo on the dark curly hair near his face and hear the even tones of her breathing. He put his right arm around her waist and pulled her tightly against him, wanting to feel the solidity of her body against his own. He drifted off again.

He was in the ECA building, in Mark Leslie's office, leaning against the wall, watching Mark type on a computer keyboard. "What are you doing?"

Mark looked up, guilty. "Creating a virus. Not to use. Just to see if we could do it."

"If I get a virus on my computer, I will not think it funny."

"It's not for your computer."

The scene shifted to Bradford's office. "Mr. Ross is going to have you trained on a new computer system he's designed."

"Why me?"

She tapped a pen impatiently. "You're good on computers. You have no family. You're solitary, rude, and Russian. Why not you?"

Then he was chained to the floor. A golf club swung down, breaking his leg.

He woke up, unsure of his location. He assessed. He was in a comfortable but unfamiliar bed, lying on his left side, his right arm draped over a sleeping Alex, his left arm under a pillow cradling his head. He tried to shift his position and realized that his left wrist was attached by a short chain to the bars of the wrought iron headboard.

He lifted his head up to take in his surroundings. It was a large

197

bedroom, furniture of a simple, tasteful design, a dresser, a bedside table. Two doors. One was closed, presumably locked; the other stood open and led to a small bathroom. He didn't see any cameras, but that didn't mean anything.

From what he could tell of his own situation: his right leg from mid-thigh to his ankle was in a cast, and he was dressed in loose blue running pants and a clean unbuttoned long-sleeved shirt. Pain was there, but less acute. He suspected that he was still under the influence of sedation. He felt groggy but able to focus with effort.

Much of the previous night was a blur. He remembered Max and his threat against Alex—and the blow to his injured leg. From that point, he had only scraps of memory, of injections, of Alex next to him, holding his hand.

Obviously, he'd received medical treatment. Leg set, his back bandaged; even his wrists, rubbed raw by manacles, were wrapped in gauze and tape. It was almost as if Cuza intended to keep him alive. Otherwise, why bother with any treatment beyond that necessary for him to remain conscious to finish the job?

Maybe there was a chance they'd be allowed to live. *Not likely, but maybe.*

From the sound of her breathing, Alex was still asleep. Good that she could sleep, both for her benefit and because it gave him a chance to think—and for the first time in days, his mind was clear enough that he could. He remembered Frick's words the day before—that Bradford had betrayed him. He didn't trust Frick, but the words had reawakened his own suspicions.

How had Cuza known enough to capture him? How had he known about Alex?

The dream was what he started with—Mark designing a virus. But it wasn't just a dream. He remembered walking into Ross's office and finding Mark on the computer.

"Creating a virus. Not to use. Just to see if we could do it."

His subconscious mind had dredged up the memory. It had to mean something. He fought the mental fog from the drugs and concentrated.

"Creating a virus. Not to use."

A virus. Why was Mark creating a virus?

He came up with an obvious possibility and rejected it. It couldn't be. Not even Bradford could be that callous. Or could she?

He ran the events of the past week through his mind: Bradford separating him out from the other agents; Cuza knowing not only what train he would be on, but knowing the location of the apartment; Cuza knowing about the computer system; Eric not intended to accompany Kolya to New York; Bradford's insistence that Kolya continue on to the apartment even after he described the risk.

He remembered Mark Leslie's mournful demeanor the last day in the office.

Creating a virus.

What if the whole elaborate computer game he had learned was nothing more than camouflage to trick Cuza into accessing a program that contained a virus—a Trojan horse—that Mark and Ross had designed?

He no longer rejected the possibility. Under this theory, everything made sense.

If the new computer system contained a Trojan, then Bradford wanted him captured, and Bradford wanted him to break. To do all that, she must have given the Intelligence Committee an account of his movements, knowing that the mole would pass it on.

Of course Bradford would want him to go to New York alone. No reason to lose more than one agent. No wonder Mark had worn the expression of a dying cow. He had been in on the plan. Bradford's idea, no doubt, but Mark had executed it, spent a week training Kolya on the new program.

But why didn't Bradford fill him in? If he'd known, he would have given in. Before his leg had been broken, before he'd spent days under torture, before Alex—

"Pizdorvanka," he hissed a Russian insult. "Whore of a bitch."

Bradford had given them Alex. He could almost understand Bradford's using him. He understood the necessity of getting into Cuza's computer. He was an agent. He accepted a certain level of personal risk. While he was angry at the lack of trust evident in Bradford's decision not to brief him on the real mission, he would, in time, have let it go—had the risk and the damage only involved him personally. He wouldn't understand or forgive dragging Alex into the business.

He owed a debt to Eric as well. Eric was dead because neither Kolya nor he had known the real purpose of the trip to Manhattan.

Bradford, Mark, Ross. And Ford, of course. If Kolya survived, he'd pay all of them back. He'd take a golf club to Ford's leg. He'd burn off Ross's testicles. He'd break Mark's neck.

He wasn't capable of doing what Bradford deserved: of forcing her to watch him hurt her granddaughter, so maybe he'd just shoot her.

Had Jonathan known? Had his closest friend allowed him to be captured and tortured? Had Jonathan actually believed him to be dead—or was that an act? If there was anyone besides Alex whom Kolya trusted completely, it was Jonathan. Now, he didn't know what to think.

He was so angry he was shaking.

"Kolya?" Alex turned over, and her gaze sleepily met his. "Are you all right?"

"*Podsirushka*." He took a deep breath and tried to calm himself. He still trembled with rage. "Just angry."

"Who the hell isn't?" She reached a hand over to feel his forehead. "Your temperature was up to 103 last night. At least, you're cooler. How do you feel?"

"Better than yesterday." That much was true enough. "I'm so sorry, Alex. It's my fault that you're here—that you were almost raped."

"If you weren't so sick, and I weren't so worried, I'd smack you. You were shot and kidnapped. You've been tortured for days, and when they forced you to work, you blacked out. You offered to have your leg broken to protect me. How is any of this your fault?"

"For not giving in sooner." For working for that *suka*—bitch— Bradford. He phrased it more diplomatically. "For staying on the job." He spat out the words.

"You were doing your duty."

"I thought I was."

He could screw up Bradford's little plot. He could tell Cuza what was really going on—or what he thought was really going on—that the computer system Cuza was so anxious to access probably contained a Trojan.

That would be funny, wouldn't it?

Alex swung her legs out of the bed. "Not that I'm not enjoying our conversation, but you need your medicine, and I need to go to the bathroom." From the bedside table, she picked up a plastic glass and pills and handed them to him.

"What are they?"

"Antibiotic." She pointed to the largest pill. "Aspirin and Percodan."

He swallowed the antibiotic and the aspirin, and handed back the Percodan, although the pain was starting to build. "It'll make me groggy."

"You're in pain."

"I dislike being groggy."

"I've never heard you object to vodka."

"Vodka doesn't make me groggy. Oh, and Alex, before you use the facilities, turn on the hot water. Wait until the mirrors fog up."

She gave a brisk nod of acknowledgement.

She disappeared, and he rested, the conversation having drained his limited energy, but continued the internal debate: tell Cuza what he now believed to be the truth? His initial rage at Bradford's unacceptable betrayal had cooled to a calculating anger.

However he would or could repay Bradford if he had the chance, they were prisoners, their lives hanging in the balance. He couldn't let anger determine his decision, any more than he could allow a painkiller to cloud his mind.

Would Cuza be more likely to spare their lives if Kolya told him about the Trojan horse? Perhaps. Cuza might be grateful at being saved from a trap, or he might consider Kolya to be a participant in the deception.

Alternatively, if the computer system did contain a Trojan horse, if Kolya activated the Trojan on Cuza's computer and Cuza realized it,

Kolya knew what Cuza would do. Kolya would be condemning Alex as well as himself to terrible deaths.

How long had Gina lived after being impaled?

Proposition three: If he did put the Trojan on Cuza's computer, would he and Alex have a better chance of survival? If his theory were correct, Bradford knew he was alive. Would the ECA attempt a rescue once the job was done? Would he and Alex still be alive when and if an extraction team arrived?

If they remained Cuza's prisoners, whether or not he informed Cuza of the Trojan, sooner or later, Cuza would have them killed.

Any way he looked at it, it was a gamble.

Alex returned with a bedpan and hand sanitizer. "Hot water's running, but it'll take a few minutes to fog up any cameras. While I'm in there, I'm taking a shower. There're towels and things. I thought you might prefer to use this now."

"Thanks. You don't have to watch."

"It's not like you have anything I haven't seen." Still, she turned her back.

Using a bedpan was unpleasant under any circumstances. Managing with one hand chained to the bed made for interesting logistics. He shifted up on an elbow and proceeded gingerly.

"The alleged doctor left antibiotic salve for your burns. In the top drawer." Alex still faced the door. "It should go on every few hours. What'd they use on you, a cigarette?"

"Cigar."

"Max. Bastard."

"He held the cigar, but it was a group performance." Kolya finished and rubbed sanitizer on his hands. "Could I have the salve?"

She removed the bedpan, washed her hands, returned, fished in the drawer, and came up with a small tube.

"Looks like the shower's ready." He nodded toward the steam rolling from under the crack in of the bathroom door. After she disappeared, he gingerly dabbed the ointment on the burns on his chest and genitals before sliding back down on the bed.

So what was he going to do? Alert Cuza to the possible nature of the program—Cuza who had impaled Gina—who was responsible for Eric's and Gina's murders —who had ordered Kolya's torture and hadn't cared what Max did to Alex? How many more people would die if Cuza weren't stopped?

On the other hand, Bradford, for whom he had worked for almost ten years and on whose orders he had repeatedly risked his life, had betrayed him. She had allowed him to be captured, tortured, and when he didn't break, she had arranged for Alex to be captured as well.

Who did he hate more, the torturer or the betrayer? Or was that beside the point?

He closed his eyes, tired and sick, but too tense to sleep.

* * * * *

Frick balanced the tray so as not to spill the two cups of coffee into the plates of eggs while the guard unlocked and swung the door open. Feinstein was nowhere to be seen. Petrov lay on his side, his arm across his eyes. Frick heard the sound of a shower, and he waited while the guard closed the door behind him. Petrov didn't stir. Frick cleared his throat.

"Want some breakfast?"

The arm dropped down, tired eyes blinked open and focused slowly. Petrov looked better than the night before, which wasn't saying a hell of a lot. He was visibly weak, and there were pain lines around the eyes and the mouth. Petrov pushed himself into a sitting position, leaned back against the headboard, winced, and caught his breath.

Frick placed the tray on the bed within easy reach of Petrov's free hand. "Poached eggs and toast for you; mushroom and cheese omelet for the lady. She's in the shower?"

"Yes."

A small bowl with cubes of sugar sat next to a small pitcher of cream. Petrov dumped two cubes into the coffee, stirred with a plastic spoon, the only utensil provided, and picked up the cup. He drank slowly.

"I'd eat the eggs first. Your system's screwed up enough as it is, which is why you get poached eggs instead of an omelet." Frick seated himself in a chair next to the window overlooking a spectacular view of mountains and forest.

Petrov finished the coffee, replaced the cup on the tray, and picked up the plate of eggs and toast, resting it on his lap. He selected a piece of toast and chewed slowly. "Is there a reason you're here?"

"Just having a friendly chat."

Petrov managed to slide half of a poached egg onto a plastic spoon and get it to his mouth, something of a feat with one hand. Frick waited for an answer until Petrov swallowed.

"I don't chat, and you're not my friend. I've capitulated. I'll answer whatever the hell you ask me, but I don't feel up to playing games." The second half of the egg followed the first but with noticeably less enthusiasm. Petrov replaced the half-full plate on the tray and gingerly slid down into a prone position. Despite the obvious discomfort, he chose to lie on his back, chained arm under his head, staring at Frick, watchful and wary.

"You can finish eating," Frick said.

"I'm done."

"Feeling sick? I can get the doctor."

"No."

The negative was for the suggestion of Stanescu. Petrov was clearly feeling worse, either from the unusual activity of eating or from the effort of sitting up.

The bathroom door clicked, and Alex Feinstein emerged, wet hair hanging down her back, wearing the clothes from the previous day. Her face wasn't any friendlier than Petrov's.

She ignored Frick and narrowed her eyes at Petrov. "You're paler than you were before I took my shower. The pain worse?"

"I'm naturally pale."

"Why are you so damn stubborn? Take the Percodan."

"We've been through this. It'll make me sleepy."

Frick knew his opinion wasn't wanted, but he offered it anyway. "Take the medicine, Petrov. You've got twelve hours until you try accessing the computer system again. You should sleep while you can."

Neither looked at him. "Why's he here?" she asked Petrov.

"I assume he wants to ask me questions. The omelet's for you."

There was only one chair in the room, and Frick occupied it. Alex picked up the plate and curled up on the bed, against the headboard, on Petrov's far side. She dug into the eggs with the remaining plastic spoon.

"You should finish your breakfast. They've been starving you," she told Petrov, as if the two were alone in the room. "It's partly why you're so weak."

"I'm out of the habit of eating."

"In other words, you're nauseous." She finished the omelet and poured milk into the remaining cup of coffee. She eyed the empty cup. "Don't tell me you drank a cup of coffee before eating anything."

"Fine. I won't tell you."

Frick cleared his throat. "I told him to eat first."

Alex glared. "You gave him coffee in his condition? He's a coffee addict."

"Hey," Frick protested. "I just brought the tray. I'm not his goddamn mother. Petrov wants to make himself sick, I'm not going to stop him."

"Son of a bitch."

"Alex, the coffee didn't make me ill. Calm down."

"Look, I protected you last night," Frick tried again.

"You think that I should be grateful?" She was furious almost beyond words. "Because you intervened to keep me from being raped—after kidnapping me? But torturing Kolya—that's okay? Jesus Christ. Look at him! Look what you've done to him! Take a look at his back. Did you hold him down to be burned or to have his leg broken?"

"Alex, I'm all right." Petrov reached a hand out to her, but she wasn't having it.

"Like hell you are." She stood and smashed the tray on the dresser. Dishes rattled. "You're hurting, and you won't even take a pain pill, damn it. Do you know how worried I am about you?"

"I'll take the Goddamn Percodan if it matters that much to you."

"Yes, it matters. You need to sleep."

"Fine." He held out his hand for the pill and swallowed it dry. "Happy?" He caught her hand.

"No, but at least you'll get some rest." She pressed his hand against her cheek. "I can't sit here and talk politely to one of the men who hurt you." She kissed his palm, released it, stalked into the bathroom, and slammed the door closed.

"Shit," Frick said. "She was so rational before. I guess being kidnapped and threatened is enough to send the average person around the bend."

"She's not thinking about herself."

"Yeah, I know, she's concerned about you. As you are about her. Although objectively speaking, she's right. She's traumatized, but you're physically damaged. How bad was it?"

"Bad enough." Petrov turned his head from watching the bathroom door to staring at Frick. "If you want details, ask your friends."

"I got the description over last night's dinner. Ruined a perfectly good meal. It's not how I get my kicks."

Petrov gave a sharp laugh.

"You don't believe me?"

"It doesn't matter what I believe."

"I was doing my job. You have information that I need. Are you telling me you've never done anything of questionable morality to get information?"

"Not like this."

"Never turned a prisoner over to another country for interrogation in a manner inconsistent with U.S. laws on human rights?"

"No. I know that's been done by the CIA, but not by anyone in the ECA and not by me."

The conversation tired him, or maybe the drug was kicking in. But he seemed to be making an effort just to speak. The area under his eyes looked darker.

"You've killed people."

"Only when they posed an immediate physical threat. I'm not an assassin. If I were ordered to do what you've done, I'd fucking resign."

The challenge hung in the air.

"You know who I am, don't you?"

"Frick."

That was correct, of course, if limited. "You didn't recognize me after your escape attempt?"

"No. I wanted to kill you. That was my only thought."

Shit. He was lying. Frick would have bet the ranch that Petrov recognized him. Cuza would be listening to this, but Cuza would have no way to double check whether or not Petrov actually knew Frick's real name. But if Petrov lied about something else, something that Cuza could check, Petrov was as good as dead.

Frick hunched over. "Let me make things clear. You know a lot about the internal workings of the ECA and its personnel, and that makes you valuable as long as you continue to cooperate. I don't want you or the lady killed, but if you're caught in a lie, you'll be considered unreliable."

"Understood."

Now for the test. "So who came up with the idea for Gina Antonia to sleep with Cuza?"

"Jonathan." Petrov's eyes closed.

Frick persevered. "I already knew that. Your girlfriend said his first name yesterday. What's his full name?"

"Egan. Jonathan Egan. Son of the former Senator. We've worked together for ten years."

Petrov had just given himself additional time to live. "And the kid?"

"Teo Lorenzo." Petrov struggled for the words. "New agent."

"Enough for now," Frick said. "Get some rest."

Petrov painfully shifted onto his side, as Frick stood and moved around the bed to collect the tray. He left the plate with the remaining toast and poached egg on the dresser. Petrov might feel up to eating later.

He knocked on the door to the room and heard the key turn in the lock.

In half an hour, he'd be on the plane headed back to the United States. He hoped he'd given Cuza reason enough to spare Petrov and Feinstein, but sooner or later, later, even if Petrov continued to provide information, both of them would be killed. Frick had known what would happen but hadn't really cared as long as it happened out of his sight.

Maybe he was lower than Max—willing to benefit from what Max did but unwilling to get his own hands dirty.

* * * * *

The path wound upward from the high meadow where the mansion had been built. Most of the trees were pines, although a few golden leaves drifted to the earth from deciduous trees. Cuza always enjoyed a walk on the mountain. Max might not be his favorite companion, but they had business to discuss.

Max got right to the point. "I thought you'd decided on tonight."

"No, I haven't decided. It is possible that Petrov may have other useful information. But if I decide to spare him for now, it's an easy decision to reverse. Miss Feinstein is an attractive woman. If we kill him, we have to kill her as well. I find her intriguing, even if she's a Jew."

"If you want her, take her. She's not going to fuck anyone but Petrov of her own will."

"Forcing her doesn't interest me. Seducing her is different—but that would take time."

"He's very dangerous."

"Do you know that certain royal houses in Africa would keep wild cats—cheetahs, lions—as pets, dangerous though they may be? There's a sense of power in having a wild and dangerous animal under your control." A golden eagle soared overhead. Cuza watched the bird's flight. Magnificent. "If I decide not to kill him tonight, I'm sure we can keep him harmless."

31

Jonathan sipped a latte. Out of the corner of his eye, he watched Teo butter a blueberry scone. "How can you still be eating? You already ate five pancakes and three eggs."

"That was three hours ago. This is second breakfast. You think you'll be able to recognize him?"

"Yep, I'll know him."

Elizabeth slipped into the third seat. "No answer to the door." She'd agreed to try Frick's apartment, just in case.

They'd arrived in New York at midnight. From midnight to five, they'd parked in a rented car half a block away, where they'd taken turns sleeping and watching. They'd eaten breakfast at a diner down the street. Now, from Starbucks, they continued surveillance of Frick's building.

Jonathan was tired. But he'd gone for days on a few hours sleep before—when necessary. Afghanistan—he didn't think either he, Kolya, or Marty had slept more than three hours a night those four days when they were trying to sneak out of the country.

God, Kolya. Even if he were alive, what kind of shape would he be in?

"How about we knock on some of the neighbor's doors?" Teo asked.

"Very discrete, boy wonder," Elizabeth said. "How about we stand outside his window and make an announcement with a bullhorn?"

Teo flushed. "Stop calling me that, damn it."

"You took it from Kolya. What's wrong? Can't handle a little friendly teasing from a woman?"

"Shut up, Elizabeth," Jonathan said. "Teo, ignore her. Act like professionals, both of you."

"Sure, but what profession?" Elizabeth asked. "We've all just kissed our jobs goodbye."

"Having second thoughts?" Jonathan asked.

"Of course I am. And you would be, too, if you didn't have a trust fund."

"I don't have a trust fund," Teo said.

"And you're not having second thoughts?"

"Kolya'd help me if our positions were switched." Teo crunched down on the last of his scone.

Elizabeth leaned on the table. "I'm willing to go the distance to save Petrov and Feinstein. But this is costing me my career. I know it, and I'm not happy about it."

"We're keeping our jobs. We have leverage. Margaret won't want this to get out—to the press or even to other agents." Jonathan didn't think that Elizabeth completely believed him. He wasn't sure he believed it. Still, move on. "We're going to have to split up. Change outfits. Three of us constantly together are conspicuous. We need to blend in." This was the problem with launching an impromptu operation without planning or backup. Normally, they'd have the agency van and at least another two to six people doing surveillance, and a cover reason for them to be hanging around the neighborhood.

There was also the possibility that Fuller wasn't coming home any time soon.

Teo stared out the window. "Milo's Pizza."

"You have a sudden yearning for sausage and pepperoni?" Elizabeth asked. "Third breakfast?"

He gave her a scornful look and leaned across the table. "I need cash, Jonathan, a lot of cash."

"I've got two hundred in cash, but if you've got a good reason, there's an ATM a block away."

"More would be better."

"Hold on," Elizabeth said. "What are you planning to do?"

"Blend in. I used to make pizzas for my uncle. For some cash under the table, the owner'll probably let me join the staff temporarily."

* * * * *

Steve Kowolsky looked up at the technician standing in front of his desk.

"If someone had wanted to obliterate any possibility of a DNA identification, they did a good job."

And there was only one reason to do so. Kowolsky dismissed the technician with a wave of his hand and picked up the phone.

Twenty minutes later, he was in the Director's office. Ben Smithson. Large white desk. Large white filing cabinet. No personal pictures. No comfortable couch. No wall decorations except a yellowed copy of the Constitution and framed letters of commendation from three presidents. Smithson looked tired and annoyed. "This had better be important."

Kowolsky leaned forward. "What if I told you that I believe an ECA agent is a mole who faked his own death?"

"How do you know that?"

"I was contacted by Jonathan Egan. They've been hunting for a mole for weeks. Here's a laugh: he thinks the mole is someone on the Intelligence Committee. Certain operations were blown by someone with inside information. Did you hear about two ECA agents being killed in New York last weekend? One of the bodies burned beyond recognition?"

"So?"

"So, the body was allegedly that of Nikolai Petrov, and it's so badly destroyed that DNA identification isn't possible. But his wallet untouched? His keys—his watch?"

"And?"

"And Petrov had access to all the data that was compromised. Egan probably told him they were searching for a mole. And then, suddenly, Petrov's dead, his body destroyed. I've suspected he might be a Russian agent for years now."

"Yes, suspicious." Smithson tapped long fingers on the desk. "This

211

is not to be discussed outside my office, do you understand?"

Kowolsky's face reddened. "Aren't you going to put out an alert for Petrov?"

"No. Not until I see Lewis. And Bradford."

"But," Kowolsky sputtered, "Petrov's a traitor."

"Is he? Maybe. You just don't like Russians."

"There was Afghanistan."

"Yeah, the ECA beat us out there because of Petrov and Egan. But you have to put that aside. If Petrov's a traitor, he'll be hunted down. I'm not saying he's not. But I'm not sure he is."

* * * * * *

President Thomas Lewis had half an hour between a meeting with the President of Mexico and a meeting with several Congressional members for some low-level arm twisting. On his desk was a copy of the latest report from his National Security Advisor on the political situations in Europe. The report on the Romanian elections had stopped him cold. Ion Georgescu, Mihai Cuza's chosen candidate, was considered strong enough that the Chinese were scheduling a meeting with him.

* * * * *

The Gulfstream was stocked with expensive liquors, a movie screen, and a flight attendant, a trim blonde with her hair tucked into a French twist—who served steak, garlic mashed potatoes, asparagus, and chocolate mousse. While he ate, Frick talked to Radu, who was waxing poetic on the beauties of Romania.

"The coast of the Black Sea, the monasteries in the north, the cities. And so much is unspoiled. In ten years, Romania will be the premier country in Europe. The Voivode will bring business into the country."

"I understand a Dracula theme park is being planned. That'll bring in the bucks." Frick drank single malt scotch with ice.

"The Voivode feels that dwelling on old folktales degrades our country. A theme park would be the ultimate insult."

"I don't see why. Mickey Mouse with teeth. No one in America thinks Mickey Mouse degrades us."

Radu laughed. "That's why I like you, Frick. You have a sense of humor. Not all of my associates do."

"Max's sense of humor is certainly limited."

"Gruesome violence can be funny. Like the scene in *Fargo*. Same with screaming. Then impaling. Talk about screaming. You know," Radu leaned forward, "I've seen two impalings. Gina Antonia and an informer in Romania. With her, we had to tape her mouth shut before we started. After all, we were in the middle of Manhattan. With this other guy, he screamed and moaned for hours."

"You displayed him?" Frick felt sick.

"Oh, sure. Half the point is to make an example. No one sees it, the lesson's lost. We put him just outside a village where there'd been talk against Cuza. Took him three days to die. No one in the village ever said another word against the Count. I should get Max to do a video when he impales Petrov."

"I thought that Cuza wasn't going to kill Petrov."

Radu shrugged. "All I know is Max told me this morning that he intends to impale Petrov. He didn't say when. Probably when Cuza gets tired of the woman."

"Christ," Frick drank the rest of his scotch in one gulp. So much for his self-congratulations at saving Petrov's life. Maybe Petrov would live another couple of weeks, but in the end, he wouldn't just die, he'd die in agony. "Whatever. I don't have to watch."

"You know viewing an impaling's like any new experience. Skiing. First few times are uncomfortable, then you appreciate the finer points."

"Maybe you're right." Frick never did get the hang of skiing. Every time he tried to get off the ski lift, he'd fall on his Goddamn face and then some ten-year-old kid would ski over his leg.

* * * * *

"Thanks for coming so quickly, Margaret." The President and Ben Smithson were both in the Oval. Lewis lounged in a stuffed armchair across from a white silk sofa where Smithson had already positioned himself. "Sit." Lewis pointed to the empty space on the sofa next to Smithson.

She slid into an armchair instead. Better to be further from Smithson.

"You should have told me, Margaret." Smithson grinned at her. "I'm speechless with admiration. I didn't realize just how devious you are."

She looked over at Lewis, who gave her a nod. "He guessed most of it, Margaret. I just filled in the holes."

"So, has Petrov accessed the Trojan yet?" Smithson asked.

She shook her head. "Still waiting. Someone tried but didn't complete the sign-on. My technical people don't know if it was Petrov or a hacker. Ross assures me that Petrov knew the system cold. So we still don't know what's happening over there."

"Damn, Margaret, what're you going to do if it doesn't work?"

"It's going to work. Everyone has a breaking point. Everyone."

She had been saying it over and over, to herself, to Lewis, to Ross, with the same conviction, but she was beginning to wonder.

Lewis cleared his throat. "We still need the intelligence from Cuza's computer, but in the meantime, I'm sending the Assistant Secretary of State to meet with Ion Georgescu. If Georgescu should become President of Romania, we'll need to have relations with him. As distasteful as that may be."

"I thought you were opposed to his election. The danger of Fascism in Central Europe."

"I'm still opposed, but what do you want me to do? If he's elected, I'll have to deal with him. And we might pursue other avenues of intelligence with Cuza."

"Such as?"

"Such as bringing in Carl Ford and interrogating him along with the undercover agent who's had direct contact with Cuza," said Smithson.

"The Trojan is the best chance to get information. I doubt Cuza would have filled in Ford on his plans, but he'll have everything in his data base." Margaret turned to Lewis. "Give me one more week."

"Three days," Lewis said. "That's when the Assistant Secretary is heading for Romania."

32

"Kolya." Alex's voice. She sat on the bed near him as he struggled up from another dark dream. "They brought food a few minutes ago. You have half an hour until you have to try the computer again." There was a tray on the bed with a noodle dish, several slices of bread, a pot of jam, and a tall steaming glass of a light amber color. A bland last meal for the condemned.

He pushed himself up onto an elbow. "Tea? They gave me fucking tea?"

"You're Russian. You're supposed to like tea."

He picked up the spoon, plastic again, as if he could fashion a weapon from a stainless steel spoon, scooped jam into the glass of tea, and stirred. If he was getting tea in a glass, he might as well drink it Russian style. "I haven't had tea in twenty years." Memories flooded in with the taste. He could almost hear the piano, a slow Mozart adagio. "My mother would give me tea with jam."

"Not Rifka?"

"She only drank coffee. That's how I picked up the habit. My first meal in America was a kosher hot dog and a sweetened cup of coffee, no milk."

"Really? For a fourteen-year-old kid?"

"She didn't know much about kids." He put the tea down and started on the wide egg noodles, cooked with butter and sugar. "She did her best, but I think she never knew quite what to do with me. Did you eat anything?"

She shook her head. "Unlike you, I've had reasonably regular meals

216

for the past few days. I'm not hungry. Are you going to tell me what's going on?"

"They want to get into the ECA computer network."

"Who's the tall, thin guy in charge?"

"You don't need to know." He drank more of the tea. His muscles ached, and he wondered if his temperature had risen during the day.

She frowned in his direction. "What the hell do you mean I don't need to know?"

"Is there aspirin?" he asked, both because he needed it and to divert her attention.

"In the bathroom." She returned with two white tablets, which she placed in his hand. "Let's try it again. If I'm going to die tonight, I'd like to know why."

"I'm trying to minimize the odds that you're going to die. The less you know, the less need to kill you." He swallowed the pills with a sip of tea.

"But you think that they'll kill you?"

"I think it possible."

"Then, why are you going ahead?"

"I'm hoping that you at least might survive."

"If they kill you, they have to kill me. So if you're convinced we're going to die, why are you giving the ring to the dark lord?"

"You're the one who convinced me to cooperate yesterday. Are you changing your mind?"

"You don't think other people will be killed because of what you're doing?"

He now was convinced that Cuza would get nothing but chicken shit from the computer system, but he could hardly say that out loud. "Intelligence is a game. A secret today is news tomorrow, and it's hardly worth dying to keep."

"If it were so unimportant, why did you let them torture you?"

"I am prepared to sacrifice my own life for my job. Not yours."

"You gave that Frick person Jonathan's and Teo's names."

Whether or not Jonathan had participated in the Trojan scheme, Kolya would never have identified him or Teo if he hadn't been

217

convinced that Frick already knew the names of the two agents who had worked with him and Gina. Frick probably even knew Jonathan from the days in the FBI. None of which he could explain to Alex in the presence of microphones.

"He's not going after Jonathan or Teo. It was simply a power game—to establish that I would answer anything he asked."

"A game? Of course. Just for the record, I hate it when you get all male-protective on me."

"You're taking care of me."

"You're ill. That's different. I'm not making decisions for you."

"Except about coffee."

"I'd let you drink goddamn coffee now if the guards had brought any and if you had insisted on making yourself sick. Tell me what's going on!"

He finished the noodles and the tea. He'd eat the bread later, if he lived. "I don't have the energy."

She studied his face, touched a hand to his forehead, and accepted that answer, gathering the tray off the bed as he rested again. He was better than the day before, but he still was far from well. The pain from his injuries, his leg, his back, the burns, was there but less intense. The fever was a nuisance, although his mind was clear enough to do what he needed to do.

They came a few minutes later. Stanescu carried crutches and three guards carried Galil MAR submachine guns, Israeli made.

Stanescu unlocked the manacle on Kolya's left wrist. Kolya straightened his arm, flexed the stiff muscles, sat up slowly, and eased first his left leg then the casted right leg over the edge of the bed. The room revolved in a blur of light, and Kolya's stomach lurched. He lowered his head towards his knees and breathed deeply.

"You've just been lying down too long." Stanescu checked his pulse. "I guess that answers whether you can manage on crutches."

"I can manage. Give me a minute." The dizziness subsided. He took the crutches, pulled himself to his feet, and balanced unsteadily.

They made an awkward shuffling parade down the hall, a guard and Stanescu in front, Alex at his side, two guards behind. Every few feet, he stopped to rest. Twice he leaned against the wall, and Alex slipped close to hold him up.

The stairs presented a new difficulty. It was a winding staircase, with a magnificent wooden banister. The chandelier he had seen on his arrival glinted overhead. He looked at Stanescu. "No elevator?"

"You can sit and slide down on your ass."

"No thanks." Apart from the loss of dignity, he had painful burns in awkward places. Maneuvering on crutches was bad enough. Bumping down marble stairs would be worse.

He handed one crutch back to Alex. She moved to a step below him. "If I fall, get out of the way."

"If you fall, I'll catch you."

With one hand on the banister, the other holding onto the crutch, he hopped one step at a time. Slowly, painfully, he made it to the bottom and received the crutch back from Alex.

They were in the front hall of the mansion. The procession moved through the living room to the office where they had been the day before.

Cuza waited in the armchair in front of the bookcase, a book on his lap. The executive chair at the desk with the computer was empty, and Kolya seated himself. He checked the room as he drank a glass of water that Stanescu pushed into his hand. Max was not present.

Cuza looked up. "Mr. Petrov, how are you feeling?"

"Well enough." He set the glass down and tapped the space bar to bring up the screen.

"Miss Feinstein, you can pull up a chair near Mr. Petrov or sit over on the couch. Mr. Petrov, does it matter to you?"

"I prefer her near me."

"Fine." Cuza waved with the graciousness of a good host. "Gheorghe, pull up a chair for the lady."

Gheorghe dragged a wooden chair next to Kolya's, and Alex sank down.

"You're sure?" she asked in tones so low only he could hear.

It was his last chance. He could tell Cuza what he suspected. He could double cross Margaret Bradford just as she had him. And then what? Cuza might not believe that he hadn't known all along and would kill them anyway. The opposite was just as possible—that if he gave Cuza real information, Cuza might keep them alive a little longer. But that was irrelevant. The slim chance of increasing the odds of survival was not reason enough. Nor was his anger towards Bradford. This could be the ECA's best chance to learn what Cuza was planning. If Kolya, out of anger and pique, didn't follow through, whatever Cuza was planning would go forward.

Cuza was a cold-blooded killer, and Kolya had the means to stop him. This would be his revenge against Cuza. If he lived, he'd take care of Bradford later.

"I'm sure."

He located the webpage and typed in Jonathan's user name and password.

At least today he wouldn't pass out. He was uncomfortable, but medical care, sleep, and food had helped.

He drank more water and waited. The first security question appeared on the screen.

Author of *War and Peace?*

He typed in Joseph Stalin.

Composer of *The Ring of the Nibelungen?*

He typed: J.R.R. Tolkien.

"Who wrote the questions?" Alex asked.

"Ross, I suspect." Ross, whose neck he intended to wring.

"Figures."

What was the last plague visited upon the Egyptians?

He typed: Gefilte fish.

Ringo Starr discovered the earth circled the sun. Combining hydrogen and oxygen created pizza. The first premier of the Soviet Union was Ronald Reagan.

"Only four left, Mr. Petrov," Cuza observed from across the room. "This must be very tiring for you. As soon as you're in, I want your hands away from the keyboard."

Minutes left to live? Beethoven composed *Mama Mia*; Dickens wrote *To The Lighthouse*.

He heard the click of a door opening. He didn't turn his head, but Alex did. He looked at her face and knew from her expression that Max was standing behind him. He took a deep breath. One more question before the bullet—unless they'd decided on a slower death.

The last question: Composer of Mozart's *Requiem?*

Appropriate. Behind him, he heard the sound of a round being chambered.

He typed: Mozart.

"Kolya, that's the correct answer," Alex said.

He hit enter. "Only in part. He died with it unfinished. It's just another joke."

The logo for the Executive Covert Agency computer network filled the screen. "I'm in." His voice showed his exhaustion. He leaned back in the chair, his hands clear of the computer, reached for Alex, and twined his fingers through hers. "I'm sorry I didn't buy you a diamond ring. I meant to." He wanted her focused on him, not on Max.

"Of all the things to regret, that wouldn't be the one I'd focus on." Her gaze stayed with him, but she'd seen the gun.

"I regret many things. I apologize for the ring."

"I love you, too." Her voice was calm, but she was trembling.

Cuza circled around the desk and looked at the logo. "Well, well, Mr. Petrov. We've wasted a lot of time getting to this point."

Kolya said nothing, his entire being focused on Alex. If they were going to be killed, he hoped they'd be shot simultaneously, so neither had to watch the other die.

* * * * *

Ross brewed a pot of coffee from his hidden stash of Starbucks, called a secretary, and bullied her into fetching him a turkey sandwich. He settled back into his chair, cradled his coffee, and waited for his lunch.

The secretary arrived and deposited the tray in front of him. He wondered if she were the one who sometimes dipped into his Starbucks supply but decided not to ask.

He ate with one hand, checking staff e-mails with the other. He was so engrossed in a suggestive e-mail from a field agent to a technician that he almost missed the computer's signal. Then he saw it. *Finally.*

He picked up the phone to dial Bradford's number.

Five minutes later, she peered over his shoulder at the monitor, as he popped gum and waited for the download to complete.

"It worked. I knew he'd break." Ross chewed rapidly.

"Can you get into Cuza's files yet?"

"Couple minutes."

"Will you be able to tell where Petrov is from the download?"

"Maybe. Probably."

"Try. I'll want a full report: everything on Cuza's system as well as possible locations for Mr. Petrov. I have to go find Ms. Owen." Bradford walked toward the door of Ross's office, her low heels clicking on the floor. "This remains highest level of classification until Mr. Petrov is recovered."

"Yeah, highest level, sure. By the way, Owen isn't in. Or Egan. Or Lorenzo. Egan's on vacation." Ross ticked off his fingers. "Lorenzo's sick. Owen took a personal day. Funny that half that team is out."

"Funny." There was not a trace of humor on her face. "Carry on, Mr. Ross."

* * * * *

Cuza swiveled the mouse and clicked. A list of ECA personnel appeared on the screen. He scrolled down the screen. "There you are, Mr. Petrov. Can't you afford a better neighborhood?"

Max was still behind them, but they weren't dead yet. Kolya turned his head to look at the screen.

Any lingering doubts disappeared. Kolya's name was listed under personnel, but the address was wrong, 1438 Cedar Street SE —a much poorer area of D.C. Teo and Jonathan, the two agents whom Cuza knew from New York, were also correctly named but with the wrong addresses. Bradford, who lived in Virginia, was given a Bethesda address.

Every other name on the list was fictitious.

"I earn ninety-five thousand a year. It doesn't go far in Washington."

"A man of your abilities? Surely you can do better than that." Cuza scrolled down the list of names.

"I like—used to like my job." Kolya was entirely truthful. "The last few days I've been contemplating a change of professions."

He glanced sideways at Alex, who had seen the screen. Her eyes widened and then narrowed. He tightened his fingers on hers, but he understood the look she gave him.

"How do I get any files on me?" Cuza returned to the main menu.

"It would be a working file. Click on operations, click on operational files, click on working files. You can search by keyword." Or at least that's what he did before.

Cuza followed the directions, and his name appeared at the top of the screen. He leaned his arm on the desk and read. "Well done. My father's background; my grandfather's background; my education; the informer. Who wrote this memo?"

"I did."

Cuza continued to read. "There's nothing but rumors about my current plans."

"That's what we knew as of the point I was captured," Kolya said.

"I had heard you had an informer in my group."

"You know we did. You had him impaled." Kolya remembered Vasily. Vasily. Eric. Gina. The list of people he had known and liked whom Cuza had killed. "I was going to New York to try to find a member of your group to recruit, but we had no one yet."

Cuza read the entire file. "Your name is mentioned, Emil. I would be careful about going back to the United States. And you're not, Max. Do you feel left out?"

"No," Max's voice came from directly behind Kolya.

"Well written. As I said, your abilities are being wasted, Mr. Petrov. It seems there isn't as much to worry about as I had thought."

Max asked, "Now?" and Kolya caught Alex's gaze again.

"Not now, Max. Mr. Petrov is being cooperative." Cuza looked down at Kolya. "I told you that if you cooperated, I would let you live. Relax."

All the tension flowed out of his muscles, and Kolya sagged, exhausted, against the side of the chair.

Cuza moved the cursor again. "How do I get into ECHELON?"

Kolya roused himself, wondering if the link was still there. "Technically, I'm not supposed to access ECHELON. They could have discovered the back door I've used and closed it. But I can tell you how I did it."

"Go step by step."

Kolya explained, and Cuza typed and clicked.

The ECHELON link was still there, still real. Kolya was relieved that for now he could give Cuza something that appeared to have substance behind it.

He closed his eyes. With the adrenaline rush over, he wasn't certain how much longer he could remain upright.

Across the room, Stanescu cleared his throat. "Petrov's about to pass out on you, Mihai, and I've got seven-fifteen. The kitchen staff will be upset if we are not at the table by eight. I understand that the meal is especially fine tonight."

"Yes, yes. I can play with ECHELON later. What happens if I sign off? Do we have to go through this ridiculous game again?"

"No. You'll get a simple password to input next time. The ECA computer will recognize the IP address and accept the password."

"Very good." Cuza printed the password and signed off. "Mr. Petrov, you look exhausted. You should go back to bed. Miss Feinstein, after you get your fiancé settled comfortably, would you care to join the doctor and myself for dinner? I'm aware that you haven't eaten. Mr. Petrov already had dinner."

Kolya, startled, looked at Alex. "She stays with me."

"She doesn't like you to make decisions for her. Miss Feinstein? It's completely your decision. There's nothing but dinner contemplated."

"You want me to leave him so you can kill him out of my presence." Alex gripped Kolya's hand.

Cuza threw up his hands in a gesture of amused annoyance. "What am I to do with the two of you? Miss Feinstein, if I wanted him killed, I'd do it now. Max is standing behind him with a cocked gun, in case you didn't know. If he were gone when you returned from dinner, you'd notice. Please join me."

"I don't think so."

"Fine. The invitation is open. From the look of him, Mr. Petrov will be asleep two minutes after he's returned to bed. You can watch him sleep or join us."

The trip back upstairs was slower and more painful. Kolya abandoned one crutch and let Alex support his weight with his arm across her shoulder. Even with her help, getting up the stairs was torturous. By the time he reached the top, he was dizzy. He collapsed against a wall and teetered on the verge of unconsciousness. One of the guards took the remaining crutch away and grasped his free arm.

Back in the bedroom, the guards allowed him to use the bathroom with the door open, although Alex helped him. He was past embarrassment. Afterward, he sat on the edge of the bed and swallowed another penicillin capsule while Stanescu checked bandages.

"His back's bleeding," Alex murmured.

"The bandages should be changed," Stanescu said. "Later tonight or tomorrow morning."

Lying down, Kolya felt marginally better. As his wrist was chained to the bed, he looked up at Alex and murmured, "I'm going to sleep. Maybe you should eat something."

He had changed his mind, realizing that keeping her with him wouldn't protect her. Whatever Cuza was up to, they needed to play for time. It couldn't hurt for her to have polite conversation with Cuza—it might help to keep them alive longer if Cuza saw her as a person and not just an enemy.

Also, she might learn something of use.

There was the other alternative. If he was be killed as soon as she was out of the room, she might survive if she were not with him.

"Your temperature's up again." She looked over at Stanescu. "I gave him aspirin before we went downstairs."

"The last hour took a lot out of him," Stanescu said. "He needs rest and quiet, which is a good reason for you to leave him alone."

Max and the other guards waited at the door.

She leaned down and whispered in his ear. "I'll go, you son-of-a-bitch. But if we get out of here alive, you're in really big trouble."

33

Jonathan slouched down in the back seat of the rented Toyota RAV4, a Yankee baseball cap pulled down almost to his eyes, while Elizabeth rustled a newspaper in front of her face. Teo, at the pizza restaurant, was two blocks south. If Fuller approached his apartment from either direction, they'd have him.

"We're conspicuous just sitting here." Jonathan put an arm around her. "If we were real, we'd be in closer contact."

Elizabeth removed his arm from her shoulder. "I've got an idea. Let's pretend we're a married couple that can barely stand each other. You probably know how to act that one."

"More or less." Jonathan accepted the rejection and crossed his arms. *Don't make assumptions based on one night together.*

It was early afternoon, and the street traffic had picked up. A young girl in her early teens chased two shorter boys across the street.

"Did you always want to be a spy?"

"I was planning a career as a tennis star."

"No kidding. How far'd you get?"

"I was on the high school tennis team in ninth grade. Won statewide championship."

"What happened?"

"Tenth grade. Anita Ellis."

"And who was Anita Ellis?"

"She was the stuck-up little twerp who beat me in the city quarter finals."

Jonathan laughed, and the corners of her mouth twitched upward as well.

* * * * *

Teo rolled out the pizza dough, just as he used to do in his uncle's restaurant on summer break. Someone at Fuller's address regularly ordered pizza. The woman at the register knew the man who answered the door of the address and who ordered the food—and in exchange for a finder's fee of two hundred dollars promised to alert Teo should he call or enter the restaurant.

With another two hundred dollars to the owner and fifty dollar bills all around, Teo was allowed to join the staff. Jonathan could spare the money. Kolya would have approved.

* * * * *

When Jonathan's phone rang, the name was concealed, but the number was familiar. He sat up straighter, pushed his hat back on his head, and shot a glance over at Elizabeth. She read his expression. "Shit." Then he answered with his name.

"Where are you, Jonathan?"

"I'm on vacation, Margaret. Where you sent me."

"In Manhattan, by any chance?"

She'd undoubtedly tracked his phone. "Of course. Just love the museums. And the theater."

"You wouldn't have other company on your tour of the Modern Art Museum, would you? Mr. Lorenzo or Ms. Owen?"

Teo and Elizabeth had turned their phones off and were using burners.

"Nope, haven't seen them. How's the plans for Kolya's funeral? Sorry I won't be able to make it."

There was a long moment of silence. "Just what is it you think you know, Mr. Egan?"

"I don't know anything."

She had to be seriously pissed. She always called him Jonathan. And Kolya was always Mr. Petrov. Kolya, for all his paranoia, may have been on the right track. Maybe Kolya had been chosen for this operation because she did regard a Jewish Russian immigrant with neither money nor political connections differently than she regarded the son of a politician.

"Let me tell what you think you know: that Mr. Petrov is alive and being held captive by Mihai Cuza."

"Why would I think that?"

"All right, Jonathan, enough. Am I correct that you, Ms. Owen, and Mr. Lorenzo are in New York to locate David Fuller? Good. Be sure you get him. He should have information on Cuza's stronghold that will be useful when we rescue Mr. Petrov."

"Damn. So Kolya did it, and you're ready to get him out."

"You mean that Mr. Petrov downloaded the Trojan, don't you? I'm not even going to ask how you know about it."

"Good. Because I'm not going to tell you, Mrs. Bradford."

"I understand that you must feel—misled."

"Misled? You betray my best friend, lie to me, and you think I feel misled? Jesus Christ, I don't have words for it."

In the seat next to him, Elizabeth pointed her forefinger at her temple and pushed her thumb down in a symbolic shot to the head.

"We had to get the information from Cuza's computer and do so quickly. I was convinced that there was no better way. Sometimes we have to make sacrifices. Mr. Petrov will no doubt be angry, but after he's rescued, he'll understand."

"Sure. He'll really understand your using Alex."

"Mr. Petrov hadn't given in, Jonathan. I'm truly very sorry about Miss Feinstein, but to save Mr. Petrov from dying under torture– it had to be done."

"Don't tell me you gave Alex to Cuza for Kolya's benefit! And don't tell me you didn't know Kolya wouldn't break easily!"

"This is beside the point, Jonathan. I am prepared to do everything possible to get Mr. Petrov out. Once he and Miss Feinstein are home, we'll discuss this."

She was right. The important thing was that Margaret was backing the rescue. "Okay. Lorenzo, Owen and I have Fuller's apartment under surveillance. Any chance that Ross could figure out Kolya's location?"

"He's working on that now, but Mr. Fuller's assistance would be helpful. I have a meeting in a few minutes to brief the Intelligence Committee on the success of the operation."

"Who's doing the actual extraction?"

"I'm requesting Seal Team Six—once we know the location."

"You tried asking Carl Ford?"

"Going to. You stay on Fuller."

"We're on him." Jonathan clicked the phone off and turned to Elizabeth. "You get to keep your job."

* * * * *

Frick had slept badly in Romania; he had slept badly on the plane, and he suspected he wasn't going to sleep all that well in his own bed. *Damn Carl Ford. Damn Mihai Cuza.* And most of all, damn his own miserable cowardly self. He stalked down First Avenue, his overnight bag slung over one shoulder, and checked the reflections in store windows out of habit rather than actual concern. He caught sight of his own image. A scary guy. The kind of guy who would let two people be tortured to death.

Close to his apartment, a druggie companion called Horse fell in beside him. "Where you been?" Horse was somewhere in his thirties, unwashed hair falling below his shoulders, a heroin addict who periodically gave Frick information on gangs and provided cover for his street identity. Horse hitched up his pants to somewhere below his hips and made an adjustment to his belt. "I've been to your place. Some woman was looking for you this morning."

"What woman?" Frick stopped and checked the street.

"Don't know who she was. Black—or Hispanic—good looking. She showed me a picture of you when I was coming out of your building. Thought maybe she was an old girlfriend. But I didn't say anything."

"Yeah, old girlfriend. Ended badly. Don't tell her you've seen me." Was it someone from the ECA or from one of the gangs he'd busted? He thought of calling Carl Ford, checking that there hadn't been any leaks, but he didn't really want to talk to Ford. Did he really care if the ECA had found out about Petrov?

Hell, maybe he'd call Jonathan Egan, tell him what's going on. He could do it anonymously and go into hiding. It wouldn't be so bad. The years in deep cover had taught him something. It wasn't like he had a wife or a family or anyone who gave a shit if he disappeared.

It was a noble thought, but he wasn't going to do it. He was sorry as hell about Petrov and Feinstein, but he wasn't interested in life on the run. It wasn't absolutely certain that Cuza would kill the two. Radu might be wrong.

Probably not.

It wasn't as if he and Petrov were buddies. Petrov would do the same if their positions were reversed. Why should he care if Petrov were killed—in a particularly nasty fashion?

If I were ordered to do what you've done, I'd resign.

Horse trotted next to him.

"What'd you want?" Frick asked.

"Thought we could get some dinner and hang. Watch some T.V." Horse halted in front of Frick's usual Italian restaurant.

And there was Alex Feinstein. If they killed Petrov, they'd kill her as well. *Look at him! Look what you've done to him!*

What the hell. He didn't do it. He didn't break Petrov's leg or hold him down or burn him.

He just tackled Petrov when he tried to escape and pumped drugs into him to keep him quiet. He just fed drugs to Feinstein and kidnapped her.

He was a hell of a human being.

Horse was still waiting. "Yeah, sure, let's order a pizza." He led the way into the restaurant.

He knew the woman behind the counter. He smiled at her and saw a smile in return. He saw something else; he saw her glance over his shoulder. He wondered why.

231

"The usual."

"One meat lovers. Want to wait?"

"Have it delivered. I'm too tired to hang around."

A young man paused from sprinkling Parmesan cheese onto a pie to glance at him. The face was familiar, but not from the restaurant. From somewhere else. The young man immediately glanced down again, and Frick felt a chill down his neck.

He'd only seen the guy once, but this young man could be Teo Lorenzo.

If he was right, Egan, Lorenzo, and God knows who else would be breaking down his door within a few minutes of his arrival home. They could try to take him now or when leaving the restaurant, but he was willing to bet against it. Too much of a danger that third parties could be hurt.

Don't panic. "I'm hungrier than I thought. Throw in some garlic knots and a second pizza with everything." Frick hoped his voice sounded normal.

He saw the calendar on the wall. Ironic. Less than a week since he had taken down Petrov. He fished in his pocket and found his wallet.

"Fifteen minutes," the young woman said.

"Great." He strolled out the front door, keeping the pace normal as he walked the two doors down to his building, Horse trailing him. He unlocked the front door of the apartment building, and they entered the hallway.

"Shit." Frick clapped a hand to his head, "I forgot beer. I'm out."

"Hell, we need beer," Horse said.

"Damn right." He handed his apartment key and his overnight bag to Horse. "Tell you what, you go up and wait for me. I'm going down to the corner to pick up a six pack."

"I'll come with you."

"Someone has to wait for the food. Oh, and a couple other people might drop by. You can start eating without me."

Horse had no objection. Frick waited for Horse to climb a flight of stairs before he headed to the back of the hall and through the emergency fire exit to the alley.

34

"*Feteasca Neagra de Uricani.* A Romanian classic." Her "host" held up a glass, demonstrating the light red liquid. "The grapes are grown in Moldavia and Muntenia. A black maiden grape. Some of the best wines in the world come from Romania, which has a reputation that extends back centuries. Legend has it that Dionysus was born in the region that the Romans called Dacia."

Alex balanced the globe between her fingers. The alleged doctor sat on the other side of the long table. The Count apparently thought he was charming her, the sadistic bastard. She gave him her best jury-winning smile.

The table could easily fit sixteen people but was set for three with white china rimmed in gold, crystal water glasses, and two wine glasses each.

Kolya was playing the situation in some way. Badly hurt and sick, he was playing the Goddamn spy game. She knew the people in the ECA, and she knew Kolya's and Jonathan's addresses. The personnel information was wrong, and Kolya had known it would be wrong. He was good at controlling his emotions but not that good. She hadn't seen even a flicker of surprise as the wrong names and wrong addresses popped onto the screen.

Kolya had sent her off to dinner with the enemy, and she didn't have a clue what she was supposed to be doing. *Son-of-a-bitch.*

She thought of him, unable to stay conscious but offering to have his leg broken—to protect her, and she softened.

She sampled the wine. Her captor was still going on about Alsace.

Stanescu, across the table from her, gave her a smile.

A young woman served them steaks, covered in a light brown sauce. Alex stared down at the hunk of meat on her plate. It looked like filet mignon, but she had never had less appetite. She picked up the steak knife next to her plate, sliced a small sliver, and tasted it. The meat was tender, almost melting on the tongue, but she couldn't eat.

She examined the steak knife as she laid it across the top of her plate. She looked up and saw *him* watching her.

"Please don't steal the cutlery." He elegantly dissected his own steak. "It would be very bad manners. If you misbehave, Mr. Petrov will pay the price."

"What could I do with a steak knife against guns?"

"As for yourself, I couldn't say. But I respect your fiancé's capabilities enough that I wouldn't want a knife in his hands."

"He can barely move." She picked up the wine glass and drank.

"Nevertheless. You aren't going to eat your steak? It's flown in from Chicago."

"I'm not much of a meat eater." She picked at the vegetables.

"You don't keep kosher, do you? I forgot that Jews have antiquated rules about food. You're a very odd sect."

The remark was infuriating in its anti-Semitism, even though she didn't follow the rules of *kashrut*, but she was too experienced an attorney to let him goad her into showing anger. "I like oysters and shrimp too much to keep kosher. But I've never been big on steak."

The Count put his knife and fork on the table and watched her. She returned his gaze.

"I just realized that I've never introduced myself. I am Count Mihai Cuza. It was rude of your fiancé to refuse to tell you my name."

"And how would you know he did that?"

"You know that we're listening to you and Mr. Petrov, and I know that you know, so let's not play games."

"And this isn't a game?" She gestured at the table. "You pretend that this is a social dinner. But you know, and I know that you know, I am here only because I'm your prisoner."

"I prefer the term guest." Cuza returned to his steak. "I know you think I'm a monster for what was done to Mr. Petrov, but it was an unfortunate necessity. He chose to be uncooperative, and he chose to be rude. He used some—shall we say—very colorful Russian phrases."

"Was that before or after you put a cigar on his genitals?"

"Both." Cuza reached for his glass and swirled the wine. "But as I was saying, Mr. Petrov was offered several options. He refused to be reasonable until your arrival. In any event, he and I are more similar than you like to believe. Suppose a terrorist had left a bomb in a public building. Mr. Petrov catches the terrorist and has twelve hours to find the bomb or innocent people will die. What do you suppose he would do?"

"I've heard this justification for torture. I don't accept it."

"You would let innocent people die rather than torture a terrorist?"

"In the first place you're assuming that the correct person has been caught. In countries that conduct torture, innocents are commonly tortured for information that they do not possess."

"I'll grant you that one. But what if you're sure?"

"There is no guarantee that a person who is tortured will talk—or will tell the truth."

"Perhaps. Mr. Petrov is, of course, an example of a person who requires more than physical pain to induce cooperation. But he is an exception. So you would be against torture, even if you knew it would save lives?"

"A society that tortures kills more people than terrorists. Besides, there are some things that civilized people simply don't do. Torture is one of them."

"I suspect your fiancé would disagree."

"Kolya wouldn't do it."

"Have you asked him?"

"I don't need to."

"You romanticize him. If our positions were reversed, he would do exactly what I've done. Mr. Petrov has physical attractiveness and intellectual abilities that blind you to what and who he really is. Have you ever asked him how many people he's killed?"

"He's only killed in self-defense."

"Everything that I've done to Mr. Petrov, I consider to be in self-defense."

A man with a gun entered and handed a slip of paper to Cuza. He glanced at it and motioned to the young woman who was collecting the dinner plates. "We'll have coffee in the library. I need to take a phone call." He pushed back his chair and rose. Stanescu stood and picked up his wine glass. Alex followed.

The library adjoined the dining room. Three walls were lined with leather tomes. Overstuffed red velvet chairs bordered cherry round tables under reading lamps. One larger, round table was set against the windows.

The two women who had served dinner set out coffee, cream, sugar, cups, and a plate of small pastries.

Stanescu settled in a chair with his wine glass. Cuza used a landline to place the call. Alex strolled to the closest bookshelf and took down a volume in Romanian with an engraved cover.

Cuza hung up and turned to Stanescu. "Ion wants to discuss the upcoming visit of the American Under Secretary of State. He'll be here tomorrow night to go over answers to possible questions." Cuza saw Alex watching him. He accepted a cup of coffee from one of the young women and helped himself to a petit four. "Ion is a candidate for office whom I am backing."

"Must be a pretty important candidate to rate the Under Secretary of State."

"I like to think so. Do you read Romanian? More similar to Italian or old Latin than to the Slavic languages of the less civilized nations that surround Romania. A melodic language."

She replaced the volume. "Unfortunately, I don't." She moved to another section of the bookshelf with English language books and ran a finger across the spines. Leather bound editions of Alexander Pope, John Milton, and Shakespeare. She took down the Milton.

Cuza remained several feet away. "You know the only difference between myself and Mr. Petrov is who and what we represent."

She opened the volume. It was dated from the early 19th century, and she carefully thumbed yellowed pages. "I know what Kolya represents." She found *Paradise Lost*, a paper clip in the margin marking the place. *Of man's first disobedience and the fruit.*

"I am attempting to create a stronger, more nationalistic Romania, one not dominated by the United States or its interests. There are people who don't want to see that happen. People who believe in an American empire."

"Kolya doesn't believe in empire building. Nor do I. We're both Democratic socialists." A paper clip wouldn't work as a weapon, would it? Then she thought of Kolya chained to the bed. She couldn't pick the lock, but he could.

"Interesting, and yet Mr. Petrov works for American intelligence. He may not set the policies, but his actions support them. Do you approve of America's policy towards Romania?"

"I don't know anything about it." If she picked up the paper clip and Cuza caught her, what would he do? Break Kolya's other leg? Kill her? "But if what you've done to Kolya is an example of how you intend to improve this country, then I worry for its future."

"America's policy is imperialism. What especially interests me is not Mr. Petrov's explanation of his job, but how you can accept both his work and him."

"That's between us."

"True." Cuza strolled back toward the coffee with an elegant shrug. "I just thought I'd point out the inconsistencies of your life as a progressive lawyer, a Democratic socialist, engaged to a man who embodies much of what she opposes."

"Kolya does a job that's necessary." It was the eternal question of how to fight evil without becoming what you fought. Intelligence agencies had stopped any number of terrorist attacks in the United States. She had her problems with Kolya's profession, but under the circumstances, she could only defend him.

Cuza's back was to her as the maid poured him another cup of coffee. Stanescu moodily regarded the empty bottle of wine. The guard near the door watched the young woman with the coffee.

The hell with it. She moved her hand smoothly across the book to turn the page and palmed the clip. *Now what to do with it.* She flipped another page, closed the book, and turned to replace it on the shelf. As she did so, her left hand slipped the paperclip into her front jeans pocket. She moved along the bookcase, studying the titles and holding her breath.

She stopped at a book entitled, *Vlad Tepes: Prince of Wallachia*. She pulled it from the bookshelf and flipped it open.

"You've heard of Vlad Tepes?" Cuza asked, approaching her. "I have the original in Romanian."

She looked at the illustration on the cover. "I don't know very much about him, except that he was a monster."

"A monster? He defended this country against invaders. He installed respect for law and order. His methods were no crueler than those of any of the other rulers of the day."

She'd had enough games for the day. She shut the biography and replaced it. "I'd like to go check on Kolya."

Cuza frowned at her. "There's no need. He's not a child."

"He's ill, and I'm worried. It's been several hours, and I'm not comfortable staying away any longer."

Cuza signaled a guard. "In that case, by all means. I don't want you uncomfortable. Anton will escort you to your room."

"Thank you." She forced a smile and turned to the guard. "I appreciate your consideration."

"One last thing. I apologize for the personal intrusion, but I do need to check that you haven't picked up any silverware—or anything else that Mr. Petrov might use as a weapon."

She turned back and composed herself. "You've been watching me. You've had a guard watching me. How could I have picked anything up? Is anything missing?"

"No. But I didn't arrive at my present position by taking chances. Maria," he gestured to the young woman, standing guard at the coffee and spoke to her in Romanian. "She'll just do a quick pat down."

Alex stood still, face expressionless, and stretched out her arms. Maria, with an apologetic air, patted her upper torso and then each leg in turn. The hands didn't hesitate at the pocket with the paper clip. Maria spoke to Cuza, who nodded, dismissing Alex and the guard.

35

Teo held out two boxes of pizza and a bag of garlic knots. Jonathan and Elizabeth, with guns in hand, stationed themselves to either side of the apartment door. With the palm of his hand, Teo knocked on the door holding his own gun, under the boxes.

A chain slid free; a bolt unlocked, and the door cracked open. Jonathan kicked the door wide. Teo dropped the food and aimed his weapon with both hands. Elizabeth, to his left, held her gun steady and level.

In the doorway, a youngish man with shoulder length hair gaped at them.

Elizabeth shoved him inside the apartment and then against the wall, while Jonathan checked the bedroom and bathroom, and Teo, the kitchen.

"Clear," Teo called.

"Shit." Jonathan returned to the living room where Elizabeth still held the man motionless, hands and legs in position against the wall. Jonathan patted him down.

"You Frick's friends?" the man asked.

Jonathan turned him around. "Frick?"

"Yeah, Frick. He told me to come up and wait for the food and some friends." He showed fear and confusion.

"Who're you?"

"Horse." Horse was not as young as he had appeared initially, and he smelled from too much time on the street and too little time in the shower.

Teo came out of the kitchen. "Looks like he hasn't been here for a few days."

"You guys cops? Frick didn't tell me nothing about no party with no cops."

"Not cops," Elizabeth said. "We have business with Frick."

With a gesture of disgust, Jonathan holstered his weapon. "What did Frick tell you about a party and when?"

Horse's hands sank to his side. "After we left the restaurant, Frick said he'd forgotten the beer. So I said I'd come up and wait for the food, and he said there'd be a couple more people. A party." He peered past Elizabeth at the two boxes of pizza. "And I'm hungry."

"Oh hell, why not." Teo retrieved the boxes.

Horse selected a slice, headed for the couch and flipped on the television.

"Goddamn it. He must have spotted me. We should have taken him in the restaurant," Teo said.

"Not with civilians around, boy wonder," Elizabeth said.

"Shut up. I told you not to call me that," Teo looked at Jonathan. "We can check the nearby streets."

"It's been fifteen minutes," Elizabeth said. "He's long gone by now."

"Shit," Jonathan said. "Shit. Shit. Shit." The television was blaring, and his head was ringing. He strode to the couch, grabbed the remote, and turned off the sound. Only then did the faint sound of a telephone register. "Is there a landline?" he asked Horse.

Horse pointed to the far side of the room.

"Answer it," Jonathan commanded.

Horse picked up the receiver. "Yo? " He covered the receiver with his hand. "Any of you named Egan?"

"Yeah." Jonathan identified himself.

Horse held out the receiver. "It's for you."

"Enjoying the pizza?" The voice was unfamiliar. "I ordered extra. I figured you'd show up with friends."

"Fuller?"

"Call me Frick. Especially in front of Horse. He's a moron, but I don't want him knowing my real name. Are you there to arrest me?"

"No. We're here to ask you some questions about a friend who's disappeared."

"Your friend named Petrov by any chance?"

"So you do know where he is."

"Yeah, more or less. Okay, Egan, here's the scoop. Cuza's a source. He gives us information on weapons and terrorists coming into the country—and I was under orders to protect him."

"Even if that means killing American operatives."

"Things kind of got out of control. Look, I don't like what's already happened to Petrov and his girlfriend. I don't like what's going to happen to Petrov, and it'd be just fine with me if you rescue him and his girlfriend."

"You offering to help?"

"I guess. I thought about calling you to fill you in, and I would have, too, except I don't want to spend the next twenty years in an eight-by-ten cell."

"I can't offer you immunity."

"Hell, Egan, I know that, but I don't want anything I do to help Petrov come back and bite me in the ass. I don't want to see you or the kid or the woman, whoever she is, on the stand, testifying against me. Just asking you to give me a jump ahead of any arrest."

"You've got a jump if you want it. That it?"

"One last point. The only thing I'm more scared of than prison is Mihai Cuza. We try to pull this off and fail, he's going to shove a stake up my ass and leave me for the vultures. Which is what he's planning for your friend."

Jonathan felt a cold chill down his back. "How much time we got?"

There was a pause. "I don't think Petrov's in immediate danger, Egan. You should know that he broke."

"And your point is what?"

"My point is—I'm taking a risk here."

"We all are."

"Okay. Don't eat all the pizza."

Five minutes later, Frick entered with a six-pack of Paulie Girl.

He looked at Jonathan and nodded a greeting. Then Frick jerked his head at Horse. "Out."

Horse, with a frightened look at Frick and at Jonathan, scurried to the door.

The door closed behind Horse, and Frick swung around to face the other occupants of the room, who regarded him with suspicion. He took a seat on the couch, extracted a beer bottle from the pack, twisted off the cap, and took a swig. "Egan, I know you and Lorenzo." He looked at Elizabeth. "I don't know you."

"Owen."

"You got a first name."

"Yes."

"Owen, then. You guys eat?" Frick selected one of the meat slices. "Take a beer, Egan, don't be a stick in the mud. You, too, Owen, Lorenzo."

Elizabeth didn't stir. Teo glowered. Jonathan thought about it and strolled over to the coffee table to pick out a beer. "Can we get down to business?"

"Okay, sure." Frick took a large bite. "I can talk and eat."

"Do you know where they are?"

"Yes and no. Romania somewhere. Don't know the town or the coordinates. I do know my way around the house and what room they're in. Even more important, a lot of the guards think of me as a friendly, so I might be able to get to Petrov before they realize a rescue is in the works."

"I still don't get how an FBI agent could get tangled up with Cuza." Jonathan sat down on the couch.

"Orders. And I was stupid. By the time I realized that Cuza was a deranged lunatic, I was in too deep." Frick took another swig of beer.

"Carl Ford gave the orders?" Jonathan asked.

"Yeah, the asshole. Told me to inform on Gina Antonia. I told him what would happen to her." Frick gave a visible shudder. "He thought Cuza wouldn't kill an American agent in the United States. Well, he was fucking wrong. Everything after that was to cover his ass. And, to be honest, my ass."

Jonathan had no sympathy. "What kind of shape is Kolya in? Can he walk?"

"Walk? He can barely sit up. He was shot in the thigh, and then they broke his leg and kneecap. They tortured him for days. People call you Jon or Jonny?"

"Jonathan." Jonathan sucked in a sharp breath. "Did you help torture him?"

"Nah, I just helped catch him. I knew what they'd do to him, but since I didn't have to take part, I didn't think about it. But when I saw him.... You don't see it, you can fool yourself. It's for a good cause; we need information. If he's not giving up information, then he's got to be persuaded. All the usual crap." Frick's words trailed off. He selected another slice. "Great pizza. You agree, Teo?"

Teo stared back stonily.

"You were saying?" Jonathan asked.

"As I was saying, Petrov broke, but I left before Cuza got what he wanted. Still, I did what I could to keep your friends alive. Then on the flight home, this asshole tells me Cuza's going to have Petrov impaled. Not right away, but still...." Frick raised the bottle to his lips, drank, and wiped his mouth with the back of his hand. "You know, when I stopped Petrov from escaping, he beat the shit out of me. He'd probably kill me now without thinking twice about it. But I got to where I half liked the bastard. And his girlfriend, too. So when we leaving?"

"Not sure yet," Jonathan said. "I'm waiting for word. You said you could help with the location."

Frick finished off his beer and twisted the cap off a new bottle. "It's stuck on the side of mountain. Used to belong to some big mucky muck in the Securitate. Can't be that many places in Romania that fit the description. You can probably use satellite images to find the place."

"That'll help." Jonathan dialed Mark Leslie, who promised to check and get back.

36

Margaret seated herself directly across from Carl Ford in the usual White House conference room and directed her words at the President. "My technical staff just completed a download of Mihai Cuza's computer files. Software installed at a number of nuclear power plants around the world had been set to give misleading readings about core temperature and other safety measures. Some plants may have been able to avert disaster by using the analog back-up systems, but some of the plants undoubtedly would have had melt-downs." She looked down at the list in front of her. "In France, Romania, the United States, Japan, Russia. Eight of the plants are in this country. Apparently the list sent out by Ms. Antonia was incomplete."

"How was it done?" Smithson asked.

"All of the plants on the list recently updated their software. A firm in France designs the software for nuclear power plants world-wide. Cuza's people infiltrated the French firm."

"But why?" Ford was gasping.

Hadn't he known what Cuza was doing?

She glanced at Smithson. "Ion Georgescu has been railing against the building of nuclear power plants in Romania—power plants that are not needed by Romania but receive financial backing from countries like Italy that want to purchase the excess power. A series of accidents would discredit the nuclear program and discredit the government's bowing to foreign pressure."

"But why would he attack nuclear power plants around the world?" Manion asked. "In the United States?"

244

"Camouflage and money. It would look like a world-wide problem with nuclear power and not traceable to Cuza. He also does have a large financial interest in a company that cleans up nuclear disasters. He would make billions."

She cast a quick sideways glance at Carl Ford. His right eye was twitching. Good. She wanted him to stew for a few minutes.

"Congratulations, Margaret." Lewis nodded his head. "We need to notify all of the affected countries, don't we?"

"Not until we get our people back. We've got a couple days, anyway."

Ford cleared his throat. "What are you talking about Margaret?"

She'd had enough of the game and turned to Lewis. "I want this man placed under arrest and held incommunicado until further notice."

"Margaret," Ford sputtered. "What the hell?"

She had not a drop of pity. "Carl, you've fed information to Mihai Cuza that has led to the deaths of two of my agents and the kidnapping of another. I believe that comes under the heading of treason and espionage."

"We do know your role in Gina Antonia's death and in the kidnapping of Kolya Petrov," Lewis said to Ford.

Suddenly Corey Manion came to life. "What are you talking about? I thought Petrov was dead!"

"Mr. Petrov's not dead. He was kidnapped by Mihai Cuza," Margaret said. "Mr. Petrov's death was faked by someone working for Carl. Mr. Petrov has been held prisoner since last Friday."

"Since last Friday?" Corey asked. "Jesus, haven't you done anything to get the man out?"

"Couldn't be done sooner." She didn't elaborate. "Right now, I have a team intercepting David Fuller, who was Carl's go-between with Cuza."

All the color drained from Ford's face.

"Does Egan know?" Corey was recovering from the news. "Petrov's his friend. God, he was so upset the last time I saw him."

"No. He knows that Fuller has something to do with Petrov's

death—and that's all." She had no reason to tell anyone that security at the ECA had been breached. And it was no longer important. Egan was tracking down one of Petrov's kidnappers.

"Why, Carl?" Lewis asked Ford.

"That's not critical at the moment," Margaret interrupted. "The important thing now is to get Petrov out. His girlfriend, I believe, is also with him, isn't that right?"

"Alex Feinstein? How'd she get involved in this?" Corey asked.

"I told Carl of Mr. Petrov's relationship with Miss Feinstein—who was devastated at the news of Mr. Petrov's "death." A day later, she disappeared. I had asked for Seal Team Six to do the extraction." She turned to Lewis.

Smithson cleared his throat. "Actually, Margaret, there's a bit of a change in plans."

Lewis avoided her gaze. "I've decided that a forceful extraction from Romanian territory could create some international—um—difficulties."

Margaret's jaw dropped. "What? What did you just say?"

"There's the base on the Black Sea in Romania, which gives us access to Eastern Europe and to the Middle East. And, Romania is in Europe, and Europeans look askance at the United States flexing muscle on their territory. We can't risk the loss of the base; we can't have a showdown with the rest of Europe. In other words, no Seal Team Six. No extraction team," Lewis said. "I'm not sending anyone. And you're not either."

"You promised me every resource would be available to get Petrov out once he did his job. He did it. We need get them both out now, before they're murdered."

"Here's the thing." Lewis toyed with his water glass. "The Under Secretary is going to Romania to meet with Georgescu. We can't afford to affront Georgescu by mounting an assault on one of his main advisors and supporters. I appreciate the job that Petrov did, but overall security for this country has to be my first consideration."

"Wait a minute," Carl Ford was beginning to revive. "Did his job? You mean Petrov was supposed to be captured?"

"A Trojan horse. Congratulations, Carl," Smithson said dryly. "Both you and Cuza fell for the oldest trick in the world."

Carl laughed. It was a grim laugh, but still qualified as a laugh. "A Trojan horse? You knew that there was a leak, and you manipulated me. Petrov didn't know?"

"He didn't." Margaret nodded.

"So, this was all an elaborate game?" Corey asked.

"I wouldn't call it a game," Margaret said. "Just a necessary maneuver."

"Let's talk about national security," Ford said. "Cuza's helped the FBI prevent terrorist attacks on U.S. soil, and you, Mr. President, by setting the ECA on him, threatened a valuable source of information. Okay, so I gave Cuza information that cost the lives of several ECA agents. But the information he gave me saved thousands of American lives. I had no idea that he was planning an attack on American nuclear power plants."

"Just the power plants of other countries?" Margaret asked.

"I had no reason to believe that he would do anything of the sort. I was assured that his only interest was in a peaceful political transition in Romania. He gave me good information, Margaret. Let's talk about MANPADS. You know that shipment that was intercepted in Newark? I received the information for that raid from Cuza."

"He gave you shit," Margaret said. "The man who imported those missiles was probably someone Cuza wanted out of the way."

"You may be right, Margaret," Smithson said. "Still, Carl did stop dangerous weapons from entering the country."

Margaret swung to stare at him. "Cuza was planning to sabotage American nuclear power plants."

"Well, he planned to have the software go haywire," Smithson reminded her. "All of the plants have back-up systems. He was throwing a scare into us, nothing more. There's something to be said to keeping him as a source, especially if Carl reports directly to me."

"Are you crazy?" Margaret said emphatically. "Cuza will know what happened the minute the plants are shut down. He's not going to keep supplying us information. And Carl should spend the rest of his miserable life in prison."

"Not necessarily." Smithson said. "A routine check of the software uncovered the problem. No reason Cuza has to know that we're on to his plan. No reason he has to know that we know about Carl. And between Carl and your Trojan horse, we'll keep tabs on him."

"You see, Margaret," Lewis said apologetically, "With Georgescu poised to win the election, we can't overtly go against Cuza."

Smithson took over. "Your people are good at small, covert operations, like this one. I'll give you credit, Margaret, you did come up with a hell of a plan. But the CIA has the resources to integrate the information from Cuza into a wider view of what's happening in Europe. I can coordinate what Carl learns from Cuza with what you've learned from the Trojan horse. I'll want all the computer downloads, too, when you get a chance."

Margaret pulled the pitcher of water over and poured herself a glass. At least her hand wasn't shaking, and she showed no outward sign of her sense of betrayal and fury. "And Petrov? Mr. President, isn't there any sense of loyalty or obligation to a man who's risked his life for this country?"

"Petrov didn't volunteer to do this, did he?" Smithson said. "It's not as if he was promised anything going into this."

"Maybe not, but he did his job. I suspect he also held out against torture out of a sense of duty and loyalty. He was tortured, wasn't he?" She turned to Ford.

"Oh for God's sake, Margaret," Smithson said. "We know the man was tortured. We know that they used his girlfriend to get him to break. We ask men to die in battle for their country. Sometimes sacrifices have to be made."

"Cuza's going to find the Trojan," Margaret said. "You can find any virus if you look hard enough. And your little plan of keeping him as a source will disappear. He'll know we found out about Carl. And if Petrov's still alive at that point, Cuza will impale him. Won't he, Carl?"

"Probably."

"At least we can try to get Petrov out." Corey waded in with support.

"We don't even know if he's still alive," Smithson said. "We could be sending a team to rescue a dead man. We could be disrupting an important relationship with the possible future President of Romania and destroying a valuable information source for nothing."

"Look," Corey said. "I hate to tell you, Mr. President, how this would look if it came out? You set up a man to be captured and tortured, and then you abandon him?"

"We would risk losing every field operative we have," Margaret put in. "I can't even begin to tell you what this would do to morale."

Lewis looked directly at Corey. "If any word of anything that happened in here is breathed outside this room, there will be charges under the National Security Act. Only a few technical staff at the ECA and the people in this room know just what happened. For everyone else, Kolya Petrov died honorably in the service of his country and is being buried tomorrow."

"And Alex Feinstein?"

"She's a defense lawyer handling controversial cases. There's no way to tie her disappearance in with Petrov's death."

"There are people who suspect that the body being buried tomorrow isn't that of Nikolai Petrov, Mr. President," Margaret said.

"Yes, Kowolsky suspects," Smithson said. "Do you know what he thinks? He thinks that Petrov was a mole who faked his own death."

"Kowolsky's a lunatic, and he's prejudiced against Mr. Petrov's nationality."

"No doubt," Smithson agreed. "And there's a little professional jealousy in there. Petrov and your other boy, Egan, beat out Kowolsky on at least one occasion. But still, there it is. If anyone comes out with the preposterous notion the President of the United States would deliberately set up an agent to be captured, the President will reluctantly give out the information that Petrov betrayed his service and his country."

"In the name of God. We can't just abandon him!"

Lewis shook his head. "I'm sorry. I know you feel badly about Mr. Petrov and Ms. Feinstein. I do, too. But I've made my decision."

37

Rifka was scolding again. He'd been in another fight, and she was screaming in Russian that he was a hoodlum, that he didn't appreciate all she'd done for him. "You're going to wind up a member of the *vorovsky mir.*"

The *vorovsky mir*, the underground Thieves World in the old Soviet Union, had been Kolya's probable destination had Rifka not brought him to the United States. But she had, and he would not repay her by becoming a criminal. Still, old habits were hard to kick. In the *dyetskii dom*, he had learned to defend his person or his honor with his fists.

"Join up with me." Sitting across from him at the Ukrainian restaurant on Second Avenue in Manhattan, Dmitri wore a tailored suit from London and a gold pinky ring with a large diamond. "I'll make you rich."

"It's all right. You were having a nightmare." Alex's voice reassured as he woke, sweating. The room was dark, as was the sky outside, but a little light filtered under the door from the hall and through the window.

"What are you doing?" His voice was thick with sleep and fever.

"Watching you. Wouldn't you be more comfortable on your side?"

"Maybe." Awake, he was aware of all his various aches and pains and of the chain attaching his wrist to the bedrail. Lying on his back hurt, but he had developed a cramp in his shoulder and arm from staying in the same position for too long. It was just a question of deciding what position hurt the most. At the moment, it was his back. He turned on his side.

"Who's Dmitri?"

He must have been talking in his sleep, not a good habit for someone in his profession. "He was my best friend in the *dyetskii dom*, the boys' home where I lived before Rifka adopted me. I taught him to play jazz, and he taught me how to fight."

"You needed to know how to fight when you were in an orphanage?"

"From time to time." He remembered Yelseyev, who only left him alone after Kolya broke his nose.

"Is Dmitri still in Russia?"

"No. He's in America. In a federal prison. I put him there."

She studied him for a long moment. "It must have been difficult."

"Yes." He appreciated that she didn't ask for details.

She leaned across his shoulder to check the back of his shirt. "You're bleeding."

"I'm all right."

"Sure you are." She slid out of bed and disappeared in the general direction of the bathroom. He closed his eyes until she returned and began to peel the bandages on his back.

"What're you doing?"

"Cleaning you up."

"No need."

"Did they hurt your head?"

"No."

"Good." She smacked him lightly on his ear. "Stop the tough act. You need help, and you can accept gracefully."

"You don't have to resort to violence. I'm not feeling particularly tough." He closed his eyes and relaxed his muscles. She gently began to sponge the welts with a warm cloth. Her hair was damp and smelled of lilac. Despite the discomfort from her efforts, he felt a warm glow at her presence. "Did you enjoy dinner?"

"Not especially."

He came awake with concern. "Did anyone touch you?"

"A maid checked me for weapons. Other than that, no." He felt the swish of the washrag. "Your back is a raw mass, and some of areas look infected. I should have done this earlier. How's the leg?"

251

"Could be worse." One spot was particularly sore, and he pulled away from her. "Not so hard."

"Sorry. Almost done." She made a trip to the bathroom to wash out the rag. "Mihai Cuza told me that you're a pawn of American imperialism."

"I try not to be. Did he try to seduce you?"

"Not overtly. He did try to impress me with his knowledge of wines and literature."

"Were you impressed?"

"I liked the wine." She resumed her work. "The American Under Secretary of State is meeting with someone named Ion. Do you know who that is?"

"Ion Georgescu. Cuza's candidate for President of Romania. He must have come up in the polls. Claims that Romania is being ruined by gypsies, Jews, and foreigners. Especially Jews. The usual conspiracy theories."

"There are still Jews in Romania?"

"Between nine and seventeen thousand. I don't know how personally anti-Semitic Cuza is, but he has no problem with it from Georgescu. Or Max." He remembered Max cursing him as a Jew during torture sessions. "Is Cuza meeting with Georgescu?"

"Yes. Here. Tomorrow night."

"I suspect we won't be introduced." Could Georgescu's visit impact the two of them? Quite apart from Georgescu being disdainful of Jews, he wouldn't want any involvement in the holding of Americans. But if Cuza wanted to get rid of them before Georgescu's visit, he would have already done so. Most likely, they'd simply be kept out of sight. And, if busy with Georgescu, Cuza would be less likely to be on the computer, exploring the possibilities of the ECA's computer network.

Alex finished cleaning and returned the cloth to the bathroom. On her return, she picked up a tube from the dresser. "Antibiotic cream."

"It can wait until tomorrow. It's late."

"No, now. You need to put it on the burns as well. That's your job." She squirted some on his hand, sat on the bed behind him, and gently began to apply the cream to his back while he dealt with the front. "You could use a shave, too, you know. The alleged doctor let me shave you last night, but he didn't leave the razor."

"Perhaps I'll grow a beard." A long blond beard. He could pass for a Viking.

"Beards scratch."

"You'll get used to it."

"No beard, Kolya." She touched an infected spot, and he moved involuntarily. "I know it hurts but stay still!"

He took a deep breath, and she continued to apply the antibiotic cream. "Are you going to be this bossy after we're married?"

"Only when you get yourself hurt."

"I didn't do this to myself."

"I know." She finished and pulled his shirt down. "You're still very hot. Have you had any aspirin in the last four hours?"

"No."

She offered aspirin, water, and the bedpan. He accepted the offerings in appropriate order and with reasonable grace. He settled himself back down, and she covered him with a sheet and blanket.

"Okay, you can sleep." She leaned over and kissed his forehead in an almost maternal gesture.

"You too."

"I can't." She slid down under the covers, still wearing the jeans and tee shirt from the day of her kidnapping, and faced him. "Not here."

He reached over to touch her cheek and settled his arm around her waist. She pulled the blanket up over her shoulders.

"You slept last night."

"Only towards dawn. When I was so tired I couldn't keep awake anymore."

"Think of something pleasant. A book. Music. You've been under stress before. What do you do the night before a trial?"

"Work."

"That's not true."

"Okay, I do sleep, but it's different. I'm not afraid for my own life or for the life of someone I love. How do you do it?"

"One of the advantages of injury and fever."

"When you were first captured—could you sleep?"

"When they'd let me." He started to drift. "I'd run musical pieces through my mind. Bill Evans. Ellington." He let his eyes close, but he could feel the tension in her body. "Run the plot of a Jane Austen novel through your head." He disliked Jane Austen almost as much as Alex loved her. Still, this was not the time to compare taste in literature.

Alex pushed at his arm. "Move. It's uncomfortable."

"Sorry." He tried to interpret the message. Too intimate under the circumstances? The arm around her waist was to offer comfort and love. Was she uncomfortable even with that?

When he moved his arm under the blanket, she slipped something small into the palm of his hand. He explored the object with his fingers. It was a paper clip. She had been trying to maneuver his arm so she could slip him the paperclip unobserved by any cameras. What did she think he could do with a paper clip? If she had handed him a gun, well, that would have been something. Still… it wasn't a weapon, but maybe he could get the chain off his wrist.

Under the bedcovers, he unfolded the clip until it was a long, straight wire. His left wrist was under the pillow. He slid his right hand under as well and twisted the wire into the lock of the manacle. He felt the lock click and flexed his arm to work out the kinks.

Wait. What was he thinking?

His objective now was to keep both of them alive long enough to be rescued, and doing so required that he not do anything foolish. Crippled as he was, he couldn't escape from a house filled with armed men. It would be more comfortable to leave his arm free, but it would be stupid. They were under constant surveillance. All he needed to do was move in his sleep, and they'd know he wasn't chained. Alex would suffer, and he'd lose the opportunity to free himself when there might be a reason to do so.

There had to be a rescue planned. There had to be. However devious Bradford might be, she would never deliberately abandon an agent.

The greatest danger to their lives would be when the Trojan was discovered or when a rescue attempt was underway. If the Trojan was discovered, they were dead. However, if a rescue was attempted, he would not want to be chained and helpless, an easy target for any guard ordered to eliminate the prisoners. That would be the time to free himself.

He moved his left wrist back into the manacle and clicked it locked again. With his right hand, he felt for the seam near the wrist in the left sleeve of his shirt. Carefully, he pushed the straightened clip inside the seam, leaving the tip bent on the inside of the cuff. He checked the outside of the shirt with his fingers. Hopefully, it wouldn't show.

"I'm sorry," he said. "The timing was wrong."

"It's okay. It'll get better."

She understood that he intended to wait to free himself.

"It will. What kind of diamond ring would you like? I still need to go shopping."

"For God's sake, Kolya, forget the damn diamond. Just tell me you love me."

He kissed her hair and told the truth. "I love you more than life."

38

The door leading from the lobby to the offices of the ECA was securely locked and required a security code and a handprint to open it. Corey examined unlabeled buzzers and the security cameras. Finally, he shrugged and hit all the buzzers at once.

"Can I help you?" A young woman's voice.

He cleared his throat. "Corey Manion to see Margaret Bradford."

Five minutes later the door opened, and a man extended a hand. He was pleasant looking with brown hair and a slight Southern accent. "Marty Davis. Ms. Bradford asked me to escort you to her office. An honor to meet you, Senator."

Corey shook hands and followed him past a receptionist.

They rode the elevator to the top floor. Corey followed Marty down another corridor, through another security door. Marty tapped on a closed door, shook hands again, and headed off.

"Come in." Margaret closed a file on her desk as he entered and seated himself across from her. "To what do I owe the honor of this visit, Senator?"

"What're you going to do, Margaret?"

When he left the Intelligence Committee Meeting, he hadn't known what he would do. He just knew that what had happened was wrong and that he had to speak to Margaret Bradford.

She picked up a folder. "This is the hard copy of Mr. Petrov's personnel file. Since he's "dead," the file's closed. If I recommend Mr. Petrov for a posthumous medal, the President would approve it. Ironic, isn't it? I wonder if it would be awarded before or after he

256

actually dies. This file," she waved at a large red well on her desk, "is the download of everything significant we have so far from Mihai Cuza's computer. Ross printed it out for me." She slapped the folder back down on the desk in front of her.

He didn't know her well, but he'd never seen her like this.

"For God's sake, Margaret, snap out of it. Two people's lives are at stake."

Her voice rose. "Damn it, Corey, I've just been given a direct order by the President of the United States."

"It's a wrong order." His own voice rose. "If I were President, I'd never abandon our people. Never."

"Maybe you'd be a better President. Maybe not. In either case, it's immaterial. You're not the President."

"You're not in the military. You can't be court-martialed if you disobey."

"Are you suggesting I directly defy the President?"

"It's the right thing to do. You know it is."

"I couldn't agree more."

"So?"

"I'm not doing it."

"You're worried about losing your job? Is that it?"

She shook her head. "I'm close to retirement, Corey. But this agency. Damn it, Corey, I've spent ten years building it. I have good people who take risks and get results. Ben Smithson wants to destroy the ECA. If I disobey a direct order, he'll win."

"Hell, he's already won, didn't you hear him? The ECA will become just another department of the CIA. If you abandon Petrov, you'll going to lose your greatest asset—your people. Don't give me this crap that no one knows, either. Egan's suspicious—he'll find out."

"He already knows." She opened the file in front of her. "Egan would go on his own, if he knew where Petrov is being held, but he doesn't."

"Was there a location in the download?"

"Maybe. It's possible we may have located Cuza from satellite pictures and information in the file, and it's also possible that the coordinates are on page ninety of this file. But if I give Egan this information, I'll be in violation of the National Security Act. Do you understand the position I'm in?" She studied him. "I have to go speak to Mr. Davis for a few minutes, Corey. Please wait here." She rose and walked to the door. On the threshold, she paused to look back at him. "I'll be exactly ten minutes."

Corey walked around the desk, sat in her chair, opened the file, marked Eyes Only, skimmed to page ninety, retrieved his phone, and snapped a picture. When Margaret returned exactly ten minutes later, he was back in his chair.

"I hope you weren't bored," she said.

"No, not really. So, what are you telling your people?"

"Officially, Mr. Petrov is dead. Certain agents are due vacation time. Mr. Egan. Mr. Davis and Mr. Menendez are also due, and there are two other agents already with Mr. Egan. I have no control over how any of them spend their vacations. Do you understand, Corey? Do you further understand that no information regarding Mihai Cuza's whereabouts has been disclosed by this agency—that such disclosure would be in violation of federal law?"

"Why are you playing games?"

"We all play games. I am not going to compromise this agency. If Mr. Egan is questioned as to the source of his information, he can with truth deny that it originated with me. You can sit there and tell me to risk the existence of the ECA and my own position while you stay safe and secure in your nice cushy Senatorial seat. I'm glad you feel so strongly, but you can put your money where your mouth is, Corey. Now it's up to you." She scribbled on a note pad and held the piece of paper in the air. "Egan's cell phone number. Remember what this will mean. You could go to prison."

Prison. Disgrace. The possible end of his political career versus two people's lives.

Corey took the paper from her hand. "Any final instructions?"

"Tell Egan not to get caught. And we never had this conversation, Senator."

* * * * *

"What the hell is going on?" Jonathan growled at Mark Leslie. "I've been waiting for two hours."

"Sorry. I had to wait for Mrs. Bradford to get back from the White House."

"Is she back yet?"

"Yes. You'd better call her."

"I need Mihai Cuza's location. Goddamn it, Mark, you did the download!"

"Call Bradford!" Mark hung up abruptly.

Jonathan looked over at the couch. Frick was on yet another beer. Seated next to Frick, Teo had finally broken down and started on the pizza. Elizabeth leaned against a wall, arms folded.

"We're screwed, aren't we?" she asked.

"You're such a damn pessimist." He dialed Bradford's office number and was put on hold. Waiting, he directed a request to Teo. "How about a beer?"

It was Frick who twisted off the cap and carried the bottle over. "What's happening?"

"I don't have a clue." Jonathan accepted the beer and took a swig. "Still waiting for a location."

"I'll check flights into Bucharest." Teo took out his cell phone.

"It's a fucking big country to be going door to door." Frick returned to the couch and thumbed on the television.

It was another minute before Margaret picked up. "It's no go, Jonathan. No rescue. Not by Seal Team Six. Not by us. President's orders."

"Screw him. Screw you, too, Margaret. Cuza's going to kill them both, you know that, don't you?"

"I know that you're close friends with Mr. Petrov, but you can't take it personally."

"Margaret, it's not just my friendship with him. For God's sake, he's worked for you for ten years. He's one of our best people."

There was a momentary pause. "I knew that you'd have a difficult

259

time accepting this order, Jonathan, so I'm giving you, Mr. Lorenzo, and Ms. Owen a week's vacation to come to grips with the loss of Mr. Petrov. Mr. Menendez and Mr. Davis have also requested a week off. They should be on a plane into Newark right now."

She's letting us go on our own. Jonathan put the phone down and spoke to Teo. "Book six seats on the next flight to Bucharest. From Newark." He then spoke into the phone. "Okay, Margaret, we're going on vacation. But I need to know where I'm going."

"I can't tell you that."

"There's a 9:00 Lufthansa out of Newark," Teo called from across the room.

Jonathan checked his watch. They could make it. But once in Bucharest, what the hell were they going to do? He tossed his wallet to Teo. "Six round-trip tickets on my Visa. Margaret, give me some help here. I'm willing to take the responsibility—even pay for the trip—but we can't search all of Romania. Cuza will find out we're looking long before I find him."

"I'm sorry, Jonathan. One additional fact you should know. Kolya's suspicions about the nuclear power plants were on target. The software at fifteen plants was programmed to produce misleading information on October 14. It's being corrected now."

"Shit, Margaret, Cuza'll figure out how we know. Give me his Goddamn location!"

"Have a good flight." She hung up.

Jonathan took a moment to gain control over himself. "Okay." He turned to face the others. "Here's the deal. We're going to try to pull off the rescue by ourselves. Pete and Marty'll be joining us in Newark, but that's it. Just the six of us. No backup. And we've got to do it fast."

"Did Cuza find the Trojan?" Teo asked.

A dead silence followed his words.

"Trojan?" Frick asked.

"Good going, boy wonder," Elizabeth said.

"Teo, you're not supposed to blurt out information. Didn't they teach you that in spy kid school?" Jonathan said.

"Screw yourselves, both of you." Teo was red-faced. "What's the difference? He's coming with us, isn't he?"

Frick bent double laughing. "This is good," he gasped, wiping his eyes. "Ford was so nuts to get into your computer—Cuza, too—and it was a Goddamn trick. I don't suppose there was any real information in it, was there?"

"I wouldn't know," Jonathan said.

"I understand you don't completely trust me. I don't blame you. But who the hell am I going to tell? For what I've already done, Cuza would kill me." He calmed down enough to take a swig of beer, but his tone remained amused. "This whole thing was a charade? Petrov was supposed to get Cuza to access your system. He took it a little far, didn't he, dragging his girlfriend in?"

"He didn't know about the Trojan. I didn't know. Only a few people knew what was going on." Jonathan briefly explained.

"Do you know what Cuza will do to the two of them when he discovers that this coveted computer system was nothing but a trick?"

"That's why we're going to Bucharest on the next flight."

"Let me get this straight—four of us...."

"Six," Jonathan corrected.

"Six of us then. No helicopters. No Navy Seals. Six of us are going to just waltz up to Cuza's stronghold, which, by the way, we still need to locate, and we're taking two people out alive, including one who can't walk. If someone else were doing this, it'd be really funny."

"Maybe you might get us inside, and we'll take it from there."

"Yeah, the men there know me, and I can come up with some bullshit excuse for being there, but what am I going to do with the rest of you? Put you under my shirt? And what about weapons? We need guns, and not handguns either. Cuza's guards have submachine guns. We might as well go in with peashooters as with handguns."

"I know a guy at the U.S. base on the Black Sea. I've obtained weapons from him a couple other times. He won't know it's not official business."

"Great. So we get some guns. We're still outnumbered. We're still going to fucking die."

"There's that possibility," Jonathan said.

"We can't leave Kolya and Alex to be murdered," Teo said.

"Assuming we can find them. But you can back out, Frick," Jonathan said.

"Hell, I'm the only Goddamn chance you've got," Frick said. "Mind if I straighten up a before we go? I'd hate for whoever cleans out my personal effects to think I was a slob."

* * * * *

Teo helped carry paper plates into the kitchen. Elizabeth sat on the far end of the couch, picked up the remote, and turned the channel from a golf game to MSNBC.

"I told you we're screwed." She turned the volume up.

"You can back out, too."

"I didn't mean that. I like a good fight, but we've got no shot of finding them."

He tried to sort out his feelings towards her. They'd shared one night together —which he'd enjoyed and would have liked to repeat—but she had rebuffed every subsequent gesture on his part. And yet, she'd risked her career and was willing to risk her life. Why was she doing it? Out of principle? Loyalty to fellow operatives? Dormant feelings for Kolya?

Could he be any part of the reason she was taking the risks?

Frick was in the kitchen noisily washing dishes while Teo asked him about the FBI. Neither of them would hear what Jonathan said to Elizabeth.

"Elizabeth. Have I thanked you for going out on a limb to save Kolya?"

"Don't sweat it, Egan. I'm not in this for you."

"For Kolya?"

"Hell, no, not for him either. Well, yeah, I mean I am doing this because I don't want two people murdered, and he is one of the two. But it has nothing to do with the fact that I once dated him. It has to do with self-respect and with who I am." This time she looked up.

"I'm watching a show here, Jonathan."

"Got it." As he spoke, his phone buzzed. The caller i.d. announced Corey Manion—not someone Jonathan was eager to speak to. "Corey, this isn't a good time. I'll call you in a few days."

"Don't hang up. Listen, Jonathan. I know what's going on. I was in the meeting with Lewis and Margaret. I know that Petrov was set up and that he's a prisoner. I went to the ECA to urge Margaret to disregard the President's orders. She wouldn't agree to the ECA's rescuing Petrov, but she walked out of the room and left the Cuza file on her desk."

"Jesus." Jonathan had the answer from a source that he had never expected. "Did you see where Cuza's located?"

"That's why I'm calling. Margaret said that you'd go on your own if you knew where to find Cuza, but she couldn't tell you. I snapped a picture of the location and I'm forwarding it to you."

"Corey, you just got my vote for President. I'll even switch parties and vote for you in the primary."

There was a laugh on the other end. "Just pull it off, would you? You switch parties, and your father will kill me."

"He's not the only one who'll be ready to kill you for this, Corey."

"If you bring Kolya and Alex home alive, Lewis wouldn't dare do anything. If you screw it up, heads are going to roll, mine and yours."

"If I screw it up, my head'll be on top of a pole in Romania. I appreciate this."

"Don't thank me too soon. I may be sending you off to your death. Laura will kill me."

"She never gave me a hard time about doing my job. I've been pretty pissed off about the two of you, you know, but it's not fair. It's my own damn fault that she walked out. If I don't come back, take care of her and Dylan." He'd never thought he'd say anything of the sort to Corey Manion. But then, he'd never thought that Corey, whom he had always regarded with scorn, would take this kind of a risk.

"I will. If I'm not in prison for my part in this."

39

Snowflakes drifted down as Mihai Cuza gazed out his living room window. "Ion doesn't like to drive in the snow."

Stanescu regarded the outside world with the weary eyes of a man who'd drunk too much the night before. "He'll come anyway. Did you progress with the lady?"

"She's not going to screw around on Petrov." Max leaned against the door. "I told you. I watched the video of the two of them."

Cuza was unperturbed. "I watched as well. At least she liked the wine. And I introduced ideas for her to mull over. Women find an injured man irresistible. I can wait until Petrov's better—and slowly work on her."

Max crossed the room and helped himself to a cup of black coffee. "That'll take time. How long you planning to keep your new pets?"

"As long as they entertain me." He liked the woman. If he killed Petrov, she'd never accept him. He'd wait. He had other more immediate concerns. The snow and Ion.

Ion would come, no doubt about that; he was worried about the talks with Under Secretary Nielson. The thing to do was to have a thorough briefing ready before Ion arrived. Also important was the entertainment.

A traditional dinner. *Sarmalute in foi de vita*, vine leaves stuffed with meat, rice, and herbs or *muschi ciobanesv*, pork stuffed with ham, covered with cheese and served with mayonnaise, cucumber, and herbs. He'd speak to the cook.

"You could have Petrov play the piano." Stanescu sipped his coffee.

"You're out of your mind," Max said. "You don't know what the fuck he'd do. And he's a Jew."

"There is that. And Ion'd be upset by the idea of my holding an American operative, especially one who evidences a rigorous interrogation. Anyway our Russian bear isn't yet tame enough to dance for company. Nevertheless—" Cuza stroked his chin reflectively, "Petrov might have some information about the Under Secretary. We'll drop by his room for a visit after I finish my coffee. Meanwhile, go find Traian, would you? Ask him to go online and see what he can find out about this Nielson person."

Traian was the most technically competent man on the premises. Of course, Cuza could do it himself, if he wanted, but he was too busy these days to see to all the details. That was why he employed people.

* * * * *

"It's really very witty." Alex sat on the chair next the bed, her legs drawn up to her chest, while reciting the plot of *Pride and Prejudice*. "Elizabeth thinks she hates Mr. Darcy because he insults her at their first meeting, whereas Mr. Darcy likes her because she insults him."

"I'm really not interested." Kolya had maneuvered himself onto his right side, the chained arm bent over his head. His leg hurt regardless of the side he lay on, but it was a relief to be neither on his back nor on his cramped left side. Still an awkward position—he felt a little like a pretzel.

"It tires you to talk. I'm trying to entertain you and keep from bouncing off the walls," Alex snapped. "What the hell else is there to do?"

There wasn't anything to do. Nothing to read. No television, no music. One of the side effects of captivity was boredom unless the captors were considerate enough to offer reading material. It was a problem more for her than for him. He could spend the day dozing. She was traumatized but healthy.

"Does it have to be Jane Austen?"

"Why not? What should I talk about? You could tell me all about your childhood, but you don't feel like talking. And even if you did, you rarely talk about your feelings or your past under the best of circumstances, and you're certainly not going to do it with people listening to us. You suggested Jane Austen."

Well, he had, as a method for her to calm herself and go to sleep. But she was right. What could they talk about in front of microphones? "Go on. Elizabeth hates Darcy."

"Do you know that you're something of a cross between Mr. Bennett and Mr. Darcy?"

"Is that a compliment or an insult?"

"A compliment. Mr. Bennet is witty and sarcastic, wants to do nothing but shut himself up in his library and read. Except for the gun, you're very similar. Mr. Darcy is rich, reserved, intellectual, romantic, and has good principles. Except for the rich part, I see similarities. So how did you manage to graduate from Princeton with a major in English without reading Jane Austen?"

"Just lucky." He closed his eyes and dozed, until the sound of the door being unlocked jolted him back to full consciousness. His back was to the door.

"Is he awake?" Cuza's smooth tones behind him addressed Alex.

They didn't know about the Trojan. If Cuza had discovered the Trojan, he wouldn't still be carrying on the polite host charade.

"Not completely."

"You were talking to him."

"I'm bored, and he's not well. He sleeps while I talk. I thought the doctor was going to check up on him last night or this morning."

"The doctor is preparing for an important visitor. He will see to Mr. Petrov later. Please wake him."

Alex touched his arm. Kolya started and blinked. "What?"

Alex indicated behind him, and he turned awkwardly.

"Good morning," Cuza said. "Are you acquainted with the Under Secretary of State for the United States?"

"I don't know him personally, but I know a little about him. Robert Nielson. Twenty-year career in the State Department. Intelligent.

Good at playing the political odds, which is how he's survived this long in State."

Kolya did know more. He knew that the vetting process had turned up a few indiscretions, but nothing so bad or so public that Nielson's position had been jeopardized. Kolya had no particular loyalty to Nielson, but he saw no reason to give Cuza more than absolutely necessary.

"What would he want to discuss with a prospective president of Romania?"

"You don't need me to tell you this. America is interested in the airbase at Constanta, terrorism, and the general stability of the region."

"You're correct. I don't need an intelligence agent to tell me what I can find in the back pages of *The New York Times*. I want to know what isn't in the papers. How to get him on our side. How to blackmail him, if necessary. Need I remind you that you only remain alive as long as I find you useful?"

It would be ironic if they killed him not because he was holding back, but because he simply didn't know enough. He decided to give what he did know.

"Reports are that he's had a few discrete affairs: one with a receptionist at a posting in Italy several years ago, another with a woman in the Department of State. He likes young and brunette. His wife knows and puts up with it. He also likes German beer, cigars, and golf, and he's decent at it. The best place to talk to him is on the golf course, but only if you can match his game."

"Beer and cigars. And possibly a pretty young woman. It's something." Cuza looked at Alex. "I'm sorry that you're bored. I'll have some books brought up with your lunch." Max, followed him from the room.

Relieved at the removal of the immediate threat, Kolya drifted back into dreams while Alex resumed her recitation of plot points.

* * * * *

Traian Arcos frowned at his laptop. It was fine until he linked up with the network, which was slower than usual. He tapped his fingers on the desk while he waited for the data to finish loading.

He printed an article that described the upcoming visit of Robert Nielson to Romania. He had already printed articles on Nielson's background. None of it was particularly interesting.

The only thing Traian was currently interested in was a look at the top-secret site with access to ECHELON. But, Traian didn't have the password to get onto the site, and the Count wanted his articles quickly. Maybe later, after he got the materials to the Count, he'd play around on Cuza's desktop, see what he could find on ECHELON.

Maybe he'd run some diagnostics on the network, see if he could find out what was slowing things down.

* * * * *

The plane landed at 2:30 p.m., Bucharest time. Jonathan Egan glumly regarded the splattering of rain against the window. Eleven hours in the air. Passengers took down small carry-on bags, fell into line, one after another, moving two feet forward. Next to him, Teo stood and stretched. Jonathan fell in behind Marty. Behind Jonathan, the rest of the team.

After customs, doors led to the outside of Otopeni Airport where Jonathan spotted a slim African-American man in a suit lounging casually against a white van. The man raised a hand in greeting.

"Allan." Jonathan motioned his companions forward. "Colonel Allan Brooks, I'd like you to meet my team. Liz. Teo. Marty. Pete and Frick."

"Frick?" Allan raised an eyebrow. "That a first or last name?"

"Both," Frick said. "Let it go."

"No sweat. Let me give you folks a ride."

Allan swung open the back of the van revealing two large canvas bags on the floor. Jonathan dumped his carry-on bag on top and swung around to sit in the front passenger seat. The others followed.

Allan, in the driver's seat, turned on the ignition. "I haven't heard anything through channels about this operation, Jonathan."

"You're not going to, either. This much you can know: We're getting two of our people out of a bad situation. We may need some help getting back to the States, too, maybe on a military jet."

"Boy, you can't just hitch a ride on military aircraft."

"Oh come on. You've worked with me before. Anyway, if we can, we'll just drive out of the country."

"You want to give me a pick-up location just in case?"

"No. The less you know and all that. I'll get hold of you if necessary."

The windshield wipers scrapped a rhythm against the glass. Allan drove to a parking lot across from the airport.

"I parked my vehicle and rented this for you," Allan said. "Don't wreck it; Hertz'll have my ass." He pulled the van up behind a Jeep.

"Thanks. I owe you."

"You owe the U.S. Air Force, not me. You got everything you asked for in the duffle bags in back: six HK MP 5s with sound suppressors and enough ammo to take the country. You got flash bangs. You got side arms. You got night vision goggles, and light body armor. I'm driving back to Constanta. If you do need that lift home, you know how to reach me."

Constanta, on the Black Sea, was the location of Mihail Kogalniceanu Air Base, where the U.S. Air Force and Army troops were stationed.

Jonathan slid from his seat and crossed to the driver's side. With a final wave at Allan, Jonathan started the engine, noting the reorganization of the car. Teo was now in the front passenger seat; Frick immediately behind him. Elizabeth sat behind Jonathan's seat, and in the far back, Marty and Pete.

Teo studied a map. "North to Brasov." He traced the lines on the map with his forefinger through small Romanian towns. "From there, we take the road through the mountains."

"About six hours," Jonathan said. "We need to time it so we go in midnight or later."

Jonathan turned the steering wheel and swung the car around.

Ion Georgescu sipped a glass of cognac. He had more of an air of confidence than he had on the last visit, looking more like a president and less like an errand boy. Cuza liked the change, as long as it was only in appearance.

"Cigars, beer, and a young woman for the American Under Secretary?" Ion asked. "I don't quite see the point."

"You're establishing a relationship. When you're elected, you'll have laid the groundwork for negotiations. Also, it wouldn't hurt to have some *kompromit* as the Russians would call it, on someone at his level, just in case we want to need it. Eventually, we want the Americans out of their base at Constanta." The base might be abandoned after the nuclear power accidents that Cuza had arranged, but Ion didn't need to know what was happening in two days.

There was a movement at the doorway, and Cuza turned his head. Traian Arcos waited for an acknowledgement. "Come in, Traian. Those are for me?"

Traian nodded as he advanced. "Articles on Robert Nielson. All I could find."

Cuza flipped through the papers. The information was about on the level of what he'd received from Petrov.

"The network's a little slow today," Traian said. "I tried your desktop, too. It's worse. I don't understand why."

"Did you run a virus check?"

"Nothing's shown up," Traian said. "But I'm still looking. Would you mind if I spent some time checking out ECHELON?"

"Go ahead."

"I'll need the password to get into the ECA site."

"It's printed on a piece of paper in the top left drawer of my desk," Cuza said.

"Maybe I can get Petrov to show me around the site, now that he's being cooperative."

"No, too much trouble." Cuza wasn't particularly concerned about

Petrov's health, but he didn't want Ion seeing Petrov, especially in his current condition. Cuza opened his cigar box, withdrew a Cuban cigar, and rolled it between his fingers. "If you want to go on site, poke around, see what you can come up with, feel free."

40

"Ploiesti," Teo announced from the driver's seat. Jonathan now sat behind him. Elizabeth rode shotgun.

Frick rolled down the window and sniffed. The air that blew in, cold and damp, smelled of acrid smoke. "Smells like oil."

"Smells like and is. Romania's biggest oil town," Jonathan said. "The world's first oil wells were built here in 1857."

Out of Ploiesti, Teo took DN1 north towards Braslow. They stopped for a meal at the Hotel Palace on Stada O. Goga in Sinaia on the border between the provinces of Wallachia and Transylvania. They ate dumpling soup, beetroot salad, and duck with sauerkraut. It was a heavy meal but they had hours to go. Teo asked for *papanasi* and carried a bag filled with cream donuts back to the van. Elizabeth took over driving, and Frick switched to the front passenger position.

"It's a nice town," Jonathan said as they pulled back onto Bulevardul Carol I, which turned into DR1. "A resort town. Good hotels and restaurants, which you can't say about every town. There's skiing nearby in the Bucegei mountain range. A German style schloss."

"I've seen enough of this country," Frick said.

"Can't blame the whole country for the company you were keeping. It's a gorgeous place, untouched mountains, interesting traditions. There are monasteries with spectacular paintings, roadside icons. When we first were assigned to Cuza, Kolya and I spent two weeks getting the lay of the land before recruiting a Romanian guy, Vasily Roman, to infiltrate Cuza's organization. Vasily loved his country as much as he hated the people who wanted to bring back the Iron Guard."

"Those are some of Cuza's supporters, now, aren't they?" Marty asked from the rear of the van.

"That's his strongest base of support. Anyway, Vasily was an amateur violinist, and he'd talk to Kolya about Mozart and jazz. He was really upset about what Cuza might do if he got into power. Nice guy. There's a lot of good people in this country, you know. Hard working people trying to make the best of a bad situation, and Cuza is just trying to exploit them."

"Was Vasily the guy Kolya mentioned?" Teo asked. "The guy that Cuza impaled?"

"Yeah. We found his body in a village in Alexmures, a ten-foot stake through his intestines. You know, the trick with impaling is to shove the stake in, either vaginally or anally, but not all the way through, because you don't want to hit any major organs or blood vessels. Don't want your victim to die too quickly. You do it right and he'll die slowly. When you plant him upright, his own weight forces his body down until the stake comes out in the stomach or the chest.

"Vasily didn't die straight off, but he'd been dead for a while when we found him. Bicaz is a little village, no public transportation or anything. Two Orthodox churches in town: the old one with paintings from the eighteenth century is falling apart, and the new one is the place of worship for the villagers. They planted him in front of the old church in the middle of the night. A little village filled with people who have nothing to do but peer out their windows at the neighbors, but that night, everyone slept soundly. Can't blame them, particularly."

"Didn't the authorities know Cuza did it?" Teo asked.

"Of course. Everyone damn well knew, but Cuza has too many supporters, and those who don't support him are scared of him. So it was hushed up. The government doesn't want any hint that a descendant of Vlad Tepes is putting stakes through people."

"How much ammunition we got?" Elizabeth asked from the front.

"Enough to do the job," Marty assured her. "Nobody here's getting impaled."

273

No. There were six of them, and they would be well armed. They might all die, but not that way. They had night and surprise on their side, and the rescue would succeed. It had to.

If Cuza hadn't already impaled Kolya and Alex.

* * * * *

"Excuse me, *Voivode*," Max, with Traian a half pace behind, interrupted the conversation. "This requires your attention."

"I still can't find exactly what's wrong," Traian said. "But the computer's still slow. A couple programs are screwed up as well. Like our program to link into the transportation system. I think we've got a virus that our software isn't detecting. And the nuclear plant in Cernavoda went off-line this morning. I checked some of the other plants. Indian Point in New York is down as well. So is Davis Besse in Ohio. All fifteen plants that we are interested in are down."

"What on earth?" Cuza's frown deepened. "Emil, please entertain Ion for a few minutes."

* * * * *

Cuza checked the backdoor into the nuclear plants that the software, painstakingly created and downloaded during recent upgrades, had left open for him. But all of the computers had been shut down, his access as well.

It was scheduled to happen in two days. In two days, Romanians would realize the incompetence of the current government and the foolishness of the policy of building nuclear power for other nations.

In two days, the Americans would have too many problems of their own to worry about the internal affairs of Romania. And he would be making billions in cleanup revenue.

Cuza typed the password to access the program that had been created to interface with the computers of the Romanian transportation system. Nothing came up.

"It's as if someone deleted it," Traian said. "But it wasn't deleted.

There's nothing in the recycling bin. No sign of it anywhere."
Cuza typed. Still nothing. "When were you last on this computer?"
He affected a calm he didn't feel.

"Yesterday morning, Voivode. Before Petrov got you the access you wanted."

"Anyone else been on the computer since?"

"Not as far as I know. I had similar problems on my laptop."

"Max?"

"I'm not a big computer person. I haven't touched it. None of my men would have touched it either. Could Petrov have done anything to the computer when he was on it yesterday?"

"No. I was watching him. All he did was type the answers to questions posed by the ECA computer. The second he was in, he removed his hands from the keyboard."

"Maybe there was a virus on the ECA site, and we picked it up," Traian suggested. "It happens, you know."

"A virus? Maybe." A new and terrible thought occurred to him. What if it was all a trick?

Couldn't be. Petrov hadn't been faking his resistance. Until the woman had been dragged into it, he had shown absolutely no inclination to cooperate. Not even the most dedicated agent would endure such protracted torture if he were really planning to give in.

Cuza dialed up the ECA site and typed in the password. The Executive Covert Agency computer network logo filled the screen. He went into working files. All the information he had viewed with Petrov was still there. What else was there? He already knew the information about his own organization. What about other covert operations that the ECA was engaged in?

He found information on Pakistan and on Afghanistan, but the reports read oddly, as if the most important information had been edited out. If he weren't already suspicious that something was wrong, he might not have noticed.

But he couldn't be sure that the reports weren't normally edited before being logged into the system. What could he check? He searched and found himself back on the listing of ECA personnel

275

names, addresses, and telephone numbers.

He took out his cell and dialed the telephone number listed as belonging to Nikolai Petrov. After one ring, a recording informed him that he had reached a nonworking number.

He printed the sheet of addresses and phone numbers, folded it and put it into his breast pocket. "Traian, I want you to go through every operating program and look for a virus." Cuza rose. "Max, I want Miss Feinstein to join me in the dining room. After she's downstairs, return Mr. Petrov to his cell in the basement. I want the opportunity to speak to them separately."

* * * * *

North of Gheorghi on DN12, a truck lumbered along, barely reaching 30 kilometers per hour. Marty was driving, and he took it with a calm patience that annoyed Jonathan.

"Go around him," Jonathan said.

"I can't see around him. Relax. Enjoy the scenery."

It was getting dark, but outside the windows, the mountains were visible.

"Have a donut." Teo held out the bag to Jonathan.

With a shake of his head, Jonathan declined. "We don't know what's happening to Kolya and Alex. They could be dead or dying."

"In which case, a few extra minutes isn't going to make much of a difference, is it?" Marty responded. "We've still got a couple hours drive, even if we speed."

"We don't go in until after midnight, anyway." Frick took the offered paper bag from Teo, fished out a donut, and bit into it. "Not bad."

Pete Menendez turned from his current position in the front and retrieved a donut.

"Nice mountains."

"If you like mountains," Frick said.

"I like the beach," Pete said. "Mountains are pretty enough, but I'm not much of a hiker. I like to swim, lay in the sun. When this is all over, I'm spending three weeks on a beach in Spain."

"My kids like mountains," Marty said. "We go to North Carolina every summer. My wife's parents have an old farmhouse that they've fixed up and it's right next to a state park and a mountain. My kids like to pretend that they're hobbits on a long journey. Your son like to hike, Jonathan?"

"No," Jonathan said. "My son likes video games and movies and pizza. He likes to pretend he's in one of those Japanese cartoons."

"I like anime," Teo said. "I grew up with Pokémon."

Marty flipped the radio on and found a classical station. "Anyone object?"

"It's boring, but what the hell." Frick stretched.

"Anyone backing Miami for the Super bowl?" Pete asked. "You seen that new quarterback?"

"I hate professional sports," Elizabeth said.

"We could play Botticelli," Teo said.

No one took up the suggestion.

Jonathan folded his arms across his chest and slouched down in his seat. "I don't know about you guys, but I'm expecting an active night. I'm going to try for a nap."

41

Alex sat by the window, transfixed by snowflakes floating to the ground. She glanced over at Kolya, who slept restlessly, his back to her. She had recounted the entire plot of *Pride and Prejudice*, scene for scene, but she doubted he'd heard more than ten words.

Without a thermometer, she could only guess at his temperature, and her guess was somewhere around 101. The welts on his back were clean and the signs of infection clearing up. It was his leg and continuing fever that worried her.

They had been given breakfast, but no lunch. She didn't really care for herself. She often skipped lunch when she was busy, but Kolya needed to build up his strength.

If they survived, both of them would have to deal with the trauma of the last week. Still, with Kolya this sick, she put all of that out of her mind. All she could do was tend to him and hope.

She jumped at the sound of the door unlocking.

She glanced at Kolya and saw that he was aware someone was entering. One of the guards she'd seen before, a gun tucked in a shoulder holster, motioned to her. She narrowed her eyes at him. "What?"

"*Sculati-va!*"

Kolya lifted his head and responded in the same language. The young man answered him curtly.

"He wants you to go with him," Kolya said. "You're invited to dinner again."

"Ask him where your dinner is."

"I'm not hungry."

"I'm not going."

"Someone bring him dinner later." The guard switched to English. "Please to come with me."

"He's sick," Alex said. "He needs a doctor."

The young man squinted down at Kolya and spoke in Romanian.

"He says that Cuza will be displeased at any delay," Kolya translated. "Alex, I'm not any more likely to get either food or medical care if you don't go."

This much she understood. *Pretend to be cordial, go along with the program.* Last night, she'd gone, and it had been fine.

"All right. I'll go. I'll drag the damn doctor back." She leaned over and kissed him on the cheek.

"Don't worry about me." He turned the pillow over, punched it up, and settled himself. "I'm all right."

Two days resting in a comfortable bed had done some good. He still had the flushed look of fever, and she could tell that his injuries hurt him, but his voice was firmer, his eyes more focused. She didn't like leaving him, but he was right. Angering Cuza wouldn't help Kolya.

The guard stayed at her elbow as they walked down the corridor, down the magnificent circular stairs, through the library, and into the dining room.

Cuza was at the head of the table, Stanescu to his left. To his right sat a stocky man whom Alex didn't recognize and who looked ill at ease.

"Miss Feinstein." Cuza waved her to a seat next to Stanescu. "We were just having plum brandy. Would you care for a glass?"

Stanescu poured and handed the crystal to her.

The stocky man glanced at Cuza. "Feinstein? Jewish? You have a Jew staying here?"

"Yes, she is, but she's American. The Americans like Jews. Still, she's lovely, isn't she?" Cuza said to the stocky man.

"Jewish women can be pretty," His tone showed distain. "But wouldn't you prefer a pretty Christian Romanian woman?"

"I'm not sleeping with her," Cuza said. "She's engaged and very dedicated to her fiancé, the lucky man. But if you want a good American lawyer, you'll want a Jew. Miss Feinstein is a prominent Washington attorney. In preparation for your meeting, you should know something about the American system of government and its judicial system."

At Cuza's prompting, Alex explained the differences between federal and state courts, the balance of power between the three branches of government, and the role of the Supreme Court, controlling her anger at the anti-Semitism. The goal was to stay alive. Afterwards, she'd process everything that had happened.

"I have never been in favor of judicial activism." Cuza lounged with the relaxed appearance of a sleepy leopard. "The courts should only enforce laws, not create them." Cuza leaned to catch a glimpse of a young man signaling him from the doorway. "Dinner should be served in about fifteen minutes. If you'll excuse me, Ion, Miss Feinstein, I have a quick call to make."

He placed his glass on the table, rose, and with a slight bow, left the room.

*   *   *   *   *

When Max and five others entered the room, carrying Galil MAR assault rifles, Kolya knew they had found the Trojan.

"We want to talk to you, Petrov," Max said. "Downstairs."

The rifles were aimed at his mid-section, and Max moved forward to unlock the chain holding Kolya to the bed.

"Where's Alex?" he asked as Max inserted the key into the lock.

"Having dinner. The Count wanted to talk to the two of you separately."

Kolya slowly sat up, with a show of puzzlement. "No crutches?"

"We'll help you." Max's voice was smooth, without a hint of unpleasantness.

Kolya eased his legs over the edge of the bed, the casted leg stretched out straight in front of him, and leaned over, as if suddenly dizzy. One of the guards slung the rifle over his shoulder, grabbed for

Kolya's left arm, and twisted it behind him. Kolya turned toward the guard and thrust the fingers of his right hand into the guard's throat. The guard made a gurgling sound and went down on one knee.

The men crowded in then, and he was hit on the head, the back, the arms, and the mid-section. He fought back, helped by an adrenaline rush but it wasn't enough to compensate for the effects of captivity and injury. Even if he'd been at his best, it was six against one.

He didn't see the blow against the back of his head that knocked him off the side of the bed and onto the floor. His arms were yanked behind him, and handcuffs fastened his wrists together.

He was pulled upright, held tightly, two men on each arm. Max hit him across the face. "You thought we wouldn't find out, didn't you?" Max hissed. "You thought you could screw us over, didn't you? You fucking Jews think you're so smart."

"I don't know what the fuck you're talking about."

Max hit him in the stomach. Kolya would have doubled over except for the men holding him.

Max turned on his heel and headed out of the room. Kolya was dragged from the room down the corridor and down the circular stairs. He felt every thump on his broken leg, and he tried, unsuccessfully, to struggle up on his good leg, to hobble rather than being dragged. But the guards kicked his leg out from under him.

To his dismay, they continued to the stairs that led back to the basement to the too familiar cell where he'd been held before Alex's arrival. They dumped him in his old spot on the floor and attached the chain on the wall to the handcuffs, his hands behind him. Stunned and dizzy from the beating, he tried to fight down his panic.

Maybe Alex'd be spared.

Three men left. Max, Gheorghe, and Eugene remained. Max looked him over with a smile of satisfaction. A moment later, Mihai Cuza entered the room, as well groomed as ever.

"You're a mess, Mr. Petrov. Again."

Kolya shook his head in an effort to clear it. "I've done what you asked me to do."

"Yes, so you did." Cuza's voice was dry. "But before we talk about just what you did for me, I have a simple question for you. Answer honestly, and you'll live."

Kolya licked his lips and tasted blood. "I've answered truthfully every question you've asked."

"Why am I not convinced?" Cuza asked the ceiling. "But never mind. Just one question, Mr. Petrov. What is your address?"

"What? Why?" The program on the ECA computer had given a false home address. With a flash of fear, he knew why Cuza was asking, and he also wasn't certain he remembered the false address correctly.

Cuza turned to Max. "He wants to know why."

Max crossed the room and kicked Kolya in the ribs. "That's why."

Kolya coughed and gasped, while Cuza waited. When he was able to speak, Kolya gave what he hoped was the fake address on the ECA site. "1438 Cedar Street SE."

Cuza pulled out a piece of paper. "That matches."

Kolya would have been relieved but for another thought. Would Cuza ask Alex the same question? Had he already asked her? It would be the logical thing to do. Would Alex remember the address? What if she told Kolya's real address? Cuza would know that Kolya had lied, but perhaps Cuza would at least believe Alex to be innocent of an attempt to trick him.

But Alex had caught sight of the computer monitor and the fake address. Kolya'd seen her expression. Even if she didn't remember the fake address, she'd try to back him up. She'd fake something, and it might not match what he had remembered.

"I moved recently," Kolya lied and amplified. "A little before you captured me."

But Cuza wasn't done. "Your phone number, Mr. Petrov."

Kolya didn't have any memory of the phone number from the computer. He told his real number. "The number in the personnel directory is incorrect."

"The number is incorrect? Why didn't you mention that when I was reviewing the site?"

"Why would my phone number matter to you?"

"Why indeed?" Cuza asked. "Well it really doesn't except that I have a problem, Mr. Petrov. Do you know what it is?"

"I don't have a fucking clue."

"My problem is I seem to have a virus on my computer. A very sophisticated virus. My anti-viral software didn't pick it up. Furthermore, it appears that this virus allowed a download of everything on my computer and my network."

The cold of the room was penetrating, and Kolya could hear the blood pounding in his ears. "You can't blame this on me."

"Can't I? You know," Cuza's tones remained silken, "the Trojan is an interesting concept. The idea of inducing an enemy to freely accept a weapon that will ultimately destroy him. Very clever of your agency. I'm actually rather impressed. Annoyed, but impressed."

"You're telling me that there was a Trojan on the ECA site?" Kolya coughed again.

"Yes, and you put it on my computer."

"I only accessed the site. You asked me to do it."

"That's the beauty of it," Cuza said. "I asked you to do it. I forced you to do it. If you'd come to me, offering your services, I would never have accepted. Your apparent unwillingness to cooperate just made me all the more eager. In a sense, you're the ultimate Trojan horse, aren't you?"

"You're suggesting it was some kind of a trick? That I allowed myself to be captured and tortured just to trick you? Do you think I would have held out so long if I were under orders to capitulate?"

"It certainly was a trick. Your role in it isn't completely clear to me," Cuza replied. "You held out for so long that it's hard to believe you were acting. I don't think you were. I also don't think you would have allowed Miss Feinstein to be dragged into this matter had you been in on the Trojan. Both of which support the theory that you didn't know, at least not initially."

"If this was a trick," Kolya let some of his real anger show, "then I was set up by my own people. I was tricked even more than you were."

Cuza looked at him impassively. "I think you didn't know about the Trojan, that your agency trained you on a new "security system," patted you on the head, and sent you out for me to capture. I think that you didn't have a clue until Miss Feinstein showed up. Suddenly, you were willing to do whatever I asked. I attributed it to the force of love, because I'm a romantic at heart, but you realized that something was wrong. I'm not sure how or why, but you did.

"I was watching you when we brought Miss Feinstein in. I don't doubt that you love her. It's touching. Still, by the time you went on the computer and accessed the ECA system for me, you knew what you were doing. Or, if you didn't know before you got on the site, you knew once you were in. I just read some of the other operational files, and the material is obviously edited or faked. Furthermore, I don't believe that you live in that section of Washington. I looked it up. It's a very poor black neighborhood. You'd stand out, and a man like you can't afford to stand out."

Kolya shook his head again in denial.

"In any case, it doesn't matter. Your agency sent you out to be tortured and killed, without asking or informing you. At some point, you realized what had happened, and you decided to go along with it. And that's why you're going to die now. Had you notified me immediately on realizing the trick, I might have spared you."

"I didn't know." Kolya made one last effort.

Cuza deliberately rested his foot on the cast on Kolya's leg. "I dislike being tricked. Every plan I had for the next year has to be scrapped." Cuza's full weight had shifted to the foot resting on Kolya's leg, and even through the cast, Kolya could feel the pressure painfully bearing down on the broken bone. "There's discipline to maintain. If you get away with tricking me, other people will think they can do the same. And I'll be frank. You've made me very angry. I'm going to enjoy watching you die. My only question is whether to impale Miss Feinstein along with you."

Cuza was close enough that Kolya could smell plum brandy on his breath. "She's not an agent. She doesn't know anything about my work. She didn't even know who you were."

"Possibly. Or possibly she's a very good actress. In any event, if she had any inkling that you were lying and covered up for you, that's a good enough reason for her to die as well."

"I'll tell you anything if you let her live."

He meant it. He would give up any ECA secret to save Alex.

"I no longer trust anything you say, and you no longer have any information I want. As for your fiancée, I find her attractive, despite her being Jewish, and I hate wasting beauty. I'd enjoy taking her to bed. But your agency has already used a woman to make a fool of me. And, you and your fiancée would make a nicely matched set of lawn decorations, at least until you begin to rot. Here's my solution: I'm going to ask her your home address before I decide what to do with her."

Cuza removed his foot, turned, and walked toward the door.

"Shall I get the men down and do Petrov now?" Max asked.

Cuza paused. "Not while Ion is here. He's squeamish, and I don't want him rattled for his meeting with the Under Secretary. And I want to be present. Later tonight. Find a pole strong enough for his weight."

Cuza left the room. Max tested the handcuffs on Kolya's wrists, and satisfied, gave instructions to the two guards. "I want two of you here at all times watching him. If he tries anything at all, shoot him in the left kneecap, but don't knock him out or kill him. I want him conscious for his execution."

* * * * *

The dinner was excellent. *Muschi poiana*, as it was called by the woman serving the dish, or beef stuffed with mushrooms, bacon, pepper, and paprika, and served with vegetable puree.

Alex hadn't eaten much all day or the day before, and the dish was delicious and unusual. "You sent dinner up to Kolya?" she interrupted a discussion in Romanian between Cuza and Georgescu.

"Don't worry. Mr. Petrov has been attended to." Cuza dissected his beef with a sharp knife.

"Excellent dinner." Stanescu stretched back against the chair, his glass held casually in one hand. "So, Miss Feinstein, are you planning a big Jewish wedding?"

She was surprised by the question. "We haven't had an opportunity to discuss it yet."

"I like Jewish weddings." Stanescu cast an apologetic glance at Georgescu. "Well, I do. The food, the drink, klezmer music, and dancing. Men on one side, women on the other."

"Those are orthodox weddings, which we're not. And we haven't made any specific plans."

"Yes, your engagement is fairly recent, isn't it?" Cuza's tones remained pleasant. "Have you discussed where you'll live after your marriage? I understand you have a townhouse in Georgetown."

"Yes," Alex said. "The building dates back more than two hundred years."

"Yes, lovely area." Cuza forked a tomato in his salad and ate it. "Much nicer than Mr. Petrov's neighborhood. Where does he live again?"

"He lives closer to his office."

"You're being vague. What is his address? I know Washington quite well."

Alex remembered the ECA personnel site and that the address for Kolya had not been correct. She didn't remember the fake address. She didn't know if this was a test or not, but she didn't want to say anything that would let Cuza know that the information on the site was wrong. She hesitated.

"Come on, Miss Feinstein, don't you know your own fiancé's address?"

"We spend all our time at my place. His apartment is so small, books crammed everywhere, and then there's his piano. Really, there's no room to move. It's on," she remembered the street, "Cedar Street. I could find the building, but I don't remember the number."

"What about his phone number?"

"He changed it recently. And anyway, he's in my contact list. Who knows phone numbers anymore?"

"Good point." Cuza finished his salad. "Do finish your meat. It's an authentic Romanian dish, unlike our meal last night." She stared down at the plate, her stomach churning. "No? Not hungry. Worrying about Mr. Petrov no doubt. Well," he tossed his napkin on the table, "if you're not going to enjoy your meal, you may as well return to him."

He extended a hand to her, still the courteous host. She knew that she had been given a test and that she had failed.

42

Gheorghe smoked nonstop and spoke to Eugene in Romanian. Periodically, one or the other would walk across the room to check that Kolya remained securely handcuffed. Gheorghe looked in Kolya's direction and exhaled smoke.

Kolya's left eye was almost swollen shut, and he watched the guards with his eyes open just a slit. Kolya's entire body hurt. New bruises from the latest beating competed with the throbbing of his injured leg and back, and his muscles ached from fever. Still, he couldn't let any of that distract him. He focused on retrieving the paper clip hidden in his left sleeve without drawing the attention of the guards.

His fingers caught the sleeve of his shirt, and carefully, he felt for the tip of the clip.

He would only have one chance after he retrieved the clip, but to do what? Had Alex not been upstairs, he would know his course of action: try for a quicker death. First: free his hands. Then, take down the next guard to come close and get his hands on a gun. He knew that at best it would be a short-lived victory. He would be shot either by the second guard or by an assault of Cuza's other men—or he'd shoot himself. Shot was better than impaled, and there was some satisfaction in the thought of killing one or two of Cuza's people. But while that would save Kolya from a terrible death, would he be leaving Alex to suffer that fate?

He'd get the paper clip into his hand and wait. If Cuza decided to spare Alex, Kolya would forego any attempt to escape impalement.

His fingers found the clip, worked it free of the shirt seam, and

288

closed around it. Gheorghe caught Kolya's slight movement, pushed himself off the wall, and approached, gun aimed. Kolya's stomach tightened in apprehension.

"Uncomfortable?" Gheorghe checked that Kolya's hands, behind him, were still cuffed.

"You coward." Kolya tried to get the man's attention away from his closed fingers, banking on the stupidity that Gheorghe had repeatedly demonstrated. "You're afraid of me even like this, aren't you?"

Gheorghe lost interest in the handcuffs and smashed Kolya on the side of his head with the butt of the gun. Kolya shook his head to clear it and spat out the traditional Russian insult to Gheorghe's mother.

Gheorghe raised the butt of the gun high for another blow. Kolya braced himself.

"Don't," the second guard near the door warned in Romanian. "You'll kill him or knock him unconscious, and it's what he wants. He's goading you to kill him so he won't be impaled. It's not a good death." The second guard flicked the burning remainder of his cigarette toward Kolya. Kolya flinched, more for show than out of actual pain. Unlike Max's earlier treatment with the cigar, the cigarette bounced, the ember in contact with his skin for only a second.

"You're right. I'll wait. Maybe I'll drive the stake into you myself," Gheorghe told Kolya.

Gheorghe returned to his former position by the wall, accepted and lit another cigarette. Kolya also waited.

* * * * *

Frick turned on the wipers to clear off the snow. He swiped a sleeve against the side window.

"Damn." Jonathan peered out the side window at the snow that was already several inches deep.

His watch read nine-fifteen. The snow and road obstacles had slowed them down, but they were close to their destination, with a couple hours left before the agreed upon time for the operation.

The van had four-wheel drive, but would it be enough on the mountain road?

They'd find out.

They continued on DN17 up through the Birgau valley, past Prundu Birgaului. Frick shifted into four-wheel mode. The van continued steadily, although the snow was now accumulating on the road.

"Turn here." Jonathan pointed, and Frick turned the van from the paved road onto a small one-lane road just barely visible through the trees. "This should go to Cuza's private airfield."

Frick turned on the road, cut the headlights, and proceeded at a snail's pace. The visibility through the trees was minimal. Wipers slapped in rhythm. The tension in the car escalated.

"Once we hit the airfield," Frick said, "the road goes straight up the mountain."

"Does Cuza keep people stationed at the airstrip?" Marty asked.

"There were people there when I landed and when I took off, but I don't know what it's like at other times."

"Best to be prepared," Jonathan said. "Stop short of the clearing."

Frick nodded, his attention focused on the dark, bumpy path. In a few minutes, the slow progress of the van stopped altogether.

"Trees are breaking ahead," Frick said.

Jonathan looked around the van and chose Elizabeth. He nodded at her, and she slipped from her seat to the back of the van. Jonathan opened the back, picked up an HK M5 and loaded it while Elizabeth did the same. He tossed Marty a radio and took two others with him.

The snow was still falling heavily as they walked the few feet to the clearing. At the edge of the trees, Jonathan went left and Elizabeth right.

The landing strip was empty, and no cars were visible. The shed had a small window, but the interior was dark. Jonathan stationed himself to the right side of the door while Elizabeth took the left. He took three deep breaths and kicked the door open.

The shed was empty.

They piled back into the van and proceeded up the road. It was steeper now, harder for the van to keep moving.

* * * * *

Alex pulled her arm free of Cuza and ran to Kolya. She put cool hands on either side of his face. "I knew something was wrong."

"I think that Mr. Petrov owes you an explanation and an apology," Cuza said from the door. "Suffice it to say, Miss Feinstein, that you knew of Mr. Petrov's deception and tried to cover for him."

"What are you talking about?" She turned angrily toward him. The two guards swung their guns from their shoulders and aimed at her.

"Mr. Petrov's address and phone number," Cuza replied.

"His address and phone number?"

"Yes. I don't know how much you know or whether you're simply trying to protect your fiancé, but your loyalties are clear and should be rewarded with a place by his side. Mr. Petrov, I'll let you explain what's going to happen. Miss Feinstein, sit down next to your fiancé. I have to see to Mr. Georgescu. You don't mind waiting, do you?" Cuza spoke to the two guards in Romanian, and Kolya understood that the two of them were to be kept alive and secure until he returned.

A few hours at best. Kolya fingered the paper clip and felt for the lock on the handcuffs, as Alex turned to him.

"What the hell is going on?"

"He thinks I put a virus on his computer," Kolya explained, his words blurred through puffy lips.

"Did you?"

"Not intentionally," he lied, hating to do it, but still trying to protect her.

She gave him a hard look. "Will you tell me the truth, Goddamn it? For once?"

"I am. I knew nothing of a virus." Which was true, to an extent. "Apparently my capture was some sort of trick by ECA technical people."

"You weren't in on it?"

291

"Do you think I would have agreed?" He could be honest here. "Do you think I would have allowed myself to be put in this kind of jeopardy, let alone you?"

"I don't know, Kolya. I don't know how far you'd go. You do insane things. Sometimes I don't know who you are."

"I am not this crazy." His voice reflected the anger he genuinely felt. "They screwed me over, Alex. Bradford, Ross, Jonathan, the entire agency. I was sent out to be captured, tortured, and killed. I'd kill Bradford with my bare hands if I could."

And this was the final betrayal. No one was coming—they had been abandoned. Once he'd done the job, there was no reason to wait to launch a rescue. Bradford had to know that the window of opportunity for a successful rescue was small—and a team should have been sent within minutes or at least hours of the downloading of Cuza's information. His ten years of service, Alex's life, his life, none of it mattered. For reasons political or practical, Bradford had consigned both Alex and him to horrible deaths.

Fresh anger surged through him, but he'd never have a chance at revenge. And the anger was a distraction. *Focus.* Under the cover of their conversation, he continued his efforts to pick the lock on the handcuffs. The wire went into the lock. He rotated the wire in the fingers of his right hand and tried to feel for the release.

"The addresses were wrong," she said. "That's how Cuza knew. I knew something was wrong when I saw them. Then when he asked me your address upstairs, I couldn't figure out what to say. I tried to cover for you. I didn't do a very good job."

"Nothing you could have said would have made any difference." No reason to make her feel like it was her fault.

"When did you know?"

He gave up part of the pretense. "When I got on the site, I saw that something was wrong—and realized the truth. But by that time, it was too late. We were screwed either way. The virus was on Cuza's computer. I thought that if I told him, he'd kill us. If I didn't tell him, he'd kill us—but maybe he wouldn't notice—for a while, anyway."

By her expression, he knew that she knew he was lying—that

he'd known before even getting on the site. But the guards were listening.

"They're going to kill us aren't they?"

"Yes." He couldn't lie about their approaching deaths, but he didn't want to describe what Cuza had planned. He still assumed that they were going to die, at least he knew he would. There was only a small chance that he could free himself. No chance of him getting away. If he freed himself and took out the guards—maybe Alex could get out. But even Alex getting out was a remote possibility. Still, if he could and if he had to, he'd kill her himself rather than allow the alternative of an agonizing death by impalement.

He was accomplished at picking locks, but the position of his hands in the cuffs made it awkward.

If he couldn't get his hands on a gun, if the guards were smart enough to keep their distance until more of them arrived, Alex and he would be impaled. No reason to tell her. She would suffer enough when the time came. No reason to let her anticipate it.

But the guards weren't so considerate.

"Tell her how you both will die, Petrov." Gheorghe spoke in English. "Or I will."

"*Eboyanna mat.*" Kolya almost had the lock opened, but the wire slipped from his sweating hand to the floor. He imagined a ping from the metal hitting the concrete floor, but there was no sound—and no reaction from the guards.

The two guards conferred while Alex focused on him. He saw the anger, but it was no longer directed at him. "They beat you up. Again."

"It's hard to fight six men. Even if I weren't already injured." His cuffed hands searched behind him frantically.

Gheorghe approached, smiling. "Not going to tell her, Petrov?"

Kolya said nothing, his entire being intent on finding the paper clip. He shifted his position again, and his fingers located the long wire.

Gheorghe took his silence as a negative. He was close enough to grab hold of Alex's arm. "Maybe I'll whisper it in her ear." He yanked her to her feet.

"Maybe you won't." Alex twisted her arm free just as Kolya twisted the wire into the lock of the handcuffs.

"Leave her alone." *Don't hurry.* He carefully moved the wire with numbed fingers and listened for the click that would signal his release. "Cuza told you to keep us secure and alive."

"She'll be alive. She'll just have some fun before we shove the stake through her." Gheorghe looked over at the other guard, who grinned in response. "Max wouldn't object to us fucking her, and I don't care if she's a Jew. We'll take turns."

The second man moved up to grab Alex's neck from behind to hold her still. Gheorghe pushed his hands up under Alex's tee shirt and fondled her breasts. Kolya concentrated and finally felt the handcuffs give. His arms were free, but the two men and Alex were out of his reach.

But an instant after he freed himself, he saw Alex slam her knee into Gheorghe's groin. Gheorghe went down. Her hands went up to her neck. She grasped the second guard's thumbs, yanked his hands off her neck, and slammed her elbow into his chin.

He fell backwards in surprise onto Kolya. With a twist of his arms, he broke the guard's neck.

Gheorghe struggled to his knees and swung his gun around into firing position.

Kolya fumbled for the Galil MAR assault rifle that the second guard had dropped. Alex snapped a kick to Gheorghe's nose that sent him backwards, and Kolya shot him once between the eyes.

"Get his gun," Kolya ordered.

"The shot. They'll be down."

"Get the gun. And they won't notice one shot. The walls are thick. Cuza is busy with Georgescu, and perhaps no one is monitoring the microphones."

She stooped down and picked up the rifle. "I never saw you kill anyone before."

"I'm sorry. But I had to do it. They were going to rape you and kill us both."

"Don't apologize. Do you think I don't know? It's just difficult."

"I know." Killing took a toll, even on a professional, and she wasn't a professional. To the contrary, she devoted her life to keeping people from being executed. Now, she'd watched him kill two people. It was self-defense, but it was still difficult, and it would be added to the already long list of emotional baggage she would have to deal with, if she survived.

She knelt next to him and wiped blood off his face with her hand. He pushed himself into a sitting position, removed the semi-automatic pistol from the second guard's shoulder holster, and shoved the body to the side.

"Do you know how to shoot one of those?" He indicated the Galil. She shook her head.

"Give it to me, and I'll show you." With immediate danger over, he felt dizzy and sick.

She handed the gun to him. "Took you long enough to pick the lock on the damn handcuffs."

She'd known what he was doing, and she'd covered for him—again.

"You try it some time when your hands are cuffed behind you." He turned his attention to the Galil. "Safety catch. Trigger." He showed her. "Hold it like this, both hands, firmly, shoulder level. Don't try to aim. It's on full automatic. Pull the trigger and you'll get a burst." He checked the magazine and handed the gun back. "Shoot at anything that moves. You know your way around the house. There's keys to the cars on a table near the front door."

She stared at him, and comprehension flooded her face. "I'm not leaving you."

"Alex, look at me. I can't walk. I can barely sit up. Your best chance is to get out quickly before any of the other guards come down to check. Once they realize what's happened, you'll be trapped. If you get away, you can get help."

"Don't give me this shit. There's no help to find. Even if there were, you'll be dead before it arrives. You can shoot them as they come in until you run out of bullets and then they'll take you and impale you."

"They won't take me alive."

"They could pump gas in and knock you out. Or maybe you're right. Maybe they'll just shoot you. Either way, you'll die if I leave."

"Yes. But if you stay, you'll be dead as well. Very romantic, but pointless. You have a chance without me. I want you to go."

"The front door's not far. I can help you. I did it yesterday."

He shook his head. "And do you remember how much time it took me to get up a flight of stairs yesterday, with you helping and I had crutches? I'm not any better today." After the new beatings, he was worse.

Her mouth set firmly. "Then I stay with you. We'll go down fighting together, or we try to get out together."

"You're so Goddamn stubborn."

"Me? Then we're a good pair, Kolya Petrov. You're the most pigheaded man I know. You know, the longer we argue, the greater the chance we'll be trapped. We escape together, or we die together. Your choice."

She extended her arm to help him up. It was stupid. He was dizzy. He hurt everywhere. He strongly doubted he could make it up the stairs, let alone out of the house. Still, if she wouldn't go alone, he had to try.

"Okay."

He slung the Galil on its strap over his left shoulder, tucked the pistol into his waistband, and hooked his arm around her shoulder. She swung the second assault rifle over her right shoulder and put her left arm around his waist. Leaning on Alex, he struggled upright.

* * * * *

"It's snowing harder, Mihai." Georgescu tossed his napkin on the table. "I don't want to get stuck on the mountain."

Cuza was disgusted. And this was the man he'd handpicked to run for the Presidency of Romania. "You worry too much Ion."

"I don't care," Georgescu said. "I'm leaving. Now."

"You're not leaving," Cuza's tone changed from pleasant to

commanding. "We haven't finished."

"Are you forcing me to stay?"

"No." Cuza softened his manner. "Of course not. I just thought—if you're worried—perhaps you could stay the night. We could continue our discussions, and you could return to Bucharest in the morning."

This would mean postponing the executions. He couldn't proceed with Georgescu under his roof. But the prisoners were secured; a few extra hours wouldn't make any difference. It'd give them more time to think about their impending fate.

"You know these mountain snows." Ion paced to the window. "We could get a foot by morning—and I'll be stuck here. I could miss the visit by the Under Secretary. I'm going—now. Why don't you accompany me to Tirgu Mures if you want to continue discussions? We can take rooms at the Continental and in the morning, I'll go on to Bucharest and you can return here."

Tirgu Mures, a small city known for its university and also for the 1990 ethnic riots, had a large number of right wing extremists, a number of whom had joined with Cuza. Cuza wouldn't mind checking on some of his people in the town, and the Continental was the best hotel. However, it had a casino. Georgescu liked to gamble.

"The casino would not be a good place for the Presidential candidate to be seen."

"Yes, of course." Georgescu shrugged.

"Fine," Cuza picked up his wine glass. "I'll have one of my own men drive us down in the Land Rover. Satisfied?" He turned to Stanescu. "Do you wish to accompany us, Emil?"

Stanescu drained his glass. "Certainly."

It was the suggestion of the Continental that did it for Stanescu. He never turned down an opportunity for good wine and food.

"Good." Cuza'd find Max and deliver the news that the prisoners were to be kept alive until his return. Punishments were important affairs, and a leader should be present. It demonstrated strength. Besides, Petrov had destroyed years of planning, and Cuza wanted to watch him pay for that act.

* * * * *

They were on foot just below the stable when they heard a car engine starting up. Jonathan signaled, and they ducked a few feet into the darkness of the woods. The snow was still lightly falling. Moments later, headlights swept past the trees.

The car passed without any change in speed. It was a Land Rover, one of the more expensive models. Jonathan could make out the shape of four people in the car, two in back, two in front.

"Think Kolya's in there?" Teo watched the tail lights disappear down the mountain.

"Unlikely." Jonathan said.

Lights were on outside the stable. Without a word, they fanned out: Jonathan, Elizabeth, Teo to the left; Frick, Pete, and Marty to the right. On the side of the stable closest to the house, a man with an assault rifle stood under the light.

Frick shot him, and the man fell in the snow.

"Check the stable." Jonathan spoke over the radio to Pete and Marty. "Get the body out of sight."

Weapons at the ready, Marty and then Pete went inside. "Only horses," Marty reported. They reappeared and dragged the body inside.

They divided into groups of two, Teo with Jonathan, Elizabeth with Frick, Marty with Pete, and circled up through the woods as they approached the house. It was huge, which made Jonathan grateful for Frick's presence. Searching the entire place for Kolya and Alex would take time and lower the odds of success.

Five cars were parked in the circular drive in front of the imposing mansion. Two of them were Land Rovers, and they would do. The other three, two Mercedes and a Jag, were flashy, but not as convenient for transporting so many people over snowy mountain roads.

The snow slowed to light flurries. They hiked through the woods to the back of the house where, in the circle of light over a door, four men stood, smoking and talking, two with rifles slung over their shoulders.

Jonathan's team, in the woods five hundred feet away, halted. Teo spoke into Jonathan's ear. "Do we take them out?"

Jonathan consulted his watch. "Too close to the house. Too many of them." He spoke into the radio. "Hold positions."

"I can try it." Frick's voice responded in the earpiece. "I've met these guys."

"No." The chances of Frick's being accepted by a group of armed men if he appeared suddenly out of the woods were slim to none. "Wait them out."

It wasn't as late as they had planned—only eleven fifteen. The men would eventually go to bed. It was better to be safe.

* * * * *

Determination kept Kolya moving. The stumbling and painful journey across the basement jolted every injury, and despite Alex's best efforts, his leg kept hitting the ground. Several times the room swam, and he thought he would pass out. He didn't, and they reached the bottom of the stairs with him still upright.

He glanced at the unbarred windows in the entertainment room and rejected that escape possibility. A wire ran through the frame of the nearest window. An attempt to open a window would bring down Cuza's thugs. The only route was the one they were taking. Besides, they needed a car.

At least, he could assist on the stairs, using the banister to pull himself along, but he made achingly slow progress. Every step took a monumental effort. Drenched with sweat, he halted at the top, just below the closed door that opened outward. He pressed his ear against the wood and heard nothing.

Alex reached for the doorknob, but he blocked her.

"Wait. Have your gun ready."

With his left hand tightly gripped on the banister, he removed his right arm from her shoulder and drew the pistol from his waistband. He knew he could accurately shoot a pistol one-handed. He was not as confident about the Galil.

299

Alex aimed her Galil at the door. He took a deep breath, reached with the hand holding the pistol, and rotated the doorknob. It turned without a sound. With the barrel of his gun, he cracked the door and peered out.

Max stood four feet away, his back to the door, talking to two other men. None of them glanced in the direction of the basement. In one hand, Max grasped a ten-foot wooden stake, one end resting on the floor, a vivid reminder of what would happen if they were caught.

Kolya raised a hand in warning. They could come out shooting, but even if they could kill all three men before any of them shot back—which he doubted—there would be more down within minutes.

Best to wait. If Max or the others approached the basement door, Kolya and Alex would shoot. There was a good chance the men would just move on.

He couldn't risk speaking to Alex, but he motioned, finger to lips. He sagged against the wall, letting a dizzy spell pass, and felt Alex's arm slip round his waist.

* * * * *

The four men remained outside, despite the cold and the snow, for another few minutes, jovially exchanging comments and laughing. A few Romanian words drifted out. Jonathan glanced at Teo to see if Teo's understanding of those few words mirrored his own.

Teo's face had gone hard. "I only caught a few words," he whispered. "But they're joking about someone who was impaled."

"You catch when? Or who?"

"No."

Were they anticipating or had they already impaled Kolya and Alex?

There was another animated exchange. "They've switched to sex," Teo said. Finally, one man tossed a burning butt into the snow, and the four trooped, one by one, into the house.

"Egan?" Frick's voice sounded in his ear. "I'll give them five minutes to head upstairs. Then I'll follow."

"Okay," Jonathan agreed. "Pete?"

"Found the generator." Pete would flip the switch and guard against anyone turning it back on.

The kitchen lights remained on, but additional lights brightened the upstairs windows. And went out.

* * * * *

The one hundred yards between the woods and the house was the longest walk Frick had ever taken. He had the HK MP5 slung casually across his back, and night vision goggles dangled on his belt. He'd considered leaving the HK; he was supposed to be a friend, and the assault rifle might dispel the illusion. On the other hand, Cuza's men, with the exception of Max, weren't the brightest lights in the world, and he wasn't about to stroll into Cuza's house armed only with a pistol. Someone might also wonder about the night vision goggles, but again, he wasn't keen on fumbling around in the dark when the lights went out.

He opened the door to the kitchen, prepared for an assault, but none of the men he had spotted earlier were visible. The cook, whose English consisted of three words, worked at the kitchen counter, pounding bread dough.

"Hey, beautiful," he called to her.

She looked at him with recognition and nodded her head. "Okay." Then she crossed the room and locked the door behind him.

The kitchen was large, two sinks, two ovens and stoves, and an industrial size refrigerator. Frick strode through and headed to the stairs at the far end leading to the second floor. With a quick glance over his shoulder at the unconcerned cook, he began the ascent, head and heart pounding.

The hallway on the second floor was empty. He scrutinized the hall in both directions and trotted toward the room where he'd last seen Petrov. He swung the HP M5 around to the front. His right hand rested on the side of the gun, his finger near enough to the trigger to shoot.

He padded on the thick carpet past the decorative staircase that led to the front hall and glanced down. Three men stood almost directly below him talking. He recognized Max from the back and picked up his pace. Max wouldn't be fooled even momentarily into thinking Frick was a friend.

Max didn't turn. Frick continued toward Petrov's room.

Egan and company would have to clear the way, before Frick could start out with Petrov. If Petrov was still alive. Frick had his doubts.

The morning that Frick carried breakfast up to Petrov and Feinstein, the room had been guarded by a man just outside the room. Not only was the guard gone, his chair was gone.

He opened the door to an empty room. The bed was stripped, and blankets folded neatly. He flipped on the overhead light and walked around the room, kneeling down to examine the rug. He recognized the stain.

Hell and damnation. They were too late.

"Egan," he said into the radio. "It's no good. They're not here. I think they're dead. There's blood on the carpet. The bed's stripped. No guards, and Cuza kept a guard on Petrov at all times. It's over. Let's get our asses out of here before we join them."

"I'm not leaving unless I'm sure. Check the third floor and the basement. Or you want us to come in?"

"Christ, no, I don't want you to come in. There're bad guys in the front hall. You'll have to come in shooting, and then all hell's going to break loose."

"Then check. Or we will."

"Okay, the third floor. But that's it. They're not there—we get the fuck out of here."

"You can get out," Jonathan replied, leaving Frick the clear impression that he was going to search the damn premises for the bodies.

The hell with him. Frick was willing to risk his life to save two people but not to retrieve corpses. Egan wanted to beat the bushes to take his pal's body home, fine and dandy. He'd take one of Cuza's cars and get as far away as possible.

He reached the door of the bedroom, listened, and froze. Even with the door closed, he heard voices down the hall. He flicked off the light switch. The voices moved closer, and then further away. Frick opened the door silently. He was near the staircase to the third floor. Well, hell, maybe they did move the prisoners to the third floor. Worth a look. If he were upstairs, Petrov would be under guard.

He cautiously climbed carpeted stairs to the next floor. Cuza and the more important visitors had rooms on the second floor. Max's room was near Cuza's, as was Stanescu's. The guards with less seniority stayed on the third floor.

In the third floor corridor, he proceeded slowly, hand on the HK MP5. If he were lucky, Cuza's men would all be sleeping. But his luck ran out. At the end of the hall, Stefan, who spoke English, stepped out of a bathroom and eyed him.

"Frick? I thought you were back in America."

His tone was curious, not hostile. Maybe Frick could pull this off.

"I was. I'm back. How's it going?"

"Good. Looking forward to tomorrow. That's why you're here, no? Voivode Cuza makes a celebration of an execution. There'll be a big meal afterwards: wine and toasting."

"Tomorrow? That's when Petrov's being impaled?"

Stefan yawned. "In the morning, both of them. The best part is when we shove the stakes through them, and they're screaming and writhing. After a while, they get quiet, even though it takes a while for them to die. We have a poll going for time of death. Do you want in?"

"Yeah, sounds like fun. Where's Petrov now?" Frick hoped he sounded casual. "Back in the cell in the basement?"

"Yes. Not going to make any trouble. You want a beer? I have some in my room."

"Sure." Frick followed Stefan to his room where Stefan flipped open a small drink cooler and took out two Bergen biers. Frick accepted the beer, twisted the top, and drank. Stefan drank with him.

"Wait." Stefan held up his beer. "Do you hear something? Downstairs?"

Frick heard a thudding sound.

"We'd better check." Stefan put down his beer and reached for an assault weapon on the top of the dresser.

"Yeah, good idea." Frick positioned the HK MP5 and shot him. With the sound suppressor, the noise was barely audible. He spoke into his radio. "Egan, in case you didn't hear, Petrov's still alive, being held in the basement. Something else is going on downstairs."

* * * * *

Standing motionless was worse than moving. With Max this close, Kolya couldn't risk sitting down, but leaning against the wall, even with Alex helping to hold him, was difficult. He was lightheaded, and his body trembled from the effort.

After what seemed like an eternity, footsteps moved away, and voices dimmed in volume.

Alex pushed her eye to the crack as he sagged, exhausted, against the wall. She put her mouth to his ear. "They're gone."

He peered out. Clear, but he knew that any of them could be just out of sight.

"You go first," Kolya said. "I'll cover you."

"We've been through this. We make it together, or neither makes it."

He didn't have the energy to argue. He nudged the door open another inch, the semi-automatic ready. Alex posed with the Galil aimed, also ready. Still clear. He swung the door open on an empty hall.

"We're almost there," she said. "And looks like there's a pile of keys on the table. We grab them all. Something will work."

He agreed with a nod, tucked the pistol back into his waistband, and encircled her shoulder again with his arm. It was maybe twenty-five feet from the door to the basement to the front door.

They started out again. Kolya dredged up all his reserves to keep going, right arm around Alex's shoulder, eyes on the goal. Keys. Door. *Twenty feet.* He shifted his gaze to the living room on his right, the library on his left. Both clear. They would make it.

He heard a whisper of sound behind him and reacted instantly. He yanked his arm off Alex and pivoted on his good leg. Alex went down, struck on the side of the head. Behind them, Max wielded the long wooden stake like a quarterstaff. After Alex fell, Max slashed the stake at Kolya.

Kolya grabbed the stake, twisted, held on, and crashed to the ground. The force of his weight threw Max off balance, and he fell as well. The fall loosened both of their grips on the stake, and it rolled across the floor, out of reach. Max grabbed for the assault rifle still strapped on Kolya's shoulder. Kolya thrust an elbow strike towards Max's throat, but Max blocked it. Kolya swung the rifle from his shoulder, trying to aim, but Max grabbed the barrel and pointed it towards the wall.

Max and Kolya struggled, both with hands on the barrel of the Galil. With a jerk, Max pulled it free, but a blow from Kolya's elbow sent the rifle scuttling across the polished wood floor.

Kolya's gun slid out of his waistband. Kolya grappled for it, but Max kicked it away.

They hammered at each other with fists and elbows. Kolya rolled on top of Max, a forearm across Max's throat. For an instant, Max was pinned and choking. Kolya, a week earlier, would have finished it then. But adrenaline and training could not completely compensate for the level of his injuries. Max broke the grip and shoved Kolya to the side.

Max struck at the side of Kolya's head with a fist, but Kolya blocked the blow. Max kicked, aiming for Kolya's genitals. Kolya blocked the kick to his groin with his left leg, but a second kick landed hard on his right leg. Kolya felt the impact through his entire body.

Max landed another kick on the cast. Kolya groaned, and his grip on Max lessened enough for Max to roll out of reach, grab the pistol on the floor, and stagger to his feet.

"Not as tough or clever as you thought you were, Petrov." Raising his voice, Max shouted for help in Romanian and aimed the gun at

Kolya's left knee. "But I'm not going to kill you. You're not escaping impalement."

Kolya rolled desperately toward the Galil just a few feet away. The bullet hit the floor where his knee had been a second earlier.

Max shouted again. Almost simultaneously, feet thudded upstairs.

Kolya shot a glance at Alex, still stretched motionless, the Galil on the floor next to her. He dragged himself toward her, but Max got there first, and retrieved the Galil. The second assault rifle lay on the other side of the hall. He'd never make it.

So close. So fucking close.

"She's still breathing, Petrov," Max said. "So you'll have the pleasure of her company when we impale you. You're done."

He tried anyway, dragging on battered elbows a body that no longer wanted to respond, toward the assault rifle that lay out of reach. He knew that Max would never let him reach it, that even now Max was aiming the Galil at his arms.

Then the lights dimmed and went out, and there was the sound, from the kitchen, of a door breaking.

* * * * *

Jonathan kicked the back door open and darted inside, followed by Teo, Elizabeth, and Marty. He saw the green outline of an elderly woman cowering in the corner of the kitchen and headed for the front hall. Teo and Elizabeth raced for the door from the kitchen to the dining room. From there, they'd circle around through the library.

Marty followed Jonathan.

Jonathan kicked open the door to the hall and was met with automatic fire. He ducked back into the kitchen. In that brief moment, he noted three figures on the ground spaced apart, one holding an assault rifle, one moving slowly on the ground toward a second assault rifle on the floor, the third motionless.

He couldn't make out the faces of any of the figures.

"One shooter on the ground," he reported to the others. "Another going for a weapon. A third on the ground is not moving."

"Is any of them Kolya or Alex?" Teo asked.

"Can't tell."

"We take out anyone with a gun?" Elizabeth asked.

Kolya had been in the basement. Could Kolya have made an escape attempt with the injuries that Frick had described? Maybe with Alex's help.

There was the sound of additional gunfire on the stairs. If Kolya and Alex were in the basement, the team had to clear the way to get down. On the other hand, there was the remote chance that they were in the hall.

"Only shoot those who pose a threat to a team member," Jonathan said.

* * * * *

In the pitch-black room, Kolya found the energy to roll away from the spot where Max had last seen him. As he rolled, he heard the sound of the Galil firing and he saw the spurt of flame from the end of the gun. Fragments of wood stung his face. Miraculously, the bullets missed him.

Max shouted in Romanian. "Intruders in the kitchen."

He couldn't see Max, but Max couldn't see him either. He dragged himself in the direction where he had last seen the second Galil. The door to the kitchen opened, and automatic weapons spewed fire.

Men clattered on the stairs. Kolya heard bursts of gunshots from the second floor but was unable to see who was shooting.

He inched forward, revolving his arms in a semi-circle on the floor ahead of him. His fingers made contact with a cold metal shape and, with an almost religious gratitude, he pulled the assault rifle close and set it on semi-automatic.

He lay flat, weapon ready. There were men on the stairs and unknown people—an extraction team, it had to be—in the kitchen. But Kolya and Alex had to survive to be rescued. Max would and could still kill them both.

Max lurked somewhere between Kolya and the kitchen. Kolya

knew the general direction where Alex lay and where he had last seen Max. If Alex should sit up, Kolya wouldn't know it. Any shots he fired in the dark could kill her.

Max was a threat to her and to the extraction team. He had to kill Max.

From the stairs, automatic fire exploded and behind him, answering fire. A man tumbled down the stairs and lay unmoving.

He knew that members of the extraction team were behind him and in front of him. The team could handle the people on the stairs. If he tried to give supporting fire, he'd draw their attention or Max's attention to his location.

He waited for the sound of Max's voice or for Max to shoot again. He strained in vain to see, concentrating on the darkness ahead of him.

Max's voice called to the men on the stairs. "Petrov is in the hall. Leave him to me." Between the voice and a shape in front of him, Kolya knew he'd located Max.

He raised himself on his elbows, aimed, his finger on the trigger, but before he could fire, a blow on his left shoulder knocked him flat again.

He lay stunned. He'd been shot. Shoulder wound. Wouldn't kill him, not unless he bled to death. Still, he couldn't use his left arm to aim the assault rifle that lay on the ground next to him. He didn't feel pain from this newest injury, not yet; that would take a few minutes.

A moment later, a quavering voice called his name.

He identified the voice. Teo.

Relief flooded his body, but he knew better than to move. Whoever had shot him—and he suspected it was Goddamn fucking Teo—might shoot again. If he identified himself, Max would know his location and finish the job.

* * * * *

Alex woke to a darkness interrupted by bangs and flashes that even in her slightly confused and muddled state, she knew to be gunfire. Her head hurt. She'd been hit or she'd fallen. She tried to remember. They had been in a hall. She'd been helping Kolya, then something had hit her in the head, and it all went dark.

Gunshots echoed, and men shouted in a language she didn't understand.

Someone offered in English to surrender, and another voice accepted the surrender. The second voice she recognized.

Jonathan. We're safe.

"Kolya?" she whispered.

There was no reply. She heard someone crawl toward her on the floor as the sound of gunfire ceased. She pushed herself into a sitting position. The hall lights flashed on and blinded her. Almost immediately, an arm encircled her throat and cut off her air.

* * * * *

The sudden brightness fell on his eyes like a blow. Teo pushed the night vision goggles off, but his eyes were dazzled. He squinted and focused.

On the stairs, Marty and Frick trained their guns on three men who stood with arms raised. Jonathan was halfway down the stairs, his gun leveled.

In the hall, a figure with light blond hair sprawled on the floor, right hand on an assault rifle on the floor, back covered in blood. Even without seeing his face, Teo knew him.

Teo felt his heart drop to his stomach. He'd fired the shot. He came to rescue Kolya, and instead he'd shot him. The emotion was so overwhelming that it took him a minute to register the rest of the scene. A few feet away from Kolya's body, a stocky man with darker blond hair crooked an elbow around Alex Feinstein's neck, pointed a pistol at her head, and yanked her up from the floor. A Galil semi-automatic rifle hung from a strap on the man's shoulder.

"Drop your weapons and let her go. You won't be hurt," Jonathan said, but the words sounded forced. "Teo, translate."

Teo's first word in Romanian was interrupted.

"Do you think I'm a fool, Egan?"The man spoke in perfect American English. He retreated toward the front door, shielded behind Alex. "I let her go and you'll kill me." He stared upwards. "Frick. I should have known."

"Good to see you, too, Max. He's the one who tortured Kolya," Frick said.

"Nevertheless." Jonathan advanced down a step. "I want to end this without risking Alex's life. None of my people will shoot you if you surrender, Max."

"Here's my counteroffer. I get to a car outside, and I'll let her go. You can take Petrov's body," he gave a contemptuous glance at the still form, "and collect his whore on your way out. Nice of you to finish him off for me, by the way."

"If he gets out," Frick said, "he'll kill her."

"Pete'll be behind him once he gets out," Teo said. "If he tries anything outside, Pete'll take him."

"Pete's dead." Elizabeth indicated the lights. "Otherwise he would have stopped whoever turned the generator back on."

Teo let that information sink in, and then he aimed his weapon at Max's head.

"If you shoot him," Jonathan said, "he could pull the trigger as a reflex action."

"Look out, Teo." Elizabeth knocked him to the side and darted to the left as someone behind them opened fire from the door that led from the dining room into the library. Jonathan returned fire from the stairs. The shooter ducked behind cover.

* * * * *

Alex stared desperately at Kolya as Max dragged her backward.

He couldn't be dead. They couldn't have survived these past three days only for Kolya to die now. But she couldn't see if he was breathing. And he wasn't moving. *Damn it, Kolya. Don't do this. Not now.* Not after she had mourned him and found him again. Then fury replaced the disbelief. Fury against all of them, the Romanians,

Kolya's people who had bungled the rescue, but above all, at Max and Cuza.

Elizabeth and Teo returned fire through the library and pinned down the new gunman.

The burst of gunfire startled Max as well as her. The grip of his arm around her neck loosened. With the strength of rage, she slammed the back of her head into his face, at the same time, grabbing with both hands the gun pointed at her head, changing the aim to the ceiling. He let go of her neck and struggled for control of the gun. She stomped on his instep and twisted under his arm, away from him.

There was the loud report of two gunshots, and Max glanced down, face surprised, at the blood running from a hole in his midsection. He glared past her, malice and hate on every feature, pushed her away, and swung the gun downward with the same motion.

Two more shots hit Max between the eyes, and he dropped.

Alex turned. Kolya lowered the assault rifle that he had shot one-armed, and collapsed on top of it. She reached him before any of the others. He was conscious enough to smile.

43

The eggs were runny, the coffee weak, the toast limp. Frick had had worse breakfasts, but not often.

He couldn't believe he'd accepted Bradford's offer. Couldn't believe that his ass wasn't sitting in jail. He also couldn't believe Carl Ford's ass wasn't sitting in jail—that Ford had only lost his job, but Lewis probably didn't want the whole sordid mess coming out, which could happen if Ford was arrested.

Frick had been a little dubious about the ECA, but Egan and the others had warmed up after the Romanian expedition. Teo was being downright friendly.

He tried the eggs one more time and confirmed his first impression.

"I told you to get the cheesecake. It's the best thing here." Teo took a large bite.

"Too sweet for first thing in the morning." Frick gave up, put his fork down, and picked up the coffee cup.

"Just remember. Cheesecake good. Eggs bad."

"Who's that?" Frick inclined his head toward a thin man just entering the doorway, chewing gum with his mouth half open.

Teo turned toward the door, and his face crinkled in distaste. "Greg Ross. He designed the Trojan horse. Along with Mark Leslie over there." He indicated a younger man who, like Tim, ate cheesecake for breakfast. "Mark's an okay guy. Ross just keeps him cowed."

Frick watched Ross select a tray and spit his gum into his hand. "Remind me not to shake hands with him."

312

"I wouldn't shake hands with him even if he didn't spit all over himself. The little creep. Allowing Kolya to be captured was his idea. Eric and Pete are both dead because of him."

Frick saw another figure in the doorway, and this one was familiar. He put his coffee cup down, not quite sure what to expect.

Frick nodded behind Teo. "Petrov's here. Out of the hospital, apparently."

In the doorway, Kolya Petrov balanced on crutches. His gaze roved over the people in the room. Frick noted the expression as Petrov focused on Greg Ross's back.

"Yeah?" Teo shoved his chair back, stood, and crossed the room. Petrov spoke a few words, looked at Frick, and gave a brief dispassionate nod of acknowledgement. It might not have been full forgiveness, but it was something.

Teo returned to his seat, and Petrov disappeared.

"I guess he's not joining us," Frick said.

"He had some things to do." Teo forked another mouthful of the cheesecake, looked over Frick's shoulder, and waved. "Hey, Greg, join us." Frick half-turned in his chair and watched Ross steer in their direction. He glanced back at Teo, whose face betrayed nothing but welcome, and understood what had been communicated.

* * * * *

Kolya seated himself in front of the computer, leaned his crutches on the edge of the desk, and tapped the keyboard. As he had suspected, Ross had not bothered to sign off before going downstairs for breakfast. He went first into old e-mail, starting with those dated a week before his capture by Cuza. He skimmed until he found those with Jonathan's address. He finished the file and went into texts on the phone log.

By the time he heard the whisper of sound behind him, he was reading over the download from Mihai Cuza's computer. Without moving his head, he said, "Put on a pot of coffee, Mark. You'll find Ross's Starbucks stash in the top drawer of the filing cabinet."

313

He turned his head to see Mark Leslie frozen in the doorway, resembling a deer caught in headlights.

"Kolya," he stammered. "I didn't know you were—H –h—how are you?"

"I'm fine, thanks. Enjoying the fucking crutches."

"What are you doing?"

"A little research. For which I need Ross's computer. Are you going to make that coffee?"

Mark swallowed. "Ross'll catch you in here."

"I certainly hope so. I would very much like to see Ross make a fuss about my using his computer. In the meantime, I could use another cup of coffee and it's hard on the fucking crutches to carry a coffee pot. You're nominated." Mark had been a minor player in the events leading up to Kolya's capture, but he'd been a player, and a little bullying was appropriate.

Mark handed him a cup of coffee. Kolya nodded a cool thanks, finished reading, and drained the cup. He reached for the crutches.

"You need any help?" Mark followed him into the hall.

"No." *Not from Mark.*

Greg Ross exited the elevator and halted. "Petrov." There was shock on his face followed by indignation. He chewed rapidly. "What the hell were you doing in my office?"

"Searching your computer."

"It's a breach of security," Ross sputtered.

"I have clearance." Kolya kept his tone deceptively calm. "Besides I'm not the one who left my computer on and unguarded. Now, if you'll excuse me."

"Wait a minute." Ross put a hand on Kolya's right forearm. "Did you do something to my computer?"

Kolya balanced himself, took hold of Ross's wrist, and twisted. Ross went down on one knee. Kolya released his grip, wobbled, and steadied himself on the crutches as Ross fell backwards. "Do you think that something as juvenile as my screwing up your computer would be sufficient payback for what you did to me? To my fiancée? Do you think I play fucking children's games?"

Ross's face went pale with fear. It wasn't as good as killing him, but it would have to do. Ross wasn't worth life in prison.

* * * * *

When he finally arrived at his office, he was too tired and in too much pain to pack up his personal items in the cardboard box that a secretary delivered. After swallowing two aspirins, he turned on Herbie Hancock and leaned back in his chair, trying to ease his aching back and shoulder. His eyes closed as he listened to the music.

He didn't know how long he'd slept when he heard a voice say softly, "That looks like a great way to get a stiff neck." Jonathan sat on his desk, arms folded, and regarded him with a questioning air. "Are you okay?"

"Just tired."

"No wonder. From what I hear, you've been busy for your first day out of the hospital. Ross's practically wetting his pants. He claims you almost broke his arm and threatened to kill him."

"An exaggeration, but I'm pleased to hear he's wetting his pants."

"You going to see Margaret? Believe or not, she still wants you to stay."

"If I see Bradford, I'll kill her." Kolya ran a hand over his face, not fully awake. "I need to pack up and get out of the office."

"So you've resigned." Jonathan's voice held regret but no surprise. "I don't blame you, but I'm sorry to hear it. You've bounced back before."

"I've been injured before and recovered. It's a little different this time." It wasn't just the physical injuries. It was the vivid flashbacks, the sweats, the trembling. The side effects of torture. The PTSD symptoms should diminish, but how much and how much time it would take were both unclear.

But Jonathan wasn't giving up. "No one expects you to be instantly back to normal. Give it some time. Think about it."

"I have thought about it." Kolya's temper flared, but he damped it down. "It's no good, Jonathan."

Jonathan shifted and looked at the far wall, which was decorated

315

with a framed poster of Miles Davis. "What were you looking for on Ross's computer?"

"For one thing, I was checking on Cuza's whereabouts."

"From what I hear, he's in the wind somewhere in Eastern Europe."

"But we're not going after him."

Jonathan shrugged. "Politics. Georgescu won the Presidency of Romania, and we're not going to hunt down his buddy. I hate fucking politics. That all you were looking for?"

"No. Did you know that Ross keeps every e-mail transmitted to any computer in this office in a master file? He tracks texts to our cell phones. And that he also writes notes to a personal log after every significant meeting or event?"

Jonathan frowned. "I didn't know that, but what does it matter?"

"It matters because he set up the Trojan horse, and he was in on almost every step of the plan. I wanted to know who else was in on it. Whether you were in on it."

Jonathan blew out a breath. "Shit, did you really think I'd have agreed to betray you?"

Kolya was suddenly tired again. "I didn't think you would, but I wasn't sure. I had to be sure." He leaned forward and turned off the music.

"Oh come, on, Kolya. Look. You were screwed over. I know that. I know what they did to you. Still, couldn't you have trusted me?"

"Not without checking." Kolya met Jonathan's gaze. "And you don't know what they did."

"I saw you."

"You saw what they did to me physically. You didn't see what they did to my mind." He laughed, but it wasn't from amusement. "Alex thinks I'm crazy, and she's right. What's really crazy is that I'll miss it." He gestured sweepingly, a gesture meant to include not only his office but his entire professional career. "If it had only been me, if I had been the only one to suffer from the *yobanich* Trojan horse, as angry as I would be at the betrayal, I might not have resigned. Do you know how really crazy I am—if Bradford had asked me to let Cuza capture and torture me—I probably would have agreed. But she didn't ask, and when I didn't break fast enough, she gave Alex to Cuza—" He trailed off and took a deep breath. "I owe it to Alex to try something else. I just had to be sure about you."

Jonathan took a long moment to answer, clearly trying to find the right words. He raised his hands, gave up, and said the mundane. "I understand. I'm so sorry. Changing the subject, have you had lunch?"

"No, but I really should pack up and get out." Kolya looked around his office. It would take him an hour, maybe more, fumbling with the crutches.

"Forget it. Teo and I will pack your stuff this afternoon, and I'll drop it by Alex's townhouse. Come on, the gang wants to take you out. And we're doing French this time, no arguing."

The gang was Frick, Elizabeth, Teo, and Marty, all of whom were loitering in the hall outside the office. Kolya surrendered good-naturedly. "As long as I'm not paying."

"What's a trust fund for, anyway?" Jonathan retrieved Kolya's crutches for him. "I'm going to miss you. We've worked together a long time."

Kolya knew he would miss Jonathan as well, but it wasn't something he felt comfortable saying. "I thought I was a pain in the ass." Kolya stood with the help of the desk and placed the crutches under his arms.

"Well, you are." Jonathan held the door open.

Kolya took a last look at his office and hobbled forward to join his friends.

* * * * *

As he played the piano that evening, he heard the front door open. He glanced at the clock. Seven o'clock. Right on time. He listened for a minute just to be sure. One set of footsteps. Her footsteps.

He played another chord of "Sweet Georgia Brown" and moved into improvisation.

"I've got egg rolls, hot and sour soup, and scallops with walnuts," Alex called.

He played an arpeggio and an F sharp scale. At least, his hands were undamaged. His fingers still moved over the keys with dexterity. He played another chord, retrieved the crutches from the floor, and hobbled toward the kitchen.

"How was the trial?" he asked, as Alex set containers of Chinese food on the table. He shook his head at her as she offered the soup. She ladled herself a cup of soup and located a spoon in a cabinet behind the table. He selected an egg roll and doused it with duck sauce.

"We settled after the jury was picked. How did it go?"

"As expected." He looked at her and knew the question. "I resigned."

"Did you shoot anyone?"

"Did you think I would?"

"Not really." She sipped a spoonful of soup. "But I know that you want to. Bradford. Ross. Lewis. Ford. You want to kill them all. Cuza, too, of course, but he's in Romania."

He didn't deny it.

"Do you think killing any or all of them will stop the nightmares?"

"No." He wasn't that naive, but his desire to kill the people responsible for what had happened to the two of them was not based on an expectation of a catharsis. Still he wouldn't do it. It wasn't worth the risk of prison, and it wasn't worth hurting Alex. He did the diplomatic thing and changed the subject. "Your piano needs tuning. And you should put a humidifier under it before the winter sets in."

"Why bother if I'm going to sell it."

"Sell it?"

"Sure." She finished her soup, set the bowl aside. "You don't think it'll fit into your apartment, do you?"

He'd forgotten the dispute over where they'd live after marriage. The wedding wasn't going to happen for another year—a year of discussing where they would live. "Don't sell it yet."

"Are you considering living here as a viable option?"

"Maybe."

If pressed, he would admit that he liked her townhouse, liked the space, the location, and, of course, her piano. More importantly, she

318

liked it and would be unhappy to move. His back and leg ached, and he shifted in his seat, trying unsuccessfully to find a comfortable position.

"You overdid it today, didn't you?"

"Just tired."

Both of them knew better, but she didn't push it. She served herself scallops. He reached for another egg roll.

"On another subject, I was thinking—I always knew anti-Semitism existed, but I never really faced raw hatred like that. Makes me think about what it means to be Jewish. I'm maybe thinking of getting involved in some Jewish organizations."

"Please don't tell me you're going to keep kosher."

She pointed a chopstick at the scallops and then expertly speared one.

"When they were torturing me," he dipped the eggroll into duck sauce and then into mustard, "Max would curse at me as a fucking Jew. So I understand the impulse."

She ate another scallop. "Aaron called last night after you were asleep to invite us to Thanksgiving dinner."

"Did you accept?"

"Not without talking to you."

"I'd prefer not." He ate half the remaining egg roll and dropped the rest on his plate.

"My parents are coming in the early part of the week so they can spend Thanksgiving with their grandchildren."

This was one of the problems with marriage. Her family would become his family. He liked her parents, but he wasn't crazy about Aaron. He also didn't know what to make of the extended family, the grandparents, the aunts and uncles, the great aunts and great uncles, the first cousins, second cousins, first cousins once removed. He could put up with it for the wedding, whenever it occurred, but once married, he was in the family. More benign than joining the mafiya, but not dissimilar. "You could tell them that I'm not well enough."

"Aaron has privileges at Hopkins and knows your doctor, as you are aware. He knows just how well you are. Look at it this way. You don't have to pretend to be an accountant anymore."

The fact that he could drop the accountant cover wasn't going to compensate for the difficulties in dealing with Alex's brother. That Aaron now knew Kolya's real—former—profession hadn't improved matters. He thought of another excuse.

"He told me not to bring a gun to his house."

"So don't. You can go without the gun for one evening."

"There are too many people who want to kill me—and who will continue to want to kill me regardless of my occupation."

"Carry concealed. He's not going to search you."

"Fine." He was out of arguments. "But I'm not drinking fucking kosher wine. Too damn sweet."

"There'll be vodka. And some kosher wine is pretty good. Anyway, I thought you liked sweets." The amusement in her face changed to concern as she watched him shift his position again. "I can get you a pain pill."

"You know I don't like them." He couldn't find a comfortable position and gave up, pulling himself up on his crutches. "I'm going to bed. You're right; I did overdo it for my first day out of the hospital. Are you coming?"

"In a minute."

He didn't bother undressing. He unbuckled his holster and placed the gun on the nightstand before he stretched out on top of the covers, arranging pillows and shifting on his side. He found the television remote, flipped to a news station, closed his eyes, and dozed as the anchor droned the events of the day.

He woke to her sitting next to him. Cool fingers slowly unbuttoned his shirt. "Why didn't you get undressed?"

"I was tired. And it's more fun when you help."

"Is it?" Her fingers traced the area on his chest that Max had burned with the cigar. He felt himself stirring at her touch. "Do you have any pain from the burns?"

"No, just the scars. It's other parts that haven't completely healed."

She finished with the buttons, and he sat up to take off his shirt, careful not to give her a view of his back. Every mark on his body was a reminder of what he wanted to forget, of what he wanted her to forget.

He lay back down, pulling her with him, and she nestled, head on his shoulder.

"This is nice."

He didn't disagree. The closeness was pleasant in itself, but it was also a first step. They hadn't made love since before Romania. The burns had healed enough; his other injuries were uncomfortable but manageable. But she'd been injured psychologically. She'd been kidnapped, almost raped, and she had almost died. He couldn't blame her if she wasn't interested in sex.

He reached for the top button of her blouse and stopped, not wanting to push, not yet. But she solved the problem. She sat up, unbuttoned her blouse while he watched, and leaned over, her dark hair falling over his face, guiding his hand under the bra. He caressed the soft coolness of her breast. "Are you sure?"

"I'm seducing you, idiot. Of course I'm sure. I just don't want to hurt you."

It would be awkward, and they would have to be careful. But what was a little discomfort compared to the joy of being together? He reached behind her back and unsnapped the bra. "It's worth it."

About the Author

S. Lee Manning spent two years as managing editor of Law Enforcement Communications before realizing that lawyers make a lot more money. A subsequent career as an attorney spanned from a first-tier New York law firm, Cravath, Swaine & Moore, to working for the State of New Jersey, to solo practice. In 2001, Manning agreed to chair New Jerseyans for Alternatives to the Death Penalty (NJADP), writing articles on the risk of wrongful execution and arguing against the death penalty on radio and television in the years leading up to its abolition in the state in 2007.

An award winning short story writer, Manning is the author of international thrillers. Her life-long interests in Russia and espionage are reflected in her Kolya Petrov thrillers. Manning is currently working on the second in the Kolya Petrov thriller series, Nerve Attack, coming in July 2021 from Encircle Publications.

Manning lives in Vermont with her husband and two cats, but frequently visits her daughter Jenny in California and her son Dean in New Jersey.